Tash y!!!
I love you girl
Thank so m
yours app
Hope you enj
Peace
Blessings,
&
Love!
Lisa!

RABBIT'S LUCKY NUMBER

PEARSON LEE

Brooklyn Girl Publishing Co., Inc.
New York

Brooklyn Girl Publishing Co.
244 5th Avenue #L231
New York, NY 10001-7604

ISBN 978-0-6151-6382-6

Library of Congress Control Number: 2008930022

Printed in the United States of America

I DON'T CURSE.

But on this uncomfortably warm October morning, a muddy stream flows freely from my lips, making a liar out of me. *Fuck. Fuck. Fuck!*

Rodney, or Hot Rod as the press loves to call him, is on the sports page of the *New York Daily News,* flashing a disarming million dollar smile. The words "Home Sweet Home" are perched atop his invisible horns confirming all that I'd hoped was a nasty rumor.

Contrary to what you may believe, the devil is not red and spike-tailed. His tongue is not black, or forked for that matter, and he does not hiss when he speaks. His disposition is not surly, nor his countenance sour. In fact, when you first meet him, you would never even guess his true identity.

He is the owner of flawless peanut butter colored skin and eyelashes that are long enough to inspire envy. He is intelligent, spirited, and charming: a Mr. Personality, if you will.

At first, I think I'm okay. It's nothing, Adrienne. Just relax. That's what I tell myself. But I feel a familiar heaviness swelling in my chest even though I hold out hope that my luck will change with the flip of the newspaper.

Factory workers from Minneapolis cheese about the Mega Money Jackpot that should have been mine. Fuck! I trash the newspaper, mulling over a new plan. A better plan. But I've got nothing.

More than splurge on my first pair of Gucci pumps and an *MTV Cribs*-worthy house for my daughter Angela and myself, I intended to get as far away from New York as I could before Hurricane Rodney made landfall.

I practically trip over my own feet running to the window. I tug and pry and push at the lock without success. My hands, paler than usual, tremble against it. I'm cold and I'm goose-pimpled and I am beginning to panic. I have to get air. I bang one more time with the palm of my hand.

As if it senses my desperation, the lock shifts. I chuck the window open and suck in maple sweet October air as though I'd just broken the water's surface.

Down below, the children of the country's elite sit on the lush Crayola green campus lawn, *noshing* on their celery sticks and granola, hopefully only worrying at the moment about mid-terms and the minutiae I overhear in passing: like how many calories there are in a single sunflower seed.

I imagine myself twenty again and instantly regret it for the shame that rushes back to reclaim its old home. I hurry back to my desk. It's eight forty-four. Adrienne Lucas does not do disarray and disorder. Ever. I collect fallen stationary and my letter opener from off the floor, straighten my daughter Angela's picture and fix the collar on my army stiff starched shirt. Like clockwork, Stacey, my southern belle assistant, peeks into my office at eight forty-five on the dot.

"*Aydree-yanne*," she calls. "Did you hear about Hot Rod?" She slaps half an apple and a new *In Touch* magazine on top of the blotter. Our morning ritual is fifteen minutes of breakfast and gossip. Halle and Britney. Halle and Oprah. Brad, Angelina and the junior United Nations. And Halle. Always the fabulous Halle.

Stacey yanks the tails of her bright purple satin shirt, drawing my eyes up from the magazine to her mid-section. Pieces of copper flesh peek-a-boo between the buttons. I think to remind her again of her work appearance, but I can't deal with the dark side this morning.

"I know what you're gonna say. But those girdle thingies squeeze my jelly in a way she just does not like to be squeezed." The two things I like most about Stacey is that she doesn't miss a trick, and that she has a way of phrasing things. I would laugh, but my unruly thoughts have drifted back to Rodney.

"Girl, you're as white as a Klansman. Are you alright?"

"I'm fine, Stace. Really." I push my glasses up on the bridge of my nose in a composed and unaffected manner. In control, I am. Janet's got nothing on me.

"So did you hear about Hot Rod? He's been traded to the Skyscrapers! Bryan is gonna be so *exsahted.* His favorite team and my favorite player! I bet the air around him is as *sahweet* as his jump shot!"

I refuse to look Stacey in the eye. If I do, I will never get rid of her. There's a resume on top of my inbox from Kennedy Rockford, the Assistant Director of Human Resources. I can tell from her "K" sticky note at the top. *Please review.* Jennifer Rockford, or *Jen*, as she put in parenthesis, was minimally qualified even for the open receptionist's position. But it didn't help her that she was related to Kennedy for whom I've never had much use. Reviewed. Denied.

"Stacey, please file this under 'never'." Stacey checks her watch. We are still in gossip time. And I would never interrupt it. But I can't keep the façade up for much longer. "Actually, Stacey, I've got a really important call to make. Mind if we catch up at lunch?"

"Alright." She steals a glance at me before she pulls the door shut. I sag in my seat. The air around him, even in my farthest memories, is not sweet. It is tainted and polluted and foul.

Stacey flies back into my office, breathless. Her bangs are flipped upward.

"Kennedy is out there saying yall are kin or something. Is that true?" I shrug, but it is enough for Stacey to run with.

"Ooooh! Why didn't you say so!" she squeals. "You think you could get good seats for me? I would love to surprise my Poppa Bear."

"I doubt it. We're not close." She shakes my shoulder playfully. My stomach struggles not to turn itself inside out at her exuberance.

"C'mon, Aydree! Can't your momma ask his momma? Pleeeease?!"

"Stacey. Will you back the hell off?" Her smile fades away.

"Madame Director, will you be needing anything else?" She slams the door behind her before the question mark is dotted.

Stacey and I are good friends outside the office, but Rodney James Barrus, Jr., a.k.a. Hot Rod, a.k.a. Mr. Personality is, was, and ever shall be beyond the realm of confiding in a girlfriend. Or anyone else for that matter.

Brooklyn 1986

THE LAST DAY OF SCHOOL was supposed to be the happiest day of the year, after Christmas, of course. No more pencils, no more books, no more teachers' dirty looks and all that jazz. All it meant to me was that I was the last girl in my graduating class to get her period. Even Puerto Rican Maritza with the mustache ran out of Social Studies with an embarrassing red spot on the back of her grey and burgundy pinstripe Lees. Lucky heifer.

My best friend Tanisha Banks and I stepped over shattered Colt 45 bottles and uneven sidewalks, just as we did everyday on our way home from school. Except today, carrying our report cards and the New Edition pictures from inside our beat up lockers, we were silent.

There were many differences between Tanisha and me. I was the color of maize, while she was the color of milk chocolate. And where I was what my mother described as hourglass-shaped, she was model slim. Yet still, everyone called us the Twin Towers. We were the same height at 5'8", we spoke alike, dressed alike, and where you saw one of us, you saw the other. But in September, Tanisha would be going to Brooklyn Tech, breaking up our duo. We'd both gotten in, but no matter what anyone including the principal said, my mom didn't want me to travel that far away for school.

"Ain't nothing wrong with the special classes at Wilcox," she said in her Brooklyn accent that challenged wrong to *rawng*, strong to *strawng* and water to *waw-tuh*. It didn't matter how many times I told her I wasn't a baby, she would not budge. "The world is cold. You stay close to home and everything will be fine." And that was that. Anyone that ever tried to change her mind would tell you the same. I kicked a pebble into the street.

"We could meet at the train station after school," I said.

"And I'll come over and study with you. It'll just be like we've got classes in different buildings."

"Yeah. I guess so."

I could see my house in the distance: two stories of yellow aluminum-sided magnificence that my Grandma Rose left to my mother. Today, instead of the usual comfort I felt on sight of it, the inside of my nose tingled. I blinked my tears back.

"Can't hang today," said Tanisha. "Uncle Roland's waiting for me."

"I know."

"I don't want to go."

"You're such a liar."

"Can't you let me at least try to make you feel better?" she asked.

"Oh boy. Here comes Sally Sunshine again." She giggled. Her perkiness annoyed me sometimes, but that was just the way she was wired. Besides, most of the time it made me feel good.

"And don't worry. You're gonna get your period soon. In fact, I'll bet you twenty dollars that you'll get it before I get back from visiting Nana in Ohio." I didn't have twenty dollars, but I locked my pinky with hers anyway. I was that sure I'd be the only period-free girl in high school. She hugged her pictures and report card to her chest.

"Don't you feel like crying?" she asked.

"Hell no!"

"You're such a liar."

"I know." She hugged me quickly, so we wouldn't end up bawling our eyes out right there on Hopkinson Avenue. She was a smart girl, that Tanisha Banks. She walked backwards down the street.

"See you in September, Ayj. Love ya!"

"Love ya, too!" I waved and kept waving until she got so small in the horizon, I couldn't see her anymore. The forecast for the summer: definitely overcast.

One month later, on my birthday no less, it turned out Ms. Sunshine was absolutely wrong. I sat on the toilet making plans for my twenty dollars. Maybe it would go toward a new pair of sneakers. Or maybe a new walkman. I almost burned the motor out of the one I had, rewinding my Saturday night hip-hop radio tapes. Or maybe it would go toward buying myself a bib and pampers because I was still just a big damn baby.

I slunk into my parents' bedroom and curled up next to my mother. Her satiny sheets emanated baby powder, Grey Flannel cologne and an odd scent I wasn't sure of. The only time I ever noticed that smell was early in the morning when they first unlocked their bedroom door.

"Happy birthday, Baby."

"Thanks," I mumbled.

"You'll get it soon, Baby. Trust your mommy, okay?" All I could muster in response was a sigh. I snuggled closer to her, relishing the rare treat. My mother was always cooking, cleaning, fixing, hustling or helping someone somehow. My father always said if someone tried to kill her, she'd probably be an accessory to her own damn murder.

Sometime around noon, I woke up from a sticky midsummer's nap and my mother was gone. My stomach was achy and I felt slightly feverish. Just what I needed for my birthday: the flu. I turned over to holler for her.

"What's the matter?" She folded my dad's undershirts, placing them one stack at a time in his dresser against the window.

"Stomach hurts."

"It's probably just gas," she said. "Maybe you need to go boo-boo." That was my mother's solution to everything. I sat on the toilet until my leg started to fall asleep, but there was nothing happening. Then again, nothing ever happened to me. All my friends had these fantastic boy stories. Tanisha met a boy in Ohio last summer and got a hickey on her neck. My friend Lizette snuck a boy into her apartment but her mother came home early and beat him with a broomstick handle. Nikki and her best friend Tasha Tee met Kangol from UTFO at the Fresh Fest. And my cousin, Kerri? She had even done it! Me? I had a city spelling bee championship and I'd been skipped a grade. Big frickin' deal.

You would have thought a burglar was coming through the bathroom window the way I hollered. My mother busted through the door.

"What in the ---?" I pointed at the pink water.

"Aww, my baby is grown," she cooed.

"So can I go to Tech in September?"

"Nope. Come on. We gotta go buy you some stuff!"

"Can I at least go to the store by myself?" She let out a huge sigh like she does when she's ready to let me have my way.

"Child, please."

Salsa pumped through La Mercado Supermarket on Pitkin Avenue.

"I wish they turn down this *La Cucaracha* music. I can't even hear myself think," she mumbled. She yelled up to the booth.

"Manny, where yall keep the girl stuff?" Oh. My. God. I shielded my eyes from the glare of embarrassment. If anybody in the store asked, I would definitely say I was adopted. Manny, with his spiky black crew cut, pointed toward the back and put up four fingers.

On our way to the 'girl stuff', my mother turned to smile at me every few steps. Her bright white teeth contrasted against smooth ebony skin that I had not inherited. Everyone would definitely believe my adoption story.

"You grown, Baby!" I shrugged like it was no big deal. After all, I couldn't even come to the store without her. But I proudly embraced the green and pink package like it was a trophy. All I ever wanted was to be grown. And to meet Bow-Legged Lou from Full Force.

I was exactly one step away from making my first womanly purchase when everything I knew stopped making sense.

Corey Robinson, the cutest of the cute, was behind the register. He was tall and slim with caramel skin, big chocolate brown eyes and a Colgate smile. He even had a straight part cut into the side of his hair. The only man that was finer than him was my Daddy. I didn't realize I was staring until he smiled. I dropped the pads like they'd caught fire, smiling back at him and blinding everyone within a five mile radius with my braces.

"So much for being grown," whispered my mother. She placed the pads on the conveyor belt.

"They ain't for my *daughtuh*," she told him with a wink.

I was halfway down the block before I realized the laughter behind me was not in my head, but my mother having a good time at my expense.

Nikki and Tasha Tee lounged on their favorite bench outside the park. Every time I passed by, if they were outside, they were sitting in the same place: Nikki on the seat with one leg folded under her, jabbering at lightning speed; Tasha Tee on the bench back nodding and maybe interjecting once or twice in the conversation.

"Wassup Adrienne? What you up to?" asked Nikki. The red strings of her bathing suit slithered down the front of her yellow t-shirt. I felt a twinge of jealousy because I wouldn't be able to go to The Pool with them.

"Coming from the store. Guess what I finally got, yall?"

"A boyfriend?" she joked. I pointed back over my shoulder.

"Yeah right. Not with The Warden around."

"Well then, that would mean you're in the club." My mother strolled up, closing the gap I'd made between us.

"What club you sposeta be in?"

"The women's club," said Tasha Tee.

My mother rolled her eyes, dismissing our claims of membership.

"Women pay bills and take care uh they damn self. When yall can do that, then come talk to me about it." She handed me the package. "Women also carry they own supplies." She sauntered off, with me rolling my eyes so hard, the whites had to be showing.

It didn't matter what she said, I was a woman. I could tell because the gaze of the cutie climbing through the hole in the chain-link fence slowly elevated past my thighs that swished past one another, up toward my breasts that bounced jubilantly in their new found glory and finally to my face. I watched him on the sly, shy but curious to read his expression. Just before I could make heads or tails of it, my mother's voice smacked the wonderment right out of me. "She's only thirteen. Go on 'bout ya business." How I would ever get a boyfriend, I didn't know.

MY HOUSE WAS LOCATED up the block from the park and directly across the street from The Pool. It was the place to be every single summer, but this year it was even better. Why? Because of the boys, of course! Cash Money and his crew would lift us up and dunk us in the water, copping free feels and hoping for a prize to pop out.

If they ever got that lucky, they would cry out, *"Ohhh!"* while Cash Money pointed and giggled; his two gold-capped bucked teeth sparkling in the sun.

As usual, the boys took things too far and went on a yanking spree.

Tasha Tee ran out of the pool clutching the front of her bathing suit like all the other girls did, but instead of crying or cursing the boys out, she came back ten minutes later with her ex-con brother, Trey Ski.

"Where he at?" The Pool was silent as Tasha pointed him out. *Oh shit. Oh shit. Oh shit.* That's what everybody was saying – Cash Money included. Trey Ski jumped down into The Pool with his jeans on, sloshing the water out of his way. Cash Money stood stock still waiting! Trey Ski cocked his thigh-like arm back and *boom*! There was blood!

"My toof! He knocked out my gold toof!" I know everyone thinks black people don't swim, but boy did we all dive for treasure!

Everybody, even Cash Money who wasn't laughing quite so hard the day after, was outside the pool. I sighed from behind lacy beige curtains frustrated at the limitations of being a woman.

"Oh no!" I cried out to no one in particular. Lashelle Johnson with her stupid pigeon-toed self was standing in the middle of the group, snapping her gum, talking to Corey. My Corey! Lashelle had long wavy hair, smooth light skin and a tiny little mole over her lip. She was the prettiest girl in the neighborhood, but she thought she was all that, just because her mother owned Klassy Kuts Beauty Parlor on Pitkin. Little did she know Klassy Kuts was only the place to be while the Jheri Curl was in style. And even when it was, my mom forbade me to go there because she said they sold drugs in the back room. I didn't understand why anyone would buy drugs from her when Mr. Schwartz' pharmacy was right across the street.

The big wire-rimmed fan blew hot air on the back of my sweaty legs and cajoled the curtains into my line of vision. I nearly ripped them from the rod.

"You watchin' them nappy boys again?"

"No. I was watching for Aunt Juicie and Aunt Say." My mother moved the window curtain to the side.

"That's the boy from the supermarket. Do he know you like him?" That heifer Lashelle hooked her pointer finger in the vee of Corey's Le Tigre shirt. Sweat beads popped up on my forehead, I was so mad. I wiped it quickly; mindful of preserving my brand new press and curl.

"I'm gonna go over there and tell him." She held my arm.

"Any boy that likes you will let you know, so it don't make no sense to be runnin' up *awnim.*"

"But Ma! She's getting him!"

"Oh Adrienne. I don't even know why we discussin' this. You need to be in ya books and not worryin' 'bout these damn boys all day."

My aunts pulled up in a beat down, rusty red, two-door Chevy Malibu that *sputt-putt-putted* even after Aunt Juicie took the key out of the ignition. My mother braced her foot on the baseboard of the car to help pry Aunt Say out of the passenger seat. Aunt Say was short and stocky with cheeks that looked like halves of a drumstick stuck to each side of her face. She'd had a terrible accident that made it difficult for her to walk. I overheard my mother saying her husband Big Rodney had something to do with it, but that was one story that was kept under lock and key. Aunt Juicie held Aunt Say at the elbow.

"C'mon, Sadie, just two more."

"Tryin', Juicie. But you know it's hard to get all my goodness up these stairs." When Aunt Juicie and Aunt Say stood next to each other, they literally looked like the number ten. Aunt Juicie was the exact opposite of Aunt Say, weighing in at maybe ninety-five pounds. She caught me staring at her shoulder blades.

"Adrienne, bring Say's wheelchair up on the porch, Honey." I went down to the car in my best girly walk, watching the boys who were watching the girls in their bathing suits. I may as well have been invisible in my t-shirt and Bermuda shorts. That sow Lashelle threw her head back and screeched, "Oh Corey. You so crazy!" How would Corey ever notice me with Lashelle being all in his Kool-Aid?

"Adrienne. How many damn teeth do he got?" asked my mother. My ears warmed up. I know everyone heard her because they turned our way.

Nikki confirmed it. "Adrienne, you coming to the park later?"

"Maybe tomorrow. We have company."

"Okay!"

I brought the old chair onto the porch and marked a criss-cross on the worn vinyl seat with my finger.

"C'mon, Aunt Say plant your big ol' booty on the X."

"Silly Girl, you're a mess," said Aunt Juicie chuckling. That's what she called me because she said I always made her laugh.

"Ain't she a mess? Aunt Flow done messed up her plans, so now she wanna take it out on me, her poor old sweet Aunt Say." I glared at my mother who pretended not to notice. Aunt Juicie held my shoulder.

"Periods just mean you're grown up, Silly Girl," she whispered.

"Periods ain't a secret, Baby," said Aunt Say. I still held my frown in place stomping to the kitchen, but I was tickled that they thought I was grown, too.

By the time I came back with my mother's famous lemonade, Aunt Say had finally dropped into the wheelchair and rolled herself into the living room. She parked her wheels in front of the fan and began cooling her bosom with an old church fan. Her gold bangles jiggled in a steady *chiddink-chiddink* rhythm. Aunt Juicie sat next to her on the pea green plastic-covered sofa swirling ice cubes around in her glass. I sat next to her and clasped my hands in my lap. Aunt Say told the best stories when she came over.

"You know we 'bout to talk grown folks business, Adrienne."

"But I'm grown now. You just said it yourself!" Aunt Juicie sighed.

"Not that grown, Silly Girl. Not yet."

I stomped off to the kitchen defeated. They were Indian givers. That's what they were. I paced the linoleum squares mimicking those hypocrite traitors.

You're grown, but not right now. Not yet, Silly Girl. But I was not a silly girl. I was smart. So smart, that I crawled behind the sofa, quiet as could be. Aunt Say's bangles jangled.

"Rhona Girl, they put us out," she said.

"What you mean put you out?" asked Mommy.

"Put us out. Sheriff, padlock, eviction notice. We homeless." I was puzzled. The bums by the train station were homeless. Not people with family.

"Sadie, you ain't homeless with all this family you got," said Aunt Juicie. When she spoke the plastic crinkled under her.

"I ain't got no address to get my mail, Judith. I'm homeless." I sat there with my hand cupped over my open mouth.

"He been spending all our money on the horses, girl. Horse named *Not So Lucky*. The kids are with my cousin for the weekend. I didn't even tell them nothin' yet. And girl, don't even let me get started talkin' about those little ---" Her glass clunked on the table and her bangles stopped jingling.

About those little what?! I yelled in my head. Something hard banged the top of my head instead. I popped up, holding the tender spot. My mother's fist was still clenched like she was rapping on a door.

"Owwwwwwww! Why'd you do that?!"

"Well, well, if it ain't a jackass in the box!" cackled Aunt Say. Aunt Juicie shook her head, as if to say *Silly Girl, I told you not yet.* My mother raised two fingers in the air and pointed toward the stairs the way she did when she was 'two seconds off my ass' and couldn't even find it in her to say the words.

"And you betta not repeat nothin' you heard here. Tellin' a secret…"

"Is like breaking the law," I mumbled.

I stomped out, head hung low and peeking sideways at Aunt Say. Her chunky cheeks hid her eyes in a barely concealed smile. She pinched her nose. Nosy. I rolled my eyes and stomped up the stairs. When I got to the top, Aunt Say cackled again.

"Ooh Lawd, Rhona, I love that girl to pieces." I blew imaginary kisses to her. *I love you, too, Aunt Say! Even though you sold me out!*

I lay on the carpet at the top of the steps counting the cracks in the graying ceiling paint, hoping for a gem. I couldn't hear much except the occasional '*giiiirl*'. Finally, I heard my mother's voice.

"I'ma talk it over with Dub and we'll have a family meeting tomorrow." A family meeting? I'd never been allowed to attend any because they were usually grown folks business, and therefore off limits.

The glasses clinked together as my mother collected them. "You can come down now, nosy." I crept back to my bedroom, the Lavender Palace, so she wouldn't know that as usual, she was right.

That night, with my mother and father looking over my shoulder, I blew out the candles on my pink and white homemade cake and made a wish, a few wishes actually. The most important ones: to be at the family meeting and to get a boyfriend.

Bing bing.

"Adrienne, put this up for me." I shoved my father's brandy bottle under the couch. He patted his low afro before he pulled the front door open.

"Heeeeey. Come in, come in," he said. I was so excited. Aunt Say's kids, Kerri and Lil' Rodney, were my favorite cousins. Their father, Big Rodney was another story.

Kerri was dressed fly in a Hawaiian shorts set. She was cocoa brown like their father, and pretty as ever with hazel cat eyes shielded by long satiny eyelashes. She was even prettier than Lashelle Johnson! Rodney, tall and lanky with eyelashes like Kerri's and pretty straight teeth, had on Adidas warm up pants, a t-shirt that was snug as a bug, and shell toe Adidas.

Everyone spread out on the couches: Kerri and Rodney on the pea green plastic, my parents on the brown velvet plastic. I jumped in my Daddy's armchair, between the couches, like I was Judge Wapner on *The People's Court.*

Big Rodney perched his wide ass on the arm of the couch, even though my mother always asked him not to. He was a bull of a man, with large flaring nostrils. He could vacuum the living room carpet in one sniff. I couldn't stand him.

"Ay Dub. You got any more of that good shit you be drinking?"

"Sorry man. That well's dry," lied my father.

"Well," said my mother, "we might as well get down to it. Rodney Senior, since it's just me, an' Adrienne and Dub living here, Rodney and Kerri can come live with us." Big Rodney snorted.

"I think Lite Brite and Kerri and Rodney should all go on upstairs and let grown folks talk." I begged my mother with pathetic puppy dog eyes. *Please don't make us leave!* My father adjusted in his seat, rustling the plastic under him.

"Alright now. Easy on the Lite Brites." He was light-skinned too, with freckles at the bridge of his nose.

"Ay Dub, you know I was just playin'. Rabbit, you know I was just playin', right?" His nose flared. My mother kicked the side of the chair.

"Yes, Big Rodney. I know you were playin'." I lowered my voice. "Wit ya ugly self." My mother narrowed her eyes at me.

"Whaaaat?" I asked, pretending I didn't know why.

"Rodney, the kids gonna stay right here and understand the *sitchation* for what it is. They parta the family, too." Big Rodney tugged at navy suspenders, sliding his thumbs down past his man tits, to his navel and back up again. We secretly called him Rerun because above all else, every Christmas he cut the fool, pop-locking to Salsoul's Christmas album. My Daddy winked at me, but I sat still like I was in church. I didn't want any parts of Rhona.

"Well shit. Seem like I ain't got no say 'round here. Nobody ain't even ax me what I want. Said 'Rodney Senior. Where you want yo' muthafuckin' kids to go?' Nope. Not even that common courtesy."

"Look. Sadie asked me to keep the kids and thas what I'm gonna do. The kids can be close to school and since Kerri is always here, sneaking my cookies up to Adrienne's room, she may as well come and sneak them into her own." Kerri scratched her arm like the dope fiend in front of the bodega on Rockaway.

Aunt Say could have stayed with us too, but her goodness wouldn't have been able to make it up and down the stairs in our house. She was moving into Aunt Juicie's tiny apartment in Coney Island and in her own words, *didn't want to see Big Rodney's black ass ever again.* Big Rodney belched.

"You an' Say always tryna gang the fuck up on me even though you my damn sister. But you want the kids to stay here? Fine then, Rhona. They can stay here. Yall kids wanna stay here?" Rodney and Kerri nodded.

"Okay, well then it's done then." He cleared his throat. "So what's the arrangements gonna be?"

"What you mean arrangements? You can see the kids whenever you want. Just don't be ringing the bell at no crazy hours uh the night. And long as they here, they got to follow my rules. Ain't no other 'rangements than that."

"Oh nah, I ain't talking bout that. My kids is good kids. They gon' listen to you even when you not talkin'. Right, kids?"

"Yesh, Daddy," said Kerri with a silly baby voice. Rodney and I looked at each other. Big Rodney ran his hands down the suspenders again.

"You know yall got that extra room in the basement, right. So I was thinkin' you can put the girls in Lite Brite's room and Rodney can stay upstairs, next door to the girls…and then I can stay down there." He snapped his right suspender with his thumb, which divided his one mammary into two. I wondered how Aunt Say felt about that breast situation. My mother tilted her head to the side.

"Why the hell you lookin' at me like that?" asked Big Rodney.

"Because I don't think that's a good idea at all."

"Who the hell said you was the judge of good ideas and bad ideas, Rhona? Huh? Who appointed you?" My mother smiled. She was a little bit crazy. Smiling when she wanted to curse; crying when she was happy.

"Let me talk to you in the kitchen, Rodney."

"Nah, Rhona. We family. Thas whatcha said right? So let's talk like family. I'm just tryna make things right. Keep family together." My mother's smile stayed put.

"Alright then. I am gonna keep the kids together, here with me and Adrienne and Dub. And I love ya, but we can't live under the same roof." He cut his eyes at my mother and turned to my dad.

"This was my mother's house, too," he said. My mother interjected.

"Was." My mother folded her arms. Big Rodney lowered his voice.

"Dub, you gon' let ya wife control ya house like this? Woman don't know nothin' bout keepin' a family together, man."

"That's what my wife say, then thas what it is, Bruh." My mother jumped up, hands on her hips. She tipped her pointer finger his way.

"Rodney gonna stay downstairs in the extra room. The room next to Rabbit is for Kerri. Girls upstairs, boys downstairs, so we don't have no misunderstandings." Everyone else sat straight-backed. If I'd had a gavel like Judge Wapner, I would have banged it. Big Rodney folded his arms across his chest.

"But they can share a room. They girls," he whined.

"And you can make your own way. You a man. Now I'm tryna be nice about this Rodney, but you pushin' my buttons."

I felt bad because Big Rodney was crazy, but he was still family. He brought candy by the house on holidays and he took Rodney to all these different basketball tournaments in the city. Mommy said it's because he saw something in Rodney that he never had. She said Lil' Rodney had drive. I didn't understand what she meant at first, since I always saw Big Rodney driving his Cutlass Supreme everywhere, sometimes with ladies that weren't Aunt Say. But then I got hip. And she was right, as usual.

"Rhona," he sniffed. "You ain't shit. You ain't worth---" *Sksssshh!*

Chunks of my mom's white ceramic vase were at Big Rodney's feet. Water dripped from the bald of his forehead and baby's breath hung from his shoulder.

"Don't you dare disrespect me in my own home, Rodney James Barrus. I don't owe you a explanation, but I'll tell you this much. Your spirit is bad. And you will not lay your head in my home as long as I am alive. Trust." She rounded on Lil' Rodney.

"Rodney Junior. You think you gonna have a problem living here and follin' my rules?" Rodney stared at the floor.

"No, Ma'am."

"Kerri?" She scratched her arm again. I never noticed that before. It was fascinating. She shook her head.

"Then it's all settled then. Blood is blood. We take care uh each other. Dinner is in a hour. Be at the table with clean hands and a good appetite." Big Rodney stomped out, slamming the front door behind him. The rest of us fell in line at the sink.

TO MY ABSOLUTE DELIGHT, Kerri and I were also inseparable. So much so, that my father took to calling us Shadow Sisters. *Shadow Sisters, it's time for dinner. Shadow Sisters, go to the liquor store for me. Shadow Sisters, be back before the streetlights come on.* After years of begging my mother to have another baby, I finally had a sister. I loved it.

At the park, I couldn't wait to introduce her to everyone.

"Wassup, Adrienne!"

"Hey yall! This is my cousin, Kerri." The response was weird. It was almost like my ears were stopped up. Kerri had her best b-girl stance in place: one hip poked out, the other leg bent just so, but her face looked like she had gas. Fuquan the Swan walked over from the basketball courts dribbling the ball. Fuquan was tall with a long neck, well-built and light brown sugar fine, but he was a loose cannon. Nobody, I mean nobody, crossed him.

"Sup Adrienne?" he asked.

"Hi Fuquan." He checked Kerri from her bone straight bangs down to her Diamond Ellesse sneakers.

"Hey Cutie, what's your name?" Kerri snapped her gum.

"Didn't she just say 'this is my cousin Kerri'? Oops, ah-doy."

"Bitch! Who the fuck you think you talking to?" Kerri scratched her arm. Of all the people to have an attitude with, she picked crazy ass Fuquan!

"Ay Fuquan. Nice kicks you got on," said Corey.

"Thanks youngster." He turned to Kerri. "Watch yourself, girl. Word to Big Bird, I'll slap the fuck outta you." Kerri very wisely pretended not to hear him. Corey stood between Kerri and me.

"What's up?" he said looking at me. I blushed.

"You're too young for me," said Kerri trying to grab control of the situation again.

"You ain't all that," I heard from in the crowd. Even Nikki, voted the neighborhood Miss Congeniality, rolled her eyes and looked away. The breeze was definitely cooler in the park. Kerri pulled me to the side.

"Don't introduce me to any more of these people. Who are the top dogs?" And so I pointed out the key players. The kids that would rob you: Julie and T-Pot from Blake Avenue; some boys I recognized as members of the Decepticons Gang; the boosters that could get fly Polo gear for cheap; Cash Money and the Cash Money Crew; and the girls sitting at the far end of the park that we wouldn't be talking to under any circumstances: Lashelle and her friends.

Even if no one else liked Kerri, I did. She was hip, she was cool, she was fly. And she was my sister. Sometimes sisters got on everyone's nerves. It was a fact of life. But I didn't take her back to the park.

Instead we hung out on the steps like Tanisha and I used to do or we sat up in The Lavender Palace.

"Your mom needs to get some AC in here. Dang."

"I know. I can hear the drums of the Congo."

"What?"

"It's hot like Africa."

"You ain't never been to Africa. How would you know? And anyway who says stuff like that?" She shook her head, giggling to herself. Personally, I didn't see what was so funny about that.

The only other place in the house where we could have any privacy to gossip was Kerri's room and she said she preferred my room because I had a bigger television. Never mind that it was secondhand with a black and white picture tube.

Even in the sizzling heat of summer, and no matter how much my father and I had argued, begged, or complained my mother did not believe in air conditioner because it was just too expensive when we could just use the fan.

I sat on the floor between Kerri's legs. It was too hot to be so close to another human being, but Kerri had promised me a miracle. In the summertime, my edges tended to frizz up giving me an afro halo surrounding my silky ponytail. If Kerri came through, I'd be fly like her!

"Anyway, Lashelle and her friends are so corny," said Kerri. "I can't believe everybody likes them."

"I don't think she's all that."

"Nope. And I already had that haircut. And I even heard her mother has a beauty parlor. She should have the latest hair styles at all times."

"Yeah. But nobody goes there anymore. Everybody that goes in comes out looking like James Brown. Ha! Kiss myself!" Kerri slapped her leg and let out a shriek that startled me.

"Now that was funny, Rab!" She giggled.

"Yeah. And Lizette came out of there once and she looked like a poodle so she never went back!"

"A poodle?!" *Bwaaaahhh-ha ha ha!* She continued to cackle and beg me for more. I was only too glad to dish as she brushed and yanked my hair back until she finally patted my head. "There. Now you can roll with me." I jumped up and ran to the mirror. My French braid was long, down past my shoulders. Perfect. I tied on my head scarf and jumped on the bed with Kerri.

"So you think Corey likes Lashelle?" I asked.

"I hope not. She's so dumb."

"I know. Because I think he's sooo cute!"

"Me toooooo!" We fell back on the bed, screaming.

"Tomorrow, I'm gonna say hi to him," I said, breathlessly.

"For what? He's not gonna like you."

"Why wouldn't he like me?"

"You're right. He might like you." She had a funny smile on her face that I wasn't sure I liked. I brushed it off. Kerri and I were the Shadow Sisters, singing *Showstoppers* into a makeshift hairbrush microphone like we were the real Salt and Pepa. She was my sister, my partner in crime, my ace boon coon.

The next day, I let Corey pass by without saying a word. Kerri was right. He probably wouldn't like me.

While Kerri and I were tag-teaming the world, Rodney was in his own. He went to basketball camp everyday, came home and went down to the bat cave. If he wasn't at basketball camp, he was at Gauchos gym or the Boys and Girls Club. And if he wasn't there, he had a tournament game over at the park where I could finally go and hangout with my friends, so long as Kerri or Rodney were going, too. On game nights, Kerri and I followed hot on the heels of his yellow and purple Converse dunks. We got to be cheerleaders for his team, the Brooklyn Bombers.

My name is Aydree. Oh yeah.
I come from Brooklyn. Oh yeah.
I look so fiiiine. I blow your mind. Oh yeah.
My sign is Leo. Leo girls' sweet as can be!

For me, the cheering was fun but the real highlight was seeing Corey. When I did my cheers, I made sure I put a little extra bounce in my steps just in case he was watching. Just in case Kerri was wrong.

The hot and sticky night that the Brooklyn Bombers smashed the Harlem Hoopsters was the night I'd been dreaming of. The game was over and everybody was giving Rodney his props as he passed by the bleachers. Corey came from behind the gate and gave him a pound.

"Good game, man." He leaned down to me. "Nice cheers." I was shocked. I kept walking, cheeks afire. Kerri, who had just been walking next to me, was suddenly arm-in-arm with Rodney.

"Great game, Roddy." Lashelle waved from the stands.

"Bye, *Rotneeeee*," she said. Rodney waved and put his head down quickly.

"Don't you like girls, *Rotneeee*?" I asked.

"Of course I like girls."

"Well how come you didn't talk to her?"

He bounced the ball on the concrete. Bap. Bap-bap. Between his legs to his left hand and back to his right. Bap. Bap-bap.

"Know what I think? I think you like boys." I teased. He grabbed me and put me in a headlock with his left; right hand still bouncing the ball in his right. Kerri snapped her Bubble Yum.

"Roddy, don't listen to her. She got all that mouth, but she ain't say nothing to Corey."

"That's different. Ewww. Rodney! You all sweaty! Get off!" I pulled away and ran. When I got far enough away, I started up again.

"And why're yall always slappin' each other on the butt?"

"That's sportsmanship, stupid."

"That's gaymanship!" I laughed like a hyena until I crouched over, tears streaming down my cheeks. Kerri shook her head at me.

Rodney tried not to, but he couldn't help but laugh, too. He kicked me in the butt and I chased him all the way home, never catching up no matter how hard I tried. He was a slippery guy, that damn Rodney.

THE NIGHT BEFORE the first day of school was too much for me to bear. I was literally bouncing off the lavender walls of my bedroom. I was going to high school. Me! Thirteen year old, Adrienne!

I had so many questions, too. What would school be like without Tanisha? Would I make new friends? Would I make friends with Kerri's and Rodney's friends? Would they treat me like a nerd for being in the gifted classes? Would they laugh at my braces? Call me brace face? I jumped off my canopy bed and went to the mirror to practice smiling with my mouth closed. And then I giggled because I looked like my dead Grandma Rose when she didn't have her teeth in.

I always envied the other kids that had their brothers and sisters in the same school. It may have been in my head, but I always imagined they had this invisible bond and had each other's back no matter what, which was cool. And now I was going to be one of those kids. I ran downstairs to see what my sister and brother were up to.

"Where're you goin' like that, Rodney?" I asked. I fell into the sofa next to my mother and Kerri, who had on the cutest pink and white polka dot pajama set. My nightshirt looked slightly yellowed and worn compared to hers. Rodney looked down at his snug white polo shirt and Levi's.

"It looks alright to me, Roddy."

"It looks fine, Lil' Rodney. Don't pay her no mind." Rodney smoothed down the front of his shirt.

"What's wrong with it, Rabbit?" I shrugged my shoulders.

"Nothin'. Never mind."

"Adrienne stop being silly and answer the boy's question."

"The jeans are okay, but you need to stop buying your shirts in the newborn section." I drew a line across my bicep. My mother exhaled.

"Well, now that you mention it, it does look a little bit tight. But it's too late to do nothin' about it now."

"Why don't you wear the red one that your mom sent you? And wear your white and red Nike dunks. The clean ones that you don't play ball in. That'll look cute. And then, maybe you'll get a girlfriend and stop slapping the boys on the butt."

"Very funny, Rabbit." When I passed by, Rodney stuck his foot out so that I stumbled. We giggled, but Kerri held her stomach howling louder than the two of us combined.

I went back to my room and tried again to smile without showing my braces, but Grandma Rose smiled back.

Kerri barged into my room with her hands on her hips.

"Kerri. How does it look if I smile like this?"

"Like it's better than blinding everybody with those train tracks." Wow. "Anyway, I don't know what your problem is. But you need to back off."

"What are you talking about?"

"You're the smart one, Miss Honor Roll. You figure it out." I snuggled between the sheets wondering what exactly my problem was besides her funky attitude. I fell asleep without the answer.

In the morning, I checked myself one last time in the front hallway mirror. Baby hair. Check. Vaseline on the lips. Check. Fly outfit. Check. I was halfway down the street, in front of my mother's friend Miss Lewis's brand new row house before my mother called out to me.

"Adrienne, I think you gonna be needin' this, Baby." She met me half way, shaking her head like I was a lost cause. Book bag. Check.

"Now, calm down. And stick close to Kerri. And --- " I booked up the street to catch up with Kerri and get away from my mother. The school was practically two minutes away. Sometimes she worried just a little too much.

Wilcox High looked like an enormous limestone castle as we approached it. The gates guarded the grass moats on the side, while the front entryway was swarmed with laughing and grumbling serfs and peasants. I giggled at my medieval observations. Kerri would definitely think me a nerd for that.

The guys were styled out in the latest brown suede Clarks with straight leg jeans. And the girls? Tight Lee Jeans with tight Le Tigre shirts. Sergio Valente jeans. Coca Cola Shirts in turquoise or red. And the jewelry? The bigger and shinier the better. Rings. Earrings. Rope chains. All in extra large. Kerri had her prep look going, defying the masses. A blue Polo Rugby. I felt like I was in uniform in my Lee's and baby pink LeTigre. I felt like I fit in for a change.

"Aren't you nervous?" I asked Kerri.

"Nope." She scratched her arm.

"How come you can't just admit you're nervous, too?"

"Because I'm not nervous!" She scratched again. Kerri was a trip.

Conversations swirled around us. Everyone but us little freshmen had something to say.

"Senior homeroom seven-oh-five. That's right. Respect your elders."

"I can't stand Miss Norwood. She a bitch!"

"Fifth period was the dopest lunch period last year. If Mr. Levy is the dean, you know it's gonna be fly!"

All of a sudden, Kerri started bugging out.

"TaQuisha! Jasmine! Over here!" I had never seen her so hyped before. She waved her arms in the air, beckoning them over. I had to admit, they were fly with their MCM bags and brand new haircuts from Black Hair Is. But they were Lashelle's homegirls from way across the park. The ones I refused to introduce her to. She lowered her voice.

"They were the flyest girls in my old building, Rabbit. So don't embarrass me." Her voice got loud again.

"Quisha, Jazzy, this my lil' cousin, Rabbit. She thirteen, but she smart. Like *Revenge of the Nerds* smart." My eyebrows shot up. "But thank God I hooked her up so she doesn't look like it."

"Hello? I'm standing right here…"

"Rabbit? What kinda name is that?" asked TaQuisha.

"My *name* is--" Kerri cut me off before my neck could make its full rotation.

"Cause she had had buck-teef. So Roddy had gave her that name."

"Rotnee? Oh word? I seent him at the park last week and his game had lookted good. He playin' again this year?" asked Jasmine.

"Yup. And he gonna be on the Varsity. That's the juniors and seniors. Only the best players be on Varsity. And everybody know Roddy is the best!

I waited against the gate by myself, disappointed and pissed. It wasn't my fault I got skipped. And why'd she have to tell them I was thirteen? Oh! And the nerd thing?! Where did that come from? I looked over at her and rolled my eyes. She didn't even notice because she was still jabbering about *Rot-neee.*

A candy apple red Jetta with a skirt and spoilers pulled up to the curb with the bass thumping. Lashelle Johnson stepped out in the freshest Nike tracksuit. Every girl in the courtyard made a mental note to get one. I know I did. Jasmine and TaQuisha squealed and ran over leaving Kerri alone at the gate. I turned my back on her treasonous ass. Rodney sat at the top of the steps with his ball player friends and a group of prissy girls that were giggling at everything he said. I knew Rodney. He wasn't that funny. But when he saw me looking his way, he yanked the collar of his red Polo and gave me a thumbs up. All I could do was laugh. Maybe he was kind of funny.

When the bell rang and the front doors parted, I spilled into the lobby with everyone else. I didn't want to look like a lame so I pretended to know where I was going. On the fourth floor, the numbers weren't making any sense. Corey laughed with his tenth grade friends near the water fountain. I ducked behind a fat girl with a ponytail to the side. I didn't want him to see that I was lost. I trudged to the end of the hallway wondering if I'd ever find my way.

"Ayyy-dreeee-yennnne!" My head snapped upward and then every last one of my brace-sparkled teeth came out to visit.

"Neesh!" We ran to each other and hugged like we hadn't seen each other in one hundred forevers. Ironically, when I got skipped to the fifth grade, Tanisha was the first friend I made.

"But what are you doing here? What happened to Brooklyn Tech?"

"My mother didn't want me to go that far." She leaned closer. "Her and my dad split up over the summer. And you know my father's crazy." He really was crazy. He was outside in shower slippers and shorts in the winter, crazy. Talk in riddles and laugh when no one else is laughing, crazy. Run the other way, crazy.

"I'm so glad to see you," she said. "Where in the world is 413B?" I showed her my schedule and we grinned like fools.

"And guess what Neesh? I owe you twenty dollars!" We jumped up and down until the dean hollered into the bullhorn.

"Get to class!"

High school was gonna be fly. Just like I'd imagined.

EVER SINCE KERRI SPOTTED Jasmine and TackyIsha on the first day of school, my dreams of having a sister in the same school faded. It was almost like we'd never even met. That was fine because I could not stand the way she spoke around them. If I had to listen to her talk about *Rotnee* for five more seconds, I would have killed myself. On top of that, she didn't really have a sense of humor. And so, the Shadow Sisters were officially defunct. But it didn't matter. The Twin Towers were back in effect.

"Ayj. It's Africa-hot in this building. Will you please hurry?"

It was hot in the building, but my bag was heavy with my dirty gym clothes and books. The closer we got to the door, the hotter it seemed to get. Tanisha began to speed walk, and then we both started running until we bust through the front doors.

"Air!!" she yelled, her arms opened wide.

"You are so dramatic." She laughed for a second and then her expression darkened.

"Ayj. Go ahead without me. I forgot my keys."

"See. That's what you get for rushing me. I'll wait for you out here."

"No, for real. Go ahead. And I have to ask Mr. Levy something about my homework." Before I could insist, she ran back inside. Strange.

Tanisha's dad sat on the hood of an old gray Buick Skylark, sporting a turquoise turban and fatigues and super shined army boots, whistling back at the birds in the tree. I walked past him, hoping he wouldn't ask me where she was.

"Rabbit, wait up." Rabbit? He didn't know me as Rabbit. I looked over my shoulder. It was Kerri. I was surprised because when I saw her in the hall at school, she would act like she didn't see me. And at home, everything I said seemed to earn me an eye-roll or a snide comment.

I walked along the edge of the sidewalk in silence, crunching the leaves under my feet. Kerri shook her head, hitching her Gucci bag up on her shoulder. "So lame," she muttered.

"If I'm so lame, why the hell are you walking with me, Kerri?"

"Cause Jazzy and Quisha had to go somewhere."

"Yeah, to Lashelle's and you weren't invited." I smashed the leaves down harder.

"That's not true!" I shrugged. Maybe it was. Maybe it wasn't. It didn't really matter. Kerri sped past me toward the house.

But instead of going inside to get out of the cold and away from each other, she and I exchanged a glance. Across the street, Cash Money, Corey, and some other boys from around our way were rapping and doing the human beat box in front of the locked-up pool.

I sat sideways on the frozen concrete, spying on Corey, but trying to look like I wasn't. Kerri leaned on the pillar next to me, in her favorite stance.

"Cash Money is fi-yi-yine!" she said. I snickered into my jacket. None of the kids had found Cash Money's gold tooth in the bottom of The Pool because it was lodged in Trey Ski's fist. Nikki said that Trey Ski wore it around his neck on a gold chain. Oh, yeah. Cash Money was fine!

"Rab, can I borrow your walkman?" asked Kerri.

"Nope. It's lame just like its owner."

"I'll braid your hair for yooou…" she sang.

"So you can make me out to be a charity case again?"

"Rabbit. What is your problem? I was just joking with you! You want me to braid it or not?"

My boo, Corey, waved from across the street. My heart flippity-flopped. We waved back. Kerri was a little too enthused for my taste.

"He's really cute," she said. I looked at her sideways for a full minute. I'd kill her. I didn't even know how. But I would. Her and Lashelle.

Corey jogged across Hopkinson and stood at my front gate with his hands tucked into his pockets. His elephant skin bomber jacket was stupid fresh. He checked out my sneakers and my bubble goose with appreciation.

"Did I pass the inspection?" I asked. "Damn." He smiled at me like he did in the supermarket: extra wide. Kerri cleared her throat.

"Rabbit. I think your mother's calling you."

"Corey, what's your favorite New Edition song?" I asked. They both looked at me like I'd completely lost it.

"I ain't really down with New Edition."

"Yeah, well my favorite song is *Jealous Girl*." Kerri turned her full attention to me, raising her voice higher than necessary.

"What's that supposed to mean?" All the boys looked over from The Pool. I lowered my voice.

"It means you're playing yourself. That's not my name and my mother's not calling me."

"Your name is Adrienne, right?" Corey asked. I nodded with a stupid smile on my face. He knew my name!

"Aren't yall related to Rodney?" My smile disappeared.

"Yeah. He my brother." Kerri boasted, ready to grab the limelight.

"If you came over here to ask about Rodney, then you can just go back across the street and *puh, ah-one-two*, with your friends." Kerri elbowed me, so I elbowed her back. She elbowed me again like she wanted to start shit.

"I didn't come to ask about Rodney. I came to ask if you're going to Tanisha's party." Every year, Tanisha had the hottest birthday parties in her basement. Her big brother, Sha-Born was a deejay and he always had the freshest records.

"I'm in there like swimwear." He leaned down closer.

"You gonna save a dance for me?" Inside, I did a cartwheel and a split.

"I gotta see if you can dance first." His gold tooth sparkled in the afternoon sun.

"Oh. You will see, girl." When he walked away, I was in my own dreamy Corey-filled world of red cartoon hearts and cupid arrows. Kerri barged into it.

"You knew I liked him first, Rabbit. That's messed up."

"What?!"

"I told you I did. And you were jealous 'cause you knew he would like me better! That's why you didn't want him to ask about Rodney. Because you're jealous of him, too. You're the one that's a jealous girl!"

The porch door slammed shut. I almost paid attention to her tantrum, when I realized all of a sudden, Corey liked me. Regular ol' Rabbit. And we were gonna dance at Tanisha's party. Tanisha! I dashed inside and as soon as I got to the kitchen phone, it rang.

"Heard you got a date for my party. Go, Aydree, it's ya birfday!"

"Well dang. I only got it five minutes ago!"

"I know. Your triflin' cousin called me."

"I didn't know yall were like that." I felt a pinch of jealousy. Neesh was *my* friend.

"We're not. You better watch that girl. She's type funny." I felt better knowing that Kerri wasn't going to be able to infringe on my friendship, but I was still anxious. Tanisha wasn't the type of person to talk about people. That was all me. I hung up with her and headed to my room. My Dad sat up in his chair. I jumped back, dropping my books on the floor.

"Daddy! What are you doing home?"

"Had a day off, Baby. Every man is entitled to a day off, ain't he?"

"I guess." I could distinctly remember him telling me, men that work with their hands don't get a day off so often, but if that's what he said, then that's what it was.

"National Geographic's on. They in the Serengeti this week. You gon' watch with your old Dad?" I gathered my books.

"I have a lot of homework and Kerri's gonna fix my hair for me. Next week, maybe?"

"Alright, Pumpkin." I ran upstairs and knocked on Kerri's door.

"Who?" she yelled.

"Who else?" I turned the doorknob, but the door didn't budge.

"Kerri? Kerri, open up." The TV was on and I could hear her laughing. I waited for her to open the door, but she never did. Heifer. I dropped my books on the desk, and noticed something else that was odd: my walkman was gone.

TANISHA WAS RIGHT. I had to watch Kerri because I never knew what she was going to do next. And she was always doing something.

Kerri bounced down the length of the cafeteria with Jasmine following right behind her and sat at our table. She glanced at the stairwell every minute or so. Her door knocker earrings glittered in the fluorescent light.

"Is something the matter, Kerri?"

"No." Tanisha sat down with her tray.

"Well, is there something you need?"

"Like I need somethin' from *you*. Psssh." She fanned me off. "Ain't nobody looking for me, but Julie Trotman looking for you." Tanisha and I looked at each other. Julie Trotman lived in the projects around the corner from me on Blake Avenue. Julie was a strange reddish brown color with hair that was sandy brown and always worn in a ponytail. She was deceptively innocent looking, dimpled cheeks and all. But Julie, her cousin Khalid and her brother T-Pot were notorious for robbing people. At knifepoint!

"What'd I do to her?"

"I don't know. But she *axed* me if I *seent* you. And I told her you had lunch this *peviod*."

"Stupid! You should've said you didn't know! Oh my God! Where were you when they were handing out brains?"

"In the beauty line, where you shoulda been at!" Kerri and Jasmine strode off, past the junior and senior spades games, seeming to enjoy my panic.

"Neesh. What could she want with me?" Julie came through the stairwell at the other end of the lunchroom. Kerri, that heifer, pointed my way. Tanisha sighed.

"If she hits you, we'll just have to jump her. That's all." As she got closer, I tried to remain calm but mostly, I watched Julie's four finger ring.

"I've been watching yall," she said. Tanisha touched her Nefertiti earrings.

"Nah! Not like that. Yall are funny!" Julie laughed until a tear fell.

"For real tho'. Yall need me to round out your crew."

"We don't have a crew," said Tanisha.

"Now you do. Miss Popularity. The Cute Brainiac. And me the Flygirl Enforcer. It works." I narrowed my eyes like my mother did when she was suspicious.

"What do you really want?" I asked. Tanisha kicked me so hard under the table, I jumped.

"What?!" Julie looked like she was going to punch me right in the face. And then she surprised us again. She laughed. Again Tanisha and I relaxed…a little.

"So spill the beans. What do you really want, Jules?" She chuckled, shaking her head.

"Jules. Yall two are hilarious." She lowered her voice. "I need tutoring, but I don't want nobody to know I actually do my work." She bit her bottom lip. "And as a trade off, I got good gossip about everybody."

"Lashelle Johnson," I blurted. Tanisha tapped my hand, but she leaned in closer than I did.

"She's fucking Fred Barnes. And anybody else that got a little status." We had no cool, Tanisha and I. Our eyes flew wide open. Julie laughed again.

"So I'm in?" she asked.

"Hell yeah. What else you got?" Julie did not let us down. She knew *a lot.* I was so glad I didn't have any business to spread.

Big Rodney's old raggedy ass Cutlass was parked crookedly in front of my house, blocking the driveway.

Even though I hated his fat-engorged guts, I wondered what he was doing here on a school night. It could only be one thing! I busted through the front door right in time to catch the drama unfolding.

Rodney was having a melt down on the sofa. My mother stayed on the sidelines, but since I walked right into the mix, I was dead center, Wapner-style like how I liked it.

"I don't know why Coach changed my number! My number is twenty-three, not thirteen!" Big Rodney put his big ham-hock hands on Rodney's shoulder.

"It shouldn't make you no damn difference what got-damn number it is! You Rodney Barrus, Jr. You a star no matter what muhfuckin' number you wearin'!"

"But isn't thirteen bad luck?" asked Kerri.

"Fuck that," said Big Rodney. "Wear that shit and wear it proud. You are lucky number thirteen! Anybody ask you, that's what you say."

"Dang, you can't say a sentence without cursin'," said my mother.

"Yes, the fuck I can."

"But I don't wanna wear it. I'm gonna sit out the game." Rodney's eyes were red. His voice was shaking. He was really upset and I felt bad for him. Big Rodney quick-jabbed Rodney's ear. *Whap!* He boxed him again and slapped his cheek with the back of his hand. I looked away, embarrassed.

"What the fuck is wrong with you, boy?! This the first home game and you playin' Lincoln High. Best team in the city. You better put that damn shit on and get out there. Don't nobody got no time to be playin' wit yo punk-pussy ass. There's a lotta money ridin' on this!" Rodney's bottom lip quivered.

"Rodney Senior, you ain't learnt ya lesson yet?" asked my mother.

"I know we in yo' house, Rhona. But this between Rodney Junior and me." My mother sucked her teeth and went to the kitchen.

"So put on that got-damn jersey. And make it happen." He clapped Rodney on the back and snapped his suspenders.

And then he was gone. Rodney sat with the jersey in his hand, bottom lip quivering, stewing in punk-pussy soup.

"You don't have to wear it, Roddy. You're the star."

"What you think, Rabbit?" asked Rodney. Kerri crossed her arms.

"Yeah, Rabbit. What do *you* think?"

"I think your Dad's right. It's just a number. Maybe, you can get you a lucky rabbit's foot and then that'll definitely make you lucky number thirteen. Or maybe I'll just come to the games and be the lucky Rabbit!" Kerri's face contorted like she'd sucked on a lemon. Rodney's was blank.

"Ummm, that was a joke, guys."

"You know what, Rabbit? You're right," said Rodney. Kerri's face was pure confusion. Her sneer was partly there, but she suddenly was trying to hide it.

"I'm lucky number thirteen," said Rodney.

"Yeah Roddy. You lucky number thirteen. That sounds real good."

When the final school bell rang, I rushed out of Global History, skimmed between and dodged the potential roadblock in front of the guidance counselor's office. I spotted Kerri heading toward the exit in a navy blue shearling leather coat. It wasn't cold enough for it, but she said she wanted to be the first one to showcase the coat in that color.

"Kerri," I called, "you're not going to the game?" She rolled her eyes like I was being ridiculous.

"It's not 'til three-thirty, Rabbit."

"Well, it's the first home game and it's gonna be packed like the park is in the summer. We're going early so we can get good seats."

"I can get good seats, anyway."

Kerri went out the side doors, while the girls and I scored seats right behind the bench, as planned. I put my bag on the seat to hold a spot for her, just in case. Lashelle sauntered over with the MCM Girls. Her pigeon-toed gait, extra pronounced.

"Tanisha, you and your freshman friends need to go sit up there with the others." Julie looked her up and down, studying her thick gold rope chain and bright white Nike Airs.

"We got here first," I said.

"I wasn't even talking to you, freshman nobody."

"Freshman nobody got here first, though," I said.

"Yup, we got here first, Lashelle. Sorry," said Tanisha. Julie studied her four finger ring.

"Well, we here now," said Jasmine. Tanisha pointed across the gym.

"You could sit on the other side by the cheerleaders." Jasmine looked to Lashelle for an answer. Lashelle flung her hair over her shoulder.

"See. I'm about to break. You know I don't stay shut for nobody. Especially not no freshmen." Julie huffed on her ring and buffed it using her shirt front. Huffed again and buffed. I wondered if she stole it.

"Those Nikes are fly, Lashelle," said Julie. "You like 'em?"

"Oops, ah-doy," said Lashelle, tapping the side of her head. "Of course I like 'em. Thas why I bought 'em."

"I like 'em, too. I think they might look better on me. We'll talk." Slowly Lashelle's face showed understanding. She looked Julie up and down. And then Jasmine's mouth fell open…because Lashelle *stayed shut* and climbed up on the bleachers, to a seat about three levels above us; up and away from Julie's covetous eyes.

At tip-off, Kerri came into the gym wearing some kind of crazy cut up jeans outfit and lipstick that was a shade too pink for black people. She had ditched the leather shearling for a bright neon pink scarf with matching gloves. The stands were packed and she was having a problem getting through.

"'Scuse me, 'scuse me!" she bellowed. Everyone had their eyes on the ball, trying not to miss the action.

Rodney, wearing number thirteen, was crouched, ready to spring into action.

"Ex-cah-use me! Could yall move over some?"

Tanisha and I shifted over, but the seat we were holding for her had disappeared. We moved over as far as we could, but she couldn't fit.

"I neet to be by Rotnee. Julie, you mind sittin' somewhere else?"

"What kinda question is that? Aydree, you better talk to your cousin 'fore she get her *feelins* hurt."

"Kerri. I told you what the plan was. What took you so long?" I asked.

"I knew you would take up for her!" She stormed along the outskirts of the gym and sat courtside with Big Rodney. She should have gone up top with the MCM girls. Unfortunately, they ditched her for Lashelle.

The game was so much fun, I didn't even have time to pay attention to her. With nine seconds left and the score tied at sixty-five, the tension in the gym was thick as pudding. Rodney brought the ball down from just about half court. Just when it looked like he was going to go for the shot, he shot the ball to Khalid. Khalid faked right on his man, went left and passed to Rodney who went for the three that swished into the basket. The gym exploded!

"Rodney! Rodney! Rodney!" Everyone chanted. He laughed and blushed and held his head down humbly while everyone else went stupid. Lashelle jumped down from the stands and threw her arms around his neck. Her feet dangled in the air. Oh really? Tanisha surprised us.

"Since when does that heifer know Rodney like that?"

"Oooh. You sound like you like him *like that*," said Julie.

"I could hook you up, Neesh." Rodney put Lashelle down and she kissed his cheek. His red cartoon hearts fluttered up over his head.

"Maybe some other time," she said with a huff. "Number thirteen has all he can handle for one day." Julie and I elbowed each other in collusion. Corey came across the gym.

"Can I walk you home?" he asked.

"If you don't mind walking with all of us."

"I ain't scared a yall. Especially not Knuckles over there." Julie chucked him under the chin. He didn't flinch. I liked him even more.

We filed out the side doors of the musty gym, into the unspoiled evening air. Excited at winning; excited at being young. Julie's eyes twinkled.

"Hold up," she said, "I see someone I need to talk to."

"Julie, leave that girl alone," said Tanisha.

"I just wanna talk to her. Yo, Lashelle!" Lashelle picked up her pace. I couldn't help but giggle. *Oops, ah-doy* to you, Lashelle.

"Rabbit!" I whipped around. Kerri waved from Big Rodney's old beat down Cutlass. Rust ate away at the bottom of the door and the paint job was dull and scratched. I turned around, embarrassed.

"I think that's your cousin," said Corey.

"It is. Let's just keep walking. And whatever you do, do not look over there." Someone tapped my shoulder.

"Rabbit! I know you heard me. My dad gonna take us home."

"It's only a few blocks away."

"Oh, I could stay at your house, but you too good to ride wit us?"

"No! But I'm walking home with my friends." She stomped back to the car, her neon scarf flowing behind her. Corey put his arm around me.

"So where were we? Oh yeah. You were saying how much you liked me and everything and I was saying that I knew that." I elbowed him.

"No, I was saying that guys that have a lame rap don't stand a chance with me."

Toot, toot, toot! I wanted to melt into the sidewalk.

"Ra-biiiiit," bawled Big Rodney. "Rabbit, c'mon and get in the car. Your mother want me to bring yall home." Big stupid lying ass fool.

"I'll see yall tomorrow," I mumbled.

Lil' Rodney put the seat down so I could climb in the back. I banged my head on the way in. My eyes watered, but I refused to let the tears fall. I watched Big Rodney in the rearview mirror, shooting poisonous darts into his head with my eyes.

"Think I wanna get me something to eat. Yall want some McDonald's?" I couldn't believe he was really driving us all over the neighborhood in the junk mobile! I shrank down in the seat.

"Yeah," said Rodney. Kerri put on a baby voice.

"Daddy, I would love shum McDonald'sh. Rabbit, don't you want McDonald'sh, too?"

"Rabbit. I'm talking to you." She poked me in the arm. I brushed my arm off like I would a mosquito.

"I bet she wants her regular: a cheeseburger, fries and an orange," said Lil' Rodney looking back over the seat. I crossed my arms.

"Then that's what Lite Brite's gonna have!" I knew I should have ignored him. For one thing, he was an adult. And because he couldn't help being stupid. But everything about him rubbed me the wrong way.

"Please don't call me Lite Brite, Uncle Rodney."

"Aww, what you gonna do Lite Brite, tell your Daddy? Well, he ain't shit." Kerri giggled. "Besides, everybody know pretty boys don't fight!"

"Don't disrespect my Daddy, Big Rodneeeee," I sang. Lil' Rodney tried to change the subject.

"Hey, Pop. Did you know---" Big Rodney cut him off.

"You know what? You could be a rapper like them Run DMC boys. And your name could be MC Lite Brite." I sighed. I should have just ignored them and walked home. I would have been in less trouble.

"Hmm. Let's see what your name would be if you rapped."

"Yeah, what would be my name?" he asked.

"I don't think we should play this game," said Lil' Rodney.

"Oh Rodney, we're just having fun!" I said with a big smile. He looked out the window, leaving the scene of the crime.

"See, this the Lite Brite, I like!" said Big Rodney. "What you got?"

"Hold on, I'm thinking." Big Rodney tapped his hands on the steering wheel, wearing a big stupid grin. I almost ate my words. It really wasn't worth it.

"Lite Brite, we ain't got all fuckin' day!" Did I say it wasn't worth it? Yeah. I lied.

"Well, Big Rodney, too bad for you, there's already a group called the Fat Boys, so maybe MC Rerun." I snapped my fingers. "Oh dang, somebody already has that name." Big Rodney's nose flared in the rearview. "No, no. I got it. MC Hoover!" I couldn't hold back the laugh that whooshed out of me. "Wait, wait. I got a rap, too. Listen." The car, except for the sound of the brakes squeaking, was silent with disbelief. "Pushed too far, said her Daddy ain't shit. Rabbit called me Hoover 'cause I just wouldn't quit!" I screamed with laughter.

"What she say?" asked Big Rodney. "What you say, Rabbit?" I doubled over again, trying to contain it.

"She ain't say nothin', Pop," said Rodney. Big Rodney slapped Rodney on the leg.

"That was a nice three-pointer. Your form has gotten better since summer, boy." I looked out the window again choking on leftover giggles. Hoover!

"You the best one on the team, Roddy. If they gave you the ball, the team would win by much more."

"Thanks, Kay," he said.

"Yeah, but you only had four rebounds," I said "I think you could have played more defense, Rod. Your man was scoring like crazy and you were standing there with your mouth open."

"Rabbit. You don't even know about basketball," said Kerri.

"Anyway, *Rot-nee*, in the third quarter, James was open and you went for a shot that you knew you couldn't hit."

"That's the same thing Coach said."

"He's gotta go for his. You don't get stats by passing off the ball."

"I get assists, Kay." I smirked. Yeah, *Kay*. I know about basketball.

"Rodney. Do you go out with Lashelle?" I asked.

"Well, technically we never went anywhere."

"I heard she's a hoe. And I heard she was going out with Fred Barnes from the football team." Kerri clapped her hands excitedly.

"Fuh reee-al? Fred Barnes is fine! He look just like El DeBarge." Rodney looked back between the seats.

"Where'd you hear that, Rabbit?"

"Just heard it, that's all." Rodney turned toward the window. His expression in the glass was confused and hurt. I felt kind of bad for telling him, but I couldn't have her trying to get over on him.

I munched on my fries and looked out the window, thinking about cutie pie, Corey. Kerri was going on and on about Fred Barnes until Big Rodney barked, "Shut the fuck up about that yellow nigger!"

When we pulled up to the house, I rushed past my mother, anxious to get away from the pending disaster. But I couldn't help but watch through the lace curtains. I couldn't make out what Kerri was saying, but that rat imitated how I brushed my arm off. My mother marched toward the house, and I flew up to my room with my McDonald's bag.

I was not about to apologize to Big Rodney. Not now, not ever. If my mother wanted to beat me for that, I'd just have to take it. I heard her footsteps on the stairs and steeled myself.

"No phone."

"But Ma! You don't understand! Oh my God!"

"And no party." I dumped my burger and fries and went to bed. Hate was in my heart. Heavy-like.

THE HATE BEGAN TO wane after a few days. But it didn't go away completely. Kerri, that rotten heifer, wouldn't stop talking about the party. Not to me, because we weren't speaking, but to everyone else.

I'ma buy a rope chain. I'ma wear these jeans I seent at Macy's. I'ma do my hair in the city. Blah, blah, blah. I tuned her out until I heard, *I'ma dance with…*

I was waiting for her to say Corey! Just waitin' for that heifer. But she didn't. She was back to checking for Cash Money who was supposedly going to buy her a Fendi bag. My mother peeked into the living room.

"Adrienne. I need you to go to the supermarket."

I picked up the phone. Maybe Neesh would be able to walk with me.

"I know you ain't tryna use that phone."

"Well who am I supposed to go to the store with? The bags are heavy and I'm not going with *her.*"

"You figure something out." I rolled my eyes. The telephone rang.

"Hi Nikki," said Kerri. "Rabbit can't talk. She's on lock down."

"Why would you say that, Kerri? I swear, I can't stand you!"

"Adrienne. You in enough trouble for lettin' your mouth have her own way," said my mother.

"Well, why does she have to embarrass me like that?"

"Well, it ain't like she's lyin'."

"Forget it. I don't know why I thought you would understand." I refused to look at Kerri. But I know she had that stupid 'I'm innocent' smile on her face. I pried the basement door open.

"Rod-naaaayyy! Come with me to the supermarket!"

"The game is coming on."

"We'll be back before it comes on! I promise!"

I put on my cutest hat and scarf, a pink, yellow and lavender striped set, and a little Vaseline on my lips, in case we ran into Corey. I still hadn't told him I was barred from going to the party. I didn't have the heart to. Besides I didn't want him to think I was this big baby who still got punished by her mother. Rodney burst through the basement door.

"If we get back one minute past game time, I get your lunch tickets for the week."

"Bet."

My heart plummeted when I didn't see Corey at the register.

"Manny. Is Corey here?" He never looked up from his clipboard.

"No here today." Rodney snickered in the background.

"That's your little boyfriend now?"

"Mind yours." We rolled the cart up and down the aisles with Rodney stepping on the backs of my sneakers, and me trying to run over his foot with the cart. I left him in the cereal aisle and went to the register.

Everything was fine until the chocolate milk rang up at the regular price.

"That's on sale," I told the mean-faced cashier.

"No. It ain't," she sneered.

"Yeah, it is. I have the circular." I knew because that's the only time my mother would let me buy it.

"That's at Metro Food. Not here."

"Well, guess what? I don't want it. As a matter of fact. I don't want any of it. I'm going to go buy *all* my groceries at Metro Food," I said channeling my mother. Rodney appeared from out of nowhere.

"Rabbit. It's freezing outside. If we have to walk to Metro, I am going to kill you. Not to mention, the game is coming on."

"Hi Rodney," gushed the stupid cashier girl.

"What's up?"

"Nothing. I can fix the chocolate milk. I need a void!"

"What?!" Manny turned the key in the register and corrected the error. When he turned his back, cashier girl dropped the milk, two Snickers bars and a pack of Hubba Bubba into the bag without charging us. I shot her a dirty look. And him, too. I did take the Snickers when he offered it to me, though. Star treatment definitely had its trickle down privileges.

But then the star treatment came home with us.

Leave Rodney alone, he need his rest. Take Rodney a soda. Ax Rodney if he need new sheets for his bed. I know it's his turn, but wash the dishes. Go get Rodney's things out the dirty clothes. I drew the line at touching his dirty clothes. If Kerri wanted to kiss his ass, she could clean up after it, too. He didn't have to take the garbage out anymore, help my father shovel the snow from the sidewalk, rake or clear the leaves from the gutter. Nothing. It didn't seem normal.

So when everyone else was kissing his ass, I was kicking it. If a zit posted up on his forehead, I taped a coupon for OxiZap to his mirror. If his underarms were funkier than usual, I left my deodorant on his bed with a note:

Strong enough for a man… ☺

We got along perfectly.

"Rabbit, c'mere," he shouted up the basement stairs. In the kitchen, which was at the top of the stairs, I cleared the table of the breakfast dishes and wiped it down.

"For what?"

"Because I need you to help me. That's why!" I stomped downstairs with an attitude.

"You always need something Rodney. You get on my nerves."

When I got to the bottom, Rodney was holding the TV over the stand. He'd moved his bed against the wall and the TV closer to the door. It was roomier, but I wondered if my mother would approve.

"Take that towel and put it on the stand."

"Nigger, why didn't you think this through before you started?"

"Don't call me nigger 'fore I knock you upside your head. Put the towel on the stand. Damn!" I put the towel on the stand and dashed up the steps to finish my chores.

"Thank you, Rabbit," he yelled.

"My name is Adrienne!"

"I'ma call you Rabbit 'til the day I die! And you can't stop me! Mwah ha ha! Mwah ha-ha-ha-ha!" he said, doing his best Vincent Price impression.

The name really didn't bother me. My front teeth were still a little bit bucked, but the braces were pulling them back. One more year.

Even though I gave him a hard time, he still treated me like a little sister. He even gave me all the t-shirts he got from the different colleges that he visited. My favorite was the Georgetown University one. Especially since I planned to go there.

Kerri bumped around in her room singing Whitney Houston off key. It was past noon, but I was still in bed with the cover pulled up over my head and I refused to take it down. If I couldn't go to the party, I may as well have been dead. If I died, my mother would be sad and crying and she wouldn't have anyone to blame but herself. And she'd be saying, "I should have just let her go. Big Rodney really does look like Rerun!" all while crying into her hankie. So I held my breath until my chest burned and then I let it out, wheezing. My door opened.

"Come down so we can press your hair," said my mother, The Warden.

"It's still good," I mumbled.

"I thought you might want it fresh for the party." At first, I rolled my eyes. Then I realized what she said. The party! I was going to the party!

My mother washed and dried my hair and left me sitting in the kitchen while she gossiped on the telephone. I could barely sit still. *Bing bing.*

"Go open the door," she said. My mom's friend and neighbor Miss Lewis held her pocketbook under her arm and her hot combs in the other.

"We ain't Jehovah's Witness and we ain't got nothin' we can afford to give away," I said. That's what she always said when we rang her doorbell.

"I'm gonna slap ya til ya sleepy, child. Ya better leave me the hell alone."

She patted my big blow-dried afro bouffant, following me back to the kitchen.

"Boy, in our day, this woulda been a hell of a fro, right Rho?"

"Mmmhmm, I keep hopin' it come back in style. My baby would be the queen like her mommy was," my mother crowed. Miss Lewis slapped her hot combs on the stove.

"It ain't comin' back. So you might as well get me a perm." They laughed like I told a joke. Hardy-har-frickin-har.

The smell of burnt hair on the pressing comb was cotton candy scented to my nose. I looked straight ahead at the wallpaper, yellow and white, with orange flowers, not daring to move.

Finally, she laid the comb on the stove. I ran to the bathroom to inspect her work. My hair was silky straight and past my shoulder; baby hair lying down smoothly. Perfect, except I still didn't have anything to wear.

I could maybe wear my pink shirt and my jeans. Oh my God. But everybody else was gonna have on something new. I pushed my bedroom door open and jumped back in surprise. My favorite Lees and my lavender Izod shirt were pressed and laid out on my bed. But I had a brand new pair of white Nike dunks! I jumped up and down screaming. I'd been secretly wanting them since my birthday.

"Lil' Rodney told me what happened in the car. I know it wasn't your fault, but you can't be disrespectin' no adults no matter what, Adrienne. I ain't havin' that."

"Yes, Ma." I hugged my mother a hundred times, I was so happy.

"Now hurry up an' get dressed so I can walk you over there and say what's up to Tanisha's mother."

"You don't have to walk me over there, Ma. I'm not a baby."

"You want ya Daddy to walk you?" I frowned and plopped down on the bed. She always had to throw a wrench in my best plans, which was to walk down the block and wave to everybody like I was the first full-term Black Miss America.

"Didn't think so. Besides I wanna see what new wig she got on this week." I went to the mirror and parted my bang; cussing very carefully under my breath, so as not to jeopardize my reinstated party plans. I owed Rodney big time.

Bangk! The screen door at Tanisha's house flew open and we jumped up and down screaming. Tanisha had on a pink and white track suit. Julie had on bleached jeans and a purple t-shirt with her name on the back, gold door knocker earrings, a gold rope chain and gold bangles from Canal Street. She was fresh.

Miss Pam came out the door behind them sporting a blonde Farrah Fawcett flip. She moved a lock off of her brown skin, patting the side.

"Like my wig yall?" Tanisha groaned.

"Came down here just to see it. It's the cat's meow, girl," said my mother. She pulled her camera out.

"Anyway, let me get a picture of yall girls so I can get out of here."

"C'mon yall. Let's get this picture of Three the Hard Way," said Julie.

"Alright yall. Get ready. One, two, three!"

"Cheese!" She snapped our picture.

"Alright, Pam. Give a call if she get outta line."

"She know better. Dontcha, Adrienne?" My mother summoned me down the stairs with the crook of her finger.

"If she offer you any of them funny cigarettes, you make sure you say hell no and bring your ass home. You do drugs, you sleep out on the porch. Trust."

I thought about Lashelle's mother and Mr. Schwartz's pharmacy and laughed inside. Aydree, you big dummy.

Tanisha had a lot of juice for a ninth grader. There were sophomores, juniors and seniors littering the steps on the way down to the crammed sweatbox basement.

The boys stayed on one side, while the girls surrounded Tasha Tee and Lizette battling in the middle. I didn't see Nikki though. I hadn't seen her since the summertime and she was never at home. Julie had said she got pregnant for some boy from Harlem that went to Washington Irving with them, but I'd ask Tasha for her later. Fred Barnes and the footballers strolled in, at the same time Rodney and his team did. The room was suddenly electrified. The girls giggled and batted eyelashes. The regular guys, kind of posted up to the side, trying to maintain their coolness, but still studying the ways of the most wanted guys in the school. Kerri and her new friends, some corny girls that listened to everything she said, followed in behind them.

"Party over here! Party over here!" Everybody looked over that way, but looked away when they saw who it was.

When Lashelle came in with her clique, Kerri and her crew swarmed to them, fawning. Lashelle smiled and laughed. But when she looked away from Kerri, she rolled her eyes to TaQuisha. Julie bumped me with her shoulder.

"See. That's why those bitches get robbed."

When Corey came in the door, Julie and Tanisha made kissy sounds. I had a million butterflies in my stomach. I'd danced with boys before, but not one that I *liked-liked*, like a boyfriend. Julie bumped me into his chest.

I was sure everyone could see the blush in my cheeks even in the dark basement. He did the moonwalk, spun around and grabbed his crotch. I giggled into my hand. I really, really, really liked him.

We danced to every single song. I felt like I was the flyest girl at the party. He was fifteen and I was only thirteen (even though I lied and told him I was fourteen). When the reggae came on, he put his arms around my waist and we were grinding real nasty. His thing pressed hard into my tootie. I felt all tingly inside and certain the feeling was different from anything I'd ever felt. As suddenly as I'd felt the rise, it was gone. Corey lifted his head out of the crook of my neck.

"You okay?"

"Yeah, I'm fine. You?"

"*Ohhh* yeah," he said with a smile.

The boys banged on the wall and sang loud about *punanny.* Corey's thing prodded me again, except this time it stayed that way until my tingling turned into pressure and pulsating and then I was breathless.

Corey grabbed my hand and led me to the first floor where it was a little bit cooler and quieter. Miss Pam sat on the sofa dragging on a joint.

"You havin' a good time, Adrienne?"

"Not as good as you." She puffed a ring in the air, sweeping her blonde bang to the side.

"You ain't lie, child. You sure ain't lie. Ya mama still lookin' like she just had you. She be dieting and stuff?"

"No, Miss Pam. But her and my Daddy exercise together allthetime." Miss Pam chuckled and took another pull. She nodded toward Corey.

"Don't you be exercising 'fore it's too soon, girl. It make ya woozy and ya get married to a crazy fool and wonder how that happened."

"Yes, Miss Pam." I pushed Corey through the screen door before Miss Pam got started. We sat on the stoop. The music pumped through the basement window.

"Party over here!" yelled Kerri.

"Party over here!" yelled her corny friends.

"Why does she act like that?" he asked.

"Like what?" He tickled the palm of my hand with his finger. I pulled my hand away. It tickled, but not in a way that made me laugh.

"Like she's special because her brother hoops."

"Is that what you think?" I wrote my name on the top of his hand with my fingertip.

"That's what everybody thinks. But I don't wanna talk about her. I wanna talk about you."

"What about me?" He tickled the palm of my hand again.

"About you giving me a kiss."

I leaned over and touched my lips to his. His lips were soft, but firm. He pushed his tongue into my mouth and my lips opened involuntarily. I pushed my tongue against his. I pulled away, nervous about my feelings. I was tingly again. Corey smiled.

"You're my girlfriend," he whispered in my ear.

"You're supposed to ask."

"Will you be my girlfriend?" he asked.

"Let me think about it. Cause I don't wanna get woozy over you." He poked his finger into my side and I giggled.

"I'll be your girlfriend, only if you're my boyfriend."

"I'm your boyfriend, Adrienne. Your one and only." He kissed me again with a little more tongue this time.

Trey Ski walked quick fast, down the block, looking over his shoulder.

"Yo, Ay-drin, get my sister for me, yo?" He kind of asked and told me at the same time. I jumped off the steps and ran downstairs. Tasha Tee was rub-a-dub-dubbing with some guy whose face I couldn't see.

"Your brother's outside." She didn't even say goodbye. She raced past me and up the stairs leaving me in the dust. By the time I got upstairs, they were gone. I didn't even get to ask about Nikki.

"Something's going down," said Corey.

"Did he say what it was?"

"Guys like Trey Ski don't ever say anything. They just do it." He moved closer to me, taking my hand in his.

The air was getting chilly, but it felt good to me. Life felt good to me. My birthday wish had finally come true and then some. I got my first boyfriend. My first kiss. My first orgasm and I didn't even know at the time. Could my world get better than that? I didn't know. But that night, my dreams were full of sweet kisses and things I couldn't wait to ask my mother about.

“DON’T YOU BE LETTIN’ them boys rub up on your tootie. Thas how you get pregnant.” My mother darned my father socks watching *Wheel of Fortune.*

“From dancing?” I asked.

“Yes.” She shouted at the TV. “Ax for a ‘M’, fool!”

“But I thought…”

“Have I ever told you something that was wrong?”

“No, but in school…”

“All them little books and gifted classes don’t tell you everything. I may not know ‘bout no Shakespeare or nunna that. But one thing I know about is life.”

My father rushed through the front door breaking up my life lesson. Pregnant from dancing? That was new! He hung up his black pea coat and beret that was – according to him - ‘like how Huey Newton used to wear’. I didn’t have the heart to tell him that it was 1986 and it was time to get with the Kangol. When he kissed my forehead, he didn’t smell like saw dust from the furniture factory where he worked, but more like the regular Grey Flannel and a touch of Miss Pam’s funny cigarettes.

“What you doing home so early, Dub?”

“Don’t mind that. Put the game on! Rho, why yall ain’t looking at the game?” He turned the dial on the television.

“Hell, Dub. I was watching that. You can’t just be turning the channel like that!”

“Adrienne, you gonna watch the game with me? Skyscrapers and Shamrocks playin’.”

"Yep!"

"The game don't start 'til eight! I wanted to solve the puzzle!"

"It was geranium," I said.

"The hell with yall! Get on my damn nerves!" She stomped off to the kitchen. The telephone rang. I jumped the sofa and table trying to beat my mother to the phone.

"Adrienne. It's that Corey boy, again."

"I got it, Ma."

"Corey. This hour is fine, but don't be callin' my house past nine-thirty no more or I'ma put Adrienne's Daddy on the case. And what yall got to talk about so damn much, anyway? Don't yall see each other in school?"

"Ma! I got it!"

"You ain't got nothin'. And you better not be thinkin' 'bout gettin' nothin' either." She hung up.

"The game is on. You gonna watch?" he asked.

"You know it."

"Me, too. Call me after. Use the code." I curled up in the crook of my father's arm until the game started.

"Mr. Fletcher, let you out early 'cause he knows you love the Skyscrapers, huh?"

"Actually, the son of a bitch is a Shamrocks fan." He rubbed the top of my head. "Stay in school, Adrienne. And if you can, don't work for nobody 'less you makin' some big decisions." I nodded like I knew what he was talking about, but I was in ninth grade. All that was on my mind was boys, basketball and what new sneakers I wanted to get. Working and bosses and all that stuff was the last thing on my mind.

I plugged my phone into the jack under my window. I let the phone ring once and hung up. *One Mississippi. Two Mississippi. Three Mississippi. Four Mississippi. Five Mississippi.* I dialed again. He picked up on the first ring.

"What up?"

"Nothin'. What ya doin'?"

"Nothin. You watched?"

"To the end. I knew they would win."

"It was close, though. As close as I wanna get to you."

"Here we go again." I sat on the floor next to my bed, twisting the cord in my fingers listening to Corey try his best.

"You should let me kiss you there. My brother says it makes girls fall in love."

"Well, that's nasty. You're not kissing me there."

"Okay. Then are you gonna let me touch you there?"

"I'll think about it."

"For real?" His eyebrows were probably raised to his scalp.

"Sike!" Kerri stuck her head in my room without knocking.

"Your turn to set the table."

I shoved the phone under my bed and ran downstairs counting the minutes before I could call my boyfriend back. My boyfriend. That had a nice ring to it.

I took all the forks out of the drawer and put my favorite fork at my seat. It was sterling silver with roses carved into the stem and the last of a four place table setting my mother bought at a flea market for five dollar last summer. I suspected that Big Rodney had something to do with the disappearance because any time he came over for dinner he asked her where she got money to afford *all this fine shit.* I looked at my braces in the back of my fork. No more Rabbit teeth. Just one more year. I couldn't wait!

My mother took her seat at the head of the table, my father at her right hand side. Ten minutes passed before we got tired of waiting for Rodney.

The table was heaped with a large Thanksgiving-type of spread. Macaroni and cheese, black-eyed peas, fried chicken, candied yams and collard greens. I couldn't wait to eat everything except the black-eyed peas.

"Aydree, go downstairs and get Rodney."

"Why do I have to get him? He knows what time we eat."

"Cause I said so. Now take ya ass down there and getcha cousin."

I rolled my eyes at Kerri. Why didn't she have to go? I stomped down the basement stairs in drawn out dramatic defiance. *Clap!* Silence. *Clap!* Silence. *Clap!* Silence. As long as I wasn't at the table nobody could eat. Ha!

"Adrienne, hurry the hell up," said my Daddy. *Clap, clap, clap, clap, clap, clap!*

"Rodney, you know it's time to eat. Why we hafta wait on you?!" I shoved his door open. Rodney sat on his bed with wet cheeks and red eyes.

"Rodney? You alright?"

"I shoulda known that fuckin' hoe bitch wasn't shit."

"Rodney. Um. It's time to eat."

"I know, Adrienne. I heard you." *Fuckin hoe bitch? Adrienne?* I'd never heard either come out of Rodney's mouth before. I turned away, unsure.

"Wait. Don't tell anyone I was crying, okay?"

"Okay. And Rodney…Brush your teeth first. Thanks." I ran back upstairs.

"He's comin'." I folded my hands in my lap and looked over at Kerri. Even though she got on my nerves, I wanted to give her the scoop. But telling a secret was like breaking the law.

I swirled my straw in the glass thinking about Rodney getting his heart chopped up into little pieces in the blender of love. Rodney emerged from the basement red-eyed, but cheerful.

"Boy, Rodney, that musta been some nap," said my father. He swirled his drink around in his glass. E&J Brandy.

"Either that, or he smokin' that stuff."

"Auntie Rho, if I was smokin' that stuff, I woulda called Uncle Dub down to share with me." My father laughed uneasily. I kept my laugh inside. Kerri smirked openly. My mother switched up.

"What you *hee-hee-in'* about Kerri? Nobody better be smokin' long as they livin' in this house. You understand?" I looked down at my plate.

"You hear me, Kerri? Adrienne? If I even smell anything that smell like somethin', it's gonna be some problems. Yall understand me?"

"Rho, you put your foot in them candied yams," said my father.

"I did, didn't I?" Thank the Lord for candied yams.

After dinner, I lay across my bed reading *Sweet Valley High.* I liked Elizabeth because she was the nice one. But I liked Jessica because she was popular and had cute boyfriends and stuff. Strangely when they danced with boys, there was no 'getting of the tootie' and certainly no babies. Kerri came into my room looking like she did when we were kids and I told her the Wicked Witch of the West lived in her closet.

"Rabbit?"

"What?" I asked with an attitude.

"I think I'm dying."

"What?! What happened?! "

"Look---" She showed me her messed up panty.

"Didn't you say you got your period last summer?"

"Oh yeah! I just forgot." She scratched her arm viciously.

"Ummhmm. Aunt Say never told you about your period?"

"Oh please. I don't listen to nothing she say."

"Haven't you ever read *Are You There God? It's Me, Margaret?*"

"Uh-uh. Is it one of those white girl stories you be readin'?"

"What does that have to do with anything? It's a girl growing up and having all her firsts. Her first period, her first kiss and..." Kerri wasn't even listening. "Never mind."

I gave her a few pads and went with her to the bathroom to show her how to use them. She showered and came back to my room.

"So you think I'll get like you now?"

"Like me?" Kerri was everything I thought a model should be and she wanted to be like me, Lite Brite Brace Face, whose forehead broke out into Braille if I ate the wrong thing.

"Yeah, you know, look at me. I'm flat like a board. The boys don't even look at me like they look at you."

"I didn't really expect to get all of this! They kinda popped up over night." I jumped up and down. "And sometimes they get in the way." I had a thought then. "Let me show you an exercise that helps make 'em grow." I bent my arms upward in an L and proceeded to open and close.

"We must. We must. We must increase our bust!" She flapped her arms open and closed.

"Where'd you get this exercise from?" she asked.

"Tanisha," I lied.

"Oh. Yeah, she knows all the fly stuff." I laughed inside because I got it from the same 'white girl story' that she was dissing. But I secretly hoped that maybe she would appreciate my helping her out and stop being so nasty to me.

When she left, I called Corey, using the code, but he didn't pick up on the first ring. That was okay with me. I was sleepy and not really in the mood to talk about him touching me. It's not that I didn't want him to. I just wanted it to happen when it felt right.

I pulled the eyelet comforter up to my neck, running my fingertips over the pattern. I chuckled to myself. Last summer, Kerri also claimed to have had sex with some boy in her building. I was willing to bet she was just as much a virgin as me. Silly girl.

I woke up sometime around midnight, thirsty as hell. My mother didn't like me to walk around the house in the middle of the night because a few years ago, there had been a string of robberies where the thief was breaking in and shooting anyone that was walking around in their own home. Our neighbor Kirk, one of Sha-Born's boys, was killed by his mom's boyfriend because they thought he was an intruder. But my room was so warm and dry, my throat was scratchy.

I crept down the hall in the dark. When my hand passed over a small nail jutting out of the oak paneling, I turned down the staircase. My mother giggled from her bedroom. They were probably exercising again.

I padded down the carpeted steps and at the landing, tiptoed down the side of the last three because they creaked in the middle.

Standing in the light of the refrigerator, I tipped the frosted glass pitcher to my lips. My mother would slap me, but the Kool-Aid looked so rich, red, and inviting, I couldn't help myself. The basement door squeaked open and I jumped. When I looked up, Rodney was staring at my heaving chest.

"What the hell you looking at?" I asked. He pointed at the pale red stain.

"Shoulda used a glass, Einstein." He handed me a wet dishrag before he poured himself a glass. "Thanks for not telling, Rabbit."

"You're welcome," I mumbled.

"Sometimes it's hard being me."

"What do you mean?" I scrubbed at the stain, wondering what could be so hard about being loved by the world.

"Everybody wants something. The team wants me to be the best. The girls want me to be their boyfriend so they can say 'Rodney Barrus is my boyfriend,' not because they really like me. And the coaches call me because they want me to go to their schools. It's just...hard." Cry me a river, Rodney. It was hard being taller than most of the boys I thought were cute. Corey was a long time coming.

"And then, you find out, the girl you like is just using you to make the captain of the football team jealous." Aha!

"That's why I like it that you always tell me the truth no matter what. Like a real sister." I felt fuzzy warm inside, glad the feeling was mutual.

"You better get down in the laundry room and change that shirt before your mother finds out you were down here after bedtime."

"Dang, Rodney. You're right." I took my slippers off and walked softly down the drafty stairwell.

Rodney disappeared down the hall, while I hurried into the laundry room to change. I had the strangest feeling someone was watching me.

"Thanks for being there for me, Rabbit."

"That's what sisters and brothers do."

"Yup. Give me a hug, girl." I slipped past him heading toward the stairs.

"No way. You used up all your nice credits for today."

"Stop being like that." I dragged across the floor and gave him a hug.

"You happy now?" I patted his back.

"Alright, Rodney. You can let go now." He didn't let go. Maybe he really needed a hug. Then I felt his thing pressing against my stomach.

"Okay, Rodney. That's enough." But he wouldn't let go. He put his hand on my butt and I felt his cold wet lips at the corner of mine.

"Rodney, stop!" He put his hand over my mouth.

"Your mother'll kill you if she catches you down here. Shhh!" My mother! Oh my God! Everything in me said, *Run, Rabbit!* And I did. Except, I tripped. I bucked and pushed away, trying to get off the bed, but he was too big and too heavy. He took his hand off my mouth.

"Ma---" I yelled. This time, he put his mouth over mine as he shoved my underwear down. He stuck his tongue in so far that I gagged. Still I tried. Tried to scream, tried to push, tried to kick. But it was useless. His leg went between mine, first one, then two. Then there was a sharp pain and darkness and white dots. Small and large. The burning intensified as he pushed in and pulled away, pushed in, and pulled away. And then his slack body fell on top of me. Funny, I couldn't see anything, but I could hear every sound: the hum of the boiler; the water in the pipes; the cars rolling by on the wet pavement outside; the tick of the kitchen clock.

"Rabbit." I didn't answer.

"Rabbit. Open your eyes." I opened my eyes so wide, they felt like they would get stuck that way. I couldn't move. I couldn't think. His telephone rang twice and went to the machine.

Rotnee baby, it's Lashelle. I just wanted to say sorry for the way I treated you. Fred means nothing to me. I was just doing that to make you jealous. To see if you love me as much as I love you.

Everybody loved Rodney. Right up until that clammy Sunday night in November, so did I.

I LEAPT OFF THE BED, looking back only to make sure Rodney wasn't following me. The blue diamond sheets were crinkled under his body and halfway off the bed from the struggle I had lost. A small circle of blood marked the spot where I lost something else; something I could never get back. I tiptoed up the stairs, looking over my shoulder for Rodney and listening for my mother at the same time. I dialed Corey's number, forgetting all about the code. His mother answered in a voice softened by a deep slumber.

"Hello?" I know it was rude to hang up on people, but I put the phone down gently and unplugged it. Besides, what was I going to say to him? Rodney just forced me to have sex? Not knowing what else to do, I burrowed under the covers and stared into the darkness until my eyes became accustomed to it. It was all a dream; a terrible dream. Rodney would never do that to me. Yet, my tootie throbbed against my fingers. Not so much a pain, but a dull ache: reminder that someone had visited uninvited.

Maybe fifteen minutes, or perhaps maybe two hours later, I thought I heard the stairs creak. I kept my eyes on the door praying Rodney wasn't coming for me again. Sleep never came.

Kerri sat across from me at the breakfast table, leaving the chair next to me open. Rodney sat to my left, but didn't dare speak. In fact the only sound at the table was Kerri rattling on about who she couldn't stand this week.

A bronze tin rooster hung on the wall next to the stove and I couldn't take my eyes off it. I felt like I was seeing the rooster for the first time, even though I know it had always been there. My mother stood over me.

"Grits, Adrienne?"

"Yes."

"Kerri? Rodney? Grits?"

"Yes, Ma'am." They both answered.

"I heard them stairs creakin' last night."

"I was thirsty, Aunt Rhona. It was really hot upstairs," said Kerri. Rodney and I both looked at her in surprise. My mother raised a brow.

"Was it hot in your room, Adrienne?" I nodded without looking up; afraid she would read me like a book.

"Why your face look like that? You ain't sleep last night?"

"No. Not really," I said. She put her fork down.

"Why you not eatin'? Whas wrong with you?" Rodney's eyes dug into the side of my face.

"Nothin'. Just couldn't sleep." I made little hills of grits along the sides of the bowl.

"Oh. You shoulda went down and got some warm milk," she said.

"Go downstairs. Don't go downstairs. Make up your mind." Her head tilted sideways.

"Watch your tone, Adrienne. I don't like it one bit. Next time, knock the door one time, so I know it's you. You too, Kerri. I don't want yall gettin' rehydrated or nothing."

"Dehydrated, *Mother*."

"That's what I said. Rodney, you got a game tonight?"

"Yeah, it's an away game. Yall coming? We're playing Brooklyn Tech. It's a big game. If we win, we move to first place in our division."

"You know I'ma be there," said Kerri. I washed the grits down the drain before my mother could pay attention to me.

"Adrienne? Didn't you hear Rodney ask if you going to the game?"

"I can't go."

"So who is Kerri supposed to go with?"

"It's okay, Auntie Rho. I'm going with my friend Lashelle and some of our friends."

I ran out of the crazy house, desperate to breathe a new air. Tanisha and Julie waited at the corner.

"You alright, Ayj?" asked Tanisha.

"Yeah," said Julie. "Your eyes look puffy. You was cryin'?"

"Allergies."

"I've got drops from my doctor. I can run back if you want," said Tanisha.

"Nah, I'm alright." Julie walked backwards ahead of us so she could tell us the latest juice face-to-face.

"Yo! T-Pot got bagged at five in the morn. He snatched this girl's rope chain yesterday and would you believe the bitch called the cops?"

"Word?" asked Tanisha.

"Yup. All I know is she better drop them charges or I'ma be up at Art and Design wit my box cutter."

"Damn, thas messed up," said Tanisha.

"Hell no, it's not. I hope they keep his ass locked up," I said. Julie stepped to me hard. Her face was in mean mode.

"Thas my fuckin' *bruva.* Take it back."

"He shouldn't have taken what didn't belong to him. I ain't takin' nothing back."

She mushed me in the face: took the palm of her hand, pressed it against my mouth and nose and pushed my head back. I shoved her hard into the chain link fence. She bounced off, and charged me. Tanisha jumped between us.

"Yo! Whassup witchall? We're girls, remember? Three the hard way."

"That's my family. And word is bond, don't nobody talk bad about them 'less they ready to thump."

"Fuck him and fuck you, too." Well, why did I say that? She slapped me so hard, the inside of my mouth bled. But you can't just be slapping people upside the head like that. I slapped her back and we were tangled up, arms swinging like windmills. There was yelling and hollering and someone grabbed a hold of me. I looked down at the hands.

"Don't. You. Touch. Me!" I screamed. Rodney jumped back. I swatted my mother's hand away.

"Adrienne. Your face is a mess. What is goin' on?"

"Leave me alone!" I yelled, walking away from her. Corey held Julie away from me. Her hair was standing up like a rooster's.

"You better not come down Blake Avenue, bitch, or I swear tuh God, I'll put your head out," she muttered.

Tanisha caught up to me and brushed my hair back up into a ponytail.

She walked alongside me quietly straightening me up as much as she could before I swatted her hand away, too.

"Oh, shoot. Rodney's gone big time," she murmured. There was a brand new blue and white banner hanging over the front doors.

Wilcox High School
Home of the Blue Rays and 'The Hot Rod'

I didn't look back when the clapping began. I ran past the gawkers and the groupies, trying to get as far away from *The Hot Rod* as I could.

Coach Berenski slammed down the window in the science lab.

"Times up! Put your pencils down. Pass your test papers forward," he said. The class groaned. "Let me take this time before the bell rings – I said pencils down Griffin – to remind you all that we must do our part to support the basketball team. Today's game is crucial to the playoffs so I hope to see you all crowding the stands over at Tech. Go Blue Rays!" The class cheered. When the bell rang, everyone except Lizette filed out.

"Whassup with you fighting with Julie?! That's crazy!" I shrugged my shoulders. It was crazy.

"Good day, Lizette," said Coach.

"Good day, Coach."

"That means goodbye, Honey."

"But I'm waiting for my friend," she answered.

"Goodbye." He ushered her toward the door. When the door closed behind her, he sat on the edge of the desk.

"Miss Fuller, are you helping Rodney with his homework? Because with practice and all, sometimes he just doesn't have time to do it."

"Rodney's pretty smart, Coach. He's handling his homework fine."

"Well you know family has to look out for one another. It'd be a shame to not get the grade you deserve, Miss Fuller."

"I have to get to class," I said lamely. I jetted out the door wondering why I was the only one being charged with looking out for family. When was family going to look out for me?

In the hallway, Julie's cousin, Khalid started up a chant that echoed through the first floor corridor.

We are the Blue Rays.
The mighty, mighty blue rays!
Don't fuck with the Blue Rays!
The mighty, mighty Blue Rays!

My so-called family came out of the stairwell and the hallway exploded into cheers and squeals from the girls: *Rodney, Rodney, Rodney!* Lashelle appeared at his side. Rodney lurched toward me. I slipped into the girls' bathroom.

My head was spinning. I locked the door to the stall and sat on the bare toilet seat defying the Black girls' public toilet cardinal rule. It didn't matter that I wasn't using it. When the doors opened, I was in *Rodneyville* again.

"He's so fine, if Lashelle turns her back, he mine." I knew that voice.

"If that's your man, you can be around all the other people that have status. No lames."

"Well, I want him to be my first."

"You ain't done it, yet?"

"What you waiting for? That's why you still flat. When you start doing it, you get big titties and you start gettin' a big butt and big hips."

"Fuh real?"

"Yup," said the familiar voice. I came out of the stall. I recognized all the girls. One of them, TackyIsha.

"Hey, aren't you Rodney's cousin?" asked one whose name I didn't know.

"No. I'm not." Yesterday, I would have cussed them all out and then dropped dime. I splashed water on my face which suddenly began to burn. I looked in the mirror. I had a bright pink scratch across my forehead and angry red welts on my cheek. My eyes were raccooned from a lack of sleep and my shirt was torn at the collar.

"She don't need to be lookin' like that. Messin' up Rodney's image," whispered TackyIsha.

"And you don't need to be frontin' like that's a real MCM. Somebody say Canal Street up in here?" A collective *oooh* went through the bathroom.

"You lucky you Rodney's cousin." Yeah, that was me: Lucky Rabbit.

The sea of blue jerseys and team jackets ebbed and flowed down the hallway, swaying we smaller vessels in its wake. Fighting it proved useless, so I rode the current until it swept past the side exit. I slipped out onto the dry and Rodney-free lands of Pitkin Avenue. Once my feet made contact, I set out on a trip that had no destination except to get as far away as possible.

The street lights were coming on and when I took note of my bearings, I was downtown Brooklyn, standing between the Dime Savings Bank and Albee Square Mall. Men and women in business wear bustled past on the way toward the subway. I really don't remember much. Not how I got there; if I had walked the whole way; if I'd crossed with the light; or passed anyone I knew. It was almost like I woke up from a nap, except I was sure I was awake the whole time. The soles of my feet were burning and all of a sudden I was shivering and my teeth were chattering. *Home.* I had to get home.

The token booth clerk looked up through the bulletproof glass.

"Hey. You alright?" I grabbed the token out of the slot with my shaky hand.

As I stood on the crowded platform, my head began spinning again. I was tired and delirious with sadness. Like no one else, I had his back. We were blood. Family. Like sister and brother.

The number three train crackled into the station, swirling the trash on the tracks into a paper whirlwind. I squeezed on board, heading toward New Lots Avenue. Back to my neck of the woods. Back to my troubles. Back to my family.

☙

COREY AND HIS BOYS huddled out on Livonia rhyming even though most sane people were indoors cuddled up under a blanket. The temperature had plummeted and the winds were strong. It was so cold, the green traffic light, three blocks away was extra sharp in focus. He called out to me as I walked by.

"Hey girl. You not gonna say hi?"

"Hi." I kept walking. He caught up to me, touching my elbow.

"Hold up a sec, Adrienne. You mad at me?"

"No." I looked out into the distance, avoiding his eyes.

"So what's up? I thought, you know…that you liked me. I waited for you outside your class. But you walked by like you didn't even know me."

"Sorry." He walked me to the corner of my block.

"Can't you at least give me a kiss?" I pecked him quickly and I didn't look back.

My mother charged down the front steps. "Adrienne, it's almost eight o'clock! Where you been? You been out there with that Corey boy?"

"No."

"Don't lie to me, Adrienne! I saw you at the corner!" I brushed past her.

Tanisha sat on the living room couch, wringing her hands. Kerri came downstairs, her bangles jingle jangling.

"You'd do anything to upstage Roddy. You knew we had a game."

"We?" I said.

"Thank you for coming by, Tanisha," said my mother.

"Call me, Ayj. Okay? Night, Ms. Fuller."

My mother closed the door behind her and sat on the couch with her hands tucked between her knees.

"What is goin' on with you? The school called to say you missed classes. You fightin' witcha friends about who knows what. You got everybody worried about you. And it seem like you don't even care. If you don't tell me what's goin' on, I can't help you."

"There's nothing going on." She threw her hands into the air.

"See. I told you," said Kerri crossing her arms over her chest.

"Can I go to bed now?" My mother waved her hand toward the stairs.

"Auntie Rho, she acts like we're enemies. But we love her like our sister."

"Yes, Baby. I know. Sometimes family just don't see eye to eye."

I put my chair against the door to keep the monsters out, the same way I saw in the movies.

It was only a few minutes after eight, but I was beat down. I put on my nightgown and lay under the covers yearning for sleep to come, but she evaded me again. Lying there, I felt naked and defenseless, like Rodney could just come up here, get under my nightgown and take what he wanted. I took my jeans off the chair and pulled them up. Then I found my sweatshirt on the floor and dragged it on over my nightgown.

When I woke up, it was still dark outside. I had to pee so badly, it hurt. I was way too terrified to go out into the hallway. I stood by the door until a little drop spurted. Rodney didn't come upstairs, but that didn't register. I searched the room frantically for somewhere to relieve myself, until finally I shoved my jeans down and squatted over the potted plant by the window. Satisfied, I got back in the bed and pulled the cover over my head. My room was hot as hell, but that didn't matter at all.

The sunlight shone through my windows. I let the rays bathe my face.

My teddy bears were scattered on the floor. The chair was still propped in front of the door. I wept like a baby. I didn't have a potted plant in my room.

I yanked the sheets off the bed and rolled my jeans and panties into the bundle. I pulled the lid off the hamper and saw the panties I didn't realize I'd forgotten in Rodney's room - white with pink hearts - resting on top. I balled them up and dumped them in the garbage can, enraged that Rodney had the nerve to come up here. I stuffed my jeans and sheets deep down to the bottom of the hamper, put on a new nightgown and then I made my bed with just the comforter and pillows. I moved the chair from the door. *Doomp, doomp, doomp!* I jumped back.

"Adrienne?" My mother eased the door open.

"I'm up." Her nose went up in the air, sniffing like a hound.

"Smells funny in here."

"Funny, like how?" I asked. She closed the door behind her.

I stood in front of the bathroom mirror examining my body for any changes. I'd done 'it', but my breasts looked the exact same. My hips, my stomach: same. I turned sideways to look at my profile. Booty: same. Those girls didn't know what they were talking about. The mirror clouded with steam.

It's not until the water sprayed my head that I remembered my shower cap. I could feel my hair contracting into the thickest of locks. But the water felt so good cascading over me that I couldn't pull away. I lathered and rinsed the suds off my body until the bar of soap melted away and I felt that some of the dirty had washed off. I stepped out of the tub just as the bathroom door was opening. I charged toward it screaming.

"What in the hell?! Adrienne, you scared the hell out of me! And what the hell happened to your hair? You don't see Miss Lewis for another week. Sometimes you smart as all hell and other times I ain't so sure."

"Will you please close the door? It's cold." She rolled her eyes and left.

As I put my pajamas back on, she peeked into my bedroom, clad in her long black church coat over a washed out navy sweat suit.

"Why ain't you dressed for school?"

"I don't feel good."

"If you don't go back to school tomorrow, we goin' to the HIP center to find out what's wrong with you."

I jumped up and went to the mirror. My afro was a huge knotted mess. There was no way I could go to school like that. I wet my hair in the bathroom sink and dug my finger into the Dax. I rubbed it between my hands and smoothed the glob onto my hair, praying for a miracle. There was no telling what a doctor would dig up.

I climbed back in bed, afraid. Afraid to go downstairs. Afraid my mother was gonna know what happened. Afraid she would blame me. Mostly, I was afraid I was going to be lonely like this forever.

IT FIGURED THE FIRST PERSON I would run into outside school would be Kerri. It figured she wouldn't ignore me like usual, either.

"Rabbit. Oh my Gawd. What happened to your hair?" she laughed.

"Maybe you could go by my mom's shop," offered Lashelle. I was surprised. I didn't expect her to be helpful.

"No, thanks." I moved to the edge of the fence, waiting for the bell to ring.

"What?! James Brown?" said Lashelle. "I rather look like James Brown than Buckwheat!" I refused to look back at Kerri, that trifling and disloyal wench.

Before I could put my books down in the science lab, Lizette leaned over the lab counter.

"If you didn't want to be my friend anymore, you should have just said so, bitch."

"What are you talking about?" She turned to face the front. I ripped a sheet of looseleaf from my Trapper Keeper and scribbled a note to ask what the hell she was talking about. She tore it into a million little pieces. I missed the entire lesson wondering what I did to her.

When the bell rang, I was too tired for the bullshit. I hoisted my bag onto my shoulders, and when I got out in the hallway, I had all the answers I needed, for Lizette and Kerri giggled up a storm.

I bumped past the swell of students in the hallway, eager to get home.

"Adrienne! Wait up!" called Tanisha. Dammit!

"Missed you yesterday."

"Wasn't feeling so well."

"You want to come over and study with me?"

"I have to get home."

"You're such a liar. C'mon. I'll make you my famous pancakes." I couldn't say no to pancakes.

Julie sat on the front steps against the gates, zipped up and fresh in a black bomber jacket. Tanisha stopped to chit-chat, but I walked past her like we'd never met, just like how I walked past Kerri in the bathroom in the mornings, in the kitchen after school, and everywhere else in that Barrus-infested house.

"Hell no, I ain't coming," she said. "I can't stand that two-faced bitch." I rolled my eyes at her. I didn't think I was two-faced. I just thought her cousin was dead wrong to be robbing people. If that made me two-faced, she could kiss my ass. Twice.

Corey waited at the corner with Cash Money, who sported brand new Gucci sneakers. I tucked my hands deep into the pockets of my jacket, praying the light would hurry up and change.

"Adrienne," said Tanisha. She nudged me with her elbow.

"Corey's calling you."

"Yeah. We broke up."

"Adrienne," he called again. "I know you hear me." Tanisha whispered.

"Well damn. What the hell happened and why am I the last to know?"

"Just don't like him anymore," I lied.

"Man. Forget her," said Cash Money. "You need to get with Caroline. She's on your jock hard, B!" I looked straight ahead and walked with the Wilcox pack up the block, tucking this experience away in the overflowing 'Why me?' memory file.

"Don't worry, Ayj. She's not even his type," said Sunshine Girl. And when we passed Caroline's building, she spoke louder and told crazy jokes to distract me.

Tanisha's room, dubbed T's World, was candy sweet and girly. She had stuffed bears and throw pillows for days and every shade of pink she could find, somewhere in that tiny-comfy room. Half my pancake sat uneaten in a filmy pool of syrup, raising Tanisha's suspicions. She kept looking up trying to catch my attention. But I kept my eyes glued to the textbook review questions, even when I heard a familiar beat come through the radio. Tanisha jumped off the bed and cranked it up to ten. *Eric B is President* was our favorite song!

I had to laugh at Tanisha doing *the wop* with her pink suspenders hanging down off the side. She could do every dance that came out without even practicing. She waved her hands and her head back and forth like the pendulum in the clock.

"C'mon Ayj! Do it with me!" The beat was so hypnotic, I couldn't fight it. Back and forth. Back and forth. With both hands, then one. One hand on the hip!

"Ayj, you're killin' it!" she cried as she spun with hers and kicked her leg up. We *wopped* ourselves into a fit of giggles, collapsing to the floor.

"Wooooo! That was fun!" she giggled.

"Definitely!" I cracked my math book back open to the exercises. I could feel her eyes on my forehead.

"You thirsty?" Was I thirsty, she wanted to know. I had all these words and ugly feelings trapped between my throat and lips. I was parched!

"A little." She came back with Sunnydale juice and her brother Sha-Born following behind her.

"What's the word, Big Head?" he said. "I got this song by a new female rapper named MC Lyte. Yall are gonna love it!" I always wanted to hear the new songs from Sha-Born, but I couldn't even sit still. I guess my uneasiness showed because mother hen, Tanisha, felt my forehead.

"Adrienne, are you sure you're alright?" I pushed her hand away.

"Yeah. My stomach feels a little funny. I need to lie down for a sec."

"I'll let yall hear it another time," said Sha. He loved to show off his new records to us. He called us the rap Siskel and Ebert.

"You wanna watch *The Last Dragon* again?"

"Yeah. That's cool." We loved Taimak, even though we knew we could never bring him to Brooklyn. Black belt or no black belt, I could see Trey Ski grabbing him in a bear hug and Fuquan choking the poor guy to death. I plopped into her funky pink armchair and watched the beginning of the movie until it was watching me. I heard her calling my name, over and over again.

"Ayj. Your mom called. She wants you to come home now." I kept my eyes closed, holding onto the wonderfully far away place I was visiting.

"You've been acting real funny since the day you and Julie got into it. Did something happen at home?" I stared at her like she had three heads partly because her face was entirely too close to mine.

"Adrienne, what is going on?"

"I hate being there." She nodded keeping her eyes focused on mine. "Kerri makes me sick and everything is Rodney, Rodney, Rodney."

"That's all?" she asked. I nodded. She kept her eyes trained on mine and then she made this face that she makes when she doesn't believe what someone is telling her, but doesn't want to call them out. It's a little twitch at the side of her mouth. You have to be quick to catch it. She sighed.

"Come on. I'll walk you half way."

As we got closer to Caroline's, on that blustery December evening, I couldn't help but think Corey wouldn't get with her. Based on all he said he liked about me, she wasn't his type. She was a dashiki wearing-Black Power girl that did African Dance in all the talent shows. Plus she had a big head and acne all over her face.

The silhouette of two bodies under the fire escape by her apartment building caught my attention. I tried to sneak a peek, but it was too dark out. But as I got closer, I recognized Caroline's bowed legs bent back and akimbo. My heart sank. I recognized Corey's blue and yellow Polo Goose. She and Corey were locked in a soap opera kiss. I focused on the sidewalk ahead of me, careful not to look in their direction. Tanisha touched my shoulder in sympathy.

"Girl, please," I said. "That doesn't even phase me."

But even if it was ten degrees outside, and I had to walk two blocks out of my way to come from the other direction, I refused to pass her building. As much as I pretended to be immune, it did phase me. It dug a second hole out of my heart.

"Whenever you're ready to talk, I'll be here. Trust me, it can't be worse than watching your father hold a loaded gun to his head."

Damn. That was messed up. Didn't matter. The rules were simple. You never turned on blood and you never told secrets. Period.

FOR ALL OF THAT FAMILY LOYALTY, I felt like a stranger in my home. I absolutely ignored Kerri, and tried my hardest to steer clear of Rodney and my parents. It wasn't easy.

"Come on," said my mother. "Let's eat like a family."

She carried two plates out to the dining room.

"Bring Rodney's plate with you," she called. His plate was grossly piled with three chunky slabs of meatloaf, damn near a can of green beans, and a mountain of mashed potatoes. Why she left his plate with me, I don't know. I wouldn't bring him food if it was his last meal. And then something special occurred to me. It *could* be his last meal. And then he'd be gone from my life and I wouldn't have to look at his big goofy ass and be reminded of the betrayal ever again.

I snatched the pantry door open and tossed everything about: vacuum bags, disinfectant, the dustpan, roach spray. I couldn't find what I wanted and I knew it was in there somewhere. No frills dishwashing liquid, furniture wax, more household junk. Aha! The little brown box with the yellow skull and cross bones was underneath the rags we used to polish the furniture. Quickly, I mixed a teaspoon of white powder into his mashed potatoes, careful to smooth the lumps out.

"Girl, what the hell you doing foolin' with that rat poison? You saw a mouse in here? I told your father to bring a trap home." She went for Rodney's plate, but I held onto it. I wanted to make sure he knew it was me who did him in. My mother tugged the plate and I let it go since she wanted it so bad. Everything on the plate skidded to the wall and floor in a diarrheal splat.

"Dammit, Adrienne. What he gonna eat now? Ain't nothin' left. Now I'ma have to give him yours." She sucked her teeth. I sucked mine, too.

"How come he can't go down to Chung Chan Kitchen and get some chicken wings and French Fries?" I asked. She said something stupid about it being my fault, but I wasn't listening to her. I'd had another thought.

Barely able to contain my glee, I cleaned up the slop grinning like a runaway slave. I'd almost made it to the first landing when I heard her calling my name. I pretended I hadn't heard, taking two steps at a time on the path to freedom.

"Adrienne!" she yelled.

"What'd I do now?"

"Since we ain't have dinner together, let's have a family TV night." I was caught off guard and couldn't think of an excuse fast enough. My freedom! My sweet freedom!

"Adrienne. You heard me? Come on back down."

"I have to study."

"Try again." I trudged back down the stairs cursing her under my breath. *The Cosby Show* was my favorite show even though I didn't know anyone like them. I didn't want to miss it because my mother thought we should watch whatever Prince Rodney wanted to watch just so we could be 'a real family'.

Rodney sat at the table eating what should have been poisoned potatoes, going on and on about his team being the number one seed in the Public School Basketball League. I plopped into the sofa on the opposite end from my mother. A hole in the plastic covering expunged air with a slow hiss.

"That's just wonderful, Rodney," said my mother. I rolled my eyes. The timer on the oven buzzed. She jumped up.

"That's my cake." Rodney stood at the arch between the living room and dining room. I could feel his eyes on me.

"Haven't seen you at the games. Whassup?" I refused to look at him.

"So you not talking to me, now?" he asked, as though his offense was as light as having eaten my last Jolly Rancher. I was sizzling inside, but I focused on the television.

"Fine. That's how you want it?" he asked rhetorically.

Rodney slammed the basement door so hard, the ceramic vase on the dining room table shook. He would have really been mad if he knew how close he came to meeting the devil up close. The thought brought a little smile to my lips.

The opening music started and my mother came back in and settled into the couch next to me. "Why you like watching this show, Adrienne?" Psssh. She'd grow old and gray before I answered her.

"Adrienne?" I shrugged. Old and gray, I said.

"I think they kinda like us, but with a lotta money." *Whatchu talking bout Rhona?* "You know, I mean like how they talk about stuff. Cause you can tell me anythin'. I'ma love you no matter what." She leaned over to hug me except she stopped midway. "Where did Rodney go?" I shrugged, leaning out of her forgotten hug.

"You ain't say nothin' mean, did you? You know he sensitive."

A Calgon commercial came on and I wished it were me, white with silky waterproof hair, in the tub. Calgon, take me away, too. And don't ever bring me back to this hell hole, I thought to myself.

"Adrienne, you see how Claire Huxtable works and stuff? Well how you feel if I got a job?" I shrugged. My mother hadn't had a job since my Daddy started working at the furniture factory when I was a little girl.

"Where are you going to be working?" I asked.

"You don't need to know all that. But I'ma need you to help out around the house while I'm gone. It's time for you to start being a woman."

"Adrienne!"

"Yes, Daddy?"

"The timer's goin' off. It's gettin' on my nerves!"

"I'm doing my homework," I yelled.

"It's gonna burn up and we ain't gonna have no dinner!"

I stomped down the stairs to find my father sitting at the kitchen table with his pals E&J. They were having a good old time. I set the hot pan on the counter, pissed off.

"Is Ma comin' home early tonight?" I asked.

"Why didn't you ask her?"

"Because I haven't seen her."

"Join the club," he muttered. I laid out his dinner and refilled his glass.

"You made a plate for your cousins?" he asked.

"They said they ate already. Can I go do my homework now?"

"Yeah, yeah." He waved me away. I ran upstairs, heading back to my room. Except their bedroom door was cracked, the moonlight shining through the window and slicing across their bed. I listened out for my father. His fork scraped against his plate in the kitchen. I detoured into their room.

I headed straight for my mother's hamper. I was going to get to the bottom of this mysterious job. Yesterday's blue sweatshirt flopped over the side. Evidence! There was a faint scent of a fabric softener we didn't use. I searched for the pink Las Vegas sweatshirt from the day before. Nothing. Just her regular baby powder scent. Her sleeve had a white bleach spot on the cuff, though.

"What you doing in your mother's thangs?" I jumped.

"I m-miss her."

"You act like she dead or somethin'. Girl, go on and do your homework and stop snoopin' around." I was cold-busted. There went my discovery mission. Except my father was still mumbling in his funny drunken way.

"…fore you end up like your Momma. Or workin' for these muh-fuckin' cracker sons of dirty cracker whores who keep shortin' my muh-fuckin' check." He guzzled the brown juice straight from the bottle. "I meet every deadline. I fill every order. I treat everybody nice. But muh-fuckers wanna treat you like you ain't shit 'cause you ain't got no fancy ass degrees an shit." Wow. I'd never heard my Dad talk like that. He was, as he liked to say, easy like Sunday morning.

"Doing laundry's not so bad," I said.

"Thas what she told you? Her and her damn secret-y ass. She ain't workin' in no laundry. She cleanin' house for a little old white lady over the other side of Kings Highway. She 'shamed cuz she say it's like we still workin' fuh Massa. Her and her damn secrets." He handed me the empty E&J bottle.

"Do somethin' with this before your mother come home. And don't tell her I was drinkin'."

I cleared my father's plate off the table and washed the rest of the dishes in the sink. Her big secret job was cleaning someone's house. I really didn't see what the big deal was. Rodney brought his plate upstairs.

"You missed one, Rab." *Rab. Like we were friends or something.*

"When are you gonna start talking to me again?" he asked. I put his plate in the drain board. "Damn. Say something. Say anything." I was mad with him, but it wasn't as bad as before. I flooded the sink with more suds.

"It's not that big a deal," he said. "Why you actin' like that?" I wheeled around on him.

"You made me have sex with you!"

"I didn't make you do anything. You're buggin'." My nostrils flared like Big Rodney's.

"Rodney. Please stop talking to me. I can't stand a LIAR!" I raged. He backed me into the kitchen sink until my head was bent upwards at an unnatural ninety degree angle. He was probably over six feet eight by then.

"I already said I ain't make you do nothin'. If you say I did, I'ma tell everybody you came down and begged me to do the nasty with you."

"I did not!" He stepped back and opened his arms, palms up.

"Who you think they gonna believe? You or me?" I stared hard, looking for any sign of the Rodney I thought I knew: my big cousin-brother who'd shown me how to play skelly when the other boys wouldn't let us; who let me ride on the handlebars of his BMX dirtbike; who stole Lotto patches off the sneakers in Sneaker King, so Kerri and I could have all the colors. But all I saw was Rodney, the Hot Rod. Mr. Lucky Number Thirteen. The manipulator. The liar. The rapist.

WILCOX HIGH HAD NOT only swept the city and conquered the state, they had even gone on to win the regional championship. Not bad for a little team from Brooklyn.

The college scouts were coming by and calling the house to the point that some nights we had to take the phone off the hook. Rodney didn't mind it at all. Especially since he got new Air Jordans and money and leather jackets and hats and none of it was paid for by anyone in our family. Somewhere along the line, he also acquired a bevy of girlfriends and a new ego to go with it all. He was Big Rodney's dream come true.

Rodney's number one groupie came home with a set of blue and white pompoms and dropped them on the dining room table.

"Auntie Rho! Rabbit! I made the cheerleading squad!"

"Congratulations, KayKay," said my mother. KayKay. Interesting.

Technically, she was supposed to wait until her sophomore year to try out, but no one was going to say no to her with Rodney being The Hot Rod. Not even my mother. I couldn't even study in the house, because she started practicing on that first day and didn't stop.

S-P! Clap, clap! I-R! Clap, clap! I-T! Clap, clap! Spirit! Team Spirit! Blue Rays! Wooo! Jumping up and down like an ass. It wouldn't have been so bad if she didn't practice in the living room. Or in the kitchen. Or in her bedroom, the bathroom, the hallway, and anywhere she realized she could stomp as loud as possible, at any time of day or night.

On the days that I didn't lock myself away in my room with my walkman,

I'd go to my little space in the back of the library, near the Greek classics and lose myself. It was far from the bathroom, the copy machine, and the microfiche. It was my own perfectly quiet nook. Sometimes, instead of studying, I'd read *Word Up* magazines just because I knew no one would bother me. A long shadow covered a picture of Prince.

"Tell Rodney that he needs to work on his defense." Yeah, yeah. If I had to choose between Michael and Prince, Prince would be my choice all the way. He was sexy! I expected whoever it was to realize he was being ignored, but he waited until I turned the page twice before he even got the hint and walked away.

"I heard some of the kids talking. And uh, my daughter needs a date for the prom. Give Hot Rod this number for me, Darlin'?" Daughter? I looked up to see who could be old enough to have a daughter. The security guard, Mr. Charlie.

I looked around thinking maybe I should leave, but everyone else seemed to be doing their own thing.

"Hey, you're Rodney's cousin. He's the man! Do you know if he needs a tutor?" I shook my head.

"No, he doesn't need one? Or no, you don't know?"

"No. I don't know."

And that was the truth. I honestly did not know if Rodney needed help because he rarely even did his own homework anymore.

My ex-friend Lizette, sat at my dining room table typing on *my* word processor that Aunt Juicie bought me, while Rodney played Nintendo on the living room television.

"Mrs. Fuller?" Lizette called.

"Yes, Darlin'?"

"How do you make the little thingy move to start a new paragraph?"

"Um. Adrienne, how you---"

"I dunno." I jumped at the ringing telephone.

"Daddy! Mr. Fletcher is on the phone!" I sat at the dining table, amidst Kerri's book bag and scraggly pompoms waiting, waiting, waiting. Lizette tapped with one finger at a time, making this stupid, I-don't-need-your-help face.

"Lizette," called Rodney. "Make sure you make footnotes and a bibliography. I need to get an A."

"You need to be writing your own paper," I mumbled.

"As usual, somebody's a jealous girl," said Kerri. She and Lizette giggled. I yanked the cord from the word processor on my way to the kitchen. Giggle at that, heifers.

My father *uh-huhed* a whole lot before he hung up. He carefully placed his beret over his mini afro, and adorned himself in his brand new leather pea coat.

"Rhona, I'm going to see a man about a horse."

"See him about a job while you at it," she mumbled.

"Daddy, doesn't have a job?"

"Of course he does. Stay out of grown folks business."

The telephone jangled again. I grabbed it off the hook. It was the call I had been waiting for.

"Ma, I'm going to Tanisha's."

"Be back in here at ten."

At the corner payphone, I put a dime in the slot.

"I'm on my way."

Rico was light skinned with curly black hair. He was Puerto Rican and Black and gorgeous. I met him the week before, on my way home from school.

"Hey Beautiful," he called from in front of the bodega. I tucked my paper bag of sour apple Jolly Ranchers into my pocket. He couldn't have been talking about me. Kerri looked over her shoulder.

"Beautiful in the green coat. I know you hear me." Kerri pulled the collar of her blue shearling tighter and put her nose high in the air.

"Bum-ass nigga."

"Whas your name?" I told him my name, my sign and anything else he wanted to know. He kept looking at my breasts, so I folded my arms over them.

"You're a Leo? Word? So you be gettin' an attitude real quick?" I poked him in the chest, smiling a little bit. He was too fine for words.

"Yup. So you better act like you know."

"You have a pretty smile."

"Yeah right." I kept my mouth closed over my braces.

"For real. You shouldn't hide it like that. Lemme see." He grabbed my hands. I lit up the whole street with my metallic grin.

"Wait a minute. You're not a virgin, are you?"

"No!" I said with the vigor of a girl desperately trying to impress the wrong boy.

"Oh. Because even if you were, it wouldn't matter. I would still go out with you. You should come over tomorrow," he said, "We can just chill and have fun. Call me later."

And there I was standing in the middle of his bedroom.

"You are so pretty. I can't believe you don't have a boyfriend." He smoothed my hair. My perm (yes, I said perm!) was laid out. I looked like I was part Puerto Rican, too. Well, half of that.

"Thank you," I said. He kissed my neck. I felt warm and tingly, like somebody turned up the heat.

"Aren't you hot?" he asked as he lifted my sweater up over my head.

"Yes. Very." He pulled my jeans down. When he put his finger inside my tootie, I froze up.

"Don't be nervous. I'ma take good care of you, Linda." I pushed his hand away.

"My name is Adrienne, stupid!" I reached for my sweater.

"Linda means cutie in Spanish, Adrienne." I folded my arms.

"For real. *Que linda* means how pretty, how adorable. Like that." He caressed my arm. I acquiesced a bit.

"Adrienne, I love you." I put my arms around his neck.

"I love you, too." He climbed on top of me and pushed and shoved until he was done. Just like Rodney, but not as disgusting and embarrassing. And this time it didn't hurt as much either. He rolled off me and handed me my clothes.

"You gotta leave before my mother gets home."

"Okay. Can I come over, tomorrow?" I asked. But then I saw a picture on the dresser. A Puerto Rican girl with a pink T-shirt like Julie had on except it had her name printed on the front. Linda. My nose tickled. But I held it in check until I got outside. Stupid me. Stupid, stupid, stupid. I got on the bus and walked all the way to the back, where I cried until I couldn't anymore.

The house was quiet, except for the hum of the refrigerator and Kerri on the phone. "Yeah, Neesh. I'll tell her you called."

She came into the living room smiling.

"Looks like you owe me and I will be collecting," she purred.

I lay across the bed, running my finger over the eyelet patterns. My eyes were so puffy, they hurt. I wished Kerri and Rodney back to their old lives and me back to my old self. The old me, that could talk to my mother about what boy I liked. About what my body was feeling. About my favorite movie star. About what was really going on under her roof.

I WENT STRAIGHT HOME after school and locked myself in my room. I didn't bother with my books. I didn't bother with the phone. I didn't even bother to think about what I would wear the next day. For hours, I just lay on the bed, thinking about how peaceful it would be to be dead. I know life wasn't all easy, but I couldn't think of one reason to hang around. I was tired. *Dooomp! Dooomp!* I jumped off the bed ready for war. If Kerri wanted to mess with me, blood or no blood, then it was just gonna have to be that way.

My mother stepped through the doorway with my father following closely behind her. Something was wrong. I could tell by the way she was scrutinizing me and the way my father wouldn't look at me at all.

"What? What happened?" I backed up to my bed in a panic. The last time they came to my room like this, Grandma Rose had passed away in her sleep.

"Adrienne, we just got a phone call. And I wanna know what the hell is going on." Kerri's door squeaked open. "Dub, close the door." I pulled my pillow to my chest.

"You been out there sharing?"

"Sharing what?" I asked.

"You know what I mean. You been giving your tootie away?" My father's ears turned scarlet. He stared intently at Ralph Tresvant's poster.

"No!" I said.

"The person that called said your number was on the boys' bathroom wall at the school," she said.

"My number can't be in the bathroom!" The only boy that had my number was Corey. And Rico, but he didn't go to my school.

"For now, only place you go is just straight to school and right back home." I looked at her in shock. "I'm not sayin' I don't trust you. But we have to guard your reputation. Only way to do that is to keep you close." My father broke his silence.

"If you don't go with Rodney or Kerri, then you don't go."

"I'm not going anywhere with them!" My mother parked her hands on her hips.

"What is wrong with you?! This is for your own protection! Know what I think? I think it's time you start coming to church with me."

"Rhona, don't start with that church shit."

"Hush, Dub. You need to bring yo ass to church, too."

"My number is not on the bathroom stall!" I yelled.

"Well, let's ask Rodney if he knows anything about this."

"Fine. I won't go anywhere."

"Don't be so dramatic. You just have to be counted for at all times." My mother turned to my father who clasped his hands behind his back. I turned my back on them. I expected my mother to scold me for being so rude, but I guess I didn't know her anymore, just as she surely didn't know me.

"Adrienne. Do you have anything you want to say?" she asked.

"The word is accounted."

"Be ready at seven."

The storefront that was New Life Victory Baptist was all tambourines and hallelujahs for sixty-seven minutes before the preacher came to the pulpit. I know because in between wondering how more than ten people fit in the shoebox church on Sunday, I counted every single second that passed. My mother sat beside me in the velvety purple pew, quietly raising her hand every now and then to catch the spirit as it flew by.

"Good evening, my brothers and sisters," said the preacher. "Tonight, we're gonna go to the book of Genesis."

The preacher started out lightly, lulling me with his words. But every single time he said amen, bloop, the lady in the church hat that doubled as a wash basin, dropped to the floor. I couldn't help but giggle. But after the third time, I started hoping she'd just stay down.

Finally, the preacher brought the congregation down from their frenzied state to soft *umhmms* and *yes, Lords*. I've never felt anything in church, except the urge to run out, but I actually languished in the peace and the calmness around me.

"Tonight," he said, "we have a special blessing and prayer dedication. Sister Fuller would you please come forward." I turned sideways in the pew, to let my mother out, but she didn't move.

"Go on, Adrienne. Stop playin' around," she said.

"Me?" I asked. The preacher hummed.

"Mmmhmm. Sister Rhona asks that we pray for a special prayer over you, Adrienne, once you have confessed your sins in front of the congregation."

The cold from the concrete crept through the soles of my hideous church shoes although I walked fast enough to burn the pavement beneath. My mother was going to be sorry. Everybody was.

The house was quiet except for a soft giggle that floated up through the open basement door.

I tiptoed up the stairs and locked my bedroom door behind me. I hated my life. I hated how the quiet of night spurred my thoughts back to *that* night. I hated how I should have listened to my mother and never gone down to get something to drink in the first place. I popped the cap off the aspirin bottle, lining up the tablets on my dresser. I turned to my nightstand. I forgot to fill my water glass.

I stood paralyzed at my door, hating myself for sinking to the floor in tears. I was too afraid to leave my own room in my own house.

In the morning, I dropped the damp bed sheets in the washing machine.

IT'S NOT LIKE ANYONE invited me anywhere, but since I was barred from going out with anyone but Kerri and Rodney, I mostly lounged in my bedroom in the company of my books.

Every now and then Neesh and I would cut class after homeroom and go to her house to watch TV and eat Chinese food from Chung Chan. Not too frequently, maybe once or twice a month, but enough for us to have some semblance of a friendship that was not monitored or censored by The Warden.

During the final days of the school year, when the heat was pleasantly present and the breeze was soft against the skin, I had a hankering to extend our ditch days into new territory.

"Neesh, I know you don't want to go. But it's the last thing I'll be able to do before I get locked down for the summer. Besides Mikey Long's parties are legendary." She sat indian-style on a plush pink bean bag picking at the seams.

"Adrienne. I don't know. He lives right around the corner. What if somebody sees us?"

"No one's gonna see us because it's at his uncle's house in Flatbush."

"Oh! Well, why didn't you say that?!"

Mikey Long's uncle lived in an apartment on Nostrand Avenue right up the block from the zig-zagging confusion of the Flatbush Avenue Junction. The taxi cabs honked and the buses whizzed by and the cars jerked to abrupt stops avoiding jackrabbit-quick pedestrians who dared cross against the light, all before the stink of the subway could evaporate off our skin.

"I don't know why I let you talk me into these things," she said.

"Oh yes you do."

Mikey's apartment was packed like the lower quarters of the slave ships. Everywhere we turned there was a body. Mikey was kickin' the willie bo-bo with some guys I recognized. He made eye contact with me and made his way over. Tanisha pinched me so hard, I flinched.

"You go to Wilcox, right?" he asked.

"Yeah." He wasn't that cute, but all the girls thought he was the shit because he had wavy hair. He was very selective and when Lizette went out with him, she said he bought her flowers and took her to the movies and treated her real nice. He pulled me close to him and we grinded for a bit before he pulled me into an empty bedroom that reeked of old lady: moth balls and flowery perfume. My hands were clammy. Mikey Long was checking me out!

"Can I get your number?"

"Uh-uh. I can't."

"Okay. Well take mine," he said. But before I could, we started kissing. I couldn't get into it. His mouth was too soft and he was on top of me but I didn't feel anything. He stopped kissing me and pulled his pants down. I scurried off the bed to my feet.

"Oh you wanna try that freaky standing up shit?" he asked. I didn't know a thing about any freaky standing up shit.

"No. I'm gonna go back to find Neesh. I've got to get home."

"Everybody's gonna think you did it anyway. So you might as well. Besides, look at what you did to me." His pants were at his ankle and his little nugget raised his tighty whities just a tad. Mikey Long was no where near, but he wanted me. When he was done, I slipped out into the crowded musky party. I tapped Tanisha, who was smooching with a slim chocolate boy.

"I'll wait for you outside."

As I lay across my bed in my underwear, staring at the ceiling, in my bedroom that was two degrees hotter than hell, I actually wondered how many days were left before we went back to school.

Doomp, doomp, doomp!

"Open up this damn door!" I pulled on the first thing I could find. My mother leaned inside in her lucky Budweiser painter's hat and aqua blue Atlantic City T-shirt.

"Me and Lewis are leavin' for A.C. You sure you ain't comin'?"

I shook my head. The idea of sitting in a smoky casino, as they prayed to God to help them win at gambling was amusing, but not appealing at all. They would holler, "Look my way, Jesus!" And I'd be giggling and coughing up parts of my inner workings from the smoke, thinking maybe they didn't really want Him to look.

"Suit yourself. Remember. No company." She fanned herself with her hand. "Goodness Adrienne, at least come downstairs and sit in front the big fan."

"I'm okay."

Hot as it was, I didn't dare to venture out with the wolves roaming about. I went to the window, hoping for a breeze.

The Pool was packed with squealing and giggling kids but it just didn't hold the same appeal, either. One because no one liked me anymore, but mostly because Corey was giving Lashelle a piggy back ride down the block. Kerri busted through my bedroom door.

"Roddy said to tell you there're no more clean towels downstairs."

"Aren't you his right hand? Why don't you take one down?"

"Because I'm going out," she said.

Then she walked right past the linen closet and headed downstairs. I yanked a towel from the closet and slammed it in the back of her head.

"What you doin'?!" she yelled. She fluffed the back of her wedged Salt-n-Pepa haircut. "You need to be careful, Rabbit. You could have messed up my hair." She patted the side of her hair.

"Me and Mikey Long are going to the movies."

"Mikey Long? Good luck."

"Thanks." The clue plane flew right over her head, missing the landing strip.

"Ker-ray!" yelled Rodney. I threw the towel down the basement stairs and immediately headed back to my room. Rodney came up from the basement in his basketball shorts and no shirt on. His arms were huge. And the rest of him was cut up even though I tried not to look. I started upstairs as swiftly as I could, all the while thinking about how dogs give chase when you start running.

"Why you keep ignorin' me, Rabbit?" He came up the stairs behind me. I looked over my shoulder. He was right behind me, taller even from two steps below.

"Go back downstairs, Rodney."

"Why do you keep ignoring me?" he asked again.

"Rodney, just go back downstairs and leave me alone." He came forward with every step I took back.

"You always gotta be so stuck up. You ain't special, Rabbit. You just like all these other hoes. You want the dick." I was horrified to hear him talking like that. I got to the top of the stairs and broke for it! I could see the safety of my bedroom ahead of me. A few more steps, that's all I needed. He grabbed my arm before I got to the door, dragging me to the floor.

"You were like my big brother! Rodney, please!" I begged.

"You took your shirt off even though you knew I was down there. I'm a man." He pushed his hand under my dress. I screamed until my throat burned. I scratched at his face, nicking him under the eye.

"I can feel you want it," he said.

"No! Somebody help me!" He pulled my panties down.

"No one's here. You can yell all you want." He waved his penis like a weapon. And then, he shoved into me.

"Tell me you like it," he said. I shook my head. He shoved in again.

"Tell me you like it," he yelled. I turned my head to the side. He grabbed a handful of my hair. My eyes watered from the indignity.

"Tell. Me. You like it," he growled.

"I like it," I cried. Three cheers for summer vacation.

BY SOPHOMORE YEAR, my braces were off. Hallelujah! I became really popular with the boys. And not so popular with the girls, except for Kerri. She did her best to include me in her life, no matter how much I tried to keep her out of mine.

Big Daddy Kane blasted through the headphones of my walkman while I did my homework. Calculus required my undivided attention. It wasn't hard, just detailed. Someone moved the earphone, so *Raw* was only coming through half way.

"When you finish doing my math homework, my uniforms need to be washed," said Kerri. Her math homework was like grade school work. She dropped her text book and her funky uniforms on top of my Trapper. The smell of them made me nauseous. I would have liked nothing better than to throw up on them. Instead I swept them onto the floor.

"I'm not your damn maid, Kerri." She raised an eyebrow.

"You going to Tanisha's tonight?" she asked. I looked up from my desk. In my mind, I punched her in the face.

"Thought so. Cold water only. Wash with whites. Need 'em for tomorrow. Thanks." I threw her nasty uniforms in the washer, and thought for a second about pitching my red socks in the load. But I didn't want any trouble tonight. I had plans.

A folded sheet of paper fell out of Kerri's text book. Red X's slashed at the sheet and at the top was a thirty seven circled in the same blazing red. I should have given it to my mother, but she would just think I was being spiteful. She would have been right.

I finished her homework, and went back down to the laundry room. I fished her uniforms out and as soon as I opened the dryer door, I heard the back door opening. Sweat sprouted on my top lip. I threw her uniforms in and ran, taking the steps two at a time. When I got to the top, I crashed right into the devil.

"Lookin for me, Rab?" he asked.

"Yeah right," I gasped. I was out of breath and glad to be out of the danger zone. Fred Barnes, Mr. El Debarge himself, was standing right behind him looking fine as ever.

"Hey Adrienne."

"Hi Freddy." I pushed my hair back. But he wasn't looking at my hair. He was looking at the twins, Candy and Mandy. He licked his lips with the memory.

"Bye Freddy," I said sweetly, peeking over my shoulder with a small wave. Rodney's eyes were on me, but I wouldn't give him even the smallest of glances.

I knocked on my parents' door. Whatever they were watching was paused on the VCR.

"How come you don't take Missy Poo to the sleepover witcha?" asked my Dad.

"Can't I have one night without Kerri being all in the Kool-Aid?" I asked.

"Have Miss Pam call me when you get there," said my mother.

"Yes, Ma'am." Kerri came in the front door just as I was coming out.

"How come you didn't tell me that Neesh and Rodney was a couple?"

"What?" Nausea bubbled up in my stomach again.

"Oh, you didn't know?" she asked. Her expression changed. A smile played across her face. "Yeah, Neesh was telling me that they were kissing in the stairway. Neesh is so funny."

"Why do you keep calling her Neesh like that?"

"Cause that's what all her friends call her, and I'm her friend. Anyway, I think she's in love with him now. That's the perfect match. The Star Basketball Captain and the Sophomore Class President, isn't it?" she said.

"Sure is." I ran out into the night thinking that Kerri should have walked around with a mask and a pair of black gloves, for she too was a thief. A stealer of happiness.

Tanisha and I took turns holding the hairbrush to sing. Miss Pam busted through Tanisha's bedroom door in a Cleopatra wig that framed her oval face perfectly. My mother would have loved that one.

"Oh, wait a minute," she said. "That's my jam." She snapped her fingers with her right hand holding her Bartles & James and ciggie in her left.

"Ma. You have never heard this song before in your life."

"You think Sha plays all these records in my house and I don't know what's good?"

"Arrrgh," groaned Tanisha. She turned the radio off.

"Yall need to be studying anyway," said Miss Pam. "I hope ya know the names of the Presidents the way you know all that rappin'." She slammed the door behind her.

"Wanna watch *Purple Rain* again?" asked Tanisha.

"Nah, not really." I checked the clock. It was nine on the dot.

"Since when don't you want to watch *Purple Rain*?" I shrugged. I tied the laces on my Air Jordans.

"Where're you going?" she asked.

"Home."

"When you gonna stop lying, Adrienne?" I sprung off the bed. I was getting really good at it.

"Why you wanna know where I'm going, huh, Neesh? So you can tell Kerri?"

"I would never tell Kerri anything. Best friends don't backstab each other."

"Best friends don't backstab each other. Blood is thicker than water. Who comes up with these phrases? They sound good, but they're not always the case, are they, Neesh?"

Tanisha looked at me like my nose had grown. As many lies as I'd told, it could have.

"What the hell is wrong with you?"

"What were you doing kissing Rodney in the staircase, Neesh?"

"What? Who told you that?"

"Is it true?"

"Well yeah, but---"

"But what, Best Friend Back Stabber?"

"Aydree, I don't understand. Why're you mad at me?"

"Cause first you tell me to watch my back with Kerri and then you confide in her about kissing Rodney, and you didn't even tell me. But that's alright. I'm strong." I flexed my bicep.

"She can't hurt me. He can't hurt me. And you sure can't hurt me." They couldn't hurt me because I couldn't feel anything. Friends. Family. Ties that bind. All a figment of the imagination. *Blood sticks together*, said my mother. But blood wasn't a glue. Blood signified pain and betrayal. And that's all.

Neesh slammed the front door behind me. I turned back to clear the air, but I changed my mind. She had a crush on Rodney since forever. I could live with her thinking I was jealous of her and Kerri. But I couldn't live with her thinking I played her out. I got to the corner and a horn toot-tooted. I climbed into the little bluish-grey Civic hatchback.

"Whassup, Sha-Born?"

"Nothin' much. You ready to roll?"

"Yup." He clamped his gold nugget rings over the steering wheel.

"Bet."

SHA AND I DROVE FOR AN hour and change, listening to KRS One for the whole ride. I wasn't sure where we were going. I just knew it was in Connecticut somewhere. On the highway, we blew past blackened trees that looked like long gnarled fingers poised to grab your soul. Neesh and I watched a scary movie at her house that had a scene that looked just like it. I closed my eyes to block it out. The scary movie and Neesh.

I always felt at home at Tanisha's. On Friday nights, we watched TV in the bed with Miss Pam. She would tape *All My Children* on her bedroom VCR and *The Young and the Restless* on Neesh's. Then we'd watch them back to back until it was time for *Dynasty*. Some nights, she would watch the Spanish novellas even though she didn't know what they were saying. She was a soap junkie to the fullest.

I had a nasty cold one particular Friday. It was so bad, my mother took an unpaid day off from work to keep watch.

Kerri and her cheerleading friends came over after school, stomping and aggravating my aches.

"Kerri, can you quiet down a little bit?" I coughed hard into my hand.

"She probably got mono," mumbled TackyIsha.

"If I do," I sneezed. "I probably got it from your boyfriend." Of course, Kerri thought nothing of bringing that heifer into my home, even though she'd ripped my shirt open exposing me to the second floor corridor. All because her boyfriend said hi to me. It's not like I slept with him after they got together or anything.

"We have a competition coming up. What you expect me to do?"

"I don't really care, Kerri. You know I'm not feeling well."

"Fine. Fine. Could you go now?" The front door opened. Rodney appeared carrying two yellow plastic bags from La Mercado.

"How about the two of you go, Kerri? And never come back." My mother walked in right behind Rodney.

"Adrienne, what kind of thing is that to say to somebody?" I huffed, puffed, wheezed and coughed back to my room. I was sick of her and her hospitality. Not a second after I sat on my bed, the stomping resumed.

"I brought you split pea soup, Baby," said my mother. It took a second for her to digest what was going on.

"Where in the world are you going?" she asked. I pulled my hat over my ears and knotted my scarf.

"To get some peace." She didn't argue. And she didn't stop me. That was the part that stung the most.

I snuggled into the pallet Miss Pam made for me on the floor.

"Chile, I can't afford to get sick, but I wouldn't want you to miss this. Alexis is up to no damn good this week!" Alexis was up to no good every damn week! That was why we didn't miss it!

She tied her head scarf on and propped her pillows up behind her, while Neesh brought me hot tea and crackers. We settled into the show, enjoying the buildup of it all. And just as Alexis raised her hand to deliver a smack, I raced down the hallway. One step away from the bathroom door, a second before I was in the clear, I lost my dignity. Sha opened his bedroom door and I was beyond embarrassed. He was the coolest guy I knew.

"You alright?" he asked.

"The flu." He mopped up the mess and sat me on the toilet seat. He knelt next to me. His face was about an inch away. I put my hand over my mouth.

"I've been hearing things about you," he said. He put his hand on my leg. Oh no. Not Sha, too. I shut down the tears that waited to spill over. And instead I smiled even though another guy I'd never thought would turn on me, was.

"And they're not good. Are you using stuff when you're out there?" My mouth turned downward. I shook my head.

"You think you might be pregnant?"

I shrugged out of denial. To throw my mother off, I'd been wrapping clean maxi pads in tissue and putting them in the garbage for five days each for the last two months. I was hoping against hope that Aunt Flow would show up, but she was on vacation.

"We're gonna take care of you."

Sha drove into the parking lot of a gray concrete Holiday Motel that was probably really nice when it first opened. Everything about it screamed scandal. From the woman standing outside the glass doors in snagged fishnet stockings, to the guy chain smoking in the Pontiac Grand Am.

"If anybody comes near the car, there's a .38 under my seat. Wave it in the air like you crazy and honk the horn."

"Okay." The woman in the fishnets walked over to my window, saw it was just little old me and walked over to the Grand Am. When she leaned over, her dimply butt cheeks peeked out from beneath her pleather mini-skirt. I was so glad to see Sha boppin' back to the car with the key.

As soon as he opened the door to the motel room, stale cigarette smoke clung to us like plastic wrap. Sha, who I guessed had done this before, pulled out a can of Lysol and sprayed until the mist covered every surface with an antiseptic dew. The room had two beds with ugly gold and green paisley spreads, a wooden desk and a phone on the night stand between the beds. I put my Jansport on the bed furthest from the door. Sha went to the bathroom and came back out in a t-shirt and sweat pants. He climbed into the other bed. I sat on the edge of the bed.

"The sooner you lay down, the sooner it'll be tomorrow and the sooner it will be over with."

"I know." He rolled on his side.

"Sha?"

"Yeah?"

"Never mind. It's stupid." I pulled the spread up over my jeans and sweatshirt. He clicked the light off. I sighed.

"Come on, Ayj. Spill it."

"How come you never tried anything with me?" I blurted it out so quickly, I'm sure it sounded like all one word. He didn't answer.

"You think I'm ugly, Sha?" I felt self-conscious even in the dark.

"No. I think you're a beautiful girl. But you're a girl. What I look like, messin' with a girl in high school and I'm damn near twenty-two?"

"Everybody does it."

"When I look at you, I see Tanisha. I don't see you in that way."

"Okay, so suppose I wasn't her friend? And suppose nobody would know? Suppose I told you that I thought about you in that way." Sha let out a deep breath.

"Get some sleep, Ayj."

I was glad the light was off because my cheeks were hot as hell. I was hurt and confused and embarrassed that he didn't want me. I fluffed my pillow and settled into night's quietude. That's the word I thought of at the time. Quietude. All that quietude was bad for the rejected heart.

When the wake-up call came at five, I was bathed, dressed, and peeking out of the smoke-tinged curtains. A jiggly woman in spandex hurried out to a doodoo brown sedan. A man in a short sleeved shirt, shoulders hunched against the cold, scooted across the parking lot and disappeared into the darkness before Sha came out of the bathroom fully dressed and headed toward the door. It was time to go, but I couldn't make my feet follow instructions.

"I'm scared." Sherron held his hand out to me. I stared at his hand, still glued to the carpet.

"I'm scared, Sha. I don't want to."

"Okay. Well let's go home. But whatever we do, can we at least get out of this nasty ass hotel?" He held his hand out again.

We drove what would probably be ten city blocks or so out onto the main highway and made a quick right into a dinky little strip mall. The plain white door with Women's Care in small black stencil paint was flanked by a beauty supply store, a raggedy bowling alley and right next door, a *botanica*, where there were candles and statues of Jesus in the window.

Sha Born tapped the door twice and the lock snapped. He pushed the door open and I followed him into the drab white room. The first thing that struck me was the sickly sanitized scent. The second thing that got my attention was the number of chairs in the waiting room. There were just too many. Two rows of fold out seats on each side, with a narrow strip that lead to the receptionist and the doctor's office. There were no pictures on the wall or any magazines in sight. When we got to the little room in the back of the doctor's office, Sha peeled four hundred dollars off his bankroll and handed it to the doctor, a little black man with small hands.

"Doctor Ogiye, this is Adrienne. Adrienne, this is Doc."

"Sherron is a good friend of my daughtah. She is a good judge of charactah," he said in an African accent. "You are lucky to have him in your cornah." Doc handed me a gown before he washed his hands in the little metal sink by the door. He pulled a blue curtain around me.

"Knock on thee door when you ah done changing."

I should have been changing, but the nosy in me, was too much to hold back. I peeked behind the blue curtain at the counter where Doc housed all his tools and medication. Everything was neatly labeled and there wasn't a speck of dirt to be seen anywhere in the room. Not a cobweb, not a dust bunny, not a crack in the tile. If I was going to die, it would certainly not be from infection. Just as I pulled the blue curtain back, I understood the reason why it was there. A needle the length of my arm posed on the tray waiting for his chance at stardom.

Doc knocked on the door. "Ah you okay in theh?"

"I'm not ready. I'm not doing it!" I pulled my jeans up and pulled my sweatshirt over my head. Sha called out from the other side.

"Ayj. Open up."

"I'm out of here, Sha. Don't try to talk me out of it."

"Adrienne. Listen to me. If you want to have a baby, then we'll leave and that's that. But if you don't want to have it, you better get undressed and get your ass on the table."

"Don't talk to me like that."

"I'm just telling you the truth, Big Head. But you need to hurry up and make a decision before all of us get into some serious trouble."

The sun was barely up by the time Doc and Sha were helping me into the backseat of the Civic. I didn't remember anything about the procedure except counting back from one hundred and watching the blue curtain fade to black somewhere around ninety-seven. I don't think the car pulled away from the curb before I was knocked out again, in a warm, black and dreamless wonderland.

I felt the car slow to a crawl.

"Adrienne. I think you'd better get up." When I opened my eyes, I wished I could go back to sleep forever.

The car barely stopped moving before Miss Pam busted through the screen door like the horses at the racetrack. Her Cleopatra wig was askew and her housecoat was flapping at the knees.

"Where in the hell have you been? And what in the hell is wrong with Adrienne?! Sherron, are you fuckin' stupid?!" Sha sprung out of the car.

"Ma, calm down." She crouched down to look into the car.

"Calm down? Yo' ass gonna go to jail for *statchatory* rape and you telling me to calm down!" My mother marched down the block in a pink sweat suit and her long black church coat over it. I locked the car doors.

"Adrienne," she hollered. "Adrienne, get the hell out that car!" I could barely move, I was so tired. Her warm breath fogged the window. She wiped it away, knocking frantically on the glass. "Girl, you high on some shit, ain't you? Open this got-damn door!" Tanisha stood at the door holding the telephone. If I had to make a guess, she had been talking to Kerri. Kerri stomped down the street, completely dressed, holding a toddler version of her cheerleading uniform. She held it up to the window.

"You know I had a competition! You did this to me on purpose! I hate your guts, Adrienne!" And then, all hell bubbled over.

My mother was in Sha's face. "What did you give my *daughtuh*?" I tried to tell her he didn't give me anything, but it wouldn't come out properly.

Out of nowhere, my mother slapped Sha in the face and Miss Pam jumped in between them and she and my mother started shoving each other and Sha tried to break them apart and my father was there and he and Sha started rolling on the ground and the sirens got louder and Sha was handcuffed and my dad was handcuffed and the cops were telling my mother to back off before she got handcuffed and Miss Pam was cursing and I was in the car trying to pull it together as Kerri yelled and screamed and Tanisha stood in the door with panic in her eyes and all the while Rodney, that Superman, that Hot Rod, that Boy Wonder, was nowhere to be found.

MY FATHER SAT AT THE EDGE of the sofa cracking red pistachios open with his bare hands. Periodically, he rubbed his raw, welted wrists. I felt guilty as hell. I never meant for anyone to get into trouble because of me.

I lay on the couch, underneath my blanket and the watchful eye of my mother. My father refused to look at me.

It was almost seven. Twelve hours since we rolled up in front of Tanisha's. My mother just wouldn't drop it.

"But I just don't understand why didn't you call us, Adrienne? We your parents."

"I don't know."

"How come Sherron didn't call us? Adrienne, why'd you run away in the first place? What were you thinking?" If I had really run away in the first place, I would have been thinking that I hated Rodney and Kerri; that I couldn't even breathe without them wanting in on it or my mother offering them my share without checking to see if I had enough; that I felt like a stranger in my own home and no one was ever on my side. I shrugged.

"I don't know."

"Every damn thing I ask you, you don't know! What the hell do you know?" she asked. I knew I didn't like her attitude, that's for sure.

"I know I want to tell people who got evicted that I want them to leave because they've taken over everything. What do you think about that, *Mother*?"

"I don't like it one bit, 'cause that's not what you do. You talk it out. That's what family does." Yeah. We talk it out. I could just imagine the conversation.

"Auntie Rho. She came downstairs and took off her shirt and she started hugging me and then she got in my bed. It wasn't my fault."

And then I would have said, "No, it didn't happen like that." And everybody would be looking at me sideways. And then Kerri would start.

"Oh please, she's such a liar. She's just jealous of us. She doesn't even come to Roddy's games. Do you know I even heard she's telling people we're not related?" And what would that get me? Another earful of family glue talk.

My mother never asked me why I wanted them to leave. She never asked to hear my side. She never thought about me where they were concerned. And for that, I would never forgive her.

Kerri stretched the telephone cord from the kitchen wall. "It's Neesh's mother." The hairs on my arm stood up. My mother rolled her eyes and went to the phone. She clamped her hand down onto her hip.

"Pamela, don't be callin' here wit that mess. Ain't nobody in this house do nothin' to that boy's car. Dub sitting right here. Dub, say hey."

"Hey," said my Dad.

"And Rodney is downstairs. So you can blame that mess on somebody else." She slammed the phone down.

Rodney came through the front door with his light blue Tar Heels jacket scuffed with dirt and car grease. Kerri scratched her arm. Shoot. I scratched mine, too.

"Rodney Junior…"

"Family's gotta stick together, Auntie Rho."

"Just drop that coat on the washer and I'll get the stain out," she said.

No one said a word. It was just as well.

"You gonna take your nose out that book and have dinner with the family?" I thought if I didn't say anything, my mother would just go away. When I looked up from my book she was still standing there.

"No," I said. "It's for school."

"It ain't gonna kill you."

I didn't bother to look up. Every night it was the same thing. Come eat with the family. Come talk with the family. To hell with the crazy ass family.

"Well, just so you know. We celebratin' cause Rodney's going to Georgetown University. But since you don't care 'bout nobody but you, you can stay right up here. Hmph. And after he tried to defend your *reppatation*…"

"Thank him for me," I said. "He didn't hear you the first twenty times."

My mother slammed my bedroom door. I opened my desk drawer and emptied all my Georgetown brochures into the garbage can. I put my History book down, and Danielle Steele was back in effect.

Everything I was going to know about life, I would find in a book. And without getting myself or my feelings hurt. I read everything I could get my hands on. Homer, F. Scott Fitzgerald, Maya Angelou, Ntozake Shange who wrote *For Colored Girls* just for me. I even taught myself to crochet from the books I read.

My mother had so many pot holders, she could make a rainbow collage on the kitchen wall. Some were ugly as hell but she said she loved them. Trying to be a good mother, I guess. But I knew they were ugly because I made them like that on purpose. Until that glorious summer of 1988 when it was time for *him* to go.

I watched from my window, not even thinking about going downstairs.

Big Rodney carried his duffle bags out to the rental. A rental, because according to him, "My son is a star. He gotta travel in style."

"Adrienne!" yelled my mother. "Adrienne, come say bye to your cousin!" I dashed to my bed and pulled the sheet up to my chin. *Doomp, doomp.*

"Adrienne," called my mother. I snored lightly. It sounded so real, I held back my giggles. My back was to the door, but I prayed she didn't come around to see my face.

"Daggone child is always sleeping," she muttered. She closed the door behind her. I heard her go down the stairs. Then I heard her on the porch.

"Rodney," she yelled. "She between sleep and wake but she said tell you bye and she love you." I ran to the window as fast as I could. It was all over his face that he wasn't sure if she was lying or if I really said it. But he hugged and kissed her and got in the rental. Big Rodney stood at the drivers' side, bellowing like he, too, was wearing a wire.

"You hear that Rodney. She love you. Everybody loves you. Everybody loves a star, Boy!" Rodney glanced up to my window, and did a double take. I stared unblinkingly, with the hopes he would clearly see the hatred and understand that no matter what nonsense my mother and his father fed him, not everybody loved him. And just in case he didn't get it, I stuck my middle finger up at him. Goodbye, you mother fucker. And mother fuck you.

THE FIRST DAY OF JUNIOR YEAR was strangely similar to my first day of freshman year. No one spoke to me.

Ironically Kerri, who was persona non grata in the park, was voted most popular sophomore in the last yearbook. She had a whole page and everything! Kerri and her crew, which now included Lashelle (yes, Lashelle was part of Kerri's crew now) and Lizette, all sported cheerleader jackets over their Guess jeans and Air Max sneakers.

Tanisha waved from on the steps, but I pretended not to see her. I was still terribly embarrassed by what happened. Every now and then she called my house to say hello, but things weren't the same. I mean after an apology, what do you say to someone whose brother went to jail because he was trying to help you? Exactly. Nothing. So as much as it hurt, our friendship was pretty much a done deal.

Lamont Hinks, the new big man on campus since Rodney left, stood with the team near the gate where the jocks always congregated. Every time, I looked over the other kids to check whether the doors were opened or not, he was staring. From what I saw on my way past the park, Lamont played the point guard position too, but with less finesse and grace than Rodney. I mean his lay-ups were decent enough. What he lacked in skill, he made up for in persistence and impenetrable defense. But he was no Rodney. Finally he came over with his little diddy bop that I loved more than apple Jolly Ranchers.

"You got a man?"

"Depends on who's asking."

He smiled like he won a lottery scratch off. The hisses from the snake pit were so loud, Lamont chuckled.

"Your fan club?" he asked.

"Nope. Definitely yours." I was already a misfit, but when I copied his phone number into my binder I officially became the girl none of the other girls spoke to. The boys, however, were another story. And not just the boys.

In his defense, Mr. Scott did not come onto me. In fact, he hardly noticed me. In gym class, I was called by my last name like everybody else. I participated fully and came to class everyday, so when we got our report cards, I was beside myself. The lowest I'd ever received in any class was an A-. Mr. Scott had given me a D.

He looked over my delaney card and my scores.

"Fuller, there seems to be an error. I'll have to change it."

"Thank you." Mr. Scott followed me to the door. He wasn't particularly tall, maybe an inch taller than me. But he was well-built and light-skinned with a small flat-top. He was that cutie pie teacher that the girls in my school daydreamed about. Our own Al B. Sure. I stopped short so that he bumped into my butt.

"Excuse me, Fuller." I didn't move. He tapped my shoulder. "Would you mind speeding it up? I have an appointment coming."

He closed the door behind me and I was shocked at being dismissed. I cracked the door open, only to find him sitting behind his desk with his penis firmly in hand.

"Ahem." He looked up but he didn't stop. His words tumbled out.

"Youshouldn'tbe…inhere." I came around his desk, and kissed him on the lips. Clear fluid formed on the tip of his penis.

"Fuller. You really. Shouldn't. Be here," he stammered.

I unbuttoned my polka dot blouse, deliberately taking my time. Mr. Scott stood so suddenly, the chair fell over. He hiked my jean skirt and put me on his desk. He stared at my tootie like it was a life preserver on a sinking ship. But when he touched me, I tingled the way I did at the party with Corey. And then he put his mouth on it.

I tried to pull away, but he held me still. His tongue pried me apart so gently and forcefully I didn't know what to do with myself except give in to the new feeling. He flicked his tongue over the little button and I could barely breathe by the time I felt the heat flowing through me. In the next motion he was inside me. When he grunted, he scared me out of my daze. I quickly pushed him away and got the hell out of there. Sleeping with the teacher was disgusting. Al B. Sure look-alike or not.

Mr. Scott aside, being with those guys wasn't something that I sought. They just seemed to come to me just like my mother said they would. I mean, Mommy knows best, right?

When they wanted me, it made me feel like I was the baddest broad ever. Badder than Apollonia. Badder than Salt. Badder than Rae Dawn Chung. And if they made the little heartbeat in my panty flutter, either with a word, or a look, or a smile, well, I had to see if they could get me there. So when they came calling, I answered. Until tragedy struck.

I got ready for school in record time. I needed to get in the building before first period. Before anyone else arrived. I tied the laces of my red Reeboks and pulled the cuffs of my jeans over them. I tried to sit back up, but the pain in my stomach was too sharp to take on.

"You need to boo-boo or something?" asked my mother.

"No."

"I would ask you what the hell is wrong with you, but I know you just gonna give your regular answer."

"Nothing's wrong," I responded.

My mother threw her hands in the air and went back to hemming my father's pants. Soon the pain became unbearable and I ran doubled over to the bathroom.

I could no longer hold my urine or the scream that burned the back of my throat.

"Adrienne?" I cursed under my breath. I forgot to lock the door.

"Baby? You okay?" Sweat dripped down the side of my face.

"Yeah," I gasped. "I'm okay."

My mother closed the door behind her. She never heard another peep out of me, but I had no idea how I could explain how the toilet paper holder got ripped out of the wall.

I came downstairs hunched over in pain. My mother stood at the door in her black church coat. She handed me mine without saying a word.

Horizon Clinic was on Pitkin Avenue in the middle of everything. I kept my eyes on the floor, nervous that someone would see me. But when the receptionist pushed the plastic cup over the counter I turned ice cold. I pushed the cup back at her. She pushed it toward me again.

"You have to give us a urine sample," she said.

"I know what it's for." I pushed it back over the counter.

"Can we just do a blood test?" I asked. The receptionist tucked the cup into her drawer.

"Have a seat in the waiting room."

Posters of uteri and various birth control methods lined the walls of the waiting room. Girls younger than me sat with hard-rock faces. Girls older, kept a poker face. Most of all, everyone kept their eyes on the floor. I was the only one there with my mother. I felt stupid and oddly, safe at the same time.

"Adrienne. What in the hell is going on with you?" she whispered. But in a place like that, a whisper was futile. If you listened closely enough, you could hear the *pffft* of a silent fart.

"I don't want to talk about it."

"Well you better talk to the doctor about it before your tootie falls off." Never mind feeling safe, I felt plain old stupid.

I sat on the counter in the restroom until my mother leaned into the bathroom. The worry lines in her forehead were pronounced. The confusion in her eyes was like a raging fire.

"It's your turn." She grabbed my arm as I passed. I looked down at my mother, my former idol, the one who knew me better than anyone else.

"You don't really want to know. If you did, you'd have figured it out."

The examination room was stark white, cold and not so different from the Doc's little office in Connecticut.

"Get on the table," said the brown-skinned lady in the lab coat. She was maybe a few years younger than my mother, with a serious face that held no expression at all.

"Can't I wait for the doctor?"

"I am the doctor. We're a little understaffed. On the table. Feet in the stirrups." I felt different with her, than I did with Doc. Nervous, like she was thinking I was dirty or stupid or something.

"Don't be shy, honey. I have what you have and I'm not here to hurt you."

After a series of pokes and prods she snapped her gloves off and threw them in the garbage.

"What do I have?"

"The good news is, you're gonna live. The bad news is you need to turn over. This will pinch just a little bit." I was hot with shame, laying face down on the table. Sometimes I wondered what I ever did to deserve the crazy things that happened to me. The prick of the needle was gone before it even registered that my skin had being punctured.

"There you go. Wait for your prescription." She scribbled on a pad and it wasn't until then that I believed she was a doctor. Her handwriting was terrible.

She handed me a pink plastic bag filled with condoms.

"Pamphlets. Condoms. All the things you need to stay healthy. Questions, call me." I left the bag on the examination table. Doctor Who shook her head thinking she had me pegged. But she was far off course.

On that cool springy day when the first green buds sprouted on the branches of grand maple trees, the curtains at the Adrienne Show were officially closed.

MR. LEVY READ HIS MAGAZINE like he did every morning during homeroom: without worry or concern about what we were up to.

"You fuckin' African booty-scratcher. You need to go the fuck back to Haiti or wherever the fuck you from."

"Don't they make soap where you come from?" I looked over my shoulder not to see who was doing the picking, but to check out the new prey. Her hair was braided in thick plaits, her plaid butterfly-collared shirt was tucked neatly into her flowered skirt. She lifted her gaze from the desktop to stare at me dead on. I looked down at my book glad as hell it wasn't me. Where I was now, no one even paid attention to me anymore. Not the Julie's, not the cheerleaders, not Kerri. No one. And I liked it just fine. Actually, that's not true. Sometimes in the hallway, Tanisha would try to make conversation, but I kept it down to an *I'm okay. The family's good* type of thing. I never asked how Sha was doing, though.

"Leave that Haitian bitch alone, yo. She could put some voodoo on your ass. Shrink your dick and then it fall off."

"His dick so small, if it fall off, he won't even know!"

"Your basehead pops ain't got no dick."

"Fuck you." *Fwap!* And then they were tussling in the aisle.

"Hey. You motherfuckers better sit the fuck down before I call security," said Mr. Levy, never looking up from his magazine.

The loudspeaker crackled and popped.

"Hello. This is Taquisha Smith with today's announcements. Today is Election Day at Wilcox. And here are our candidates answering one last question before the vote. The question is: Why do you think you are the best person for the job? First, my best friend, KayKay!"

"Why? Because I'm KayKay Barrus, that's why. And I'm a winner."

"Okaaaay. Same question, Tanisha."

"If you have been to my parties, you already know why I'm the best person for the job. Tanisha Banks for Senior President!"

"Vote for KayKay!" yelled Taquisha.

"That will be all Taquisha," said Principal Zeno. "Ladies and Gents, voting for Senior Class President opens in the cafeteria at the start of fifth period lunch and closes at the end of sixth. Please place your vote during your normal lunch period. Cutters will be detained. That concludes our announcements." *Khhhhcrrrk.* And then he was gone.

The cafeteria had changed since I last saw it, some three years ago. The spades games were on the far end near the soda machine. There was graffiti on the wall. A dollar sign. The dean barked into his bullhorn.

"Take a seat. Get off the table. Take that hat off. Take a seat. Get off the table. Take the hat off." He was like a recording.

The ballot table was way down at the other end where Tanisha and I used to sit. Neon pink oaktag boasted her name. I could see it from where I stood at the main staircase. Kerri handed out flyers and t-shirts with a picture of her and Rodney on the front. "Free t-shirts. Vote for me!" She accidentally pushed one toward me, but it fell on the floor.

"Rabbbbbit! Hey cousin!" she squealed. TackyIsha squeezed a smile out of her twisted lips. "So glad you came down to support your family!" Tanisha held her flyers to her chest.

"Hi Ayj."

"Hi Tanisha."

The ballot box sat at the end of the table manned by the security guard. I had the ballot in my hand, sure of my vote. Kerri was in my pocket, breathing my air.

"Hey cuz. What's up with you?"

"You haven't said two good words to me in three years and now you wanna claim me, huh KayKay?"

I checked the name on the ballot and dropped it in the box.

"I hope you did the right thing," she said.

When Principal Zeno's gritty voice crackled through the loudspeaker at the close of last period, the hairs on my arms stood on end.

"Good afternoon Ladies and Gents. This afternoon, I'm proud to announce…" I squeezed my eyes shut. "…the winner of the Senior elections by one deciding vote, Miss Tanisha Banks!" I smiled to myself. The cheers that echoed through the building were tempered with groans from the Kerri supporters.

On my way down the hallway, I snatched a Kerri poster off the bulletin board with joy and dropped it on the floor. Kerri stood at the front door with her clique. As I approached, her eyes narrowed, undoubtedly trying to read if I was that deciding vote. She couldn't help herself, she followed me out the front door and down the stairs.

"Rabbit, I know the votes are a secret…"

"And they will always be a secret." I left her standing on the sidewalk.

The next afternoon, I went back to the library and locked my face inside my books, glad to be back in my safe zone; my sanctuary.

At the library, I saw the same faces every day. Actually I saw the tops of their heads because their faces were book locked.

One of the regular faces was Omar Lippincottle. He and Tanisha and about half of the library crowd were in most of my other classes except gym. In the library, he sat in the same spot every day. So when he sat at my table, I was surprised. I pointed my pen toward the window.

"I think that's your table over there."

"No. I think I like this table, too."

I took my books to his old empty table. Like mine, it had *Johnny loves Isabel* scratched into the wooden table, along with 3D cubes, tic tac toe and the name "Ski", whoever he was. When I sat down, Omar rested his bag down.

"Look. Don't start no shit with me."

"Shhhhhhh!" The librarian pointed her finger at us.

"I wanted to share that table with you. I didn't see you in here yesterday. I thought you'd abandoned us." I gave him the eye. "Plus you look like you can talk about something besides school." He put his hand out to showcase the library clientele. Super thick glasses. Crazy clothing patterns matched up, that didn't exactly match. Nose pickers. Stutterers. Basically, my fellow outcasts. I looked him over. He was cute, actually. He had on a Polo rugby shirt, Guess jeans and Polo Cookie boots. I never noticed his gear before. I guess because he spent all his time in the library.

"All you have to do is tell me that on top of being the smartest girl I've ever known, you're a basketball fan and I'll be your friend for life."

"I am not a basketball fan. I am *the* basketball fan."

My mother was a little too excited that I had company. It seemed like just yesterday, she was steering me away from boys. And now today, she was practically trying to marry me off. I could hear the refrigerator door opening and closing; the cabinet doors slamming shut; the clanging of pots and pans on the range. Something good was brewing. I could smell it. Every time we started talking, she came back to the door.

"Omar. Do you go to church?"

"Yes, Ma'am."

"Omar, you want something to eat?"

"No, thank you, Ma'am."

"Omar, you want something cold to drink?"

"No, thank you, Ma'am."

My mother pranced into the living room with a tray of chicken wings still glistening with sizzling hot grease and homemade biscuits with butter melted into the tops.

"Just in case," she said.

"Don't mind her," I said to Omar.

"It's okay. She's nice. I like her." He liked my mother. Interesting. Kerri barged through the front door with her red Gucci bag from Cash Money slung over her shoulder while we watched Guy's video and licked our greasy fingers.

"Nerds," she sneered on her way up to her room. In five minutes flat, she was back down in a black spandex cat suit and red Gucci boots gliding to the front window with her ass poked out.

"Kerri, what you doin' down here in that onesie? You gettin' a lil fast, Kerri. Watch yourself." *Finally*. Kerri rolled her eyes and mumbled.

"Ain't nobody faster than Rabbit." Omar's expression didn't change at all. In fact, his eyes appeared to be glued to the television. My mother smoothed the front of her sweatshirt and went back to the kitchen. I know they heard her. How could they not have? Kerri's eyes locked on his boots.

"Are those Cookie boots?" Omar smiled.

"Yeah."

"Nice. You have a lil' flavor, Bookster." She sat down on the arm of my Dad's chair, shuffling through the mail.

"Don't mind me. I'm just looking for my acceptance letter from Georgetown."

"Really? I didn't know they offered special ed classes," said Omar. Kerri flicked the envelopes at us and stalked off.

"Nerd nobodies make nerd nobody babies," she said. "Remember that." When she got to the top of the stairs we burst with laughter. She slammed her door. And just in case we didn't get it the first time, she slammed it again.

When my parents went upstairs, I kissed him lightly on the lips as a little thank you. It was nice to have someone in my corner for a change. I snuggled up under his arm feeling like he could really be a keeper. He ran his hand down my arm and rested it on my breast.

"Let's get to know each other a little better, okay?"

"Okay." He put his hand back on my arm. A minute later, he sat up.

"Don't you like me?" he asked.

"Yeah, I like you. Why're you asking me that?"

"Because I just don't understand why you're frontin' on me." Slang words sounded square coming from him. It sounded like 'frun-tin' instead of 'fruh-in.'

"I'm not frontin' on you. I'm just not ready for all that," I said. He exhaled, slapping his leg.

"Sorry. It's just that I really like you. I guess I'm just not fly enough for you." He stood up.

"Where are you going?" I asked him.

"Home. My feelings are kind of hurt right now." I put my arms around his neck.

"I do like you." I kissed him on the cheek. "A lot." I kissed him on the neck. He didn't kiss me back. I pushed him back on the sofa and straddled him. He kissed me hard. A little too hard. I pulled away. He sucked his teeth, sounding like Aunt Say.

"Are you trying to give me blue balls?"

"No," I said. He squeezed my breasts. Too hard again. I got off his lap, giving up on the kisses. He unzipped his jeans and yanked his penis out. I really wanted to take it slow with him. I wanted this to be different. But I really didn't want him to leave.

I knelt before him, taking him in hand, but something was not quite right in the way he trembled. I backed away, not swiftly enough, making it worse for myself.

"Oh man. They were right," he whispered.

"Adrienne," called my mother, "it's gettin' late." I wiped my face with the back of my sleeve.

"He's getting ready to leave." My arms were folded and I was already standing in front of the open door. The now fattened snowflakes were beginning to stick to the sidewalk. I handed him his coat.

"Are we studying tomorrow?" he asked.

"I don't think so." I couldn't even look at him. I was so angry, I was sweating. I shifted my bangs from my forehead, only to draw back sticky fingers.

"Do you have plans?" he asked.

"No. Um. I don't think we should see each other anymore."

"What? We can't break up yet! I didn't even get a chance to---" I slapped the spit out of his mouth. Droplets sprinkled the front door. He looked so surprised, I thought he would cry. Instead, he slapped me back.

"I heard everything they said about you and I still went out with you."

"Lucky me."

"Even though you did it with your own cousin," he said. I pushed him as hard as I could and slammed the door behind him. My mother came down the stairs.

"I heard the door slam. Everything alright?"

"Yeah."

"He's a nice boy, Aydree. He got good manners. He'll be good for you."

I stared at the reflection of my clean scrubbed face and towel wrapped hair, at the dumbest smartest girl in Wilcox High. I kicked myself for thinking that that herb Omar really liked me for me and for thinking Rodney was a part of my past. I locked the door to my room and dug through my tape drawer until I found my De La Soul tape. I hated men. Actually I hated everyone. But I hated myself the most for letting my guard down. I turned out the nightlight and turned my walkman up to ten as De La Soul sang, it's just Me, Myself and I. Once again.

Bing bing. Biiiing bing.

"Who's at the door, Adrienne?" asked my mother. I pulled my jacket on, peeping through the peep hole.

"Looks like the mailman." I pulled the door open tightening my scarf before I picked up my school bag.

"Do I need to sign?" I asked him. His already pink face turned scarlet red. He handed me the small bundle and pointed toward the snow blanket in the front yard. A blue liquid spelled out *WHORE* in the snow. I dug away at it until my fingers and the cuffs of my yellow down jacket were stained and until the word was reduced to a light blue slushy mess.

I didn't look at anyone at school. Not even when the giggles were as deafening and as agitating as television static. Not even when Tanisha called my name and I wanted to stop but knew the pity would reduce me to a teary mess. Not even when *skeezer* or hoe was uttered with so much frequency that if I wasn't sure they were talking about me before, I knew for sure then.

So, I turned off the sounds and tuned everyone and everything out. That is, until the bus horn blasted me out of my haze so that I teetered on the edge of the sidewalk, with the wind from the speeding bus pushing me away from harm instead of smashing me into oblivion and ending the nightmare once and for all.

As I got closer to my house, though, I hid my soiled sleeves behind my back hoping to avoid a confrontation with my mother. I couldn't take another hit. I even contemplated doing an about face, but she was waiting at the door. She smiled and waved me forward. She waved a letter in the air.

"Come! It looks important!" My pulse raced.

"You read it," I said. She hesitated.

"Ma. Please read it. I can't do it."

"Dear. Miss. Fuller. We. Are. Placed. No. Wait a minute. Pleased. We are pleased. To. Offer. You. Ay. Full aca-aca-academy. Here, you do it. I'm too nervous." My mother's eyes darted away from mine.

"We are pleased to offer you a full academic scholarship for Personnel Management at Maryland University." She jumped up and down, her breasts flopping about under her bathrobe.

"Baby, you did it!" My mother was crying and screaming and laughing and hugging me. I didn't feel her joy, but I hugged her back. Every time, I tried to escape to my room, she dialed someone else and said, hold on tell her yourself. So far, I'd spoken to Aunt Say, Aunt Juicie, Miss Lewis, and two of her church lady friends that I'd never met because I refused to go back.

When my Daddy came home, she beamed with pride, handing him the letter.

"This is good, Baby, but how we sposed ta pay for this?"

"Well, we know you can't pay for it."

"Why you gonna go say some shit like that?"

"Anyway. That's what scholarship is Dub. The school's gonna pay for her to learn," she said repeating what I'd told her.

When Kerri came in and placed her pompoms on the table, my mother shared again. "Adrienne got a full scholarship to Maryland University."

"Oh. Not too far from Georgetown. Guess you won't be getting away from us after all, Rabbit."

“I SMELL CANDIED YAMS in here. Somebody better make sure I gets me a Tupperware,” said Aunt Say. Kerri unlatched the lock on her wheelchair.

“Ma. That’s why you so fat. You ain’t even eat yet and you axin for a Tupperware.” Aunt Say wheeled her chunky, but funky self into the living room with Aunt Juicie following in right behind her and dropped her heavy pocketbook on the pea green plastic couch that was still holding on for dear life.

“Adrienne, what you doin’ over there sittin’ so quiet? You should be celebratin’! You the valedictorian!” said Aunt Say.

“Silly Girl. You’re lookin’ like you lost your best friend. I’m not used to seein’ you like that,” said Aunt Juicie.

“I know! Ain’t you happy to see your favorite Aunties?” asked Aunt Say. Kerri sat on the sofa next to Aunt Juicie.

“Of course I am,” I replied. I kissed Aunt Say’s drumstick and the sharp cheekbone protruding from Aunt Juicie’s face. Kerri patted her cheek.

“None for me, Miss Valedictorian?”

“I got something for you.” My mother wound her camera.

“Oh. That would be so cute! Give your cousin a graduation kiss!”

“Yeah, Rabbit. It’ll be cute,” she giggled. “Let’s be a family for the cameras. Act like we really give a damn about each other.”

“All right, yall. Put these on and say cheese!” I donned my graduation cap. It was a big old party on Hopkinson.

“Adrienne, get that phone,” shouted my mother over the TV.

“Hello.”

"Ayyyyy Lite Brite! Your cousin bout to be a superstar, you know!"

"Hold on." I passed my mother the phone.

"Who is it?" she asked.

"The devil."

"Hi Rodney Senior. We already watchin' it. We ain't gonna miss it."

What we weren't going to miss was the National Basketball Draft. I sat on the edge of my seat, anticipating what could possibly change all our lives.

"Lawd! I hope he come to the Skyscrapers!" cried Aunt Say.

"Nah-uh. The coaching ain't been right since Coach Patterson left," said my father. He was right. And it didn't help that the Assistant Coach didn't know enough about coaching to be effective.

"Roddy should go to Detroit. They the champions and he should play with a champion team," said Kerri.

"They have a winning formula already," I said. "Besides. They won't be picking early because they won the title."

"I think Detroit would be best for Roddy. Winners should be with winners."

Aunt Juicie added her two cents for good measure. "Well God is good. He'll put his behind right where he's supposed to be."

"Oh my goodness," yelled Aunt Say. "Look at that big fool!"

"At least that big fool is supporting his son," said Kerri. No one reacted. For a second, I wondered if maybe the things I heard her say were in my mind, except my mother smoothed down the front of her apron.

Big Rodney's big old schnoz came into focus on the television screen, as did his purple and green suspenders. He was still a joke, that damn Big Rodney. Lil' Rodney held up his purple and green jersey smiling like he was touched.

"Los Angeles Chiefs are proud to have Rodney Barrus Jr. as the number one first round draft pick!"

My parents and I jumped up and down. I hugged them all with a fervor they hadn't seen in me for a long time. Kerri flung her Georgetown acceptance letter in the air.

Aunt Juicie was right. God was good, indeed.

ଓ

I HAD TWO DUFFLE BAGS at my feet and a backpack full of my mother's fried chicken. My Daddy's brand new white sparkling Cadillac posed quite nicely for the camera, but I frowned. The argument we were having had been going on since the Caddy arrived the day before and I was tired of it. My mother wound the camera again.

"Dub, get in the picture." My father sauntered down off the porch in his best cool dude walk. "Adrienne, I don't know why you won't just let me and your Daddy drive you down to school. You know he wanna get this brand new Caddy on the road." That brand new Caddy was a gift from Mr. Hot Rod, himself. It followed a brand new washer and dryer set for my mother and a diamond bracelet that I dropped down the sewer grate at the corner. There was no way I was placing my Lite Brite ass in anything that came from Rodney.

"My ticket's already been bought," I said.

"We can get a refund. Don't you wanna give your Daddy a chance to drive his daughtuh somewhere for the first time?"

"Okay fine." I opened the back door. "But I get car sick. So if I throw up in the back, don't say I didn't warn you."

I scrambled into the front seat on the Greyhound, even though after awhile it was clear no one else wanted it. I needed to see the new road on the way to my new life unfold in front of my eyes.

When we cleared the clutter and jumble of crammed up tall buildings and the congestion of the metro area, I found myself exhaling. I never once closed my eyes for fear that I might wake up and be right back on Hopkinson

Avenue. I waved goodbye to the skeletons hiding in the brush on the side of the road. And to the ghosts floating about in the clouds. In my mind, I saw myself running through a field with a pretty white sundress blowing in the breeze; every thought, an image of some kind of peaceful existence I hadn't had in a long, long time. I didn't even unpack the lunch bag my mother sent. I didn't want the smells of my old house to interfere with my new dreams.

My roommate Laura, a springy red-haired freckly white girl from Long Beach, Long Island, met a guy named Luke in the lobby of our dorm Logan Hall on the first day. "Ohmigod, like Luke and Laura from General Hospit-ull? It's like fate, Adrienne!" She and I got along fine. She stayed on her side. I stayed on mine. Three times, she brought Luke over and three times I remained either at my desk or in my bed reading with my headphones on.

"Aren't you gonna get out and meet people?" she asked me one morning when we were getting ready for class.

I shrugged. I had a brand-new slate to re-create myself or remain anonymous. Whether I met people or didn't, was entirely up to me. It was a beautiful feeling.

I strolled the tree-lined campus with my walkman on. From Wegman Hall where most of my classes met, back to my dorm and then maybe to the Tullman Dining Hall, nodding back at the black people who nodded at me. Black people were really friendly outside New York. It was annoying and refreshing at the same time. Still, my only company was Mariah Carey and A Tribe Called Quest blasting through my earphones. I know people thought I was weird, but that was okay. I had peace. I had calm. I had all I needed.

And then this chocolate skinned brother with a bald head walked into my Economics class. I'd noticed him the first day because on sight of him, my tootie fluttered. But I kept my legs pressed together until she died a silent pulsating death and made sure to keep my eyes trained on the Professor at all times.

He skipped over a row of empty seats, and sat right next to me.

"Can I borrow a *pee-en*?" he asked with a southern drawl. I ignored him.

"Okay. So maybe your momma taughtcha not to talk to strangers. I'm Terrell. Now I'm not a stranger. May I borrow a *pee-en*?"

"A what?"

"A *pee-en*. You know…to write with. I know you have one," he said. I fixed my eyes on the front of the lecture hall.

"You're from New York, ain'tcha?" I rolled my eyes.

"Keep your pen, Big Head. I don't need it anyway." I smiled inside. Sha-Born used to call me that.

Every day, he sat next to me. Every day he asked me to borrow a pen. Every day I told him no. For a whole month, this went on.

And then he stopped. He sat a row ahead of me and didn't even look back to say hi. That was fine with me. He was starting to get on my nerves anyway.

A week later, I arrived in class and found Terrell already there. My heart quickened, still I walked past him to my row.

Everything would have been fine if my pen hadn't fallen…down one row into his. He picked it up, slowly inspecting it. I sat with the nastiest of Brooklyn attitudes plastered across my face.

"I believe this is yours," he drawled. I battled hard against smiling at him, but I lost. That was all the encouragement he needed.

Terrell met me in the Tullman Dining Hall. He showed up at the gym in sweats so he could work out with me. He waited outside my night class on the far side of the campus, so I wouldn't have to walk back to Logan Hall by myself. He stayed up with me playing Uno and watching *Harlem Nights*. And of course, we watched basketball together. He even stayed on campus with me during Thanksgiving break when I made up one hundred two reasons why I couldn't go home.

But he couldn't stay for Christmas. On Christmas Eve, he gave in to his mother's demands.

"I'll call you when I get there," he told me.

"When are you coming back?"

"Two days from now. What you gonna do while I'm gone?"

"What do I always do?"

"Eat, sleep, read, eat, watch movies, read, eat, study, watch the lazy Skyscrapers, read, eat."

"Bye, Fool."

After a sumptuous dinner of Ramen Noodles and Doritos, I lay across my bed fingering the eyelet on my old bedspread, counting the hours before he'd call again. I'm serious. I watched the clock. I yanked the phone off the hook on the first ring.

"Hello."

"Damn. Did it ring?" he asked.

"Nope. Are you tired?"

"Not really. It's a straight ride to Columbia. Can you drive, Ayj?"

"Well. The only time I drove was the time my best friend Tanisha and I drove her big brother's car around the corner, but didn't know how to park to put it back."

"Was he mad?"

"Hell yeah. He cussed us out and made us wash his car in the dead of winter. We didn't care. Everyone saw us driving!"

"You never talk about your friends."

"We all went our separate ways. What'd your mother cook for dinner?" I asked moving onto safer subjects. We stayed on for hours until Terrell started babbling in sleepy-speak. It was so cute.

We hadn't slept together or even kissed, but there was something about him I trusted.

I let the rest of his calls go to the machine.

I was propped up on my pillows, eating popcorn and watching *The Color Purple*. Celie had just begun to let Mister have it at the dinner table when the banging on my door scared me out of the bed.

"Who?"

"Campus Police." What the hell? I searched frantically for a weapon, just in case. I held the scissor behind my back, peeking through the cracked door. Terrell leaned out from behind the cops.

"Is something wrong with the phone?" asked the short cop.

"No." The taller of the two cops tipped his hat to me and they left.

"So you weren't answering on purpose?" asked Terrell.

"I just didn't want you to be worrying about me."

"And you didn't think I would worry that you were here by yourself and suddenly not answering?"

"I don't want you to care about me, Terrell."

"Well, ain't that some shit. You met somebody else?"

"In one day? Don't be ridiculous."

"Then what is wrong with you? I've been sniffing up behind you every single day and now when I get all into you, you want me to leave you alone. I left South Carolina in the middle of the night, not even packing up any of my momma's leftovers."

"I just don't want you to hurt me, Terrell. I can't." I tried to close the door, but he stuck his foot in the crack.

"I said, no leftovers! From Christmas dinner! You know what that means?!"

"Terrell, I'm sorry," I cried.

He scratched underneath his black skull cap. "If you can't tell by now that I won't hurt you, then I don't know what to tell you."

I closed the door softly, gently pushing him out of my life. *I could love him*, I thought. I could. He didn't know anything about the old me. He was kind. He was thoughtful. He was funny. He was everything I needed.

I lay on the bed thinking about how everything I ever cared about always got contaminated somehow. I was lonelier than I was before I met him. But life goes on, I thought. It had to.

I stood under the shower spray trying to drown my troubles. I felt just as agitated and lonely when I turned the water off.

When I turned the key in my door, the door at the end of the hallway creaked. I heard his keys jingling before Dante Truman, the Men's Resident Assistant entered the Women's wing. Dante was a senior, who usually came by to tutor one of the girls on my floor. He was a dirty beige complexion with thick eyebrows and a mischievous gap between his front teeth.

"What are you doing up here?" I asked.

"Just doing rounds. Making sure everything's alright. You alright?"

"I could be better."

I moved my arm, so that my lavender bathrobe fell open. My nipples stood erect, calling him to stand at attention. We barely got the door closed before he tweaked. And I touched. He used the space between his teeth as he licked. And I sucked. He pumped slow and then fast and then slow. And I bucked. In the simplest of terms, we, well you know. All night long.

That night, I was tutored in the art of riding and amazed at how easy it was to feel so good so quickly. I'd never imagined. I closed the door behind him and went to bed feeling just a little better.

EIGHT WHOLE DAYS HAD PASSED since I'd seen Terrell. Each day I watched from my dorm room to see if he'd pass on his way back from the dining hall, but he didn't. I watched the phone, willing it to ring. The one time it did, I answered right away.

"I ain't done nothing to you for you not to accept my calls."

"Oh. Hi Ma."

"Don't do me no favors, Adrienne." She hung up. And I didn't call her back. I wasn't mad at her. I just didn't have anything to say to her. I didn't know what I would say to Terrell either, but I was starting to think I would never get the chance. I had to get out of that room before I went crazy.

I sat in the picture window in the lobby of my dorm watching the snow flurries quietly flutter down from the sky. I jumped when the mailbox behind me slammed shut. Not many people were back from Christmas break yet, but occasionally, someone came down to see if anyone sent anything worthy to a college student. Like a care package that the other kids got. Or a little extra cash for this and that. I heard Dante's keys jingling down the hallway.

"Hey Cutie," he said walking up behind me.

"Dante."

"You haven't called me."

"I didn't know I was supposed to." Terrell turned down the cobblestone path in front of his dorm. I ran outside.

"Terrell," I called. He kept walking in this slightly bow-legged stride I'd never noticed. I also never noticed that his shoulders were that broad.

"Terrell!" I called again. I was practically running behind him. When he stopped mid-stride, I slowed down, unsure of what to say.

"You didn't want to talk to me?" I asked.

"I didn't hear you." I wrung my hands.

"Do you have something to tell me, Adrienne?"

"I know you won't hurt me." He looked out over my head, with his hands jammed in his pockets. I studied my black Reeboks, poised to run back to Logan Hall to hide from the humiliation of being exposed, and conflicted because I wanted him to at least acknowledge me.

"Terrell, I don't know what else to say."

"You don't have to say anything else. That's enough for me." In my mind, I was Apollonia and he was Prince. That's how excited I was.

"Come by later. I have something for you."

"Something like what?" I kissed him sweetly at first, then sucked on his bottom lip. His eyelids lowered, letting me know he was with it. I left him in the courtyard watching my hips sway back and forth. He'd never seen that side of me. That sexy side. I couldn't wait to show him more.

I was expecting the regular twenty dollars in an envelope from my mother, but instead there was a small package in my mailbox. I ripped it open. Inside, there was a thick envelope and a Bible with a sticky note.

For quiet times and times of need. Love, Aunt Juicie.

I dialed my parent's house, but they didn't pick up. They must have been working lots of over time to send me that kind of money. Either that or my mother hit it big on the slots in Atlantic City.

I opened my underwear drawer and poked around looking for something sexy. All I had were flower prints and pastel stripes. I took a few bills out of my fortune and headed out to the campus bus stop smiling all the way.

"Hi," I said to the brown girl that lived three doors down.

"Hey," I said to the brother carrying his laundry down to the basement. I was Maryland friendly. I liked it. It felt good on me. Two sisters standing at the bus stop tittered.

"Looks like somebody's in L-O-V-E."

"Is it that obvious?" I asked.

"Umhmm," they said in unison. I was thrilled. They could see my cartoon hearts. I had cartoon hearts! Me! Adrienne Fuller! The lights in my life had been turned back on.

Victoria's Secret overflowed with soft scents and pretty little things scattered about. Today was my lucky day. They were having a sale. I could buy a few sexy panties. Maybe a g-string like I heard the white girls in my dorm talking about.

The mannequin sported a lacy black teddy thing that I thought would look great on me. I took it off the rack and I picked out a few silky panties and a red lacy triangle attached to two pieces of lacy elastic that I found out from the tag, was in fact a g-string.

The sales clerk, a café au lait Black girl with big chocolate brown eyes and black hair pulled into a big French roll wouldn't stop staring.

"Hello," I said with a smile.

She snatched the teddy from me. I didn't know what to make of it, so I didn't. Maybe she wasn't from Maryland.

"Sixty-eight dollars and fifty-five cents." She snatched the twenties from my hand.

"Do you have a problem?" I asked. She held up the teddy.

"You planning on seducing someone else's man? Or have you moved up to charging for it, hoe?" My chest seized up.

"You don't remember me, do you?" she asked. I searched her face, clueless.

"You remember Lucky Corner Deli on Ralph Avenue? Ayende Brown?" I remembered Ayende Brown and his tall, dark and gorgeous self. And then I remembered her and her friends crowding around me.

"Karen," I said.

"Yeah. That's what I thought. You lucky I need this job." She threw my bag across the counter at me. "You worn-out pussy hoe."

I watched the cars roll by, and scanned faces at the bus stops, wondering if anyone else from my past was going to show up. All the excitement I felt on the way to the mall was replaced with concerns about my worn-out pussy. Terrell didn't deserve that. I didn't even want to do it anymore. But I knew I would. If he left me now, I wouldn't make it through school.

So I did what I'd been trained to do. And he loved it.

THAT WAS ALL TERRELL needed to take off running. Frankly, he was wearing on my nerves. We carried our trays to a dining table near the window that looked out over the lake in the dining hall.

"If I thought you were intruding, I wouldn't have invited you," he said.

"But what if they don't like me?" I asked.

"They will."

"How do you know?" I put my tray down.

"Because I love you. So they'll love you, too. It'll be fine."

"You love me?"

"Since the first day I saw you."

I smiled to myself. Dante Truman walked past the dining room table twice, smiling ever so indiscreetly.

I went home to Columbia, South Carolina, with Terrell for every holiday up to the Thanksgiving of our senior year. He was right about his folks. They welcomed me with open arms. Especially his mom, Ms. Lucy Mae Lucas. His dad, Wooly, well, he would have if my gag reflex didn't kick in every time he came near me.

Ms. Lucy was teaching me how to make a sweet potato pie from scratch.

"Baby," she asked, "don't you miss your own Mama an' 'em?" She mashed the sweet potatoes by hand. "I'm sure she'd wanna pass her eyes over you, right quick. Soak you into her memory."

"No, Ma'am. We aren't that close." She pushed the sweet potatoes over to me, pulling out a rolling pin for her homemade crust that she'd been bragging about.

"That's a shame. But well, that's how life is. Sometimes, what's supposed to be is not what is. And sometimes what is, is not supposed to be."

"Well, if it's not supposed to be, then why is it, Ms. Lucy?" She put her rolling pin down on the counter.

"Terrell! Terrell, bring your ass in here." Terrell brought his ass.

"Yes Ma'am?"

"Why you ain't tell me this girl was some kinda philosophical fool?"

"That's my Adrienne. I'm going back to watch the game. Ayj, the Chiefs are beating the pulp out of your Skyscrapers. Hot Rod is giving those boys a problem."

"Yeah. I bet."

"I don't know why you don't give him his due. He's the best."

"Tee, I think you give him enough due for everybody," I said. Wooly loaded the dishwasher.

"You sure do. Just a one man cheering section. Personally, I think he could play more defense," he said. I might have really liked Wooly right there in that moment, except his gnarled hand rested on the edge of the table. He was skinny like Aunt Juicie, but it was different on him. It was creepy.

"Wooly, you know you cain't eat none of this with your sugar."

"I don't want none of that sugar," he said as he patted Ms. Lucy's butt. I tried not to cringe, but Wooly was scary to me. His eyebrows were bushy and unkempt. And his hands …ugggh! Ms. Lucy caught me staring at them.

"Wooly was a carpenter. He made me that bookcase I have my cookbooks on." The bookshelf had beautiful rose carvings on the side panels and rose feet at the bottom.

"Mmhmm. And he made that beautiful headboard in my bedroom. Come, I'll show you." Ms. Lucy wiped her hand in the towel. I followed her down a hallway decorated with wooden frames that had Wooly's signature rose carved into it. Black and white baby pictures of Terrell were inside. Ms. Lucy opened her bedroom door.

"The workmanship is beautiful," I said. I ran my hand over the swirls.

"He used be fine, too. But he got sick. He had a mini stroke. And I stood with him, just as he stood with me and raised Terrell like he was his own. Sacrificing and teaching him everything a man is supposed to be. He is all the family I can count on besides my son." She handed me the telephone.

"You should at least call 'em and wish 'em well," she said. Ms. Lucy closed the door behind her. I sat for a good five minutes, holding it in my hand.

"I don't hear no talking," called Ms. Lucy. I dialed my mother's number.

"You're where? You don't know them people. They could be axe murderers and all and your silly ass wanna be down in the country withum."

"They're not axe murderers."

"How would you know? You think axe murderers wear a sign on they head sayin' I'ma axe murderer?" asked my dramatic mother.

"No. But they're not. They're nice. I like them. And they like me. Besides, they would have killed me already, don't you think?"

"Well, if they put you out for overstaying, don't come here with no sad ass face."

"Would you say the same to Rodney and Kerri?" I asked.

"Whas that supposed to mean?" I could see her hands on her hips.

"How're you gonna tell me not to come home? When you took them in?" I was boiling inside.

"See. Now you bein' silly."

"Yeah. Well, I have to go. I don't wanna run up their long distance."

"If you were here you wouldn't have to be worryin' about that." No, Ma. I'd have other things to worry about. I opened the bedroom door.

"Ms. Lucy. Do you mind if I make one more phone call?"

"Of course, I don't." I sat on Ms. Lucy's bed and dialed.

"Hey Aunt Juicie."

"Adrienne, is that you? Hold on. Say, pick up the jack in there." The phone crackled.

"Hey, Old Ladies," I said.

"Adrienne, oh my Lord! It is so good to hear your voice," said Aunt Say.

"It's good to hear yours, too. Happy Thanksgiving."

"Got a lot to be thankful for, too. Thankful to hear you after all this time; thankful God kept those ungrateful kids away from me for another year. Don't think you know how glad that made me," said Aunt Say. "Ungrateful asses. Last time Your Highness came here, she asked me for money to replace some cheerleading uniform that shrunk in the dryer." I giggled at one of my best mistakes yet.

"I told her, hell no. She get enough money from the state and her Daddy each month. She start talkin' 'bout 'Oh Auntie Rhona's so stingy with the state money and she be using the money to buy grocery.' Like it's free to feed her and Rodney's greedy ass. My son eats like he ain't gonna eat again for another week."

"She stopped talking to you?" I asked.

"Child, if you gonna get the scoop, you gonna have to learn how to get the scoop!"

"Yes, Ma'am." *Woooo-oooh-weee! I had arrived!*

"Anyway, I told her I would give her half, but she would have to wait 'til my check came in. She start talking about how that's all the way on the first and how she don't have that kind of time. And on and on. Until I just told her to get out. Whew." Her bangles jiggled. I could see her fanning her bosom. Aunt Juicie piped up.

"Girl, Kerri turned Big Rodney on her. Yellin' and hollerin', 'You ain't nothing. You ain't never gonna be nothin' and that's why Daddy left you!' Til Sadie slapped her dead across the face with that big ham of hers. You know Say got them big ol' hands."

"Mmmhmm. She ran outta here 'bout she was gonna call some BCW on me. I told her 'Girl, I know Child Welfare number by heart'. And that boy? He ain't call nor come and see me since he moved in by yall. Last time we was by your mother's house, they act like they just met me. All friendly and polite and all. Ain't surprise me one bit. The two of them always been funny." So said Tanisha and now their own mother. Well if they were so damn funny, then why the hell wasn't I laughing?

"Adrienne Baby, why you not sayin' nothin'?" asked Aunt Say.

"Because I'm sitting here wondering why the hell didn't anybody say this before they moved in?"

The jangle of her bracelets paused. The only sound I could detect was her labored breathing and some lady in the back ground asking to buy a vowel. I placed the phone on the cradle.

Ms. Lucy pushed the mixing bowl toward me. The more I tried to steady my hands, the more they trembled.

Ms. Lucy didn't press me any further about my family. But Terrell would not let up on his latest plan to go to Brooklyn together for Christmas. The more I argued that we weren't close, the more he insisted I should try to fix things. "Don't you miss them?" I shrugged. But he kept going.

"It'll make your mom happy and believe it or not, it'll make my mom happy, too. She worries about you."

Ms. Lucy didn't hesitate to add her two cents.

"Just go on home and let them soak you in, Baby. It'll be good for all of you. I promise."

TERRELL'S HOOPTIE ZOOMED UP I-95 like it had rockets attached.

"Adrienne, you're speeding again."

"Am not. Mind your business." But the further north we got on the Jersey Turnpike, the more I was looking forward to seeing my parents. I was most excited because I was one hundred percent sure Rodney was on the road with the Chiefs and Kerri was on the road with Rodney.

At the corner, we waited for the light to turn green. Terrell watched the men huddled around a garbage can fire warming their hands. A homeless man in a tattered army jacket banged on the hood of the car.

"Kinda rough around here, huh?" asked Terrell.

"Not so bad. It's getting better."

"I got the light, muthafuckaaah!" the man shouted.

When he was on the sidewalk, I rolled slowly looking in the rearview mirror at Mr. Banks, Tanisha's dad.

"And this right here, is my house," I said.

"Okay. What is that?" he asked, pointing to my father's plastic light-up Christmas tree in the front window. I imitated my father's voice.

"You know you put anything out there look halfway decent, crackhead just gon' run off widdit."

Before we got out of the car, the front door swung open. My Dad came down the steps.

"Missed you, Pumpkin," he said.

"Missed you more, Daddy." When my mother came to the door, she started to cry. I tried to hold my tears in, but they seeped out anyway.

"You don't just be goin' away and forgettin' the people who love you, Adrienne. You just don't do that. It's wrong. It's wrong and it's selfish."

"I know," I said, still wrapped in her arms. Terrell zipped his parka up to the neck watching this odd showing of animosity that I'd claimed to have with my family.

"Mom, this is my boyfriend, Terrell. The son of the axe murderers." My mother smoothed out the front of her jogging suit.

"Adrienne, what kind of thing is that to say about those people?" Funny lady, my mother. Terrell kissed her and shook my Dad's hand.

"It's a pleasure, Mister and Misses Fuller." My mother whispered to me.

"Adrienne, he has good manners." I cut her off.

"Let's all go inside out of this cold."

"Terrell, you can take the bedroom in the basement," she said. I frowned.

"Don't worry, Rodney left it in perfect condition when he went off to school, Adrienne."

"It's not that. I just think he can sleep in Kerri's room." *And I can sneak him into mine.*

"Girls upstairs, boys down. You know the rules," she reminded me.

"Yeah, Adrienne. Because I don't want to have to worry about you taking advantage of me." I cut him up into little pieces with my eyes.

My bedroom looked the same way it did the day I left for school. I fell across the bed and rolled myself up in a new eyelet cover that was spread over it. My lavender walls still had posters of Ralph Tresvant and MC Lyte tacked up next to Rakim's first album cover. I'd have loved to bring Terrell up there to see a little bit of my world, but my mother was a menace with her rules. He really could have stayed next door. I jumped off my bed.

Kerri's bedroom door was still adorned with a glittery pink butterfly tacked on at eye level. It was also closed tightly. I nudged the door once. Nudged again. It gave! Yes! I flicked the light on and stepped back in surprise. I shouldn't have been shocked, but a fly could have flown into my open mouth.

Old clothes were scattered everywhere, ripped posters were on the wall, dirty plates and cups on the dresser and floor, and it reeked of old socks and Doritos.

I closed the door quietly behind me, careful not to knock the pretty butterfly off and careful to keep my mother from knowing I was up to my old tricks. Tiptoeing back to my bedroom, astonished that I'd never imagined her private space to be so nasty inside, I came to a quiet realization that her bedroom described who she was better than anyone ever could. Wow.

At midnight, I crept down the stairs, careful to avoid the three creaky steps.

I eased the basement door open and stepped down onto the linoleum. The first thing that hit me was the smell. It was exactly the same: baby scented detergent mixed with the smell of oil from the boiler and basement mildew. I opened the door to Terrell's room and saw the sheets on the bed: light blue with dark blue diamonds.

"Terrell, let's change those."

"Your mom just put them on."

"I know, Tee. But let's change them anyway."

"Adrienne, there's nothing wrong with the sheets."

"I want to change them!" I yelled.

"Your mother's gonna hear you," he whispered. He wrested the sheets off. I went to the laundry room and came back with a new set.

"Acting like a maniac," he muttered as he tucked the new sheet under the mattress. "And I was just getting toasty!"

He had no idea, not even a clue of what I had been up to in this basement. On this bed. In this house. More times than I cared to remember. I snuggled into him even though the ghost of an aftershave Rodney used to wear rose from the dead.

"Are you okay? You feel funny?" he asked.

"What do you mean?"

"You feel tense all of a sudden. Like you're worried your mother's gonna come downstairs."

"I am."

"Do you wanna go back up to your room?"

"No. I want to stay right here with you."

Terrell kissed me so sweetly and so calmly, reminding me of how much he loved me and cared for me. He caressed my body and kissed every part of me until I cried.

Sometimes I wanted to tell him so badly, about everything that happened to me. But that little part of me that was ugly and worn-out, didn't want to risk it.

I crept back upstairs just as the sun cracked through the darkness, careful not to make any noise.

"If I was still a gambling woman, I woulda won twenty dollars from your Daddy. I guess you grown enough to take care of a baby on your own now."

"Ma, I've been grown for a long, long time." Since I was thirteen years, four months and four days old to be exact.

I was overjoyed that it was just us sitting around on Christmas Eve: cooking, tasting, sipping on a little something. My father played an old Nat King Cole record on his old phonograph and burned an incense that smelled like pine. Our Christmas tree was the kind that got stored in the basement on New Years Day.

Watching my mother make an apple crumb cake to take back to Ms. Lucy, (not anytime soon, she said, but in the future) I wondered if I might even come home more often. Maybe even visit for a weekend each month to catch up with my mom. Maybe we could get to know each other again.We'd lost so much time and wouldn't ever get it back. The thought made my eyes water.

"Why're you crying?"

"I'm not."

"I ain't blind, Adrienne."

"I'm just happy to be home, Ma. That's all."

"Oh. Well that's good."

Dinner was beautiful. Terrell and me and my mom and dad, all sat at the dining room table discussing President Clinton being in the White House.

"Personally, I think that boy's mixed wit' somethin'," said my Dad. "Like maybe his Daddy ain't his Daddy. You know what I mean, Tee?" *Tee?* If hearts had teeth, mine would have smiled.

"I think you're on to something, Mr. Fuller." My father filled his own glass and pushed the brandy bottle across the table toward Terrell.

"Call me Dub. Everybody does." Terrell touched my shin with his toes.

"Help yourself, Tee," said my Dad. All I know is he had my vote when he went on Arsenio Hall playing the sax. The man got soul."

"Me? I vote for anybody who eats French fries," said my mother. "You ain't a real American if you don't eat French fries."

"That's your criteria for a good president?" I asked. "What about the fact that he is concerned with the state of the economy?"

"Yes," she said. "That makes him a good cannidate. But I--"

"Vote for anybody who eats French fries," we said together. Terrell sat there with this questioning look on his face.

Bing-bing. My mother jumped out of her seat.

"I think that's Miss Lewis. She said she was gonna try and stop by and see you since she ain't seen you in years." She opened the door.

"Oh, my Lord! Oh my Lord!" she said. Terrell looked over the table at me.

"Miss Lewis must have bought her a hell of a Christmas present." Kerri stepped into the living room, dressed in black leather pants and a leather fringe jacket.

"Hey Cuz," she said in a flat monotone.

"Cuz? Who's that Rabbit?!" Rodney peeked around the door. He kissed my mother quickly and took giant Rodney steps toward me. He seemed to have grown a few more inches since the last time I saw him.

"Rab! What's up, Girl?!" He grabbed me up out of my seat and into a bear hug.

"Hey," I said. I felt self-conscious and disgusting and transparent; like they could see that Rodney had lain on top of me. Rodney appraised Terrell who was significantly shorter, at only six feet tall.

"Hey man, how you doing?" Terrell stepped out from around the table.

"Ay, you're Rodney Barrus. Ain't this some shit?! Terrell Lucas." He held out his hand, grinning.

"Good to meet you, Terrell Lucas. Auntie Rho! What we got to eat?" He bounded off to the kitchen behind my mother.

"Adrienne, why didn't you tell me you had some famous family? You know he's my favorite!"

"Yeah, Adrienne, why didn't you?" asked Kerri with a funky smile.

My mother refreshed the table, smiling like her number played in the lottery.

"The family's all here," she said. "Just like old times."

Just like old times, I pushed my food around on the plate, wishing I were somewhere else.

"You wouldn't believe the women that come to the games," said Rodney. "Pass the collards, Uncle Dub?" My dad passed the collards across the table.

"A buncha skeezers," said Kerri. "On the lookout for some sucker to take advantage of."

"Rabbit. I wish you could see them. You'd have a field day! Yo, Tee," he said, making my stomach clench. "Rabbit used to keep me hip to the game. Had this girlfriend named Lashelle. Rabbit told me she was a skank hoe from jump."

"You called somebody a skank hoe?" laughed Terrell.

"Not exactly."

"Didn't I tell you she was a skank hoe?" asked Kerri.

"Yeah. After she cheated and dumped me for the third time and after she stopped speaking to you, yeah. But Rabbit warned me. You remember in the car, Rab? And you were saying she was with Fred Barnes?"

"Didn't you mess with him?" asked Kerri.

"Nope." Technically he messed with me. And Candy and Mandy.

"I think she did," said Rodney. "Ol' El DeBarge lookin' nigga. Saw him during my first year at Georgetown at a frat party over at Howard. He was one of those pretty boy Kappas. He came up to me, showing me mad love, like we were tight."

"Weren't you friends with him?" I asked.

"Nah, I didn't really like him. He was real cocky about his looks. Talkin' bout how all the girls was on his jock. He liked you though, Rab. Said you were sweet."

"Never figured you for a pretty boy type of girl, Ayj," said Terrell.

"She did like 'em pretty. What was that boy's name? The real smart one with the cute boots? The one you slapped in the living room," added Kerri.

"You slapped somebody?" asked Terrell. "I'm learning a lot about you."

"Was he being fresh, Adrienne?" asked my mother.

"How'd you know I slapped him, Kerri?"

"Duh, I saw him at school. He told me."

"I wondered what ever happened to him. He had good manners," said my mother. I pushed my seat away from the table.

"You didn't finish your dinner, Baby."

"Not hungry any more."

I was shivering so badly I could hardly get the key in the ignition. Terrell knocked on the glass. I stared straight ahead. He tapped again.

"I have your coat. Let me in." I unlocked his door, grateful that he had more sense than I did.

"Got-damn, it don't ever get this cold in Carolina. Your Dad and Rod gave me a little glass to keep me warm."

"Give me that." Terrell watched me guzzle it down with this look of amazement and confusion that he had been sporting since we got there.

"He's not who you think he is. They're not who you think they are." We sat in the fogged up car in complete silence. The needle on the heater was still on cold. Terrell drew his balled up hands up into his sleeves. His teeth clacked together.

"Let's go inside," I said.

"You feel better?" he asked.

"Yeah. I'll be okay." But I didn't feel better. I just felt bad that he was going to freeze to death and then I'd have to call Ms. Lucy and tell her I killed her son because my family was crazy.

My mother pushed my bedroom door open. Kerri stood behind her.

"I put the rollaway bed downstairs with the boys, so you girls gonna have to share the bed."

"What's wrong with Kerri's room?"

"That room is too childish for her now."

"Mmmhmm. That's okay. Kerri can have the room to herself."

"That's kind of you, Adrienne. What's come over you?"

"Acknowledging a kind gesture, Kerri? What's come over you?"

"Botha yalls asses need to stop this. Yall are family."

I carried my fuzzy blanket past my family and trucked downstairs to the living room where I wrapped up in the covers like an egg roll, and lay on the sofa to watch a videotape of every *Martin* that ever aired. My Dad loved himself some Martin Lawrence. Terrell and Rodney stumbled into the living room.

"Oh, Rab. I didn't know you were up here."

"Man, I told you I was gonna come up to see my gur-rullll," he slurred.

Terrell climbed onto the sofa and lay behind me, throwing his leg over mine. I pulled my arm out from the blanket and hugged his thigh. At that moment, I knew he was the one. He was not intimidated by Rodney, he could relate to my parents, and he was sweet and affectionate and all about me. I hadn't really thought about getting married but I allowed myself to dream.

"Adrienne," he whispered.

"Yeah, Tee?"

"I don't feel so well."

When he stood up, he lurched forward and wobbled before he sat back down. His breath smelled like he could gas a plane. I turned my head to the side and helped him up off the sofa. He sat again. I'd never seen Terrell drunk.

"C'mon Baby. Let me help you."

"Too much E&J puts you on your ass," said Rodney. "I got him." He slung Terrell's arm around his neck and got him down to the basement. The toilet downstairs flushed and then I didn't hear anything else for a while. I wrapped myself up again and lay on the sofa. At first I was watching *Martin.* And then *Martin* was watching me. Sometime later, Terrell came back upstairs and climbed on the sofa behind me. I kept my eyes closed.

"Feeling better?" He nodded into my back. He put his leg over me. I started to pull my arm out and realized that that long ass leg was not Terrell's. I tried to get out from under, but Rodney's leg clamped over me. I turned on my side to keep the blanket wrapped under me. Rodney straddled me and pulled the cover up from my feet. I kicked out at his face, but the angle was such that it caught him on the side instead of dead on. He yanked the cover off angrily and positioned me face down on the sofa. The Christmas tree on the porch blinked and I kept my eyes focused on the flashing lights. Terrell was out cold and I was so sad. Strangely, Rodney's breath did not reek of E&J like Terrell's. Just the stench of evil.

If the drawer and closet door slamming shut woke Kerri, she didn't say a word. I wished she would have though. I wished hard.

By five am, I was packed and ready to go. I went downstairs and was surprised to find Terrell sitting up in Rodney's bed. Rodney was knocked out on the rollaway bed, snoring under the blue diamond sheets. Not surprising for the 'team player'. Anything for the guys. Terrell was trying to wrap a present.

"C'mon get up. We've got to go."

"But I'm trying to wrap your present."

"Let's go."

"Question marks. Lots and lots of question marks, Adrienne."

"We'll talk about it in the car."

"But we didn't have breakfast and open the presents and wasn't that the plan? To spend Christmas with your family? I'm not used to all this unrest. What in the world is going on?"

"Nothing."

"Well if it's nothing, why can't we stay? I like your people."

"He likes us, Rabbit. Why can't you accept it?" Rodney grumbled from under the sheets. I kicked the edge of the bed.

"Shut up, Rodney. Terrell you can stay if you want to. But I'm out."

"Blood is blood, Rabbit! Call a brother some time!" called Rodney.

My mom stood at the door in big pink sponge rollers, clutching the front of her velvet turquoise bathrobe.

"Aydree, it's Christmas day," she said. A cloud of cold air puffed out of her mouth.

"Yes, but we have to get back," I said. "I'm sorry, Mom. I forgot we promised Terrell's mother." Terrell didn't look up.

"You're not gonna say goodbye to your cousins?" she asked.

"I said goodbye to them a long time ago."

"You need a just-in-case bag for if you get car sick?"

"No. Love you. Call you when I get there."

"Rabbit," he said.

"Don't ever, Terrell. Don't. You. Ever."

I cracked the window and coughed against the icy air hitting the back of my throat. Terrell stared, waiting for what I wasn't about to give him. Instead, I watched Mr. Banks walk along the wall of The Pool talking to himself. I waved to him, but he didn't see me. Finally, Terrell pulled out of the space and I blinked back tears.

"I didn't know you got carsick."

"I don't." I watched the house get smaller and smaller in the rear window and then it was gone.

THE BABY SAT WITH HIS or her knees lodged in my side. I was already irritable from not being able to sleep through the night. And what should have been a joyous final semester was instead a nausea-ridden, midnight snacking, stomach-stretching, swollen footed ordeal. But of all the people to be having a birthday party, my mother wanted me to go to Big Rodney's birthday party.

Now if she'd said it was his going home party, I would have been on the first thing smoking. I'd have even volunteered to read his eulogy…my revised MC Lite Brite version, of course.

"Adrienne," said Terrell. "You shouldn't be like that. That's your family. And it's gonna be our baby's family."

"You go. Let me know how it was." Why he didn't remember how swiftly we bailed out of Brooklyn at Christmas, I don't know. Maybe because he was one of those let bygones be bygones type folks that I admired.

A month or so later, she called back leaving messages about a retirement party for Aunt Juicie. I called her back with the quickness to get the details: namely whether or not *they* would be there.

"Before you start, all I'm saying is Rodney is throwing it at a big fancy catering hall and he's inviting everyone we know and his celebrity friends, so you have to come."

"Hey Ma. Let me call you back." I sent Aunt Juicie a card and a plush pretty sky blue bathrobe that I bought at another Victoria's Secret, way across town. I'd see Rodney again when hell had a skating rink.

My mother left one last message on my machine.

All that was supposed to be for a surprise baby shower for you. But as usual, you only thinkin' about ya self. By the way, happy birthday.

Click!

"Tee, have you seen the yellow pages?"

"On top of the fridge." I waddled my big ass to the kitchen, stepping over loose parts of my baby's new crib.

"Why are there so many screws still left over?"

"Go do what you're doing and let me do what I'm doing."

"I can see Baby's gonna be sleeping right between us in the bed. Tee, can you get it for me? My belly's in the way."

"What you need this for anyway?"

"Do what you're doing and let me do what I'm doing."

"Touche." I waddled back to my bedroom and closed the door behind me.

"Bell Atlantic, how can I help you?"

"I'd like to change my phone number and make the new one unpublished. Can I do that?"

"I'll be happy to help you with that."

And then I set about creating a peaceful life for my new family that didn't include the Barrus's or the Fuller's.

Terrell was asleep in his little dusty taupe recliner that we got at the budget furniture store. I held the baby bag in one hand and my overnight bag in the other one, heading to the door.

I didn't mean to scare him, but the contraction hit me when I tapped his shoulder. I grazed the side of his head with my clenched fist. He jumped up into a fight stance.

"It's time," I gasped.

"It's time?"

"Yes, Tee. It's time."

"It's early. It can't be time," he said taking the bags.

"Terrell. It's time, got-dammit!" He held my hand, walking me to the car.

"Wait! We forgot to call your mother." I choked his hand so hard his knees buckled.

"Damn. That contraction must have been bad. Let's hurry up and get you to the hospital."

Angela Monique Lucas came into the world after twenty-six hours of labor on August 14, pasty white, her face looking beat down like Marvelous Marvin Hagler. She was beautiful.

I fell in love with her ten perfect little toes and ten little fingers and the dimples in her tiny chubby hands. I wondered what she would do with them; what kind of person she would be. I wondered which of us she would finally look like. I wondered if my mother thought all these crazy things when she had me. I wondered if I was wrong to not have called her, especially because Ms. Lucy, enraptured and engrossed by Angela, cradled her to her bosom purring sweet words and coos in her baby ears.

"You wanna hold her, Wool?" she asked. I stared daggers into Wooly.

"Naw. She's too little. I don't think Adrienne would forgive me if something happened to her baby girl."

"Mmhmm."

I knew I would never allow the same things that happened to me, happen to my daughter. I bet that on my life.

At three weeks old, Angela was Terrell's creamy cocoa complexion.

"She has my feet. And she has your mother's cheekbones," said Terrell.

"Mmhmm."

"She called by the way."

"Who called?"

"Your mother. Did you think you could just change the phone number and I wouldn't find out?"

"It's just that…"

"It's just that you may not want to be in contact with your family, but I want to be in contact with mine. And on top of that, it would have been nice if you had let me know before you did it."

"Sorry Dad. I didn't know I needed permission." I tucked Angela's feet into her blanket, snuggling her up against my chest.

"To change *our* phone number? Not permission, but you could have told me before I tried to call *our* house to see if you were okay. Or before my job let me know I missed overtime hours that *we* need because they couldn't find me."

"Blah, blah, blah. Move on, Terrell."

"Fine. Speaking of moving on, I don't want to stay in Maryland anymore. Why don't we go up North? I've always wanted to live in New York."

"So my changing the phone number doesn't clue you in to the fact that I want nothing to do with New York, huh?"

"Yeah, but Ayj if you can put that aside, I can make probably five more dollars an hour with DeliverEase and get a job in my field that's paying real money."

"You can get a job in accounting here making real money."

"That's true, too. But we have nothing here. What about Anj? Who's she gonna grow up with?"

"I don't want to live there, Terrell. Are you listening to me?"

"I could ask you the same damn question. Shit Adrienne, I'm twenty-one years old. I've got a girl that's not working. I've got a baby that eats more than I do and takes a shit on the hour. I don't even know how we're making it."

"All that matters, is we are."

"Okay, but what about when you get a job? Who's going to keep her? You trust strangers with our baby?"

"Stop pressing me, Terrell."

"Fine. What about moving down by my mom?"

"I don't want to move! I want to stay right here!"

"I'm not gonna be the bad guy on this. That's all I'm saying."

He kissed Angela on the forehead and went to the bedroom. I cuddled my baby into my arms and leaned back in the sofa. Columbia was lovely, except for Wooly, and a little bit slower than what I was used to. Ms. Lucy would be happy if Terrell came back, I guess. Whatever. I had a pending job offer here in Maryland, and I was staying in Maryland. Period.

Everyday after that, he asked me the same question.

"What's it gonna be?" And each day I gave him the same answer.

"It's gonna be what it's gonna be."

"Keep playing, Adrienne. Keep right on playing."

I spied on Terrell and Angela from outside our bedroom door. I adored the way he was with her. Angela smiled her gummy smile and giggled, kicking her legs in the air. His voice was high and animated.

"Angel Cakes! Do you know what today is?" She giggled until she hiccupped. "It's your seven-month birthday!" She hiccupped again.

"Ayj, can you bring her some water?"

An orange U-Haul card was posted on the refrigerator underneath an Empire State Building magnet. I slapped the postcard into Terrell's waiting hand.

"What the hell is this?" He didn't look up.

"Oh. That. We can stay with my mother until we find a place."

"I want to stay here, Terrell. Professor Daughtry promised me a job in my field. He'll come through."

"Unless he calls by the weekend, it's a done deal." He peeled his uniform off in front of the bathroom.

"I'm working twelve hour days. I'm getting paid like I'm working half that. Every night I want to quit, but we need the insurance. I'm tired." He closed the bathroom door. "Three more days, Ayj. And we're gone." Angela hiccupped and giggled.

I called Professor Daughtry's office the very next morning. And repeatedly after that for two days straight. By Thursday, I was panicking. He wasn't in and his secretary, Paula, was trying to be nice, but her tone was curt.

"Hi Paula. This is Adrienne Fuller again."

"He. is. not. in. Miss. Full. Er." But I just couldn't stop. I even called his private line, but that was a bust.

Terrell brought another packed box to the front of the apartment. He scribbled on top.

"Bedroom stuff?" I asked. "Can you be a little more descriptive?" He scribbled again. Terrell's. The front of my t-shirt was damp. I didn't realize I was sweating. I leaned over Angela's portable bassinet.

"We're staying here. Right, Angie Boo?" Terrell tapped my butt.

"Not if he doesn't call by tomorrow, Aydree Boo." I sucked my teeth. I knew he would call. I was his favorite student. He wouldn't do me that way. Not after the way I did him. Terrell came back out of the bedroom smiling.

"I guess you got along at least long enough to take this picture. Who are the other girls?"

"What picture? What girls?" He held two pictures out to me.

Kerri and I were mugged up for the camera in our graduation caps. My smile was plastic, but her smile looked to be perfectly sincere, down to the sparkle in her eyes. But the other picture was of 'Three the Hard Way' on Tanisha's porch before her party. Tanisha was in the middle, her arms flanked around us, cheesing. Julie was trying to look tough but her dimples negated her intentions. And I was smiling so hard my braces sparkled like gems. Our excitement burst out of the picture. I couldn't help but smile.

"Are those your friends?" he asked. I forgot Terrell was there. I felt my smile slide downwards.

"Yeah. What were you doing in my stuff?"

"I was emptying the drawers. I wasn't in your stuff. Is one of them Tanisha?"

"Yeah. In the middle. Don't pack anymore of my stuff. I'll do the rest."

"Excuse me for trying to know you."

"You know me just fine." Terrell slammed the bathroom door.

Professor Daughtry's silver grey Volvo was parked in the faculty lot, adjacent to the building. Paula pursed her lips in a thin line.

"It's his first day back from vacation, Miss Fuller. He can't see you today."

"This will only take a second. You mind?" Before she could protest, I placed Angela in the bend of her arms, laid a diaper across her shoulder, and strode inside to see the professor.

"Knock, knock!" Professor Daughtry stood fully erect, smiling from sea to shining sea.

"Ms. Fuller. It's been ages. Do come in." His grey eyes sparkled.

On my way out, I thanked Professor Daughtry for putting in a word for me.

"I should have an answer by this evening, my dear. Never you fret."

Paula was more than eager to hand over funky Miss Angela.

"Oh Anj. What is your Daddy feeding you?!" I teased. Paula grunted.

At a quarter to five on Friday evening, I rocked Angela in my arms, pacing the floor.

"Terrell, I don't want to go. I can't. I can't live there. Please Terrell, I'm begging you." I clutched the baby so hard she belted out a loud cry that startled me.

"Adrienne, I'm sorry. But I can't be the only breadwinner. If you got that job, we could figure something out." I bounced Angela in my arms, tears sliding down my face onto hers, co-mingling.

"But Baby, I can't do this by myself." Terrell went to the telephone. When he called my name I waved him off. He covered the receiver, smiling brilliantly.

"I think you wanna take this call." He traded me the phone for the baby.

"Hello?" My emotions were all over the place.

"My dear Miss Fuller. This morning was a pleasure."

"Indeed, Sir."

"Good news. I've gotten hold of the position I had in mind for you. It pays a mere forty-four thou, with plenty of vacation time, and a great benefit package at a prestigious university." I flashed four fingers at Terrell, twice. He nearly dropped my poor baby on the floor.

"Are you interested?"

"Of course I am! Is it Georgetown?"

"Oh now, that's prestigious. But the school I'm talking about is the iviest of Ivy League Schools." When he said the name, my heart jumped from the penthouse and landed on the first floor with a thud.

"Oh. Wow."

"You don't sound very happy, darling."

"No, Sir. I am. I'm just very surprised."

"Well, my dear, I'm glad I could help. My friend is the Director of HR. So all you have to do is meet him and the position is yours." I took down the telephone numbers and the address.

"If you're ever on campus again, look me up."

"Thank you, Sir. I will." Terrell was all in my face.

"Ayj, forty-four thou! We shouldn't even unpack. We can buy a house!"

"We're not unpacking, Terrell. The job is in New York."

There was only one small problem. Terrell didn't have a job. DeliverEase in New York was on a hiring freeze.

"Maybe I'll just wait 'til we get there, then I can hit the streets."

"It's no rush. I still have some money saved."

"How do you still have money saved?"

"From school. When my mom used to send me extra book money. I really never spent it."

"Dang. I didn't know they were livin' large."

"They're not. They work hard."

"Alright. Well, in the meantime, I can stay home with Angela and we'll save even more money."

"You'll never find a job staying home all day. We can put her in day care."

"I don't want my baby at daycare! You don't know those people! You see those specials on TV with the hidden cameras?!" I tried to calm him down, but I was panicking myself. I didn't know how I'd get out of having Terrell keep the baby all day. He didn't know how to care for her for long periods of time. And what if he turned out to be…I shook the thought out of my head.

"We'll work something out. I'm going to book us at a hotel."

"Whatever you say, Miss Moneybags." I called my mother to let her know we were coming. I missed her. A little bit. She sounded strange though.

"Adrienne, tell Terrell to pick up the other end."

"He's busy right now. Just tell me what you have to say. I'll run it by him."

"I ain't even busy, Adrienne. What don't you want me to know now?"

"Just come here," I said rolling my eyes at him. I put the phone between us. I thought she was going to curse us out for staying away. Instead she rambled about the house being too big for them and how much it cost to heat the place.

"Is there something you're trying to tell us?"

"We bought a new house!"

"Ma, that's great!"

"Yes, and me and your Daddy was just thinking that you and Terrell and that sweet baby that I can't wait to hold could come back to New York and move into the finished basement. It has a different entrance and everything." Terrell jumped out ahead of the train.

"Sounds good to me!"

"Hell no!" I said.

"Adrienne?" said my mother.

"I wouldn't want to take advantage, Ma. Besides, what if people come from out of town and want to stay. We would be in the way."

"Baby, your cousins are big and grown and rich and they can take care of they damn self now." Terrell thought about it for two seconds.

"Done."

MY PARENTS' NEW HOUSE was brick with a green aluminum awning. There were rose bushes in the little front yard, and a driveway on the side that they shared with the house next door. The front walkway was concrete with a brick pathway and little begonias along the sides. It was only a mile or so from our old house on Hopkinson Avenue, but it seemed a different world.

Our entrance was off to the right of the front walkway: a tiny doorway from *Alice in Wonderland.* But I didn't complain. I carried my baby inside and got to work on making our house a home.

"Baby. I got a job," said Terrell.

"I thought you had a job already. You got something better?"

"I still have the construction job. I got another job. At the drive-thru."

He held his uniform shirt up in front of him. I held Angela over my head. I jiggled her a little, until drool splattered on my face. "Oh shoot, Angel! Tell Daddy you want a Big Mac, Filet-o-fish, Quarter Pounder, French Fry!" Angela gurgled and cooed.

"Angel Cakes, tell Mommy, it's only *temporare* and would she rather I sell crack."

"I know it's tem-pore-rare-reee, but you don't have to do it, Tee. We make enough money together."

"Yes," he said, "I do."

New York College's campus was landscaped beautifully. Majestic and leafy maple trees flanked the ivy-sided brick buildings, shading the sunbathers and the studious. The scenery was the one perk I looked forward to each morning.

Especially because my co-worker was this debutante chick named Kennedy who was the laziest, most shiftless and conniving girl I'd ever met. Except for Kerri, of course. Everything she didn't know how to do, she passed on to me and then took the credit after. I even caught her snooping around my cubicle.

"What are you doing?"

"Oh. I was looking for a health insurance form." She cleared her throat.

"By the way, a little birdie told me your mother's maiden name is Barrus. Any relation to Rodney Barrus?"

"Were you looking in my file?"

"Well, Adrienne. It's your emergency contact."

"My mother's name is Fuller. Like my father's."

"Well you know the College does background checks. You never can tell who people really are."

"Don't we do background checks on prospective employees? And not their families?"

"Adrienne. You're taking this too personally. Besides. What's the big deal? It's not like he's Jack the Ripper or something. He's a superstar!"

The minute she left, I picked up the phone.

"Maintenance? This is Adrienne Fuller in HR. I need a lock installed."

It was like being with Kerri all over again.

On the subway ride home, sandwiched between a woman wearing too much Obsession and a man who read the newspaper out loud, all I could think about was robbing a bank and running off to some Caribbean island to live for the rest of my life. It had barely been a year since we got to New York and I was ready for a change. Particularly, no more Kennedy, no more hour and a half commute, no more living downstairs from my parents.

I walked down the block cursing the thick summer heat. Even under the shady branches, I longed for a splash in The Pool. My only good thought, was that at least I'd get five minutes to myself to take off my sandals and lay in the air conditioned oasis before I went upstairs to get my baby.

Terrell sat at the kitchen table with a stack of money in front of him and his uniform rolled up in a ball. "Tee, what the hell did you do?" I peeped out the tiny window looking for the cops.

"Don't be *ridicyuhlous,* Adrienne. I want you to be my wife."

"You planning on bribing me if I say no or something?"

"I told you last year I had plans. This is savings for a house. I want you to be my wife. I love you."

Me. Rabbit. A wife. I never thought I'd see it happen. Never really ever expected it to. Marriage never came for girls like me. I was surprised to hear the words coming out of my own mouth.

"Let's do it."

Ms. Lucy tapped her glass with her spoon. "I'd like to propose a toast." Everyone at Romano's Restaurant turned in our direction.

"Momma, don't go embarrassing me," said Terrell.

"Hush. Most Mommas get sad when their boys marry off. But today, I am so very happy. God has finally given me my chance to have the daughter I have always wanted and a beautiful grandbaby. To the two sweetest things that have ever happened to my baby. Cheers!" My nose tingled.

"Cheers!"

My mother raised her glass.

"That was so beautiful. I just wish all our family was here to ---" I raised my glass, and my voice.

"To new beginnings!" I toasted.

"To new beginnings!"

TOASTING TO NEW BEGINNINGS lit a new fire under Terrell.

"It ain't right. A man has to be the head of his household," he said.

"I've never seen that work out for anyone I know."

"My parents. Your parents. What about them? And speaking of your parents, I want to invite folks over without worrying them."

"What folks? You have friends in New York?" I asked. He laughed.

"Actually yeah. But I know how anti-social you are so I don't bring them around." I unfolded my dress on the ironing board.

"I'm not anti-social." He twisted his lips to the side.

"You're not anti-social?" he asked.

"No!"

"You don't even have a phone book. If it wasn't for your mother, you wouldn't even use the phone."

"What about Alicia?"

"She's your assistant. She's not your friend."

"Yes, she is!" I yelled.

"Your dress."

"What?"

"Your dress. It's burning." Grey smoke spiraled upward off the dotted triangle on the back of my favorite frock.

"Look what you made me do! Talkin' 'bout I'm anti-social. What else you got?"

"What else? If I wanna holler when I'm makin' love to my woman, I sure don't wanna be thinking that your Daddy is hearing me."

"Tee, since when do you holler?"

He pulled his t-shirt back over his shoulders so that his chest was bare. I don't know when he started working out, but his chest and abs were cut up. I stared at his sexy frame so closely that I knocked the starch can off the ironing board. I got down on all fours.

"I'm sayin'. If I wanna holler, then I should be able to holler." He jumped on top of me, humping my leg like a dog.

"Whose is it, girl?! Huh, huh? Whose is this?" I started to laugh.

"Stop playing, you're gonna wake the baby."

"I wanna holler 'bout my Baby!"

"Will you stop it and listen to me?" He lay with his arms clasped behind his head in his thinking pose.

"We saw six houses, and what's our complaint?" He held his hand out in front of him.

"Seller's shady. House needs too much work. Bad location. Too much money. Too far from your Momma. Too close to your Momma. Yeah, yeah, yeah." He pulled me out into the living room. My body was flush against his. His hands tugged my shorts down. He ran his hands over my legs. I pulled my t-shirt over my head.

"And if we buy a house that we can't afford and don't actually love, then we're not gonna have any peace. And you ain't gonna get a piece." I kissed the tip of him and took him in. He gasped. I stayed at it, enjoying his pleasure.

The way he looked at me was like he was hungry and I was two chicken legs and two biscuits. I sat back on the couch.

I parted my legs in a perfect V. He rubbed his finger along my slit and drew it back slick. He spread my legs further and got between, putting my legs on his shoulders. His entry and execution was swift and strong. Exactly how it was meant to be. I moaned my pleasure as he worked his hips in delicious circles.

"Tell me you like it." I closed my eyes, pushing those words out of my mind.

"Baby?" he hummed against my ear.

"Mmm?"

"Tell me you like it." Instead, I squeezed my eyes shut and raised my hips to meet him; pumping faster, faster, faster, until he collapsed on me.

"Damn." I eased him off me and went to the bathroom where I sat on the toilet reading from Aunt Juicie's Bible while the water ran in the tub and until I thought he'd fallen asleep.

Sure enough, his mouth was lax when I opened the door. I got in the bed and made sure my foot was touching his leg. I closed my eyes.

"No dirty talkin'?" he asked.

"Makes me uncomfortable."

"Got it." He pulled the sheet up to his neck. "You should tell me these things, so we don't have to both end up feeling fucked up." He scooted over to his side.

He was right. But I never knew when *it* was gonna come out of hiding. Or how I'd react until it was too late.

"MA, THE STOVE IS OUT AGAIN," I sighed.

"Come on up." I hung up with her and put a veil of tin foil over the oven roaster.

"C'mon Anj. We're going up by Grandma."

"Gamma!! Gampa! Yay!" She clapped her hands together.

Angela ran top speed up the basement stairs and jumped into my dad's brand new La-Z Boy recliner.

"I know one thang. Somebody gonna have to pay to sit in my seat."

"I no ha' no money, Gampa!" She raised her hands in the air.

"Well then, you gonna have to pay me with a kiss!"

"Mwahhhhhh!"

"You have paid your debt, Little Miss Lady." He sat on the floor in front of her tickling her feet with his mustache.

"Look at his old ass playing with that baby. Keeps him young. Keeps me young, too."

I put the roaster in the oven and sat at the table with the newspaper.

"Heard Terrell down there the other night, yellin' 'bout a Baby. 'Bout time yall start workin' on number two." I just shook my head. I wasn't about to touch the topic of number two or Terrell's yelling.

I flipped through the paper with purpose until I found the Real Estate section. When Terrell was right, he was all-the-way right. I scanned through, seeing houses that were still on the market; houses that weren't in our price range. And then a listing for a familiar address jumped off the page. I know what I said about living too close, but this was too weird. When I looked at the price, it was exactly what we were looking for. I jumped up and went to the window. Terrell had double parked in front of the Century City For Sale sign and was standing out there staring at it. Our new house had a red awning and no front yard. Instead, it had an inclined driveway that Angela could use as her roller skate ramp, or for sledding when it snowed. Terrell turned to the window with this weird questioning look on his face. And in my heart, I knew that house was ours.

"Okay, Ma. Well, we have a guest room, so you and Wooly can come stay with us," he said. I cringed in my seat, looking up from my book. Angela raised her arms in the air.

"Yay! I'm gonna have two Grandmas in New York!"

"Thanks for asking me if I minded," I whispered.

"Momma. Hold on." He covered the mouthpiece. "It's my mother."

"It's my house."

"Our house."

"Exactly."

"Here. You tell her she can't come stay in *our* house."

"Oh, you are playing yourself!"

"Momma, hold on. Adrienne wants to talk to you." I snatched the phone away from him.

"Hey Ms. Lucy."

"Now that I'm retired, me and Wooly gonna come to New York for a while so I can get a fair shot at being a Grandma."

"Well, as Terrell said, we have a guest room but we have to do some work to it first and I don't know how long that's gonna take."

"Oh no. We comin' to live for a spell. Been in Columbia my whole life. Time to get me a piece of some of that Big Apple."

She and Wooly rented an apartment right off President Street and Utica Avenue in the Caribbean slice of the Big Apple. I tried to tell her that maybe she was going to experience a serious culture shock coming from the southern fried state of South Carolina, but her church lady friend had a church lady friend who could get her a great deal on an apartment. And you know church lady friends have the inside track on all that is right with the world.

"I have one question though. Just what in the hell is a jerk chicken?"

"When you find out, you're gonna wonder how you ever lived without it," I told her. She held Angela on her lap and beamed.

"I wonder how I ever lived so long without my grandbaby! Looking just like my boy!" Terrell rushed into the kitchen. He knelt in front of Angela.

"Angel Cakes. Me and Wooly are playing gin and I'm losing. So call me in two minutes." he whispered.

"Okay, Daddy!" she whispered. Less than a minute later, she cupped her hands over her mouth. "Daddy, are you losing, yet?"

"Yes, he is," said Wooly. "Come be his good luck charm." Angela jumped down off the couch and ran into the front room. Ms. Lucy took the glass top off her cake plate. She cut us both a piece of apple crumb cake.

"Better than your Momma's."

"Not while she's alive." She rubbed her hands together.

"See? Now you gonna make me kill the poor lady. That ain't right, Adrienne."

Angela shrieked from the other room. I flew out of my seat so fast, my plate fell off the table. Angela sat on Terrell's lap partially covering her eyes.

"Mommy! Wooly put his eye on the table. It was dis-cus-ting!"

Wooly grinned. "It was just a grape."

"That's not your eye, Wooly?!" He blinked his eyes. She put her hands on her hips.

"Oh, Wooly. You're such a player!" We laughed, but I stayed at the door.

"He was only playing with her, Adrienne. You can go back in the living room." I stood at the door. Terrell dealt three hands.

"Bye, Adrienne," he said. His forehead creased with irritation. Ms. Lucy came to the door.

"Can't overprotect, Baby." She led me back to the kitchen. Angela shrieked again and I jumped. And then she giggled in a way that made me smile. A tiny piece of my paranoia melted. A teensy, teeny, tiny piece.

“I NEVER BEEN ON A CRUISE ship before. I am so excited. This is a great anniversary present. I ain’t never had one uh those either.”

“Had what?” I asked.

“An anniversary present. Somebody said they don’t believe in that. But he gon’ believe it when we get there. And Rodney said it’s gonna be real nice.”

My mother folded a leopard negligee into her designer bag and I chuckled to myself. I guess they were still exercising after all these years. Ha. Miss Pam would have loved to hear that. I wondered how she was doing.

“It’s going to be fun. They have games and food and tours of the islands.” My father tossed some loud tropical shirts on the bed.

“Yeah, mon. Rodney mon say we going to tour dee eye-luhnd, Angela, mon. What you tink about me accent, Adrienne?”

“I *tink* they’re not going to mistake you for one of the locals.”

“I told him he sound like a fool. How you think the food’s gonna taste? I can’t be eatin’ no white people food all day.” My father forgot his accent.

“Yeah, I’ma need my grits in the morning. I can’t be eatin’ no granola or none of that mess.”

“Angie Baby, you gonna miss me and Grandpa when we gone?” asked my mother. Angela stayed snuggled under me. She nodded.

“Whassamatter, Baby? Don’t you feel alright?” I felt her forehead.

“Oh my goodness. You’re burning up!” My mother touched her forehead and pulled her hand back like she’d just touched the iron. She was so dramatic. She leaned over me to open Angela’s sweater.

“Get this sweater off. Oh, Dub, we can’t go now! Who’s gonna keep the baby while Adrienne goes to work?" Angela sat in her t-shirt. Her little face was flushed and she was perspiring at the neck.

"Don't be ridiculous. Of course you're gonna go." My mother left and came back with a cool rag.

"We're gonna stay. I can't leave my Angie like this!"

"The hell we are. Angie got a momma and a daddy. She gon' be fine. And we gon' be on a island somewhere sippin' on somethin'."

"She'll be fine," I said. "I'll just use one of my sick days."

Except I had a report due first thing in the morning. I called my assistant at home.

"Alicia, my daughter has a high fever, so I won't be in in the morning. Do you know how to pull up my reports?"

"Yes, Adrienne, but I was just about to call you." The telephone dropped and she screamed in pain.

"Aye. Dios. Mio. Baby's early, Adrienne." She hung up. My new assistant, Stacey was not set to start for another two weeks.

"I can't take tomorrow off, Tee. I think maybe I should just take Angel to work with me."

"She has a fever. That's the whole reason she's got to stay home. She can stay with my mother."

"No, that's asking too much."

"Adrienne. Angela is her granddaughter. She left her beautiful home, her *warm*, beautiful home to be here. She can go to my mom's and be warm and toasty under the covers all day. I just don't understand you."

"Whatever."

I stood under the shower spray.

"Would it be better if I stayed home with her?" asked Terrell. I let the water beat down on top of the shower cap. He stuck his head into the shower.

"Adrienne. Would that be better for you?"

"No. I'll stay home. I'll just call the Dean in the morning."

"What in the hell is the matter with you?! I can't stay with my own daughter. She can't stay with my mother. You're not the only one that cares about Angela. The last thing I would do is let something happen to her." I reached out for his hand.

"Tee. It's not a problem." He pulled away.

"It is, too. It's always a problem. You couldn't even relax when she was in the next room with me and Wooly. If you wanted to raise her by yourself, then you shouldn't have had a baby with me. I am not that nigga."

"I hate when you use that word."

"I hate when you make me feel like Angela is not my daughter."

He jerked the curtain closed. I peeked out. He stood at the mirror edging up. The key to a clean look was a man's haircut, he always said.

"Will you do me a favor?" I asked.

"What?"

"Close the door. There's a draft." He left the door wide open.

When I got out, I oiled my body and took care to pick a nice nightie from my special drawer: A black teddy with a matching panty. When I climbed in the bed, Terrell was on his side with his back to me. I snuggled up behind him.

"Will you make her soup?" He didn't answer.

"Terrell, Baby. I'm talking to you."

"What?" I ran my hand over his bicep.

"Will you make her soup and read her a story?"

"Yes." His abs flexed when my hands skimmed his hairline.

"And give her the antibiotics every four hours?" He nodded.

"I love you, Tee. I'm sorry for making you feel like I don't trust you with the baby." I buried my nose in the crook of his neck and shoulder.

"I love you, too. It's just sometimes, I gotta feel like you need me like how I need you." I kissed the back of his neck. I ran my hand down his rippled back.

"Is it okay if I need you now?"

He turned over on his back. Terrell was wearing his weight especially well. My husband was sexy and grown and loved me to no end. He pulled me on top of him and I made love to my man. The love of my life.

“ADRIENNE. THE BABY’S FINE. She’s had her medicine. She’s had a little bit of soup and now she’s sleeping. Every time the phone rings it wakes her up.” I held the phone in one hand while I googled spy cams with the other.

“Okay. But what’s she doing now?”

“I said she’s sleeping. I said she’s fine.”

“What are you doing?”

“Watching All My Children.”

“I’ll leave that one alone. What’s the baby doing?”

“If you call back one more time, I’m gonna take the phone off the hook.”

“Alright, alright.”

The first thing I noticed when I jumped out of the taxi was that Terrell’s car was not parked in the driveway. I shoved the front door open and ran into the foyer like I’d escaped the G Building at Kings County’s Psychiatric Ward. Their coats weren’t in the hall closet. The house was silent except for a *shhhh* noise coming from Angela’s bedroom. My heart bumped against my chest. Mother fucker. I grabbed a knife from the kitchen and tiptoed toward her bedroom. The heater clanked and the steam let out: *Ssssh.* I slammed the door shut, relieved but still pissed. The answering machine flashed.

“Hello Mommy. Grandma said I can’t call you. But I wanted to say hi to you. I remembered my phone number like a big girl. Okay. I have to say bye now. Bye Mommy. I love you, Mommy.” Click!

All the way to Ms. Lucy’s house I swore like my Daddy when his paycheck was short. I was out of breath and red-faced by the time I leaned on the buzzer. She yelled into the intercom. “Who. In. The. Hell?!”

"Angela's mother!" *Bzzzz!* The steel and glass security door unlatched. I flew through the door knocking over a little boy and his laundry bag. Ms. Lucy held the apartment door open.

"Where is she?" Ms. Lucy grabbed my arm.

"What in the hell is your problem?"

"My problem is my baby's here and you're telling her she can't call me."

"That's right. I din't want her little germs all over my phone."

Angela sat in the bed in a pink sweat suit, playing concentration. Her hair was in two lopsided pig-tails.

"Grandma, I'm gonna win if you don't come ba-a-ck," she sang.

"Hi, Mommy. Did you get my message?" I put her dolls in her book bag and looked around the floor for her sneakers.

"Wooly's not here," said Ms. Lucy.

"Wooly doesn't have anything to do with this."

"The hell he does." She took Angela's sneakers out of the closet, along with her coat, hat and scarf. And extra sweater and outfit. And coloring books and flash cards. The doorbell buzzed. Ms. Lucy left me scrambling to gather Angela's things.

"Adrienne, what are you doing here?" asked Terrell.

"You lied to me," I said. "I can't stand a liar." I bundled Angela up and carried her downstairs, as big as she was.

"Adrienne, you need to stop and listen to me." I jogged toward the bus stop, hoping to catch the one that was waiting. Terrell grabbed my arm as I put Angela on the bus steps. I yanked my arm out of his grasp.

"Adrienne," he said. "I won't be home tonight." I looked over my shoulder at him. The bus doors hissed closed in his face.

"Ms. Lucy, it's Adrienne again. Please call me."

Angela's medicine was in Ms. Lucy's fridge and I had no idea how I would get it. Angela was knocked out and I didn't want to wake her. But every time she coughed, she winced in pain.

"Ms. Lucy, Terrell, Wooly, this is Adrienne again." I slammed the phone down. Angela coughed so hard, her body shook.

"Angela needs her medicine! Call me, dammit!" Angela wheezed and I couldn't take it anymore.

As I started the car, I said a hundred prayers that my baby didn't wake up and find me gone, that nothing happened at the house or that those coughs didn't kill her.

True Pharmacy was swarming with the stuffy nosed, sniffling type.

"It's going to take one hour to refill, Ma'am," said the clerk.

"I don't have an hour. My baby is sick!" He pointed to the waiting area.

"Everybody else is here because they just loooove True Pharmacy so much. One hour. Maybe forty-five minutes if you're a good girl. Next customer!"

I grumbled to myself, but I waited on the side like a good little girl. Just as I was told.

There were no fire trucks on the block, no police cars, when I pulled up. It was worse. Terrell's car was in the driveway.

"What in your Miss Perfect mind, would let you think that it was a good idea to leave our baby alone in the house?!"

I turned the True Pharmacy bag over on the bed. Dozens of cold medications and aspirins were piled high.

"What the hell is that?" He picks up a bottle out of the pile. "This is for adults! Are you trying to kill her?"

"You're the one who didn't bring her medication!"

"Why the hell do you think I'm here?! I sure didn't come back here to see you!" He slammed the bedroom door shut. When I busted the door open, Terrell's work shirts were strewn about the bed. He pulled a suit from the closet and sweaters from the dresser.

"What are you doing?"

"What does it look like?"

"Fine. Run on back to your momma with your lying ass." He went to the bathroom and came out with his toothbrush and clippers. He chucked them in his gym bag. "You knew damn well you were going to work all along!"

"Yeah, I lied. Play back the machine."

"For what? It's Angela saying your mother forbade her to call!"

"You are one crazy chick. Play the *saved* one."

"Fuck you, Terrell. Mother-fuck-youuuuuu!" He slammed the door behind him. "And I'm not checking the damn machine either, Liar!" I yelled at the back of the door. Asshole.

Of course, the blinking red light was a beacon for my angry heart.

Time. 3:45pm. Hey Terrell, it's Dave. We know you have your daughter, but we have a little emergency. We just need you for a few minutes. An hour tops. Call me back in the project room. Extension 8128.

I went to Angela's room to unpack her bag and realized that Terrell packed everything I would have packed for her, plus an extra outfit, underwear and flash cards. I felt more stupid by the minute.

I leaned across the sofa, watching the phone, again willing it to ring. Angela turned over her flash cards on our living room floor. Terrell didn't even say hello when he walked in the door.

"Daddy!" Angela sprung from the floor into his arms. He held her tight, rocking from left to right.

"Anj, I need to talk to Mommy, okay?" She held on tighter until he pried her arms from around his neck. "Go on, now." Angela walked backwards to her bedroom, never taking her eyes off Terrell. He blew her a kiss and she blew hers back quickly before she closed her door without a sound.

"Wooly wasn't there. He works. I would have told you, but you didn't really want to hear it. I debated about going in. But I trust my mother to do right by my baby."

"You can't come in here after four days talking to me like---"

"Shut up and let me talk!" he barked. My face got hot.

"I'm sick of it. You didn't want me to bathe her. Fine. You didn't want me to change her. Fine. Everything I say, you have to override in some way. I'm tired of the controlling. This is the last time."

"The last time? You're leaving me?"

"What do you expect me to do, Adrienne? I've been fighting you for you. Fighting you for us. I'm tired."

What I would have responded turned into gibberish that only made sense to me. But he pulled me close so that my tears soaked the front of his jacket.

"I'm sorry, Terrell. I'm so sorry."

"Okay."

"I'm sorry," I cried, rubbing my body against his. He stepped back.

"It's not gonna get solved that way this time, Adrienne."

I DIDN'T NIT PICK OVER ANGELA staying with his mother for a few hours every now and then. And I allowed her to play cards with Wooly, so long as I could hear their conversation at all times. Ms. Lucy gave up having conversations with me because I could never pay attention.

Terrell kept his mouth closed when I know he wanted to lay into me. He *was* tired. I could see it in the way everything he did was mechanical. Technical. Dry. Or as my old English professor would say: perfunctory. Dry kisses on the cheek for Angela. Dry, on the forehead for me. No passion. No feeling. No nothing.

Sex was the same way. Once a week, maybe. Kiss. Kiss. Rub. Rub. Legs open. Pump. Pump. Over. Good night. Sleep tight.

Many nights I waited until he was asleep and touched myself until I pleased. But that was getting as lame as our shared encounters. I tried my best to keep my mind off it, but it was always there on the forefront, waiting, for say a grocery cart to crash head-on into mine in Metro Foods, and startle me out of a trance.

The brother at the other end of the cart was light-skinned with flawless skin, a Black Caesar haircut and an impeccable goatee. His suit jacket was unbuttoned and his tie was open at the neck. He was easily 6'2", 220 lbs. and regularly taking advantage of his gym membership. Took me two seconds to take it all in and know he was indeed doable.

"My apologies," he murmured. I kept walking, but turned back to find his handsome ass looking back. He left his cart in front of the canned vegetables.

"My name is Joel. Can I take you out?" My lonely tootie palpitated.

It was Friday night. A young lady like me deserved to be going out on the town with a handsome and virile man.

"Page me."

Three hours later, I toweled off and went to my bedroom to get dressed. Angela sat on my bed, Indian style, leafing through my Bible.

"How come Aunt Juicie put a note in this book? *For quiet times and times of need.*" She read. "She's nice. I always liked her."

"She put it there as a reminder." My drawer was full of unworn thongs and pretty little things that were going to waste because of Terrell's wanna-be-dry ass. I picked a lacy fuchsia g-string and bra.

"Mommy. How come you're wearing those? You only wear that kind when you're going somewhere with Daddy."

"What?"

"The lacy ones with the string. When you and daddy go out to dinner, you wear that. But Daddy's not here. So where are you going?"

"Out with my friend, Anj."

"When are you meeting her?"

"Supposed to be at eleven. Let me get myself together. Okay, baby?" I practically pushed her out the door. I was bubbling with pent up sexual energy and she was making too many connections for her own good. Ten minutes later she was back with the Bible again.

"The Garden of Eden sounds beautiful."

"Yes, baby. It is." In my mind I was also naked as Eve and ready to tempt a man with my fruit.

"Mommy. Please read me some of it before you go. You know I can't sleep if you don't read with me." The clock read ten o'clock and I hadn't even put my contacts in, or put on any makeup. I wasn't sure if she was trying to stall because she knew I was up to nothing righteous, but I couldn't say no to my baby. I opened up to the middle and read a passage about God's grace.

"Alright, Baby. Ask Grandma to read you the rest." My mother called out from the living room.

"Don't pull me into this mess, Adrienne."

"Just one more, please?" I flipped it open and landed on 1 Peter 3. *Wives, in the same way, be submissive* – I slammed it shut.

"Baby, read it to yourself. We'll discuss it in the morning." I shoved her out of my room and locked the door behind her.

Tight jeans, tight sweater, 4-inch stilettos and one lip gloss application later, I was at the door primed for what I knew would be a thrill.

"Be good for Grandma, Angel." My mother tsked from the sofa.

"It ain't her that needs to worry 'bout being good."

Traffic on the Brooklyn Bridge crawled through one lane because of an accident. By the time I got into the city, it was already eleven. The yellow taxis and lawless pedestrians in the Village blocked every intersection. I rewound my Jodeci tape hoping to keep my buzz going, but it wasn't working.

I rolled into the driveway at the Marriott Marquis and hopped out. The valet sped off in my car. I checked my watch. Eleven twenty-two. I was disgusted with myself. I don't do disorder. Or lateness.

Instead of handing me the key, the concierge handed me a folded note.

Time is of the essence. J. The time stamp read 11:15pm.

"Great." I looked down at my outfit. It was too cute to waste.

"Is there a bar in here?"

"It's in the Atrium. Take the elevator to eight."

The blonde model-thin bartender placed a napkin in front of me.

"E&J, straight, please."

"One of those nights, huh?" I sighed.

"It's been one of those lives."

Terrell came home in an odd mood. There was no dry, boring kiss. There was nothing. He didn't even speak.

Terrell turned the water on in the bathroom. Steam and Ivory soap wafted out. He would be soapy and slippery and I could feel my body tightening with excitement. I dropped my nightgown to my feet.

I slid the shower curtain back a bit before he grabbed it. Just before he pulled it all the way shut, I noticed a purple bruise on his neck. Mother fucker! I went back to the bedroom and picked his polo shirt out of the hamper. White Diamonds floated off of it. I sat on the bed and waited.

The minute he came out of the bathroom, I was all in his face, head rolling, finger pointing, and lips smacking.

"I can't believe you're cheating on me!" Terrell dried his back.

"As you like to say, Ms. Marriott, don't play yourself." I dropped the shirt to the floor ready to get down and dirty.

"Well if you'd give it to me like you used to..."

"Stop."

"No, I'm not gonna stop. You treat me like…"

"Stop, Adrienne."

"No Terrell. You stop. Stop acting like you're rationing out your damn dick and do what you're supposed to do to keep your family together."

"Adrienne. I'm not in love with you anymore." I stared into his face, glowering with rage. "I'm sorry."

"You punk-pussy mother fucker." He squeezed my face in his hand.

"Don't you ever, *ever* disrespect me like that," he said calmly. I pulled away from him, terrified by the coldness in his eyes.

"Get the fuck off of me. And get the fuck out of my room."

"There are two names on the deed of this house, Lady. And I use that term loosely. Ain't nobody putting me to sleep anywhere but in this bed that I helped pay for, in this room that I helped pay for, in this house that I helped pay for." He fluffed his pillow and got under the blanket.

"But you can do what you feel, Adrienne." And then he turned his back on me. I got in on my side and huffed and I puffed and I could have burned that bed down. I stared at the ceiling, seething, hurting, blaming, worrying, pondering, denying.

"What the hell are we doing?" Terrell asked.

"Don't even fuckin' talk to me."

I WOULDN'T SAY OUR relationship was ruined after that, but we were definitely on eggshells for the next few years. Terrell said he wasn't seeing anyone, but I didn't really care one way or the other. He did fulfill his duties, albeit lamely.

The morning of my baby's tenth birthday was sunny and pleasantly warm. Not stay-in-the-shade hot or hair-in-a-ponytail humid like early August tended to be. Angela came downstairs to the kitchen holding a brochure.

"What is this?" she asked suspiciously. Terrell shrugged. I stirred my tea.

"Guys, stop playing," she begged with a tentative smile. I held out the spoon like it was a microphone.

"Tee, it's Angela's birthday. What are we doing to celebrate?"

"We're going to Disney World!" he yelled. Angela jumped all over us so that we all fell to the floor laughing. I don't know which of us was most excited. We'd never been on a vacation before.

The Bali Beach Hotel was an exact replica of the island retreats of the rich and famous that I saw on TV, minus yachts parked in the marina.

The room was a cabana on stilts, resting about five feet above Disney's man made Caribbean blue lagoon over sparkling white sand. There was a hammock on the outdoor balcony and huge palm fronds swaying about in the breeze. As far as I knew, I was in paradise.

"Can we go in the pool, Ma? Please?!" She tugged on my arm jumping up and down.

"Well, I don't know…" I teased.

"Mommy, pleeeeease?!"

"Yeah, Mommy, pleeeease?!" teased Terrell.

"Oh. Okay, I guess we can." I fished out my suit. Terrell came back from the bathroom in these hideous neon green trunks. Angela shuffled around and around in her suitcase.

"Uh-oh."

"What's the matter?"

"You forgot my bathing suit," she whined. I checked and double checked. I could have kicked myself.

"Don't worry, Baby. We'll get you another one."

The TikiTaki Gift Shop was packed with swimsuits. Bikinis and tankinis. Sports suits and suits with skirted bottoms. You name it, they had it. Angela decided she wanted a two piece suit. Terrell scratched his goatee.

"I think a one piece would be better since you're athletic."

"But look. The two-piece has a racer back strap in the back and I could pull it over my head instead of snapping or tying it," she reasoned.

"Fine," I said.

And it would have been, except when we got upstairs to the room, we realized Angela had sprung some breasts over night and the suit was doing these outrageous things. Like making cleavage.

"I still think she should have gotten the one piece. It would control her breasts better," said Terrell.

"Ayj. Go get your towel and stuff." She trotted to the bedroom looking down at her new friends.

"Why are you watching her breasts?"

"Because they need to be contained. If we see them, then other people, *men*, see them too."

"Yeah, but I'll take care of that."

"Yeah, but I said we should get the one piece and as usual, you vetoed."

"So you've been checking out her breasts from before?"

"Are you listening to yourself? Because you're sounding crazy. Do you realize what you're asking me?"

"I'm asking you a simple question. Were you checking out her breasts from before?" Terrell let the hotel room door slam behind him.

"Where's Daddy?" asked Angela returning from the bathroom.

"He'll meet us at the pool."

Terrell checked into a new room at the resort. To say the rest of the trip was strained would be an understatement.

When we got home, the whole mood of the house was cautious. Terrell spoke when spoken to and watched TV all night until he fell asleep. He wouldn't even go in the room to kiss Angela good night like he used to. In the morning he ate in silence; barely looking up over his newspaper.

"Is Daddy mad at me?" asked Angela when he'd left the table.

"No."

"Then what did you do to him to make him hate me?" I went back to washing the dishes.

"How come you never tell me anything?!" she yelled. "How come nobody tells me anything?!" She sprang from the table and out the front door. Terrell came out of the bedroom in his suit jacket, with his tie loosely knotted.

"Terrell. I'm sorry I offended you."

"No, you should be sorry that you even thought I was sick enough to be checking out my own daughter and that you still don't think enough of me to tell me what the hell happened to you to make you this way." He handed me the divorce petition.

"I only waited this long because I didn't want Angela to associate her birthday with us splitting up." I stuck it in the desk drawer with the bills.

"You don't have anything to say?" I shook my head.

"We're ending our marriage and you don't have anything to say? Ten years down the drain and *you* don't have anything to say?" I shook my head.

"So you don't care?"

"Did you do this to find out if I cared, or because you can't deal?"

"Adrienne. You're cold as ice."

"You want to know how I feel? I'm going to tell you. I'm relieved. I thought I would be sad when this day finally came, but I'm relieved, Terrell."

"Relieved?!"

"Now I can stop wondering about the inevitable."

I wished I could have stopped being Rabbit. But we were two of the same fucked up kind. I proved it when I turned away from Terrell and pretended I didn't notice he was crying.

THE PRESENT

ANGELA RECITES THE *GETTYSBURG ADDRESS* while my mother and I cook dinner. She's twelve, tall, built like her brickhouse mama, and she's in the eighth grade. And just like me, she got skipped in elementary school.

Unlike me, she's enrolled at a private prep school in white bread Bay Ridge with other brainiacs like herself. She seems to like it, even though as she puts it, she's only one of four chocolate chips in a tub of vanilla ice cream. But I'm worried. Unlike me, she is fragile. Her words fall out of sequence.

"Start over," I say.

"This is so not *coo-ull.* It's not going to help me become an astronaut, Mom."

"The kids at your school will know it. So you need to know it better."

"Mom, it's 2008. We're all *equaaal.*" I look over the top of my glasses.

"Ohmigod. I hate when you do that. Four score and seven years ago..." I wonder about my decision from time to time because although it's 2008, the idea of electing a black man still makes the folks nervous. Black folks included. Things have changed. But a lot more has stayed exactly the same.

My mother is mumbling something about my being too hard on her, but I'm on to something else. Will my little chocolate chip come home with little pink-faced Jimmy and his little pink penis, talking about '*Ohmigod, I love hemm!'?* I chop tomatoes like there's a medal to be won.

"Oh! I almost forgot! Rodney sent tickets for us to come to his game tonight." I chop at warp speed now. Perhaps I could win the gold.

"It's his first night in town. We should support him."

"Not tonight," I say.

"Why can't we go, Mom? Cousin Kerri's kids get to go all the time and I'm way older than they are."

"Not tonight."

"Okay, well how 'bout me and Dub take Angela to the game and we'll tell you how it was."

"Angela has a test at the end of the week and she needs to study. Plus, it's a school night. For the last time. Not. To. Night!"

"But Mom, I could take that test with my eyes closed!"

"No game." My mother slams her knife on the counter and grabs her hips.

"What the hell is wrong with you?" I keep at my tomatoes. *Kop, kop, kop! Kop, kop, kop!*

"Is this how you treat your family, Adrienne? He's been nothing but good to me and your father. And he always asks for you. I would think you'd be a little more grateful." I look over my glasses at her, too.

"Grateful for family. Your family's all you got, Adrienne. Hmph. I didn't wanna say nothing, but you ain't got Terrell no more, cause you ran him off. You treat Kerri like a stranger. You come to holidays late and leave early. Now you don't want to go to the game. What you think you teaching Angie with all this?" She tsks which annoys the hell out of me.

"I just don't understand you."

"It's been awhile since you've understood me."

"Whas that supposed to mean?"

I drop the knife in the sink. "Angela, when you're done eating, come right home. No game." I yank my pocketbook off the chair back.

"Daddy. Where do you keep your stash?"

"Top of the cabinet. You okay?"

"I will be."

Stacey and I pow-wow at my desk. Today, her shirt is still snug, but her buttons are less likely to take someone's eye out. To her credit, she's even chosen a soft pink polyester shirt instead of the lime green and fuchsia specials that she prefers. I am proud. One day, I'll get her into a natural fiber.

She separates the resumes for credentials, past experience, education and skills. The ones that make the cut, she passes on to me.

"I found another qualified sister."

"Are you sure she's a sister?"

"LaCandria Bradbury."

"Get her in here." I look over the top of my glasses. "She better be an excellent interview." Stacey and I shake our heads.

I think of my Dad and how his advice from way back influenced my decision to work in Human Resources. It was weird, but even though I was making decisions, they were still tempered by the old guard at the College and the expectation that we jump that much higher and be that much smarter just to get in the door.

Kennedy bounces into my office with a gorgeous bouquet of orchids.

"You got a new Boo, Kennedy?" asks Stacey.

"What's a Boo?"

"A snookums, a pooh bear, a sweetheart."

"Ohhhh! No, I don't have a Boo." She places the blooms on my desk and plucks the card out.

"For my favorite cuz." She waggles her brows. "Cuz. Spelled c-u-z. How colloquial and phonetic. Missed you at the game." I snatch the card.

"Was there something you needed Kennedy?"

"Actually, the Dean would like two tickets for next week's Skyscrapers vs. Mystery game. His son is a die-hard fan."

"That's unfortunate."

"It can be unfortunate for you, as well." She pats her silky black mane. "Angie's private school is pretty expensive, Honey." She saunters out of the office. Stacey moves her bangs to the side of her forehead.

"Oh huh-ell no. She can't get away with that!"

"I'm not studying Kennedy." I stack the resumes in neat piles. "Tell me more about Bryan's friend, Rob."

"Oooh. Rob is so fine. He's also really nice and charming and he has a daughter from a previous marriage."

"Oh. A divorcee like me."

"Yeah. I figured that was a common link." I laugh louder than I've ever dared to laugh at work.

"What? Failure at marriage? Yeah, that's a conversation piece right there. *So how'd yours end? Oh, she cheated. How bout you? Didn't love him anymore. You know I heard it's cheap and quick to get one in the Dominican Republic now. Isn't marriage a trip*?" I slap my knee. Stacey snickers.

"Sometimes, you're too smart for your own good. He's nice and he's fun and he's gonna take up some of that spare time you been lugging around."

"And you say he's fine?"

"No. Rob is foi-oi-oine!"

"What should I wear?"

"The biggest smile you can fit into." It'd been a long time since I smiled at a man. I could try one on.

My desk is cleared of the day's tasks. I hate to arrive at work in the morning and find a messy desk. The only thing left are the flowers from Rodney. They really are exquisite in their lavender splendor. I empty the water out the window and drop the stems in the trash can. Fuck Rodney. Except, I can hear Stacey's voice in my ear.

What happened to the flowers, Ay-dree-yanne? As it is, I'm sure she is biding her time before she begins the inquisition. I fish them out of the garbage, cursing my little heart out. Fuck you, Rodney. Fuck you.

After circling the block a few times, I find a parking space in front of Stacey's Harlem brownstone. I am too nervous to go inside, so I sit in my car, fiddling with the radio. Rodney is on two of the five programmed radio stations where they are replaying a clip from his press conference. I change to the AM station and there he is again.

"*I'ma bring style back to New York. My crossover is mean, my jump shot is pretty; I'ma make the lights shine brighter in New York City.*"

The sportscaster pipes in.

"*Do we have a basketball version of Muhammed Ali on our hands? Is the world ready for it?*"

I push the knob, killing the sound. That is not what I need right now. I hadn't been on a date since Terrell and I did a 'one last try' date that ended with me walking across the Brooklyn Bridge and him calling my cell phone every two minutes trying to get me to be reasonable. Reasonable was to allow him to take Angie down to South Carolina with his parents for Spring Break.

"I can't bear to be away from my baby for that long," I said. The wind on the bridge tossed my scarf around my head. "No," I said. "I can't."

"I guess it's a done deal then." I hung up on him and kept across the bridge with the wind whipping my hair in all directions and the cold burning my cheeks. Terrell waited at the foot of the bridge.

"Get in the car, Adrienne." I walked past his car and kept going until I got to the train station. My baby was not leaving the state without me. Period.

As bad a memory as it was, I still smile into my rear view. A shy smile. A happy smile. I try out my interested, but not too interested smile. Yes. It is true. I am losing it. The shot of juice from my little friend settles the jitters in my hands and the queasiness in my stomach almost immediately. I tuck it deep down in the bottom of my bag and man the alarm on my car.

Stacey swings the door open so fast, I don't even have a chance to get my hand out of my pocket to ring the doorbell.

"You look a little crazy smiling at yourself like that."

"You were spying on me?" She takes my coat and bottle of Riesling.

"No. I heard the car pull up and wondered what was taking you so long. You look fab! Catwalk!"

I model my outfit for her, a chunky charcoal sweater dress, black tights and ankle boots, down her hallway and back, swinging my shoulder length hair back and forth.

"Work it, work it, work it!" she shouts, clapping her hands. "I love it." She links her arm in mine. "Come let me show you my house."

The hardwood floors, and the lighting gives the first floor a spa-like feel. Her walls are a pale teal and her furniture a nice grey. She has vanilla candles burning. It's beautiful.

"You thought it'd be a hot shiny mess, huh?" I shake my head at her crazy and correct assumption.

"No. Of course not."

"Well, it would have been, if I had anything to do with it. But you can thank Mr. HGTV for the décor."

Bryan, her big teddy bear husband, comes up from the basement, carrying a case of Coronas. Stacey puts her hands on her hips.

"I thought I told you to put those in the fridge since last night. Dang, you don't listen." She takes the beer and walks to the kitchen mumbling. He cups his hands over his mouth. "You ain't my mother, girl!"

"If she'da taught ya better, I wouldn't have to be tellin' you what to do all the daggone time."

"My buddy should be here any minute. He's a good guy. I know you're gonna hit it off." We're standing in the foyer, about to sit in the living room, when the doorbell rings and Stacey runs from the kitchen, her bangs flying every which way.

"Well damn, you sure this hookup is for Adrienne?" asked Bryan.

"Sometimes, I wish it wasn't, smarty." I almost want to run to the bathroom and hide because I'm standing in the foyer with Bryan, like I'm desperately awaiting this date. But I'm glued to the spot. When my blind date steps through the foyer, I feel shy and thirteen again.

"Hi Rob."

"Adrienne Fuller. It's been a long time." I smile, no practice necessary. Lord, have mercy, Corey Robinson is still fine. He smiles and my tootie jumps alive.

He's gained a good thirty pounds, in all the right places and his hands look powerful and able. I don't know why, but I can't take my eyes off his hands. *Down girl!* I command, but she has a mind of her own, that damn Tootie.

"I'm Adrienne Lucas now."

"Adrienne Lucas. What happened to you? You just upped and disappeared one day." I look everywhere but at him.

"Long story," I say. Stacey steps between us.

"Why don't we have dinner and talk about the here and now before we stroll down Memory Lane. Okay, yall?" I send her a silent thank you with my eyes. She winks, but the questions are etched all over her forehead.

“DINNER WAS OFF THE HOOK, STACEY,” says Corey. Stacey blushes in her lemony hued sweater. She has a gorgeous luminescence about her.

“Still finessing the girls, huh, Corey?” I tease. I am tipsy off the Riesling and feeling loosey goosey.

“Couldn’t seem to finesse you. Do yall know I had a thing for this girl?” My bottom lip drops. Bryan sits back in his seat rubbing his hands together. I don’t even look at Stacey because I know she is all eyes.

“Sure did. It took me a whole year to even ask her out.” I nearly choke.

“A whole year?” I probably only noticed Corey that thirteenth summer when it seemed I noticed everything. All those times I went to La Mercado, we could have been an item sooner!

“Yup. But you were off limits. Rodney said so.” *Rodney?!*

“Rodney?” asked Stacey. “I thought you said you guys weren’t close.”

“We grew apart,” I said quickly. “But you didn’t even know me. Remember that day on the steps?” He smiled.

“I just wanted to see if you were hypnotized like everybody else.” His cell phone rings.

“Excuse me for a sec.” He opens his phone. “Hi, Honeybun. No, Daddy’s not coming by now. Do you see what time it is?” He smiles at us but my emotions are so divided, I want to split myself in multiple parts. On the one hand, I feel so cuddly warm inside at his way with his daughter. But the warmth turns to the heat of anger because Rodney was running interference on me. I look up again and see the joy in his face as he talks to his daughter and I feel a stab of envy for Angela and Terrell. I force a smile when I realize he's staring back at me. I jump up immediately to follow Stacey to the kitchen.

"Girl!" she squeals. "Get out there and rekindle or something!"

"We are not rekindling anything! That's in the past!"

"Well, sign up for a one-nighter or something. You better not waste the opportunity." I tingle at the thought of my first orgasm in Tanisha's basement. And Lord knows Tootie is a restless animal. Before I can tilt the bottle toward my glass, Stacey holds my hand. I take a water bottle from her instead. That will hold me over until my next bathroom visit.

"Tell my Poppa Bear to bring his big behind in here and help me so yall can have a lil' privacy." She pushes me back into the living room, into Corey's line of x-ray vision. The fact that he refuses to blink is making me even more uneasy. I'm hoping he'll stay at the far end of the sofa, but he's come so close, I can smell the detergent in his sweater. His voice is full of low quiet rumble.

"You played me."

"That was so long ago."

"It feels like yesterday."

"Why'd you go with Caroline?" He looks silly in the face.

"She told me she'd give me some."

"What ever happened to her?"

"I have no idea. But I have a better question: one you haven't answered. What ever happened to you?"

"If you don't already know, I'm not going to ruin the night by talking about it. You need another drink?"

"No. I'm good."

"Well, give me a sec. I need to get back where you are."

Through the front window, my living room is dark except for the blue light from the television. I put my key in the door gingerly; careful not to make any noise in case my girls are sleeping. Actually I'm hoping they are. I'm not up for the conversation. Of course, my mother and Angela are curled up on the sofa together in their pajamas, flipping through the channels.

"You should wear your hair down more, Adrienne. It makes you look young." I hiccup in response.

"You drunk?"

"Hell no, I'm not jurrrrr-runk." I giggle.

"You and your father and that damn alcohol." Angela bolts upright.

"Ohh! There goes Cousin Rodney!" My mother raises the volume so we can hear the news anchor.

"The Skyscrapers point guard has been fined for missing practice but insists the fine is racially motivated."

Rodney, in a blue Yankee cap and white T-shirt, pops up on the screen.

"If I were a lighter shade, we wouldn't be having this conversation right now."

"Mmhmm. Amen, Rodney Junior. You gotta watch white people."

"He's full of shit!" I shout at the TV. "Angela. Bedtime. Now!"

"Why you sendin' her to bed? She need to see how the white man sabotages young black brothers."

"Oh, puh-lease. He's full of shit and you're full of shit if you believe him!"

"I'd like to know who in the hells you think you're talking to," she demanded. Rodney comes back on the screen again.

"I mean, I'm just a Brooklyn boy who visits his mother in the hospital, even if it means missing a practice."

Now I am confused. That doesn't sound anything like Rodney James Barrus, Jr.

"See! I knew there was a good reason. Let me call Juicie and find out why them heifers ain't call and tell me Sadie wasn't feeling good."

She pulls out a brand new lavender Blackberry pearl. I wait. I will be at the hospital first thing in the morning to see my favorite girl.

"Sadie? What you doing there? I thought you was in the hospital." My mother's lips are pursed tightly.

"Oh. Well Rodney said…"

I slam the door to my bedroom. If there's one person I know better than anyone on this planet, it's him. Not that I'm proud of that. But it is what it is. I sit my wobbly ass on the bed and I wonder what exactly he's up to before the lights in my room dim on their own and I pass the hell out.

Jackie Onassis shades are not enough to block the blazing daggers of light that dance around the edge of the window shades threatening to split my head wide open. There's a battering ram banging into my door.

"Umnnn." Stacey shakes her head at my shades.

"Was that, come in, honey?"

"Umhmnnn."

"Told you bout that Riesling, girl. Professor Levine is here to see you."

"Tmrrwww?" She flips the light switch, disregarding my state of disgrace.

"No, ma'am. He's here. You have five minutes." I hear her tell him that I'm on a call, and will be with him shortly. Bitch! I stick my shades in the drawer. I have no idea what he wants and I really don't care. And then I remember.

Professor Levine had been hired to teach Arab Studies in the International Studies Department. Somehow Kennedy decided he was a perfect fit and somehow, his file had never crossed my desk until it was flagged for not having the proper tax forms signed. Coincidently, after he complained that his rate of pay was not in line with his contract.

He has a Ph.D. in Middle Eastern Studies, yes. But background checks in his file reveal he is an Israeli Nationalist. Red flag. Big ass, flaming red flag. She's just asking for the Gaza Strip to be relocated to our campus. The phone in my office won't stop ringing. I buzz Lori Ann, the temp, four times. The damn girl is never at her desk.

"Excuse me for a moment." I pick up the receiver. "Adrienne Lucas."

"How long you gonna take to call Rodney. He been calling the house for you," says my Dad. Oh hell.

"Dad, I'm at work right now." I say, apparently to myself. He plays the message anyway.

> *Hey Auntie Rho. Just calling to let you know your tix will be at the will call. There's tickets for Rabbit and Anj, too. Tell that girl to call me.*
>
> *Hey yall, this is Hot Rod calling to say hey. Can't wait to get up witchall again.*

"Baby, it ain't nothin' but a basketball game."

"Dad, I don't think I want to be involved with the family right now. Just some things I need to work out."

"It'll make your Momma and Angel Cakes happy if you go."

I am tired. Tired of the pressure. Tired of the hiding. Tired of fighting off my family. Tired of Rodney manipulating my life.

"I don't want to go. And you can't make me," I say sounding like I'm thirteen again.

"I'm sorry about that," I say to Professor Levine. I feel stupid and unprofessional and stupid. Did I say stupid? He doesn't respond. My ears are hot.

"My wife is from Saudi Arabia. Our family functions, the rare ones we are invited to, are hell. It hasn't gotten much easier in ten years, but we make it work. They're all we've got beside each other."

And suddenly his background is just slightly nerve-racking as opposed to explosive. No pun intended. Maybe Kennedy isn't quite the idiot I've made her out to be. I walk the Professor to the door. Partly out of respect, but mostly so I can turn the light out. My intercom buzzes.

"Yes, Kennedy?"

"Is Lori Ann out to lunch?" Kennedy and Lori Ann shared an office suite. It's only ten o'clock and if anyone would know where she was, it would be Kennedy.

"I thought you both were." I call my Dad back.

"Make sure Angela finishes her homework by the time I get home and we'll go to the game."

"Your mother's gonna be so glad." I lay on the office couch with my Jackie O's on. My mother would be glad, I'm sure. Ah, what the hell. What's a few more lies and phony smiles among family.

My office phone intercom buzzes, waking me out of a violent dream that has me sweating and shaking. I don't know what exactly was happening, but I know I was fighting for my life.

"Whuuuuut?" I moan.

"LaCandria Bradbury is here."

"Give me five minutes."

"Well. You seem overqualified, Ms. Bradbury. What would make you want to take on an entry-level position, with your past education and lengthy receptionist experience?" I ask. If she answers in the way I hope a sister should answer, she has the job. I'm sure the old guard would frown on my tactics, but it's my way of evening things out.

"At a prestigious university like New York College, it would be in my best interest to get in the doors doing entry level work and learn the structure of the University from the ground up, spend one year in that position and then seek to move up another level, eventually using my degree and perhaps drawing a pension from this fine institution."

"Well, we need to check your references, but when can you start?"

"Today?" We break out into giggles. Kennedy pops her head into my office. She's heard something forbidden.

"Who do we have here?" She's so unprofessional, it irks me. Or maybe it's just Kennedy that irks me.

"My name is LaCandri-uhhh. Rhymes with Alexandri-uhhh. That always helps pee-pull to rememb-burrrr." I nearly choke. She sounds like my daughter!

"Coo-ulll," says Kennedy. She even flashes a huge grin before she closes the door.

"Prep school?"

"Yep. And four years at USC."

"Coo-ulll."

Two sippy sips and one hour later, I am snoring on the office sofa. I know because my own snores have awakened me twice already. This damn hangover and pending family drama is taking a toll on me.

ANGELA CAN'T KEEP HER BOTTOM LIP from dropping when she realizes our seats in the Garden are pretty much on the court.

"Better than our seats for Lil Roof Roof, huh?"

"Bow Wow, mom. Oh my God, you are so embarrassing!" The Garden is loud and bustling with sports fans decked out in blue and silver Skyscraper jerseys and foam Skyscraper hats with the buildings on top. The vendors hawk t-shirts to the passing fans.

"Vintage Hot Rod pictures! Get 'em here!" Rodney's Skyscraper jersey has a high school year book picture from Wilcox superimposed over it. Angela and I pass the hawkers and gawkers looking for the concession stand.

"Mom, do you think he'll sign my t-shirt for me?"

"Yes."

"And do you think he'll come by and say hi."

"I'm sure of it." A voice I surely didn't miss comes from behind us.

"Oh my goodness, Rabbit has finally decided to join the rest of the real world." Kerri's floor length fur coat and sunglasses are so over the top, I giggle into the collar of my bubble jacket. But none of it is as crazy as her hair weave. It's a long black wavy mess that stops at her butt. She puts her hand on her neck and pulls the hair to the front, knotting it.

"This hair is gettin' on my nerves. Whassup, gur-rulll?" She kisses me twice, once on each cheek. She looks me up and down.

"I know a nice Dominican shop on Fulton where you can get a little wash and set. It's only ten dollars on Wednesdays." I know a little Dominican shop, too, but there is nothing wrong with my ponytail. My own homegrown ponytail. Yall know I don't bother anybody unless they bother me.

"Stopped doin' the exercises, huh, KayKay?" She has the nerve to look hurt.

"That was rude, Rabbit. But more than a mouthful is too much." So says the President of the Itty Bitty Committee.

"Hi, Angel."

"Hi, Cousin Kerri." Angela stays at my side.

"Just as rude as your mother." She gives Angela both her cheeks to kiss. "Air kisses, baby girl. Don't wanna smudge Auntie's make-up." She smiles.

"Your mother and I grew up together. Just like sisters. Call me Auntie Kerri, Baby." I pinch the hell out of Angela and give her the I-wish-you-would look, topped off with a smile. She twists out of my reach and runs over to her cousins.

"Where's Aunt Say? I was looking forward to seeing her."

"Sorry Boo. She's still not feeling too well." She says that so smoothly, I almost believe her.

"Marquez and Marquise, bring your sister and come over here. The twins are nine years old, going on thirty. They think they're grown." One of the Mars's calls back.

"She don't wanna come with us. She wanna stay with Daddy." Kerri shoves her shades on top of her head.

"Honey! Bring the got-damn girl over here! Don't you see my family is here, you ass!" Honey looks like a guy I knew in school except he is twice the size of the guy I remember. When he gets closer, I realize I do know him.

"You remember Michael, right?" Mikey Long in the bloated flesh.

"No," I say. "I don't."

"He went to Wilcox, too."

"Wilcox. Riiiight," he says propping Merri up on his hip. She is the spitting image of Kerri: smooth brown skin, gorgeous lashes and a perfect weave ponytail.

"Hi, Merri." Merri looks past me, not even bothering to answer. Kerri slaps her leg so hard, her head whips around to scowl at Kerri, and her ponytail slaps Mikey in the face.

"The hell is wrong with you? Say hello."

"Hi," she mumbles without making eye contact. Even her attitude is cloned from Kerri's.

I look around for Angela. She's talking to Marquez, I think, while Marquise turns the diamond bezel on his watch.

"Anj, let's go find the concession stand." Kerri flips her weave.

"Guuuurl, with these seats, they bring food to you!"

"Okay. But I really have to use the bathroom," says Angela. She hooks her arm in mine and we escape.

"Mom, Marquez is nice, but the rest of them are a little bit loco. That means crazy in Spanish."

"Hon. They are crazy in every language." We walk all the way around the rotunda, stopping at the different stands to look at the Skyscraper T-shirts and key chains, until we make a complete circle.

"Baby, you didn't go to the bathroom." She grins at me.

"By the way, next time you don't have to pinch so hard." I pinch her again, this time with affection.

"Wait for me right here." I step into the stall and immediately take out my little silver friend. A shot warms my hands and steadies the shake a little. Everything is going to be alright.

"And nooooooow the all-star point guard for the New York Skyscrapers. Lucky number thir-teeeen. Hot Rod, Rodneeeeey Barrussssssss!" *Rahhhh!* Angela's eyes are huge with wonder. She's on the edge of her seat, clapping her hands in anticipation.

She has an innocence about her that I'm jealous of and grateful for at the same time.

"Go Cousin Rodney!" she hollers before she high-fives me. My mother gives me an I-told-you-so look.

"Whatever, Ma."

Unfortunately, the Skyscrapers suffer an embarrassing defeat at the hands of the all star point guard. Worse yet, the Sphinx are the weakest team on the planet. Unruly fans call them the sphincters. No one speaks and that's okay with me. Still, Angela darts back and forth between my parents and me, and Kerri and her family.

"I'm still proud of him, Mom." *Yeah, yeah.*

"That's good, Anj. Zip up." I check for my car keys.

"How you think Rodney would feel if he knew you left," asks my mother. I think he'd understand. "Just so selfish," she mutters, closing her red leather jacket which matches her red leather shoes.

Rodney struts down the ramp in a grey suit and mint green dress shirt; his caramel colored gators, placed one in front of the other in a confident swagger I'd never seen before. His face is set in a scowl. I keep my eyes on him. Looking for what? I don't know. When he sees me, his expression lightens. He kisses my parents, playing the role like usual. He jabs my dad's belly in a playful fight combination.

"Still eatin' them grits every mornin', Dub?"

"Heh, heh. Still smokin' em joints in your bedroom?"

"Not with random testing. But I do gets my E&J on and poppin'!" My father claps him on the back.

"Nothin' like some E&J." Tell me about it!

"Auntie Rho, you making fried chicken and macaroni this Sunday?"

"Only if you have a home game, Rodney Junior."

"Then it's gon' be on and poppin'!"

"Rabbit. Whassup, Baby Girl?!" He squeezes me in a bear hug. I want to throw up on his gators. Just *bleccch*...let it all out. He is so disgusting to me. It angers me that I still have ugly feelings for him. He lets go and steps back with this stupid grin on his face.

"It's been mad long, damn. You lookin' good. Hey, I want you to meet somebody. Britt. C'mere." A super slim, super young Hispanic girl in a coat like Kerri's walks over on Christian Louboutin heels that are so fierce I want to yank 'em off her feet Julie-style, and run.

"This is my fiancée, Brittany."

"How you doin' Tiffany," says my Dad.

"Brit-tany," she says through perfectly capped teeth. She's about twenty-two with big silicone breasts and collagen lips. Angela stays behind me, shy all of a sudden. Rodney taps Angela on her head.

"Did you like the game, even though we lost, Anj?"

"Well, yes, but, um...never mind." She looks at me.

"But what?" he asks. She stands at my side, a little more confident.

"But your jump shot was pretty weak. Maybe you should actually show up to practice." She and I high-five. I am tickled by her.

"Dang, she reminds me of you at that age, Rab." I pull Angela behind me.

"Um-hmm. That's my baby. Is everybody ready?" I ask my parents.

"It's a school night. We have to get Angela home."

"Awww, too bad," says Kerri. "Good night!" Rodney persists.

"But we usually go get something to eat and go back to the crib, Rabbit. Yall should come."

"Maybe next time. Good night, everyone," I say. Angela and I head back to the car. My mom mumbles to my father.

"I swear, if I didn't know better, I think she jealous of him!"

"I am *not* jealous of Rodney!" I shout.

"Rabbit, hold up. I got something for yall." Fuck! He is right behind us. My ears are burning. Angela starts forward, but I stop her in her tracks. He hands us a booklet of tickets each and then he opens up a Skyscrapers jersey and shows Angela his signature scribbled on the back in silver sharpie.

"In like five years, this shirt will be worth a few grand. We're about to be like the Shaq and Kobe Lakers. The Jordan Pippen Bulls. Three-peats, Baby."

"Thanks, Cousin Rodney! But I was watching Sports Center and they were saying your knees are really bad now…"

"Baby Girl, Hot Rod is a machine! Nothing can hold him back!"

"Okay…but you have to be realistic. You might win one, but three championships, I'm not so sure." Rodney cracks up.

"Like mother, like daughter! You sure yall don't wanna hang out with us?" The last time I saw Rodney was at Christmas Eve, some thirteen years ago. Everything he ever did to me remained a vile and vivid movie in my mind.

"Why're you looking at me like how your mother looked at us when we threw up the Halloween candy she told us not to eat?"

"No reason. Would love to hang, but Angel's got school in the morning. As it is, she gives me a hard time to get out of the bed."

"Well, maybe next time." He spins on his heel and bops back to his family.

"Don't know why you treat that boy the way you do," mumbles his cheerleader. "He been nothin' but kind to you. People would kill to be that close to greatness." I ignore her all the way home, even though she sighs for the rest of the trip. When I let her ass out in front of her house, I breathe a sigh of relief. I've made it without putting her out on the side of the road.

"I'm gonna pray for you, Adrienne," she says.

"Thank you."

AS IF I DIDN'T HAVE ENOUGH to worry about, *The Cork*, our campus newspaper was reporting slashes in jobs and budget cuts across the board.

"Don't get all worked up, Adrienne. It's probably just a rumor."

"All rumors have a little truth to them, Ma. So if it says no job is safe I have to wonder how I'm going to get my half of Angela's tuition together."

"I would just talk to Rodney about it. You know he'll help ya out if it ever came to that."

"I see you've been sippin' with Daddy."

"Well that's what he tell me and your Daddy. Hell, he helped us fix the roof last winter. Said he ain't want it back or nothing."

"You didn't tell me something was wrong with your roof."

"It got fixed so fast, it was like if there wasn't nothing wrong with it in the first place. Once Rodney made the call, they was here in no time. Adrienne, he would help you if you asked. He don't hold no grudges against you no more."

"Grudges against me? He told you he had a grudge against me?"

"If he did I couldn't tell you. But you know yall ain't always get along."

"So you're saying he did tell you."

"I'm not saying he did. I'm just saying you know the rules."

"But why would you say that? If he hadn't said anything, you wouldn't have said he don't hold no grudges no more!"

"I ain't up for all this dissecting. He don't have no grudge against you. That's all."

"So he told you he doesn't have a grudge against me? How would you know if he does or he doesn't?" *Click*. I sit at my kitchen table sipping. I grab my phone. But I don't have anyone to call. I mean, there's Stacey, but where would I start? I bring the bottle closer.

"Well my friend. It's just you and me tonight."

"Mom. Come on. You have to go in your bed." The living room is blurry and spinning. My glass is tipped sideways and there's a dark spot in the carpet.

"I made a mess."

"Yes Mom. Come on." She grabs me around the waist, holding me upright.

"I'm sorry. You're not gonna hold a grudge against your Mommy, right?"

"No." She lets me fall onto the bed.

"Lift your legs." She pulled my covers over my legs and up to my neck.

"You sure you don't have a grudge against me?"

"I'm sure. Nobody has a grudge against you, Mom. We love you." I start to cry.

"You love me?"

"Yes. You're the best." She wipes my tears. "No more grudge talk. It's time to go to sleep."

Dean Paris's door is slightly ajar. Even though I knock, he is looking off into space, the way I often do when no one was watching. Instead of barging in, I step back to give him a chance to put on his game face.

"Dean Paris?"

"Come in!" he calls. He shifts the papers in front of him and places his folded hands in the cleared space of his massive cherrywood desk. "What's the trouble, Adrienne?"

"No trouble, Sir. Kennedy mentioned to me that you and David were huge Mystery fans. I was able to pull some strings for tonight's game."

"Courtside seats?! That's awesome!" He leans back studying the tickets. Then his eyebrows meet and his demeanor turns pensive. "Even though David has made it clear this summer, that he would much rather watch paint dry than watch sports."

"Really?" I am genuinely surprised. David was one of those paint-your-face-the-team-colors, kind of guys.

"Yes. How can I put this? Um, it turns out he's not a man's man."

"Ohhh-kay." The Dean taps a silver gilded pen on the desk.

"Apparently, he's been faking it all these years, pretending to like basketball and hockey just to keep the peace. My wife and I had no idea he was gay. Aren't parents supposed to know what's going on?"

"I always thought so, Sir."

"But why didn't he just tell us?" It's surprisingly easy to say the words to him that I hadn't said out loud to anyone.

"Maybe he thought you'd hate him for breaking up the family or for not being who he thought you wanted him to be."

He seems to mull it over before he places his clasped hands in the empty spot on his desk blotter.

"Well, um, that was awkward and embarrassing, huh, Adrienne?"

"Eh, don't worry about it."

"Well, um, thanks for listening. And for the tickets."

"Don't mention it."

"Oh. And Adrienne?"

"Yes, Sir?"

"Your name wasn't on the chopping block." I smile bashfully, closing the door behind me, satisfied that I had killed one of my two birds.

Kennedy waltzes into my office and sits on the edge of my desk, never once acknowledging Stacey who is taking a letter. She files her nails, dropping fine white dust on my desk.

"I didn't get the tickets, Lucas. The Mystery's playing tonight."

"I left them with the Dean."

"Why would you do that?" she asks, like I'm an idiot.

"Didn't you say they were for the Dean and his son?"

"I didn't say the Dean. You're mistaken."

"Clearly." My phone buzzes.

"Adrienne, is Kennedy in with you?" I put my hand over the speakerphone.

"Speak of the devil."

"Kennedy, cancel my dinner with the wife. I'm going to the game with the mayor."

"Yes, sir." She storms out, snatching a pack of cigarettes off Lori Ann's desk. She punches the elevator buttons repeatedly until the doors finally open. The minute the doors close, laughter squeals through my office.

"That was *sahweet*! You really handled her!'

"Shoot, I'm from Brooklyn, girl! She better recognize!" We bend over laughing. Stacey picks up the buzzing telephone.

"Adrienne Lucas's office. I'm sorry, she's in a meeting. Can I take a message?" She scribbles the number eight on a post-it note, giggling like a schoolgirl.

"Good luck tonight!" She squeals with delight before she hangs up. "Oh my God, even his voice is foine!"

"Why won't you take his calls? He seems so cool." Stacey is my friend, I decide once and for all.

"Let's just say Rodney and I had some serious issues growing up."

"Aydree, we're grown up now. You either have to hash it out or let sleeping dogs lie. If you hold on to it, it's just going to take over your life. Besides, maybe he wants to apologize or something." As soon as my hands get clammy, I hold them up to end the discussion.

"Here we go again." Stacey sighs and leaves my office. I buzz her.

"What does this eight mean?"

"Number of times he's called so far." She turns her intercom off. I hear the elevator doors ding and I know she's left the office. I wonder what the hell Rodney wants. Calling someone eight times is excessive. But then I wonder if it has something to do with Aunt Say. I call the number on the post it.

> *Rodney James Barrus the Second at your service. If I know you, I'll call you back. If I don't, my people will.*

I hang up without leaving a message and crunch the post it note into a tiny ball. If it is an emergency, my mother will let me know, I'm sure. I grab my coat and scarf since getting out of the office seems to be the thing to do.

I take the long way around the campus, down the back pathway, past the Law Library. There aren't too many students hanging out in the frozen tundra. Everyone seems to be hustling to get inside, but there is that one white boy in a sweatshirt, shorts, and a baseball cap walking toward the Student Center with no urgency in his stride whatsoever.

I don't know why I don't do this more often. Even though it's brisk out, my head is clear and I am captivated by the sky's clarity. It is a silky shade of blue with one clump of gauzy cotton complementing its beauty; similar to the

9/11 sky before the planes attacked. If Tanisha were here she'd ask why I couldn't just relish the beauty of the day. I want to. I really do. I can't see any reason not to.

I sit on the brick wall at the edge of the campus, swinging my feet like a little girl. I can't see the defiant winter birds, but I can hear them chirping from their nest that is tucked between the stark limbs of the oak tree. It feels good, this relishing thing. Or as Stacey would say, *sahweet!* Maybe she was right, too. Maybe I should just let sleeping dogs lie. It's not like I had to see Rodney more than once or twice a year. Right? The cold settles into my bones and it's time to get back upstairs. On my way back to the building, I realize the balled up post-it note is still in my hand. I flick it off the tip of my finger.

Stacey is flying back and forth with her bangs flapping like crazy. Lori Ann is actually sitting at her desk for a change. Rumor has it, her normal seat is underneath Dean Paris's desk. Telling secrets is a sin, but that is no secret around here. She's on the telephone whispering excitedly. Kennedy comes out of my office sporting a huge smile.

"Oh, you're back," she coos.

"What were you doing in my office?"

"You have a guest." A guest? I walk past her wondering who could be here unannounced. The King of New York is sitting at my desk.

"Hey Girl! What up?" Kennedy is still squealing in the corner.

"I can't believe it's him!" I shut the door.

Rodney comes out from behind the desk with his arms outstretched. I dodge the hug with a quick slap on the back.

"Heeey," I say.

"I see you got my flowers!" Fuck. Fuck. Fuck!

"Yeah. Thank you."

"They came all the way from Hawaii."

We both remain standing in front of my window. He is intimidating in my little office. I take a step back, hopefully in a way that does not convey fear. But I can feel the sweat rushing to my pores. I don't take my eyes off him. I am struck by how put together he is. He has on a navy Armani suit with a crisp white dress shirt and Gucci loafers. His watch, a platinum Rolex, sparkles, as does his championship ring from last year. Life has been good to him.

"What are you doing here?"

"Well, you wouldn't talk to me. Haven't in a few years." If he fanned his hand in front of my face, I wouldn't have blinked.

"I, um. I came here to apologize." Wow. Just like Stacey said. I would have liked to have hashed it out in a more private place, but I am ninety nine point nine infinitum percent sure that I will never be alone and within ten feet of Rodney ever again.

"Apologize for what?" Angela's picture smiles at me. My Angel Cakes.

"It's been a long time," he says, "but not that long." My eyes snap up to his. Then they narrow a la Rhona Fuller. He looks away.

"Okay, okay. I'm sayin'. I'm sorry for taking advantage of you."

"No." I cross my arms over my breasts. "Be sorry for raping me." His eyes are the size of golf balls.

"I'm not saying that!" I'm breathing hard now. I don't want to lose control in the office.

"Please leave."

"You can't just throw me out. I'm apologizing!"

"No. You're minimizing the situation to make yourself feel better about being a rapist." My words are harsh, even to my own ears.

"You're buggin'!"

"Get out! Get the fuck out! Security!" Stacey busts into the room.

"Mr. Barrus, you're going to have to leave." He throws his hands in the air, walking backwards to the door.

"I don't even know what happened. She just started trippin'." Before I can even think, I throw the vase at him. It shatters against the side wall and showers him with water and orchids.

"Security! Security!" He single-handedly ruined my teenage experience and all of a sudden, he doesn't know what happened.

"You're crazy just like your mother!" He storms out of my office.

"And you're fucked up just like your father!" Everyone is looking at me. Stacey. Lori Ann. Dean Paris. Kennedy. The lookie-loos from across the hall that are pretending to have some business in our office. Kennedy plucks tissue from Lori Ann's desk and runs after Rodney. I am embarrassed at being made into a public spectacle, but I am angry that he has turned my job into his stage. All sleeping dogs lying about these parts are about to be awakened.

ଔ

RODNEY'S GALL SHOULDN'T HAVE surprised me at all, but sitting on the FDR Drive in bumper-to-bumper traffic, I still can't get over the fact that he had the nerve to come to my job with a half-ass apology. I find my old DMX CD in the glove compartment. The volume is so high the bass line feels like it could be my own heartbeat. It is unfortunate for the man that cuts me off, that this is my theme music. The way I curse him out is the equivalent of an ass whipping.

When I pull up in front of my house, there's an unfamiliar car, parked in my driveway. This is the wrong day to play, but no one seems to have gotten the memo. I fish around in my junkyard pocketbook for my cell phone. Someone is heading to the pound to-mother-fuckin-night. Except, I can't find the damn phone. I can't find my keys either. This is so not me. It's scary. Angela comes to the door with a huge goofy grin on her face. It's contagious.

"What are you so happy about?" I ask, grinning back.

"We have a visitor!" My smile dissipates and angry girl returns. I come through the front hallway ready for war. I put my spear and shield down.

"Terrell. How've you been?" Terrell gets up from the love seat and places both hands on my shoulders.

"I've been well, Adrienne. How about you?"

"Honestly, I've been better." I turn to the woman sitting next to him. A plain looking light skinned woman with a pleasant face.

"Hello," I say. Terrell's voice is strained.

"This is my wife, Patricia." Patricia remains seated.

"A pleasure," she responds.

I am surprised. In our brief conversations, Terrell has never even mentioned Patricia. Angela must not have known either because she stares at Patricia with her mouth slightly open. Guaranteed she'll be able to tell me what color socks Patricia had on.

"Can I offer you something to drink?"

"No, no. I'm okay," says Terrell.

"Patricia?"

"No thanks, Sweetie." I tense at her familiarity with me. Today is not the day for cuteness from new wives visiting my home unannounced. I feel the Brooklynian tendency surfacing for the third time in a day, but I hold it in check. Maybe she's just being nice.

"Terrell. Is that your car in the driveway?" Patricia leans forward.

"Sorry, Sweetie. We didn't think you'd mind."

"It's not a problem, *Sweetie.*" Patricia smirks and I know that she is indeed being facetious.

"What brings you two over?"

"I wanted to talk to you about our arrangements." The last time anyone discussed arrangements in my presence, there were flying vases and curse words in the air.

"Right now, I get to see Angela for a few hours every other weekend. But I feel--" Patricia taps his hand. "*We* feel we should be able to have more visits. Maybe sometimes for a weekend or so." Angela claps her hands with glee.

"Mommy, that would be so coo-ull. Can I?"

"This is so sudden, Terrell. You could have at least given me some time to think on it. Angela has a routine that keeps her on top of her school work and chores."

"To hell with the school work and chores, Adrienne."

"Now you're playing yourself."

"Don't you realize the two of us are being cheated out of a real relationship?"

"Yes. And don't forget about Angela, Rell," says Chief Haventaclue.

"You never said you wanted weekends. You didn't say anything. Now you wanna come up here, and get fly without giving me a chance."

"I've been walking on eggshells with you because I know how daggone sensitive you get about the baby."

"But now you think you should just spring it on me?!"

"Adrienne. I don't want to fight with you." He stands, pulling an envelope from his back pocket. I open it and two words jumped off the page. Joint. Custody. Everything is spiraling out of control.

"I didn't stick it to you on the divorce, but this time, I will fight you." Patricia links her arm in his. A united front. Yeah, whatever. I open the front door for them.

"Oh no, she didn't," said Patricia.

"Oh yes, she did. And she's being nice because her daughter is here, but that's not gonna last much longer. C'mon now. Put some pep in it, Sweetie." I slam the door behind them.

"You always try to keep me from Daddy! You mess up everything!" screams Angela. "I hate you!" She storms off to her room. Boom! The door slams. I am exhausted. And suddenly starving. I peel the Spanx down to below my pooch and sit at the kitchen table picking cold candied yams out of last night's leftovers.

Angela is mad at me. Terrell is mad at me. My mother is mad because Rodney told her that he came to see me at work and I embarrassed him. I should have had a banner made up so they could have a got-damn Get Mad at Adrienne parade. I go to the cabinet and realize I'm all out of drink. I slam my own bedroom door. I don't need this shit.

I'm disappointed when I listen to my messages in the morning. Stacey is under the weather and not coming in. I really need her pep in my life. And her ear. To see if maybe she thought I was being unreasonable. I'm also disappointed because Lori Ann the temp is still sitting at the front desk filing her nails like she doesn't have a stack of files on her desk to put away. I check my top drawer, but LaCandria's file is missing.

My intercom buzzes. "Adrienne. Your breakfast is here."

At the front desk, Lori Ann fishes through her brown paper bag.

"Do I have any messages, Lori Ann?"

"Not that I know of. That one's yours," she says pointing to the bag with the grease at the bottom. I am so excited.

I peel the wrapper off the sexiest thing I've seen on my desk since Terrell and I called it quits: scrambled eggs with cheese on toast. Stacey would never let me order that. Egg whites know nothing about consoling the blues.

All day, I run around like a chicken with my head cut off. The end of the semester is an administrative nightmare.

By the end of the day, my nerves are frazzled. If I cared to drink in the company of others, I would have gone down the block to Bottoms Up and gotten twisted. But the more I think about it, the more I realize that what I really need doesn't come in a bottle. I turn on my cell phone. I have five new messages that I decide not to listen to. Instead I call a new old friend.

"Corey, it's Adrienne. What's up?"

"Adrienne. How you doin', Babe?" Babe. He called me Babe! Man. If I were the swooning type, I would have.

"Good. You busy later?"

"Why? You wanted to see me?"

"Yeah. I guess I do." I giggle like I'm thirteen again.

"Okay. Well I'm on a bus route right now. But I'll be off at eight."

When I emerge from my office, the reception area is dim and Lori Ann is gone. I didn't realize it was after eight o'clock. There are five messages from my mother in the inbox. I crinkle them up and drop them in the garbage. I just want to go home, hug my daughter and soak in my bathtub until Corey gets to my house. In that order. There are a stack of messages in Kennedy's mailbox, too. As I snoop, I realize some of them are addressed to me. Those heifers! Two are from LaCandria. I copy her number down and put Kennedy's messages back where I found them. I dial her number from inside the elevator.

"LaCandria? It's Adrienne Lucas at New York College. Have you reconsidered taking the position?"

"I am sorry, Adrienne, but I can not take nineteen thousand a year. Not even to get in the door."

"It pays twenty-nine a year."

"Oh. That's a huge difference." She exhales. "But this doesn't seem like the right move. There's too much strife going on up in there. I am still going to have to pass on the position. But thank you for considering me, Adrienne. Good luck up there, Girl."

I stop at the newsstand on my way to the subway, furious at the bullshit. I need a fix. My girl Halle is on the cover of *OK!* looking fabuloso. I snatch up a copy. I notice the devil is on the front page of the *Daily News* this time. I turn back to the magazines. He is the last person I want to concern myself with. But the caption jumps off the page at me.

Instantly, I think of Kennedy and her trifling, eavesdropping ass. Or was it Stacey that overheard our conversation? After all, she came into the room the minute I was throwing Rodney out and on top of that, she's out sick, coincidentally, on the same day that the story breaks. Where the hell is my phone?

This is Stacey. Let me know something good!

"All my life I've been stabbed in the back. And just when I start letting my guard down, you go and sell me out. I'll give you a good reference, but you need to look for a new position immediately."

You've reached Kennedy Rockford, Assistant Director of Human Resources at New York College.

"Kennedy. This is Adrienne. Please put up a posting for a new assistant on the job boards." I am sick and tired of shit falling apart around me.

I pick up the newspaper. This time, Rodney's killer smile is gone and he sits on the bench scowling after a loss.

Rape Allegations Strike Lightning Rod.

When I open to page three, my head gets fuzzy. The alleged victim is a fifteen-year old Los Angeles girl who happened to be in Houston, his old stomping grounds. His teammates proclaim his innocence, as do Big Rodney and my mother. I whip out my phone again realizing I missed something in my haste. I dial into my voicemail.

You have eight new messages.

Baby. It's your mother. Family meeting tonight. It's an emergency.

Family meeting, my ass. The hell with the family. I call Stacey back. She is the only friend I have and I've probably ruined it.

This is Stacey. Let me know something good!

"Stace, um---" *The voice mailbox you are trying to reach is full. Please try your call again later.* Great. Just fabulous.

ANGELA IS STANDING GUARD at our front door when I get home.

"Grandma said not to let you take your coat off."

"Let me just get something to drink."

"She said come over the minute you get here, and I don't want Grandma to be mad at me."

"It's just a drink. It will be fast." Angela folds her arms over her chest.

"You don't have anything to drink."

"What do you mean I don't have anything to drink! I just bought a new bottle!" I push past her into the house. My cabinet is stark naked.

"I'm gonna take that shit right out of your allowance."

"Fine. Whatever Mom. Grandma's waiting."

Rodney's shiny black Escalade is parked in front of my mother's house. The only reason I don't kick a dent in the door is because Angela is with me. The window shades in the house next door shift to the side. I wave. The hand has the nerve to wave back.

Before I get to the top step, he opens the door, the devil does.

"Angel Cakes!" he says with a big smile.

"Hi, Cousin Rodney." She follows closely behind me.

"Rabbit. What's up?"

"Adrienne," I say. Kerri peeks out from behind Rodney.

"Oh Rabbit, you're here. Good. Now we can get started. Daddy, come in here. Bring *mommy*." The word sounds alien on her tongue. Her eyes say the same.

"Don't nobody gotta bring me nowhere. Back up, Rodney Senior. Back on up." Big Rodney pulls his right suspender. Apparently, no one's going to tell him the damn things aren't coming back in style.

Aunt Say pulls her wheelchair into the dining room right next to me. When I bend to kiss her drumstick cheek, she holds my face.

"Baby, I ain't seen you in a month-a-Sundays." I look at my feet. Big Rodney comes up on Aunt Say's other side, whispering, but not low enough.

"Sadie, you still mean as all hell and thas why you still in that wheelchair."

"If I start talking 'bout me and this wheelchair, we gon' set something else rollin' other than these here charges. Now git out my face." He catches me staring at him.

"All in grown folks business, ain't ya, Lite Brite."

"Still a big ass freeloading joke, ain't ya, Rerun."

"Haaaaa! Ooh, no she didn't," crows Aunt Say. Big Rodney slides away from us to lick his greasy chops on the other side of the dining room. Kerri raps her knuckles on the dining room table.

"Alright now. Settle down everyone. Marquez, let that damn dog down and come over here. Marquise, I'm gonna take that watch away if you don't quit." Her weave is in two jet black Pocahontas braids down the front of her too tight Dolce and Gabbana t-shirt. The braids look like Big Rodney's suspenders. Kerri has no idea how much amusement she is bringing me for once in her life. She bangs on the table, this time with the flat of her hand.

"This ain't a court room, Kerri. Don't bang on my table again."

"It ain't nothin', Auntie Rho."

"It is something. Don't do that again." Kerri rolls her eyes.

"Anyway. We are all aware of the allegations surrounding Rodney and we must, we absolutely must band together." She looks at me.

"Now during this time if anyone is approached by the press, the proper response is 'no comment'. Nothing more, nothing less. In the meantime, we have to rally around Roddy and be his support system. You have anything you want to add?" Rodney steps forward looking stupid in the face. Or maybe it's just me.

"All I want to do is thank all of you for supporting me over the years. I appreciate it and I love yall."

"So did you do it, Cousin Rodney?" asks the light of my life. Caught off guard, his eyebrows shoot upwards.

"Of course not!" snaps Kerri. "What the hell kinda question is that?"

"I wanted to know. I'm sorry, Cousin Rodney."

"Ain't nothin' wrong with the girl asking questions," says Aunt Say. "Don't be sorry, Baby."

"She's a hater," says Marquise. "That's what my mom says."

"I am not a hater. You're a hater. You're a stupid hater." She sure didn't get her comeback skills from me.

"Alright now. Enough," I say. "I think that at a time like this we need to have a little bit of prayer flowing through here. So let's bow our heads." Big Rodney pops his suspender.

"Lite Brite done went and got saved?"

"Hmph. Woulda done her some good," mumbles Kerri.

"I *said* let's bow our heads, got-dammit." I look around the room at all the faces. Rodney is staring at me. I've never done this before, but it feels like the right thing to do. I bow my head and begin to thank Him for His grace and mercy. A loud 'amen' comes from Big Rodney's corner of the room. I pause. My mother touches my elbow silently prodding me to continue.

"God watch over us all during these trying times."

"Ay-ay-men!" He shouts.

"Rodney. Can you please let the child get through the prayer?"

"You can't tell me how to praise my God, Say. Go' head, Lite Brite." Woo-weee! The devil in me yearns to curse the predatory sperm of my grandfather for hunting down my grandma's unsuspecting egg.

"We pray Lord, that the evil is rooted out at the core and all the lies and untruths are exposed, Lord. In your name, we pray a special and urgent prayer. Amen."

This time Lil' Rodney amen's the loudest. Kerri throws in a 'thank you Jesus'. I look into Lil' Rodney's face, certain I will see mockery, but for the first time I see a trace of remorse. Then it's gone.

"I'm starvin' like Marvin in a vegetable garden. Chung Chan Kitchen for everybody!"

"Rodney Junior, you one of a kind," says my mom, his biggest cheerleader.

"It's the least I can do. Besides, there's no other Chinese food like Brooklyn Chinese food," he proclaims. Kerri, of course, co-signs.

I sit next to Aunt Say and catch her up on Angela's progress in school and my accomplishment at making Director even though I know she already knows. Big Rodney straightens her wheelchair against the side of the love seat.

"Big Rodney, you need something?" she asks. He shakes his head, retreating over to Kerri and Rodney on the leather sofa.

"Where's my girl, Juicie?" I ask. She shakes her head.

"She's not talking to me." It seems to pain her.

"Uh oh. You steal her boyfriend?" She shakes her head, again. This time, she closes her eyes. I want to ask her so many questions and I think she'll tell me. But Big Rodney hovers again, this time picking off her plate. I leave her to deal with him.

My mother loads the dishwasher gingerly, holding the small of her back. When she hears my footsteps on the tile, she snaps upright in a way that's got to hurt. I take my coat off.

"I think Aunt Say's calling you."

"Alright then. Let me go see what that old heifer wants." Kerri comes into the kitchen, Pocahontas braids hanging down her back now.

"Girl, I didn't know you were so spiritual!"

"Lots you don't know about me, Kerri." I continue to load the dishes.

"Not really."

"What the hell do you want?"

"Rabbit." I shoot her a look.

"Adrienne. Sorry. I forget sometimes."

"What. Do. You. Want?"

"Dang. So hostile. I just came to say I'm glad you and Rodney made peace. I miss how we used to be."

I can't really remember a time after they moved in when I didn't hate them. I mean there were those summer months when she and I exchanged clothes and gossiped until the dark hours of the night. Or the time we threw Halloween eggs at Miss Lewis's door and ran. And then she came out and caught us hiding in the driveway and made us scrub the door, all her brickwork and her front walkway. And we couldn't stop laughing because her dentures kept slipping forward when she yelled at us. No. After that everything was downhill.

"I'm glad you could forgive him and move on."

"I beg your pardon?"

"I'm glad you forgave him for what he did."

"Rodney told you what he did to me?"

"Yeah."

"And you didn't think anything was wrong with that?"

"No. He said you were out of control."

"Wait. What are we talking about here?"

"He said you were too boy crazy and called your mom and dad anonymously. It was for your own good." The glass I'm holding slips out of my hand. Kerri bends to pick up the large pieces.

"As a team, the family can be that much stronger." She pats me on the back. "Let me go to get the kids ready." She leans into the kitchen again.

"Take care, Adrienne. And remember, no comment is the only answer. Okay Cuz?" The light bulb finally comes on and I'm sick about it. After all these years, they are still working our family. When the magnets on the fridge go out of focus, that's when I realize I'm crying.

I sit in my bed with my head tie hanging down the front of my face like rabbit ears, googling every article I can find about this whole horrible fiasco. From what I can gather, the girl alleges that she and her family were staying at the Hotel Montero in the Galleria section of Houston for a family reunion, which had also been the same place the Western Conference Championships party was held. I'm googling Rodney. I'm googling the Hotel. I'm googling everything I can think of. I hit a link at the bottom, randomly because I'm hoping to find something I haven't already seen. It's a gossip blog where people post their amateur pictures of celebrities. There's a picture of Rodney sleeping on a flight from LA. That piques my interest. Who in the world could have gotten close enough with the rest of the team around? The phone jolts me. And who in the world could be calling me past midnight?

"You stood me up, Adrienne. I won't do this with you again."

"Corey. We need to talk."

CR

COREY SITS ON MY SOFA with his feet planted firmly on the floor. His broad shoulders jut out and his hands are clasped tightly in front of him. I sit in the loveseat opposite him, with my legs folded under me, waiting for him to say something, anything.

"You mean to tell me," he starts. "And more than once?" I nod.

"And you didn't tell anyone?" I shake my head no.

"You're the first person I've told." I kind of expect him to ask why I decided to tell him, but he doesn't. I'm glad. Because I do not really know the answer myself.

"So in a way you let it happen." I am erect in the chair.

"How the hell do you figure that?"

"You coulda gone to your mother!"

"That's exactly the kind of reaction that kept me from telling. Because somehow I must have asked for it, deserved it, or let it happen. Do you remember what it was like to be in school with Rodney?"

"It was a phenomenon. Everybody loved him. They still do."

"So imagine living with him. Who would take my word over his?"

"But that was your mother. You could have said something."

"No one ever puts themselves in the position of what if it happened to me. And if they do, they convince themselves that they would have done it differently, and somehow they would have come out on top. Tell me, Corey. If your daughter came to you--"

"I would kill the mother fucker that touched my daughter."

"Yeah. But since it's not your daughter, you can't see how it could have happened?"

"My daughter knows she could come to me about anything."

"I didn't tell my mother because in her own way, she told me not to."

He didn't ask me to explain and I didn't volunteer. But the things that made her special were the things that kept me from confiding in her.

"I still think my daughter would tell me."

"Not if you don't let her know that there is room for mistakes and bad judgment calls. Not if you don't acknowledge your own mistakes along the way." I hand him his hat. "Not if you present yourself as this perfect person she can't relate to."

"Are you going to tell your daughter?" I shake my head.

"Why not? I don't think you want her to hear it somewhere else."

"Because she is a child and this is none of her business. I'm only telling you because---" I stop in my tracks.

"I'm only telling you because you needed to know it wasn't anything you did." He drops his eyes.

"Can I call you in the morning?" he asks. I grab his hand. I feel like the old Adrienne that needs someone, anyone, to hold her and make her feel like she is special. I feel like Rabbit.

"You could just stay and hold me." Corey opens the front door. There's a thump behind me. It sounds like it's coming from somewhere in the dining room, but I don't see anything...or anyone.

"I'll call you," he says. "I will call you." My heart's being squeezed in an invisible fist. He walks down the stairs with his hat in his hand.

It hurts more than I thought it would, this coming clean stuff. It is highly overrated.

I stand at Angela's door, watching her get ready for bed. She tucks her braids under her satin cap. I hate how she won't look at me.

"I feel like a broken record asking you the same question more than once. How much did you hear?" I sit at the foot of her bed.

"I'm not leaving until we discuss this." She lets loose one of her long braids and begins twirling it around her pointer finger the way she does when she is nervous. Her voice is a low and unrecognizable mumble.

"I heard from when Cousin Rodney first came upstairs and that he kept on..." The Chris Brown posters on her wall have her undivided attention.

"I'm embarrassed, too."

"Well, how come you let him? That doesn't make any sense."

"I didn't let him. Rodney was very strong, Angel. I don't know how to make you understand it, but it was wrong. And I was wrong for keeping it a secret for all these years."

"But if you told you woulda been a snitch. Tommy Slowinsky at school…he told that John Burke stole the money from our class treasury and nobody liked him anymore."

"Guess what? I didn't tell and no one liked me anyway. And now it has happened to someone else."

"Are you going to tell now?"

"Do you think I should?" She shrugs but she still won't look at me.

"Tell me what you would do." Now she looks at me like I'm crazy.

"I'm not crazy," I shout. I grab her arms.

"Tell me, Angela! What would you do?" Tears well in her eyes.

"I don't know! You're hurting me!" She tries to pull away, but I won't let go. I can't.

"Mom, please let go. You're hurting me," she cries. I fling her arm away and slam out of her room, hurt that even my own daughter blames me.

I can hear her sobs on the other side of the door. Frankly, I don't care.

I TOSS AND TURN all night, until I can't take it anymore. I am tired as hell, but I can't get settled. I sit on the floor with my back to the dresser, crunching the new peach carpet between my toes.

I don't want to cry. I don't want to yell. I don't want to break the furniture. I just want peace. I just want to bury my old demons and walk in light again. I'm not even sure I know how. I open my closet and pull out a pair of jeans and a sweatshirt. When I close the button on the jeans, I climb into the bed where I fade away.

Somehow, Rodney is standing at my window. He keeps tapping on the glass and every time I look his way, he disappears. Tap, disappear. Tap, disappear. And then he smashes his face into the glass, distorting his nose and mouth. I can't see his face anymore. I keep spinning around and around to the beat of this crazy beeping sound. *Ekk, ekk, ekk, ekk, ekk!*

My first instinct when the alarm goes off is to run down to Angela's room to make sure she's okay. She's sitting on her bed working diligently on a Sudoku puzzle.

"Don't you think you should get up and start getting ready for school?"

"Mommy? Is it because of what happened to you with Cousin Rodney, why you won't let me stay over with Daddy?" She twirls her braids again. I start to deny it, you know, smooth it over. But I don't think at this point, I have anything else to lose. Above all, I trust that she can handle it.

"Yes."

"Then I think you should let Daddy know what happened. Because I think you really hurt his feelings." I watch her walk to the bathroom, thinking that somewhere along the line she probably sapped up all the common sense I should have had. She leans out of the bathroom door. Her voice shakes.

"I'm sorry I blamed you." I swallow the lump lodged in my throat.

"Go get dressed."

I call Dean Paris to let him know I won't be in and then I call Kennedy to cancel my request for a new assistant, but I get her voicemail. I call a number I've been calling for two days straight. Finally, the voicemail picks up.

"Stacey, it's me. That was a complete misunderstanding. Give me a call when you feel up to it, so I can explain what's going on."

At Angela's advice, I take the day off from work and go to Terrell's job. The morning sky is bright and sparkly. I'm swaddled in a heavy wool coat and chunky scarf, but I feel lighter than I've felt in years. Walking down Sixth Avenue, I smile at everyone. Surprisingly, some smile back. They probably think I'm crazy, but I don't care. My daughter is on my side.

The receptionist buzzes me through the glass doors. Sherman, Lark & Lucas is stenciled in gold. The reception area is wood paneled and a fresh vase of yellow tulips is sitting pretty. Terrell has come a long way from McDonald's and the construction company.

"I'm here to see Mr. Lucas." Esther, his long time secretary comes out of a side door with her arms extended. Her tweed suit is fabulous.

"Mrs. Lucas, the first." I hug her

"How are you, Esther?"

"Still kicking up the dirt. How's Little Miss Angela?"

"Wiser than ever. Is Terrell in?" I follow her through a frosty set of doors into the privacy of the back offices. Pretty swanky for a country boy. I am so proud of Terrell. I am bursting to tell him so. Esther buzzes him on the intercom.

"Mr. Lucas. Your wife is here."

"That's impossible, Esther."

"The first wife." He comes to the door. His eyebrows are joined together. He closes the door behind us and turns the door shades downward.

"Before you say anything, I have to tell you that the allegations against Rodney are making Patricia and me leery. That environment can't be good for the baby. We're thinking of filing for full custody."

"For full custody of whom?" I look up over my glasses.

"Of Angela. Who else?"

"Have you lost your mind? Or have you let Patricia lose it for you?!"

"You need to keep it down."

"Keep shit down! I'd like to see you try and get my baby!"

"Adrienne, this is a place of business!"

"Shee-it! You and Patricia. Like that's supposed to scare some damn body! Boy, I'm from Brooklyn. And in the words of Beyonce, *you must not know bout me!*"

"Adrienne. It's times like this that I don't regret the divorce for one minute."

I slam out of his office and out of the office building where I hail a yellow cab.

"I'm going to Flatbush."

"Oh no. This cab does not go to Brooklyn." I read the driver's ID on the back of the partition.

"Fahid. Let's go to Brooklyn so I don't have to call your boss. And I don't want to call your boss. Because that can mean a whole lot of problems. Problems that we can avoid if you just take me where I want to go!"

"What is the fast-fast way?"

"FDR Drive. Brooklyn Bridge."

I sink into the back seat and watch the looming grey skyscrapers of Seventh Avenue zoom past. Superman could leap tall buildings in a single bound. I'd be able to leap tall buildings, too. If only I had answers to the questions that held me down. I tap on the partition.

"Change of plans, Fahid."

"Whatever you want, Miss. Whatever you want."

THE YELLOW CAB COASTS down Surf Avenue, past The Cyclone and Nathan's. In the winter, you wouldn't believe that this beat down park brings so many people out during the steamy summer months of Brooklyn; Angela and me included. Angela especially loved the Cyclone. I didn't love it so much because it was around when *I* was a little girl. As a matter of fact, I lost my keys and wallet on the Cyclone on a day when I was cutting classes with one of my boyfriends.

My mom answered with a towel wrapped around her head.

"Where the hell are your keys?"

"I lost them at school."

"How could you be so careless? Come in this damn house."

We sat at the dinner table in silence. She was pissed and slamming the cookware. Her latest job had let her go because she complained about a pay cut. She had simmered down to a low boil, until my father told her to chill, which made her bubble over again.

"I ain't chillin'. I'm hot as all hell right now. Got-damn Puerto Rocks and Jamaicans come over here and work for pennies. So when you ax for the whole dime you supposed to get insteada the nickel they tryna give you, you ain't got nothin' to stand on." The phone rang and she got up from the table.

"Thank the Lord," said my Dad. "Maybe Sadie got some gossip for her. Calm her ass down a little bit."

"Lost and found, you said?" My mother's voice was high-pitched and squeaky. "Umhmm. Umhmm. Thank you, Sir. I 'preciate it."

"Sounds like you got good news," said my Dad. My mother didn't answer.

She sat down and folded her napkin over her lap like we were at a restaurant.

"Dub," she said. "We been raising a liar." I was cold busted and so uncool about it.

"Somebody must have stolen them out of my locker." My mother jumped up from her seat and started slapping me. One of my gold shell earrings flew across the room.

"Empty your pockets."

"For what?" She slapped me again and again and tried to drag me out of the chair. I pushed her off me and jumped to my feet. My mother's eyes widened at the contents on the table, least of all the two red carnival tickets.

"Where you get all that money?"

"Definitely not from you!" I shouted. I waited for her to lunge at me, but she turned her head.

"I don't even know who the hell you are now. I can't even look at you. Just go away." Memories.

Aunt Juicie answers the door in a pink velour sweat suit. She hasn't gained any weight, but her eyes are bright and her skin is glowing. My mother said she had a little boyfriend. Ain't love grand? She holds my face in her hands.

"Let me see you," she coos, turning me around.

"You are still a beautiful child. How have you been?"

"Could be better."

"Sadie! Come out here. Adrienne is here to see you." I look around the living room taking it all in. I'd never been to their apartment before. The walls are adorned with dozens of photos of Aunt Juicie and Aunt Say, back when they were Judith and Sadie; both of them coke-bottle shaped, Aunt Say a little more ample. There are pictures of Aunt Juicie in cat-eyed glasses, looking like Eartha Kitt; Aunt Say, perched on a home made tree swing, her face unlined and worry-free; Aunt Juicie curled around a handsome man in a naval uniform; Aunt Juicie holding Lil' Rodney in her arms and standing at Aunt Say's bedside when Kerri was born; Big Rodney's Hoover vacuum cleaner nose taking up all of their wedding portrait. Aunt Say walks into the room hunched over on a walker. I hurry to her side.

"Where's your chair? What in the world? Aunt Juicie?"

"Let her be Adrienne. It's about time she helps herself." Aunt Say pulls herself to the floral armchair and stops. She lowers herself into the seat with a lot of difficulty. I start toward her, but Aunt Say holds her hand out.

"Whew. That wasn't easy, child. Juicie can you --" Aunt Juicie comes from the kitchen with a tall glass of cloudy water.

"Coney Island's finest. Would you like some, Adrienne?"

"Yes, please."

It seems Aunt Juicie is back with my glass before I can answer. Aunt Say gulps down the entire glass.

"I've been expecting you." She fans her bosom, then she scratches her arm. Wow.

"This won't be easy but I'll try to explain best I can." I settle into the couch and Aunt Juicie fades out of the picture.

"I used to work overnight as a Nurse's Aide. I know you didn't know that, put it in your rolodex. Or your *StrawBerry*. Whatever you damn kids are using these days." She looks to me for a reaction.

"Whew! You're a tough crowd. Anyway, I worked hard all night. Everyday, I come home, eight in the mornin'. Big Rodney be all fat and sprawled 'cross the couch. Kerri just be knocked out in her bed, snoring with her mouth open, even though the alarm was buzzin' all over the place. Rodney would be sittin' his ass on his bed waiting for me to iron his clothes for school. I tried to teach him how to do it, and you know that boy told me that that was woman's work? Yes, he did. When I asked him where he got that from, he said that he never saw Big Rodney iron nothin', so that's how he knew. I would slap Big Rodney out of his sleep sometimes because he was so useless." She sips from a new glass of water.

"There was always dishes in the sink. The toilet bowl was always dirty. Because Rodney wouldn't pick up after hisself, neither would Kerri. 'If Daddy and Roddy don't have to, why should I?' I was too tired to fight with her.

"Anyway, it took all I had to keep the house together. After I sent them off to school, I would bust my ass to pull it all together again and cook dinner and pay the bills and sleep for about four hours and go back to work. By the time I came home again, the house was blowed apart. I even went on strike. And would you believe Rodney is the one that stepped up? Um-hmm." She nodded.

"But only for hisself. Washed and ironed his own clothes. Tidied his room and kept to hisself. And then one day he came home and told Big Rodney he was playing basketball for the school and he wanted to practice and play some more. Big Rodney jumped on it. He was the father I didn't know he could be. Taking him to games. Picking him up from practice. Asking him about his life, you know really caring about him. The next thing you know, Kerri started acting more of a fool. She din't wanna wear this type of thing and that wasn't name brand. There was a song she used to sing. 'Shout. Shout. Lee's are played out. Lee's are the jeans we could do without.' I'll never forget it. She decided she wanted to wear these, um, what the hell was they called, Juicie?"

"Guess Jeans."

"Yes, thas what they was called. Those jeans was fifty dollars each. So I didn't pay her no mind. Then, she would cry these big crocodile tears and Big Rodney would bring his sorry ass in the room and start up some more shit. 'Just buy it for the girl, Sadie. Damn. You could afford it. Just work another shift or something.' His big lazy unemployed ass running all over the city with pompoms in his hand and he talkin' bout workin' another shift. Shee-it. I'm wipin' asses all day, flippin over people who can't turn by they self. Takin' blood from people who mighta had AIDS and stuff. And we was just scared, cause we din't know nothin' like how they know now." She fans her bosom.

"But why? Why did you send them?"

"There's no one answer."

"Tell me one. Tell me two. Just tell me something Aunt Say."

"Gettin' to it, Baby. Gimme a second." Aunt Juicie folds her hands in her lap.

"So now at this point, Big Rodney started gettin' money for Rodney to play in these games. You have to understand that Big Rodney never had no money. Even when he was working. Soon as he got it, it was gone. Now all of a sudden he handing me two hundred here and one hundred there, 'til we kinda rollin' in it. And he had to be gettin' more than that because he would never give me all the money he had in his pocket. Now at this point I've been doing everything. Working, keeping house, raising the kids. So Big Rodney tells me one day, 'Give me all the bills, and your part of the money and I'll take care of everything.' I say no. Tell him I'll take care of it. I ain't never trust him with the bills. I like my lights on when I come in. You feel me? So he leaves out, with a attitude, but when he comes back, his ass is drunker than the apostles at the Last Supper. Calling me out my name and telling me that those ain't his kids and he know it.

"Talkin' bout how they don't have his nose, and maybe, just maybe, Kerri was his cause at least she got his complexion. By then, I had enough. I told him get his ugly ass out my house and don't come back. And then he went crazy." She slaps both her hands on her knees and leans forward a bit. She looks me in the eye.

"I ain't never been afraid like I was that night. Something in the way his eyes was looking told me, *Say, you better get up on the good foot.* I ran for my life. Out the apartment and into the hallway. And you know what that fool did? Back then, I was small like I was in them pictures. Only thing round on me was my cheeks and my cheeks. You feel me, girl? Well that fool caught up with me and slammed me against the wall. I tried to get away and this time he slammed me, flat onto my back, right there on the marble floor. Still I got up and ran again. I was gone, flying down the hallway. I didn't know that son of a bitch was right behind me. And that's when he grabbed the back of my neck and he just shoved me down the steps."

Every time I pick my jaw up, she drops another bomb. I remember hiding behind the sofa as a little girl wishing I could find out the truth, but damn if I wish I didn't know. I press my pointer finger into the corners of my eyes.

"I spent two weeks in the hospital. And when I came home, them kids wouldn't even look at me. Hardly helped me. Just moved past me like I was in the way. I had to remind Rodney I was hungry or needed to pee or do number two. But Little Rodney would bring me a newspaper every now and then. And when I would open it, I would see wanted ads circled. Big Rodney would peek in the room. 'Time to get back on your feet, Say. Can't just be wasting away like this,' he said. And he would go back out in the living room, sending the kids in with KFC for lunch and Chinese chicken wings and French fries for dinner. That's where alla this came from." She fans her hand up and down her body. I am tired. Any energy I had when I sat in that couch is now depleted. Consequently and unfortunately, I can't even move to escape.

"Anyway, I started gettin' disability. But that wasn't enough. He would come in the room every week, with the check stub and say 'Sadie, I need you to be working, Baby.' When the AFDC check would come in, same thing. Then he would go back out to the living room. The day I asked him about a home nurse, he went crazy, talking about how I wanna use up all the family's money.

'You just selfish!' he yelled. 'Me and the kids is here slaving over you and you tryna keep all the money fo' ya self!' He went back out to the living room, cussing under his breath. A little while later, he there yelling at the TV. I flip through the channels until our TV's match up and I see the stupid horse coming in dead last. There was a loud crash from the living room.

"Next morning, people start calling the house and knockin' on the door. I hear Big Rodney tellin' the kids: 'Tell 'em I ain't here. Get from that door!' Few days later, I feel like I got enough strength to go to the kitchen. I go to make myself some tea, but the stove ain't workin'. I pick up the phone to call the gas company and we ain't got no dial tone. So I carried my broken up self downstairs to find out what's going on. First thing the neighbor Mr. Johnny tells me: 'I thought you was dead.' Second thing he says: 'Lil' Rodney gonna get hurt if Big Rodney don't pay soon.' I was sick to my stomach 'cause Big Rodney was upstairs sittin' on the couch in front the broke TV, not even trying to make sure his own son was safe. I opened up the mailbox and it was jammed up with past due notices. One thing I see is a letter from Housing Court that say we ain't answer no other notice from the court and we gonna be evicted. The date on the paper was the very next day. I wobbled my broken ass down to the payphone and I called Judith to come get me and well you can figure out what happened after that. I wasn't me anymore, Adrienne. They would have killed me."

"So you unleashed them on us?" I ask quietly. Aunt Say starts to cry.

"I thought Rhona was built stronger than me." She covers her face with her hankie. "I just hoped…" I want to jump up and run out, but I sit still, trying not to fly off the handle.

"As a mother, I don't know what I would have done. But I think I would have at least given a warning."

"Baby, I didn't have to warn your momma. Tell you now like I told you before. She already knew."

I call my only friend in the world. I get the voicemail.

I AM GRATEFUL FOR the annoying buzz of my cell phone because it allows me to break free of a dream that has pinned me to the bed though I felt like I was awake the whole time.

Still, I don't answer the phone. It's five-thirty in the morning. The news can't be good. It rings again. And again. I hit talk.

"Two more girls came forward Adrienne. From Tampa Bay and San Diego. Why don't these people just stop trying to disrupt everything? They playin' with people's lives."

"Are you crazy?" I ask because I really want to know. The dial tone hums in my ear. I knew I shouldn't have answered. But there are two more girls. Two. Of course, I can't go back to sleep.

I weed through my e-mail, trashing forwards and junk mail. I don't have time to get my gossip fix. I could get on *YBF,* but it's not as much fun without Stacey.

I check my cell phone to see if I've missed her call, but she still hasn't called me back. I feel like a jilted lover. Kennedy barges into my office.

"Have you read today's paper?"

"No, not yet."

Kennedy slaps the *Daily News* on my desk. You-know-who is on the cover.

"Looks like the family's got some trouble heading their way." I look over my glasses at her. I turn back to my computer. *Ignore this simple bitch, Adrienne.*

"I'd keep my daughter away from him." I spin my chair back to face her. I wonder if she is just that clueless. Lori Ann pops her head in the door.

"I can't get it, Kennedy. Eighteen-fifteen, right?"

"No, you retard. Eighteen fifty-one."

"Yeah, so anyway. What are you guys gonna do?" She has the nerve to rest her chin in her palm.

"What would make you think I would discuss this with you?"

"He's a good guy." I smile, but I am seething.

"You know something Kennedy. If I slept my way up the career ladder and was granted any wish my little white heart desired I might feel like I had a right to intrude in other people's affairs, too. So I'll excuse you this one last time for overstepping your boundaries."

"How dare you say that to me!" Her skin turns bright pink and her grey eyes water. "You don't have to be so mean. I was just making conversation."

"Yes. On the state of my family. People that you do not know."

"No, you misunderstood."

"Don't I always?"

"I think he's innocent." I stand up.

"I'll be sure to let him know you think so."

"Really?" I close the door behind her.

I have bad family blood, not a friend in the world, and a stack of work on my desk. And here comes Kennedy, thinking she can't get some of this here Adrienne Surprise that is well past overdue.

She doesn't come back in my office. In fact she stays at her desk, which is just as odd as Lori Ann staying at hers. Kennedy holds her forehead, talking fervently into the phone. I feel a little bad for blasting her. Maybe she's not all bad. Lori Ann hands her her messages, which she snatches away. I don't feel bad at all.

"You're the last one here. Make sure you lock up. Nighty-night, Adrienne!" She smiles too brightly for someone who was on the verge of tears just a few hours ago.

I turn off the lights in my office and head out for the night. I rest my bag on Kennedy's desk to find my keys. Her message light blinks twice for an in-house message. I'm the last one in the office. I'm like a moth to a flame.

Lori Ann's handwritten messages, the ones that Kennedy snatched away are tacked to the wall of Kennedy's cubicle. I punch in eighteen-fifty one on a hunch.

You have one new message. Yes!

"Presidential Pussy, this is your big Eiffel Tower waiting to hear what the plans are for you, me and Super Girl tonight. The wife's off with the Prince and the University has no need for my services this evening. Use the bat phone."

"Woooooooo-Oooh-weeeee!" I holler in the empty office. I don't know what I expected to hear, but that is some serious business! And who the hell is Super Girl? I forward it to my voice mailbox. Wait 'til Stacey hears this!

In the lobby, I can't see anything but white bursts of light.

"Mrs. Lucas. We understand you are related to Rodney Barrus. Are the allegations true?" *Pop, pop, pop!*

"How close are you? Did he tell you what really happened?" How they got past campus security is as much a mystery as the answer to the question of Rodney's innocence.

"Is it true he lived with you? And your young daughter? Do you bring your daughter around him? Does he sleep in his lucky jersey? Mrs. Lucas, over here!" I rush past them and jump in a musty yellow cab.

"Please, get me out of here!" I am terrified. And pissed as hell. That damned Kennedy had a surprise for me, too. Heifer.

Angela waits at the front door.

"Not again," I say.

"Yes, again. Come on."

Big Rodney stands in front of my mother's china cabinet. The dishes are white and pristine behind his big greasy ass. My hate for him doubles; triples even.

"Gold digging whores." Kerri sits in the armchair with Merri on her lap.

"Daddy, please. But it's just a shame what people will do for money."

"Gold digging whores I tell you. Tryna get what they can. Just givin' up the pussy!" he crows. Quadruples, the hate does. He's so crass and classless. For a second, I'm hesitant to open my mouth because this crowd is pro-Rodney, but I remind myself I've been the odd man out since forever ago.

"You ever think that maybe it's true. That maybe he took advantage of these girls?"

"Hell to the nah!" bellows the wildebeest.

"Not one girl came forward, but three. And there may be more."

"Oh, here we go," says Kerri.

"I was reading the paper and there's speculation that he paid the last two girls to be quiet and that one of the conditions of them accepting the money was that he was traded away."

"He got traded because Houston sucks as a team and he was tired of playing for them," says Kerri.

"Ummm, *Rot-nee's* championship rings say otherwise," I said.

"He said he didn't do it," grunts Big Rodney.

"Actually, Kerri said he didn't do it."

"Gold diggers. Money grubbin', broke ass, schemin', whorin' gold diggers. That's what they are."

"That hotel caters to Fortune 500 clients. It's not even in your local Triple A book. I think her people have money."

"Last week you was all prayin' for my boy, now you defending them hoes. You born-agains are all the same."

"So what if he did do it? What do we do then? Pretend he didn't?"

"You shoulda asked that when he was here to defend himself," says Kerri, who lays down her throwback Gucci bag and takes center stage in the living room in her skinny jeans and pumps.

"But I'm not even surprised at you, Rabbit. You always did hate on Roddy. 'Oh Rodney. Your jump shot needs work. Oh Rodney you need to play more defense.' You even trained your little daughter to hate."

"Maybe if you all wasn't there praising every damn thing he do, he wouldn't be in this mess," says Aunt Say.

"Really? And where were you, Miss Mother Fuckin' High and Mighty?" asks Big Rodney. "You his mother." Kerri stomps her foot.

"This is about Roddy!" Everyone's eyes shift from Aunt Say to Kerri. "This is about Roddy and how Rabbit is trying to turn us against him."

I throw my hands up in the air.

"We all know Rabbit's not normal. She was loose back then and that's why she can't keep a man now. And that's why she's siding with these hoes. Takes a hoe, to love a hoe."

I don't want my daughter to think badly of me. I really don't. But I jump all over Kerri. Her eyes fly open in surprise. I can't stop hitting her. And when I feel hands pulling me back, I grab hold of those stupid Pocahontas braids and try to choke the life out of her. Mikey pulls her away from me and she starts yelling and thrashing about. Her cat eyes shimmer with rage.

"Let me go! I hate you, Rabbit! I hate your spoiled rotten guts."

"You girls need to stop this mess right now!" screams my mother.

"And I hate you, too," she spits at my mother. My mother's hands go to her neck in surprise. Everyone is on their feet.

"I hate all yall." She turns on Aunt Say. "Especially you! Who leaves their kids like that, huh? Who does some fucked up shit like that?" she cries. I'm crying, holding Angela who is crying into her hands.

Aunt Juicie's eyes are pressed shut. "The Lord is my shepherd…"

"Shut the hell up with that shit!" hollers Big Rodney.

"Rodney, you go to hell! All this shit is yo damn fault!" hollers Aunt Say. "It's you! You the one who did all this shit!" My father drains his glass.

"Yall need to go." Big Rodney pokes out his chest.

"You can't be putting nobody out of my sister's house."

"Unless you wanna leave in an ambulance, all of you better get the hell out," he says in his calm baritone. He opens the door. "Get these kids and get that damned dog off my back porch and go. I had enough of this mess." The flashes pop like lightning on a stormy night. My father shuts the door.

Angela sits next to me on the sofa, close enough to make me feel she still loves me. My mother stares at the walls, as though the answer is scrawled somewhere.

"After all I've done," she whispers over and over and over again. "After all I've done."

I'm tempted to reassure her. She is, after all, my mother, my blood. But that goes against the small sense of satisfaction that wells in my heart.

I SHUFFLE THROUGH STACKS of paper trying to make heads or tails of the mess that has become my desk. I can't even remember what I'm supposed to be doing. I rest my head on the desk. Kennedy opens my door without knocking. I look at my clock. It's only a quarter to nine.

"Need something?" She smiles just like she did on Friday night before she sold me down the river.

"Adrienne," she says. "This is your new assistant, Jen."

A tall blonde preppy girl of about twenty stands next to Kennedy; her hair pulled back with a bandeau.

"I needed a temp last week. Not this week. Isn't Stacey coming back today?"

"She's not a temp." Stacey smacks a cardboard box on top of her desk. She's talking in an exaggerated tone.

"Would have been nice if you had warned me, *Mrs. Lucas*. Guess I expected too much."

"I told you I didn't need a new assistant, Kennedy," I say. Her voice is soft and her eyes are doe-like.

"When did you tell me that? Because I got your message saying you needed a new one ASAP." She steps to the side of Stacey's desk.

"Jen. This will be your desk when Stacey is done. Stace, I've gotten you an interview over at admissions. That suit you?"

"Suits me fine."

"Good. Then we're all set. Jen, come with me. We have some paperwork to fill out. Stacey, after you pack up your stuff, I need you to train Jen on everything you know and we'll get your transfer under way."

Kennedy winks at me before she slinks out. I sit in my office chair and stare out the window. I feel like I am thirteen again arguing with Tanisha. But I am not thirteen anymore. I am a grown ass woman.

Lori Ann shifts the same sheets of paper back and forth, taking everything in.

"How was your weekend, Adrienne?"

"Sucked. Yours."

"Super." I look at her sideways. Stacey jams her files into the cardboard box, mumbling about 'this got-damn place' and some other stuff that has so much southern drawl laced into it, that my Brooklyn ears can only tell that whatever it is she is saying is not good.

"Stacey. Can I talk with you outside for a second."

"I'm not sure that's a good idea."

"Please?"

The elevator doors barely close before everything spills out.

"I thought you betrayed me. I thought you overheard something in my office and told everyone. But when I realized my mistake, I called you back."

"Yeah. I got that. And I was not pleased about it. No. I was pissed about it, Adrienne. I never gave you any reason to think I would turn on you. But I let it go. But *then* I came in this morning….this is humiliating!"

"I know and I'm sorry. But well, you know how Kennedy is."

"Yeah, well I thought I knew how you were. Will you press the button for us to go back up? I have packing to do." I can feel my heart racing. The elevator doors open on our floor and Stacey marches off, leaving me in the proverbial dust.

My life is not going as planned. I have heartburn and the beginnings of a headache. I close my office door and crack open my pocketbook. I rummage through it until I find my juice. The first thing that pisses me off is that I don't smell liquor. The second is that it's filled with water. My office seems smaller, my desk larger. I squeeze my eyes shut.

I get up so fast, I feel dizzy. I pass Stacey who keeps her back to me and Lori Ann who watches me like a hawk. Before I get to the Dean's door, Lori Ann is on her feet.

"You can't go in there!" Lori Ann is so close, she steps on the back of my heel, so my shoe comes off. "I tried to stop her!" she yells. I elbow her in the stomach, so that she will literally get off my back. The Dean's black stockinged feet are on the desk. Kennedy and Jennifer lounge languidly on his couch, just a *hee-hee-heeing.*

He looks back and forth between the Barbie's and me.

"Don't start any trouble, Adrienne. This was all your idea to find a new assistant." Kennedy is up and leaning against the edge of his desk.

"Dean Paris, there's been a misunderstanding. I would like very much to keep Stacey as my assistant."

"I knew she was going to do this." Kennedy punches some numbers into the Dean's telephone. My voice plays back clearly. "And she doesn't want Jen because she's not a *sista*." She makes quotation marks with her fingers. Dean Paris steeples his fingers listening intently as Kennedy prattles on.

"I gave her Jen's resume weeks ago. And I found it tucked away in a drawer." I'm about to lay into her for being in my drawer when the Dean nods his fat, pink balding head at her.

"Is that true, Adrienne?"

"Hold on a second here," I say. "Jennifer, can you step out for a second?" She looks to Kennedy.

"Now. How about you step out *now, Jen*?" She pauses, the heifer does. I hold the door open for her. I wave her forward.

"C'mon now, honey. Put some pep in your step." Jennifer bumps into the door frame, looking back at Kennedy for direction. I close the door.

"Don't you think it odd that I've never even met the person who would be my right hand?"

"Adrienne. Let's settle down and see how it all works out. I've met with Jen and I can say she's a nice girl. We're giving her a probationary period," said the Dean. "And that's the final verdict."

I'm as calm as I please on my way back to my desk. I smile at Lori Ann who doesn't look so super right now. I dial into my messages.

Presidential Pussy, this is your big Eiffel Tower. Just checking. I send it to my home phone and cell phone and then I re-save it. I dial the Dean's extension.

"Adrienne. I've made a decision."

"Sir, I understand that. But I don't think Jennifer and I will be a good fit."

"That's absurd. She's a good girl. Now you be a good girl and we won't remember that there are budget cuts."

"Okay, so you won't remember that and I, Kennedy's senior, the only *Sista* holding a Director's position at New York College even though many qualified Blacks and Latinos have applied, won't remember to mention to Mrs. Eiffel Tower that there are super-international relations going on while she's away with the Prince." I can hear him breathing on the other end. "All I want is to have my assistant back."

The door to his office bangs open. Kennedy barges into mine.

"You conniving *betch*!"

She charges out of my office again. I watch her through the glass. Stacey slams her box down.

"I'm not a yoyo, Kennedy. I am not a pawn and I am NOT a damn yoyo!" She grabs her purse and stalks off toward the elevator.

"I'm using a personal day. I'll be back tomorrow when all of you get your act together!" The door to the suite slams shut.

NO ONE IN THE OFFICE speaks to me. No. That's not true. Everyone speaks to me as little as possible, but mostly through Lori Ann. The Dean, if he passes me in the hallway, is saccharine sweet, but distant. It's cool. I've been here before.

Stacey doesn't look me in the eye though. And that pisses me off. I remember those days when my father was ashamed of me and wouldn't look at me either. My mind wanders and I wonder if she's spoken to Corey. And that maybe he's told her what I'd confessed. My stomach hurts. Maybe she thinks I'm a hoe too, and doesn't want any parts of me. I'm buggin' out. I know I am. But I can't shake this old shit off my back.

Stacey drops off office supplies and the employee handbook we've been revising for the next academic year.

"Thank you." She's back minutes later with a typed up memo.

"Please ask the Dean to sign off on this one. I will not put my name on anything that hires Lori Ann full-time. It's going to start a whole new issue that I'm not ready to deal with at the present moment." Strictly professional, with not a splash of sister girl to be seen with the naked eye.

"I will see to it that he does." This could get funny with us trying to out-polite each other. I don't hear my door close. Stacey straddles the doorway, one foot in my office, one foot out.

"Is there something else, Stacey?" I try to read her face; figure out if she's quitting, about to lay into me again about the whole mess, ask me for a raise. I haven't a clue.

"Don't you miss me yet?" she asks. I laugh out loud.

"I take that as a yes. I really don't appreciate you shutting me out all the time, Adrienne. I mean your life is your business and all, but I just never learned how to be only half a friend." I don't say anything.

"How are you?" she asks.

"Terrible."

"I can imagine. Those are some ugly charges." I make circles on my notepad.

"You don't have to go along with the machine, you know."

"What are you talking about?"

"The Hot Rod-is-innocent machine."

"What makes you think he's not?" I ask, surprised though I shouldn't have been.

"It's in his face. Rodney has the Uncle Fred face." She pulls the chair around to the side of my desk bringing us face to face. "Oh my goodness. You don't know how much I missed this!"

"I missed it, too. What's an Uncle Fred face?"

"That's what I'm about to tell you, girl! Every Sunday, the family would gather at the dinner table. Without fail, Nana Belle would always send one of the kids to wash their grubby little hands. Well one day, when I was about eight or nine, it was my turn. So I went down the hall. But when I got there, it was slightly ajar. I didn't hear anyone, so I peeked in and Uncle Fred, God bless his molestin' soul was at the sink. 'Hurry up before Nana has a hissy fit.' So I hurried up. Next thing I know, he says, 'My sausage hurt. If you touch it, it feel much better.' Girl, why silly me touched it and he let go on my hand?! And then he started crying, telling me not to be mad at him." I sat there mouth open wide.

"It was the crying that bothered me the most. 'Cause it was like the crying we used to do before we got a beating. That don't-beat-me-so-bad, crying even though we knew we did something wrong.

"Now, I didn't know what wasn't right about it, but I knew it just wasn't right. So I waited and kept watch. I started to notice that my cousins Bootsie and Marcella would wash their hands in the garden hose before we came inside from playing, so I did, too.

One Sunday, I forgot. I kept my hands under the table, wiping furiously on my jeans. I woulda licked the dirt off before I went back to that bathroom. But then Uncle Steve excused himself, so I followed him, thinking it was safe. When he pushed the door open, that fool Uncle Fred said, 'Hey man, wait your turn!'

"And I turned and ran back to the table before ol' Freddie could see me. I was livid! So that night I plotted. Marcella and Bootsie were scared, but not me! I was giving him the evil eye, so that he knew it, too!" She shakes her head at the memory.

"So we talked it through and decided that I would fix his old crusty behind. We waited and we waited and we waited. But it's like he knew we smelled his lecherous scent because he was always at the table before dinner. And then finally, he felt comfortable again. The next Sunday I went in the bathroom, and guess who was at the sink? Ol' crusty butt, talkin' about, 'Hurry up, girl. You know Nana's gonna have your hide!'

"And when he pulled out that old sausage, I put the point of this old rusty Swiss army knife right in the middle and promised him that Cajun hot dog would be on a bun on the buffet table if he didn't quit it." I laugh like hell. That sounds just like Stacey.

"He kept his ass out the bathroom, but I kept watching his face. His eyes always darted around to see if people were watching him. And that's what Rodney's doing." I keep my eyes on my desk.

"He's your Uncle Fred."

"He's worse."

STACEY'S STORY DOESN'T make me feel better. It makes me feel worse because I wish I had her moxie; her strength. I can't help but think if I had at least threatened Rodney from the beginning, he would have never tried again. It makes me feel worse because I wonder how many other girls out there have been through some mess like this and will probably go to their graves with it. I even wonder if those other women have problems with relationships the way I did. The way I do. And now I feel angry, enraged actually. I pick up the phone.

"Hi Ma."

"Hi Adrienne. You okay? Nothin' ain't happen to you did it?"

"No."

"You spoke to your cousins?"

"Yep. I just hung up with them. They said they're coming to my house for dinner."

"You think that was funny? 'Cause it wasn't."

"I just don't understand why you would ask me that."

"Can you believe she had the nerve to say that to me?"

"For the hundredth time, yes."

"But how come I didn't see it?"

"Maybe you didn't have your special glasses on? I don't know."

"I didn't need no special glasses. If there's anything I know, it's you kids. Did you call to kick me while I'm down, Adrienne? Cause if you did, you doin' a good damn job."

"Actually, I called to tell you I'm going to the Garden to see Rodney. Don't be surprised if he calls you upset."

"Don't be mean to him, Adrienne. You know he sensitive."

The Garden two hours before the game, looks like someone served bacon frittata at a Muslim eatery.

"I don't know how we're gonna make it to the locker room without getting caught," whispers Stacey. We skulk around ducking behind pillars, until we can find someone we can trust to help us.

A young light-skinned sister with a super long curly weave down her back and breasts squeezed up inside her too tight uniform shirt stacks cups behind the concession stand. She cracks her gum.

"Excuse me. Where in the world is the locker room?" She looks at Stacey and me in our less than hoochiefied work attire and giggles to herself.

"Two exits down and to the left. Then go down to the bottom and it's the two beige doors." She looks us over again and shakes her head. I am offended! She just doesn't know! And I guess she doesn't know about Stacey, whose hands are anchored to her hips, either.

"Little girl. I'd run circles around you." Little Girl holds up a W, with her fingers.

"Whatever. If yall do manage to get in, tell Hot Rod that Rabbit says hi."

"What did you say?" I ask.

"She said to tell Hot Rod Rabbit says hi."

"That's what I thought she said."

"Crazy name, right?"

The two double beige doors are manned by a large and in charge security guard posted out front. That little heifer didn't say anything about a security guard. He sizes us up and reburies his head in his newspaper.

"We're looking for Rodney Barrus. Number thirteen," Stacey says.

"You ain't his type. Beat it." Stacey sticks her finger in his face.

"Rodney is my cousin, you hog."

"Tell him Adrienne is out here. Better yet, tell him Rabbit is here to see him."

"Rabbit? Isn't that that little girl?" asks Stacey. I don't confirm or deny her question. He picks up the red bat phone to the right of the doors. When he hangs up, he cracks the paper open again.

"He says he doesn't know any Rabbit."

"Tell that lousy jump shot missing, non-defense playing son of a bitch that he had better---" He holds up his hand.

"Come on."

"Go get him, Girl. And remember, you're from Brooklyn."

"Yeah. Brooklyn," I croak. I think about Trey Ski and Fuquan and Julie, all the people who passed fearlessly through my life and still, my fear overrides the Brooklyn bravado.

The locker room is nicer than I expected the men's locker room to be. It actually looks like the wood grain paneling I'd seen inside luxury cars, except that it's only around the individual cubby holes.

Rodney comes from a door in the back and stands a good distance away from me. Maybe remembering the flying vase, I don't know. But I'm fine with it.

"You cussed Gus out?"

"No, I cussed you out." He opens the door to a small conference room. I hesitate, but Gus is right outside in case I scream. Besides, I've got pepper spray in my bag. My throat feels like I've swallowed a handful of sand.

"You come here to apologize for bad-mouthing me at your mother's?"

"Like hell I did. But I came to make peace."

"Now this sounds like a new and improved Rabbit. The kind I might like."

"This is a joke to you?"

"I'm not laughing. I'm just waiting for you to tell me how you wanna make peace with Hot Rod."

"The only way I can make peace with you, is if you admit what you did to me and apologize."

"Fuck outta here. You bitches kill me." You could have blown on me, and I would have toppled right over.

"Thas right, you bitches. You bitches want to be noticed. Want to be associated with big niggas, doing big things. You wanna live off the land and then you want to come in and start making demands."

"First of all, I didn't need shit from you, Rodney. And the only thing I'm here for today is my apology. My real apology."

"Bitch please. You got tuition money. From me. Rent money. From me. Your mom's and 'em got that house. From me. Piece of your house. From me." He thumps his chest.

"I had scholarships. And my mother sold her house to buy the new one."

"Your moms and them ain't get no real money in that crack-infested area. And you didn't get no scholarship."

Something is wrong, but right about what he's saying. I signed for my scholarship money every semester, so I know he didn't pay my tuition. My mind flashes back to the envelopes with extra money that my mother would send me: the money Terrell and I lived on for a long time and some I still had in the bank. My face burns.

"Yeah. Exactly."

"You think I'm gonna roll over because you did something nice? You owed them. They went to work everyday to take care of all of us."

"Let's call your Daddy right now, let him tell you about how much he went to work everyday. Our checks put food on your table, Baby Girl." He chuckles a bit. "You're really feelin' yourself, Rabbit. Actin' like your family had it all together and mine wasn't shit. But at least my father protected me." I wince.

"So fuck you, Ay-drienne."

"No. Fuck you, Rodney. My mother should have let Big Rodney take your ass with him. See how you woulda turned out then. Who knows, maybe he would have done you like he did Aunt Say."

"There you go on your high horse again. Actin' like your mother saved the day. But whatever he did to my mother, she deserved because, *taadaa!,* here's another family secret. Big Rodney told me a long time ago he is not my father. She's a hoe. And as I said, she deserved whatever he did to her."

"I didn't forget you didn't always want to wear number thirteen, Rodney. Is that why he fucked you up? Because you were a hoe?" His jaw clenches with rage.

"Big Rodney made a man out of me! I'm a fuckin' star, Rabbit! Do you see me? I am Hot Rod and I am a mutha-fuckin' star!" My mind is brimming with too much information. I'm tired.

"Fine Rodney. You're a fuckin' star. But you owe me an apology and I'm not leaving until I get it." Rodney's smooth features turn animal-like. His nose flares, and his canines appear sharper.

"I don't owe you shit. I told you once and I'll tell you again. You wanted that shit. You all do. Just a bunch of dirty fuckin' hoes. Now get the fuck out before I call…" I bring my arm from way back and smack his face.

"Security!"

"I could have killed you!" I yell.

"Security!"

"You were this close! This close to mashed potato surprise! I should have killed you!" His hand moves to his stomach.

"Security! Come get this crazy groupie bitch!"

Gus grabs me from behind; just picks me up off my feet and carries me out of the locker room. As we exit through the common area, I recognize Luke Davidson, Pooh Cameron and Sinclair Thomas from the team. I kick my legs all over the place, but Gus keeps walking.

"He's a rapist!" I scream. Gus clamps his hand over my mouth. Still I scream unintelligibly. Still I kick and writhe in his arms until he dumps me out on my knees on the wet pavement like trash.

Just before the door slams shut, he spits on the sidewalk.

"You girls never learn."

The door bursts open again; this time coughing up Stacey.

"You haven't seen the last of me! I'll be gettin' Jacoby and Meyers on your ass! This is not over!"

I LET MYSELF INTO my parents' house. The light from a humongous flat screen TV brightens the otherwise darkened living room. My father is reclined in a brand new Barca Lounger.

"I ain't know you was comin', Aydree. Where's Angel Cakes? She ain't wanna come see her Granddad and watch the game?" My mother flicks on the lamp next to her. I feel like an intruder.

"Why you look like that? Adrienne. What's going on? It's not that custody thing is it?"

"Do you believe Rodney is innocent?"

"Oh, Adrienne. Stop it. Stop, stop, stop it. He didn't do nothin' to them girls. It's crazy already. Just stop. He's your family."

"Rhona, you always want shit to be a certain way. But you ain't seein' shit for what it is. Look how your family treated you after all those years you sacrificed everyone else for them." My father's glassy eyes gleam with pent up anger.

"You shut yo mouth, Dub! You don't know a thang about family. What you do for us except bring home your little chump change when you was sober enough to remember where home was?" My eyes dart back and forth between them thinking maybe they were right in not telling me much of anything as a kid because I am paralyzed and partially sickened at what they feel free to say in front of me now.

"Watch what you say to me under my roof, Rhona," he warned.

"No, it's my roof. My nephew bought it for me. And the house on Hopkinson, my mother gave it to me. If it wasn't for them, we woulda been just as homeless as Sadie and the kids was. So watch what you say bout things being yours around here."

"I did my best," he said quietly. "I did my damn best." He turned the top of the E&J bottle.

"So it's true then."

"What's true?" asked my mother.

"I went to see Rodney and he said all these ugly things about how we've been using him." My mother and father exchange a glance.

"Don't look at me. That's *your* family, remember?" My mother smoothes the satin of her pajama pants in her lap.

"It's not what you think."

"You have no idea what I think." She smoothes them again.

"Aunt Say benefits got cut off. And we needed to get her some money, but he wouldn't send none. But for some reason, when we mentioned we had to get you some books and stuff, he got all generous. And we thought we were helping. We didn't keep none. No. We didn't keep *any*. Matter fact, I sent the extra to you."

"He said we were all living off him."

"When we need something, we ask him. He told us, no matter what, he was helping us out for helping him out," says my Dad.

"The family is falling apart!"

"Hush, Rhona." My father looks at his shoes. He offers no explanation. And I don't push. I can tell by the way he empties the E&J bottle into his glass and throws it back in two swallows that he is ashamed. Or maybe it's his bright red ears that let me know. But I am embarrassed for him, remembering the days he was home early from work.

"Is there something else, Adrienne?" I should be bursting to tell them. Bursting to let it all out and clear my mind. But it hurts to let it out.

"When Rodney moved in here, he took something from me."

"He stole something from you?" asked my Dad. I nodded.

"Baby, what did he steal from you?" asks my mother in this tiny little whispery voice that is almost scary. I don't answer right away.

"Baby, don't say what I think you're gonna say. Cause if you say what I think…" says my Dad. I can tell they know what I mean, but I have to say it.

"Rodney raped me."

"Aww Baby, no," cries my mother. Her eyes fill. "Aww nooooo!" My father put his hands on her shoulder. "Noooo," she wails in pain.

She puts her hands to her face and her shoulders bob up and down, the way it might look if you were laughing hard.

Then she starts babbling. "We could have a family meetin' to hash everything out. What you think, Adrienne?" Her eyes are hopeful. I'm not even mad at her. She hasn't said what I'd hoped she would say, but what I truly expected.

"It's okay, Mom. Look out for the family. They're the ones that really need you." I say. Her eyes are wild. She searches my face and I can tell by her reaction, she's surprised there's not an ounce of emotion on it. As she realizes what I'm really saying, oh how she bawls. Even my father breaks down and I've never seen him cry. Not even when his baby brother Elton passed away a few years back. I walk out the door so very, very numb to it all, without the aid of even a droplet of brandy.

The girl from Tampa Bay has dropped her lawsuit for undisclosed reasons. I've read the article three times already hoping that's not the case, but I really don't blame her.

There's been a quiet, subtle pressure in the air. It comes in the form of a 'thinking of you' card signed in Merri's four year old scribble. Or in the form of my parents' mortgage statement that is 'mistakenly' mixed in with my mail. It comes from my own thoughts about Aunt Say's care. Or Angela's being embarrassed at school if it gets out about Rodney and me. Rodney's shame and embarrassment. The idea of being made a spectacle of.

My sleep is tormented. And when I'm awake all I want to do is go to bed.

Every night, Angela cooks macaroni and cheese from the box for dinner and does her homework at the foot of my bed. If my mother has called, I don't know because my daughter fields every call like a pro. Her favorite line is that I'm indisposed. I love her more than I think anyone could possibly love another person. She's not like me. She's ten times better. Rodney's picture pops up on the muted TV. "Anj. Turn that up."

"Allegations of another pay off surface in the case of Rodney Barrus. The father of the Los Angeles victim has brought new charges against the superstar alleging that Barrus accosted the victim after her class at a local college in an attempt to bribe her into dropping the

case. This case may prove to be a roadblock for the Hot Rod, yet."

And then I am lucid. "I can't believe I hadn't thought of that!"

"Thought of what?"

"Anj. Pass me my laptop!" I google until I find the little blog with the amateur pictures of celebrities. And I understand that that is how Rodney was able to be photographed so closely. He was not with the team. And he was not with Aunt Say in the hospital. He was in LA trying to cover his ass. I check my planner against the night I had dinner at Stacey's. And it is indeed the same date. He was still slippery, that damn Rodney.

Yes, Tampa Bay may have dropped the case, but it is time for Hot Rod to pay the Piper.

Stacey and I rehearse what she has to say, until finally it sounds perfect.

"Are you sure you want me to do this?" she asks.

"Never been more sure." She lowers her voice to a whisper.

"Hi. Um. I work with this woman who is related to Rodney Barrus and I just overheard some information that is going to make me rich. Oh! Here she comes! Give me your address. Oh come on, Lady, hurry." She puts the receiver down. I hug my dear friend at the door. I'm surprised at how hard her stomach feels. Her cotton knit empire waist sweater dress gave nothing away.

"Why didn't you tell me?"

"Well first of all, I couldn't stand your ass. And secondly because you needed me. We got time before she gets here, Auntie Aydree." She puts her sweater over her shoulders and disappears into the elevator.

Stacey and I are locked in my office at eight-thirty in the morning for a special edition gossip session, reading and re-reading the two page spread.

"Reliable sources, that would be you Stace, claim an adult family member was abused as a teen, that would be me, after her family had taken him in. The alleged victim, me again, has refused to comment. Rodney Barrus's spokeswoman, Kerri Long has categorically denied the allegations and refused further comment."

"Can you believe this? You're in the rags! You're part of gossip time! How does that feel?"

"It's…I don't know. It's very surreal. It still feels like I'm reading about someone else's life."

"That's some heavy shit. Speakin' of heavy, this calls for a nice greasy breakfast. We haven't had one of those in ages."

"Speak for yourself, heifer!"

When I come back to my office, I dial into my messages.

"Groupie whore! I hate you." What the hell?

"So sorry to read this has happened to you." Who were these people?

My mother's number shows up on the caller ID.

"Adrienne, these people are outside my house! You need to tell somebody this ain't true or I'ma throw some hot grease out the window! I called Rodney to see if he could send summa his security, but my calls is going to the answering machine."

"Call 911. I'll be home soon."

"We in a black neighborhood and ain't nobody dyin'! They ain't comin' here!"

"Fine. Then throw the hot grease out the window. They'll be there faster than you know."

I am thinking about how we could spin this, but the phone starts to ring off the hook. Lori Ann is at the reception desk scribbling message after message.

My message light blinks twice for in house messages. I dial in my password. Stacey brings the messages in from Lori Ann. I put the phone on speaker.

"You fucking lying hoe." Stacey sits on my couch.

"What the *hale* was that?!"

"Trust me. I've been through this before. It'll pass."

"I sure hope you're right. This is terrible!"

Lori Ann stands in the doorway with a grim look on her face.

"Adrienne. Your daughter's school called. Something's happened." I dash past her knocking all the messages onto the floor in a pink flurry.

"Oh my God. My baby. I forgot about my baby."

For the entire ride home, there is silence. I don't know what to say. I hadn't even factored her into my decision to out Rodney. The only thing she has said to me since I stepped into the principal's office is, *I'm okay.* Even though the principal has spewed tolerance rhetoric about violence not being the answer.

Even though the little white boy is silent, red-faced and seething.

The horde of reporters outside my house raises my shackles even higher. I want to put my car in reverse, but this is my house, my home. A lifetime ago, I was forced to give it up and would never do it again.

I toot the horn for them to get out of the way. Some move, but the overzealous ones stand in the way. I don't step on the gas like I want to, but I ease my foot off the brake every now and then. My driveway, my property, right? I think for sure someone is going to try and slide under the garage door with us, but they don't. It shuts behind us and closes out the clatter of the photographers and the reporters screaming our names.

"Are you okay?"

"No. I'm scared. Timmy Melder's dad is friends with the owner of The Garden. They weren't very nice when that case happened with that lady and the head coach. And then Timmy was in class saying that black girls bring it on because they dress like hoochies."

"But did you have to knock his tooth out?"

"Hell to the yeh-uh. He was talking about you, calling you a *betch*. That is so against the rules," said my Angel.

Angela and I retreat to our bedrooms where I call the firing range and then my job. Given my last encounter with the Dean, I am not optimistic.

"Lori Ann. Please put Dean Paris on the line."

"Sure thing, Adrienne."

"Adrienne. Is everything okay?" I lift my chin from the floor.

"Actually, Sir. It's not. That's what I wanted to talk to you about."

"I'm sympathetic to, ahem, your problem. And well, you know the publicity is not the kind the College encourages. So if you need more time than a week, to straighten out your family affairs, please let me know."

"I don't know what to say. Thank you, Sir."

"By the way, you were right about David. He thought we'd hate him."

"I bet he's relieved to know you don't."

"Yes. He was quite flamboyantly exuberant actually."

"Give him my regards, Sir." And I mean it. At least his story has a happy ending. I have no idea where this crazy ride called my life is going.

WHEREVER IT WAS GOING, I had no intention of running. But my mother and father moved out of their house…and into mine.

"That house was bought with blood money," she said. But the big screen TV was leaned up against the wall in my basement.

And that wasn't all she had to say.

"It ain't time for dinner yet? Don't you dust your television screen? Why you turn the blinds down like that. They should be *turnt* the other way." All this within the first five minutes of us unloading her last box in my basement.

"If you want them that way, then put it that way."

If I tried to help her out, she had more to say than if I didn't help her in the first place.

"You put these curtains up?"

"Yes."

"Well why you put 'em up backwards?"

"I did? I didn't notice."

"See." She raised the bottom of the curtain up to my face. "It got a hem on it. You wouldn't wear a dress with the hem on the outside, would you?" She rolled her eyes. It wasn't big, but it was enough for me to know the arrangement was not going to work.

So I packed up my family and we moved with half of the proceeds of our leak to the press, to a two-family home in Canarsie, where Angela and I spend an awful lot of time with my parents. And when they begin to irk, we escape upstairs to our oasis. Well, when my mother begins to. My father still doesn't say too much. It's hard to when the glass is always to your lips.

My mom and Angela sit on my sofa together watching TV while I go through the monthly bills. They're cuddled on the sofa looking like two peas in a pod.

"Damn, it's tuition time again. I know one thing, somebody better become an astronaut, because her mommy's gonna be in debt for the rest of her life so it better be worth it!"

"What you do with the money from the house?" asks my mother. "That blood money." I look up over my glasses.

"What does that have to do with anything?"

"I'm just curious."

"I donated it to a rape crisis center in his name."

"All of it?"

"Yup. All of it." Actually, I kept some for a rainy day fund, but I didn't tell a soul. I don't care what Rodney said, or what my mother thought, after all the years I suffered, I deserve to live comfortably.

"Try again," she said.

"You can see through me, huh?"

"Like glass."

"When you wanted to or always?" She doesn't answer and I go back to working out the bills. Try again. Ha. She was a funny one, that Rhona Fuller. But she's not smiling. Her eyes are downcast, staring at her ebony hands in the same way that I find her staring out of the bay window of her living room sometimes. Whatever she's looking at is not outside that bay window or in her hands. Her eyes well. But she doesn't let the tears fall. I am sorry to have hurt her. I just can't say the words.

The air conditioner sits unopened in the living room. She still refuses to use it even though I'm losing water weight by the second. I'm going to be Mary Kate Olsen's size by the time she's done baking this cake for my birthday.

"How did you know Big Rodney's spirit was bad?"

"What you mean?"

"You said he couldn't stay with us because his spirit was bad. How did you know?" She wipes her brow with the back of her hand, leaving a flour smudge on her forehead.

"Girl please. Rodney was a son of a bitch from the time we was kids. He stole. He lied. He tricked anyone he could trick, Daddy and Grandma Rose included. If he couldn't trick you, he was just beside himself. Made it his business to watch you and study 'til he found a weakness." She taps the spoon. "He almost got the house, you know."

"What house?"

"Our house. On Hopkinson. It was the only thing my mother ever gave me." She nods. "Umhmm. But Grandma Rose had a lawyer that called us every time Big Rodney came to his office about the will. She was ahead of her time, your Grandma."

"Wow."

"Oh yes. A son of a bitch."

"Well, I think you know what my next question is gonna be."

"Ain't nothin' happen to me like what happened to you. But it was bad enough."

"You're not going to tell me who it was, are you?"

"You know me well, Adrienne."

She mixes and stirs and sifts and cracks eggs with a speedy vengeance. But she doesn't speak again. She beats the batter so hard, I feel sorry for the spoon.

She slams the spoon down. "Sometimes I thought God put them with us so they wouldn't turn out like they father. I thought I could save them. I don't know. I thought God helped the just, I guess." She's back beating the mess out of the batter. Her telephone rings.

"Get that phone. My hands is full."

"Hello?"

"Mrs. Fuller, please." The voice is vaguely familiar, but it seems like the woman is disguising her voice.

"Who is it?" asks my mother.

"I'm not sure. You want me to take a message?"

"No. Give it here. Better not be one a them *telemarkers.* Hello?" Her expression changes from exasperated to straight-up pissed.

"I am fine, Kerri."

"Let me talk to her." I reach for the phone, but my mother turns her back, boxing me out.

"No, I didn't see a diamond bracelet at my house when I packed up. I would have to ask Dub. If you wasn't so evil, then you wouldna lost it." She puts the phone on speaker, and commences her cake batter beating.

"I wasn't being evil, she attacked me."

"That's right!"

"Adrienne, shush. You know she ain't gonna admit she did anything to deserve that ass-whipping."

"She did not whip my ass. Anyway ---" My mother gasps.

"Oh my Lord. You know all these years there was something I couldn't figure out. And now, I can't believe I didn't see it."

"I don't have time for your epiphanies, Auntie Rho. My publisher's calling on the other line. So could you just find out if you have my bracelet?"

"You knew what happened and you didn't say nothin'." I didn't know what the hell my mother was talking about.

"With Rodney and Adrienne. You knew what he did to her."

"Rodney didn't do nothin' to that girl. Besides, if I knew that, I would have told. That's just nasty. I gotta go."

"Hold on now. Don't you sit up here and lie now. You knew. 'Cause that night was the night it was hot in the house. And you said it at the table. When I asked which of yall was creepin' around downstairs. You said you was hot and it was you. And the only reason you admitted it was 'cause you thought you was protecting Rodney from somethin'. You ain't know that Adrienne wasn't gonna say nothin', so just in case she told, you could say you was down there and nothin' had happened."

I'd forgotten all about that. I am struck silent.

"Okay. Let's say I did hear or saw something. Why would I jeopardize my future for Rabbit?"

"Well, you don't have much more of a future with that man going to jail, now do you?" Kerri slams the phone down.

"For all these years, I couldn't figure out what bothered me about her confession. But that was what it was. She just wasn't the type to confess."

I THOUGHT AFTER COMING CLEAN about Rodney, I'd be done running from my problems. But there's one pesky problem that continues to give chase.

I manage to dodge Terrell for a good while. He's called my parents who have asked him to be patient. He's called my job and spoken to Stacey who urges me to stop running. Again. He's even called Angela, who I overhear in the kitchen.

"Daddy. She's just not ready yet. She'll call you when she is." I'll never be ready to speak that truth to the only man I've ever loved, but I've wasted enough time.

"Sherman, Lark & Lucas."

"Hello Esther, it's Adrienne."

"How are you holding up, honey?"

"I'm just holding, Esther. It's all I can do."

"Well, Terrell is gone for the day. He said he had something to do. But I'll tell him you called, Doll. Take care of yourself."

When I get home from the supermarket, Terrell is sitting in front of my house in a brand new Mercedes. Terrell is not, or should I say, was not a Mercedes guy.

"Nice car."

"Picked it myself."

"Really?"

"No. But Patricia thought this fit in more with our new home."

He kills the ignition. I stay far away from him even though today his face reminds me of the first day I saw him at Maryland University in our Economics class. Thankfully he does the same. Terrell blows a kiss to my mother in the bay window. She catches it in her hand.

When we get upstairs, he stands in the doorway of my apartment, scratching the side of his head before he finally steps inside. He looks around the cozy sage green and cream living room, but his eyes focus on a black and white portrait of Angela and me above our faux fireplace. It was taken on Memorial Day on Myrtle Beach. She was pulling me into the water, but I had dug my feet in the sand, so it appeared I was pulling her. We were both laughing. Our joy is so real that every time I look at it, it warms my spirit.

"I've never seen you like that. You look very much alive." I draw back the shades and sit in the light of the picture window. Terrell sits on the sofa, his hat on the coffee table.

"Start from the beginning."

I lead him through the days of hurt, to the nights of anger and sleeplessness, to the search to fill the pockmarks in my heart. To the disappointment. To the loneliness. To the defiance. To the denial. To the day I met him. To Karen and Victoria's Secret. To that awfully hasty Christmas departure. To the scene at the Garden. To the hurt in my mother's eyes. To right then, that very moment. And he listened. Sometimes with his eyes closed. Sometimes looking at the ceiling. Sometimes searching my face. When I am done, the sun has shifted from the back of my apartment to the front. Terrell contemplates for a bit. He stands and sits again. He keeps wiping his hands on his slacks.

"I only have two questions."

"Go."

"Is Angela my biological daughter?"

"That…is debatable." He shakes a crook out of his neck.

"What's your other question, Tee?" He holds both my hands in his. Terrell is a man.

"Are you okay?"

"Also, debatable." He cocoons me in his arms and pulls me into the crook of the sectional couch with his face lodged in my neck for a hug we both desperately need. We stay that way for what seems like eternity.

When I wake up, tears roll down my cheeks, but I swipe them away. I am underneath a blanket and the last thing I remember is Terrell holding me. I am so sad, because for a few moments, I felt safe again. Loved.

I swing my feet off the couch and pull them back up immediately. Terrell is lying on the floor with his hands clasped behind his head.

"You're here." My voice cracks.

"Yeah. Just laying here. Thinking."

"About?"

"How good we were together and how much better we would have been if that mess didn't happen to you." He looks into my face. "You're still crying."

"A little bit," I squeak.

"You think things would have been different?"

"It's just like your mother said. We were what we were supposed to be, when we were supposed to be."

"Do you think we're supposed to be apart?"

I didn't say anything. I didn't know.

"Yeah. I don't know, either." He kisses me on the lips. I try not to kiss him back, but I can't stop it. It is almost like there is a magnet between us. I welcome him between my legs. He is warm and heavy in a good way. I've missed him terribly. His cool hands go up the back of my shirt warming me. His cell phone chirps.

"Tee, you have to go," I say against his ear.

"Hmmm?"

"Patricia. Your wife. You have to go."

"Oh yeah, Patricia. Shit." I put my hands on his shoulders.

"Come on, Tee. Get up." He leans back on his haunches. I pull myself upright on the couch until he gets himself together. "You straight?"

"Not in a way that's helping me right now."

"C'mon fool." I don't feel as heavy as I did when he got to my house, but the closer we get to the door, the sadder I get. Terrell leans in for a hug, but I shift sideways to deflect the regret and sorrow that is flooding my heart. He keeps his arms raised, not allowing me to run like I do. I step into his embrace.

"That's a big step, what you just did." It sure is. And of all the people who would have noticed a change in me, I am delighted that it is Terrell. One of the sweetest things that ever happened to me.

I STAND IN THE BATHROOM mirror with my glasses off. I can see my imperfections better that way. I have fine wrinkles at the corners of my eyes, crows feet, I believe they're called. I wouldn't have been scrutinizing myself this way, but when Angela came to my room this morning and asked me if I had any pads, I felt old. Like a mother. My mother's mouth and nose look back at me; looking exactly how she looked when we lived on Hopkinson and she insisted on going with me to get my first set. I smile at the memory.

I am still perky on my way out the door. I even find myself whistling. The summer air is fuel to my soul. That is, until I bump into the Con Ed technician, a bulky girl with a tattoo on her neck

"The meter's around the side."

"Are you Adrienne Lucas?"

"Yes. I am."

"You've just been served, darlin'."

I turn down Hopkinson and see my old house standing mighty and yellow still. It means everything to me that she is still standing and not ravaged by time and disrepair. The front porch needs to be painted, but she is still standing. We are still standing.

I slow down as I pass The Pool with the kids screaming, yelling and laughing inside. That and the faint scent of chlorine take me back to a time when my life was simple and clean. *Eric B is President* comes on the radio for the Old School at Noon and I am all smiles. Classic music.

I tour my old neighborhood for the first time since that Christmas morning when I drove past Pitkin Avenue and didn't look back. What strikes me is how different every thing is and how much it's still the same. I pump the radio louder, rolling my windows up as I crawl past the kids jumping in the spray of the open fire hydrant.

Wilcox High is now called the High School of Public Services, but it is still home of the Blue Rays. The banner outside reads *Home of "Hot Rod" Rodney Barrus*. RAPIST is spray painted in red. Call me stupid, but I am embarrassed for him.

I drive down Pitkin Avenue, reminiscing. Klassy Kuts is now called Lashelle's Hair Shack. Good old pigeon-toed Lashelle was still around. It was sandwiched between El Banco and a mom and pop hardware store. Mr. Schwartz's drug store is now called Big Pitkin Drug Store and there is a little boutique selling sparkly video girl tops across the street. A girl of about sixteen stands at the bus stop in tight dark denim jeans like the Lees we used to wear. Her door knocker earrings glint in the summer sunlight. It's déjà vu.

I park my car and get out. The neighborhood still smells the same, too. Like four chicken wings and French fries from the Chung Chan Kitchen. I'm just kidding. Kind of. It smells like hard work and hustle and my history. The store front I am looking for seems to be closed. But I know I am at the right place because as soon as I start to walk away from the door, I hear my name being hollered.

"*Ay-dreee-enne!*" Her smile stretches so damn wide across her face. It takes me back to the first day at Wilcox, when life was still uncomplicated. "Oh my God! Adrienne! Sha just asked for you this morning." She hugs me with her model thin arms and I squeeze her back with my arms that have a little extra padding on them.

"How is my big brother doing?"

"He owns a record store up in the Bronx. His two brats should be here any minute with my two. Oh my God!" She screams again.

"How are you? Oh girl, you have to come inside." She unlocks the gate and pushes it back. Her ring sparkles in the sunlight.

"Councilwoman Tanisha Banks-Carter," I read.

"That's me."

"Wouldn't surprise me if you were plotting this all along." She rubs her hands together.

"Councilwoman's all a part of my plan to take over the world. Next stop, White House! Mwah-ha-ha-ha!" She's joking, but I can see the vision clearly.

"Oh my goodness. I'm so glad to see you. But what brings you back out this way again? No one knew what happened to you once you broke out for Maryland."

"I came to say I was sorry."

"Really? For what?"

"For shutting you out and for lying to you. I was lying to you and I felt guilty because I knew you liked Rodney." She chuckles to herself.

"What's so funny?"

"It's funny because I did like Rodney. Until I realized he was crazy." My eyebrows shoot up.

"But I thought yall were seeing each other."

"God, Aydree. That was so long ago. But you know Neesh don't forget a damn thing." She chuckles again. I remember it like yesterday, too. And after all I'd been through, the little hurts still smarted. Even the ones I'd inflicted.

"I *was* kissing Rodney in the staircase, it's true. I wanted to tell you, but I thought you would think I'd been using you to get closer. It didn't happen like you think. Julie said that if I liked Rodney, I would make a move."

The front door opens and a mini-football team rushes in. The smallest one climbs up in her lap.

"Boys, say hello to my oldest friend in the world, Miss Adrienne."

"Hi Mith Adrienne," says the youngest who has two missing front teeth and her smooth cocoa skin.

"Where's Daddy?" she asks.

"He went to drop Nana Pam home."

"Go on in the back, have a snack and then we'll go to The Pool. And don't make me have to come back there." We watch the kids push and shove each other. We are moms. Grown women, with families of our own and memories of days gone. I whip out my wallet and show off my pride and joy.

"Ayj! She's adorable! She looks just like you!"

"No. If she looks like anybody it's her Daddy."

"What's up with her Daddy?"

"We'll get back to that. Right now, I need to hear your story."

"Anyway Julie and I made a bet. And she wouldn't get off my back. So I pulled him into the staircase and made it happen. Julie tells me afterwards that she was peeking through the glass to make sure I was really doing it. And so was Kerri." I felt stupid at the fact that she played me like a fool.

"What made you think he was crazy?"

"Because he started following me around and calling my house. Then he started cussing me out when I said I didn't like him anymore. We had enough crazy from my father to see the signs. But Sha shut that down with the quickness."

"With the .38?"

"Yes! He stole it from my father when he started, you know..." She trails off. "He's gone. After five years clean. A heart attack."

"I'm so sorry."

"It's life. It's hard. It's fucked up sometimes," she says.

"But there are bright days," I say. She feels my forehead and I, hers.

"Talk about *Trading Places*," she says before she laughs. "What happened to us?"

"I don't know. I almost don't recognize this Tanisha. But I like her though!"

"Oh! You haven't seen anything. Julie and her husband, Dave Goldshmidt have three kids and they're living in the suburbs in Westchester."

"A white guy?! And she's a soccer mom?!" I scream.

"You know it!" I cannot contain my giggles. Good old Jules from Blake Avenue. "She respected you, Ayj."

"I don't know what to say to that."

"You don't have to say anything. But it's true. Oh man. It is just so crazy to see where everyone ended up."

"Yeah."

"What's the matter?"

"I just never envisioned I'd end up being a witness for the prosecution."

"Do you think he did it?"

"I know he did."

"I would have still been your friend if you'd told me, Ayj."

"I know. But he was my family. Even now, I feel like a traitor. He's still family."

"No, Adrienne. You've got it mixed up. The people who love you and cherish you? They are family."

"I hear you. Anyway, let me get out of here." She grabs my hand.

"You've been running for a long time. Aren't you tired yet?"

I ease my hand out of hers. She's right, but I'm overwhelmed. I give her a quick hug before I'm back out on the sidewalk

"The troubles don't disappear. Doesn't matter how fast you run."

I walk away thinking about how right she is. I look back at her again to make sure it wasn't a dream. But she stands at the office door, Tanisha Banks, in the flesh. My friend. My family.

So why am I sitting in my hot ass car, with the windows rolled up, feeling like I am about to destroy a man's life? A strange number comes up on the caller ID.

"Hello."

"Adrienne?"

"Yes? Who's this?"

"It's me, Rodney. Rodney Junior." I look back at Tanisha's office, but she's gone.

"I don't expect you to say anything. But I just called to apologize for…raping you." A humongous lump forms in my throat.

"Can you forgive me? Adrienne, you there?"

"Yes, I'm here."

"Do you forgive me?"

"Yes, Rodney. I do."

"I'm sorry for everything we ever put you through."

I hang up softly. I think about Trey Ski again. Why I think of him so often, I don't know. Maybe because he wasn't a talker, but a doer. Maybe because as far as I'd seen, he never let fear get in his way. Maybe because the last time I saw him, outside Tanisha's party, he was all about handling his business.

One thing's for sure, I am tired of talking. And I'm tired of being afraid.

I pull out of the parking space, knowing once and for all, that it was time to handle mine.

“WELCOME TO GEORGE BUSH International Airport. Please be careful opening the overhead compartments, as the contents may have shifted during the flight. Thank you for flying with JetWay. We hope you enjoy your stay in Houston.”

I was jittery and anxious for the entire ride. Terrell had promised he would come with us, but he hadn’t made the flight. It didn’t help that my mother fussed for the entire ride.

How long is this flight? You have to pay to eat? The movie, too? Next you gon’ tell me you gotta pay to use the toilet. The flight attendant leaned into the row.

“No Ma’am. You already paid for that.”

As we taxi to the gate, I turn off my ipod, my buffer between sanity and the family. I check my phone. No texts. No messages. My hands tremble.

“George Bush is everywhere, huh, Grandma?” Angela says over the aisle.

“Everywhere where there’s money to be made.” The white-haired white lady next to my mother mumbles under her breath.

“What? You don’t believe that? Ax them folks in New Orleans if George Bush is everywhere. See what they say ‘bout that.”

“We have a big fight ahead of us. Why do you have to start one now?”

“The baby axed a question. We just answered it. It’s our right to say what we feel in America, right?”

The plane pulls into the gate. I take our bags down from the overhead bins and drag Angela off the plane. Add irritated on top of nervous.

The U.S. District Attorney’s Office is a short ride away from the hotel, maybe ten minutes if I had to guess. In ten minutes, I have managed to talk myself into and out of testifying. I'm terrified that I'll go through all this hoopla and testify and he will still walk away unscathed. And that no one will believe me. And I'll be a pariah, yet again. I survived the first time, but now my daughter would be involved, and I couldn't stand that.

Any thoughts I had of running are immediately shucked by the presence of a large group of women on the other side of the police barricade.

"No Gold Diggers!" They shout. One especially gaudy woman in gold spandex and a bright purple shirt, parades back and forth with a sign that reads, *Groupies Get Lost!*

"You must really like my company," says the driver. "And I like yours, too. But Darlin', I've got to run."

"Oh! I'm sorry!"

"No problem. Good luck to you, Darlin'." I slam the door shut behind me.

"Hot Rod! Hot Rod!"

I feel a small glimmer of hope in the three women standing on the opposite side holding up signs and chanting, *No means no!*

As ol' Hot Rod would say, it's about to be on and poppin'.

Right away, Isaac Scholer gets my Spanx in a bunch. Starting with his sloppy toupee that sits on his front lobe tilted downward, to his darting tongue that constantly slithers out to wet his chapped lips. He clears a space on his massive glass desk.

"Good to meet you. Coffee, tea? No? Good. Let's get down to business. Does Mr. Barrus have any distinguishing features?"

"He has a scar right under his eye. And a tattoo on his arm that says *Sadie.*" He scribbles on a legal pad.

"How do you know this?"

"I gave him the one under his eye. The tattoo is on every magazine cover and website."

"Anything else. Maybe on his chest. Around his genitals."

"Rodney was not my lover, Isaac."

"Right, of course. And what about the size of his genitals."

"I suppose he was average."

"A big guy like that?!" I look over the top of my glasses.

"Isaac. How long have you been the DA?"

"I ask the questions, Sugar." He shuffles his papers on his desk.

"Tulani Bell, the plaintiff, has danced in music videos so she comes across like a groupie."

"Why are you telling me this?"

"Because if you're going to come across as a whore, then I don't want to put you up there. Is there anything you want to tell me?"

"How in the world did you become the DA?"

"I have friends in white houses."

The morning of the trial, I see who I believe is Tulani Bell for the first time in the waiting area outside the courtroom. She is that Black hybrid that the young brothers seem to go crazy for. Her mother is maybe Hawaiian or a Pacific Islander of some kind. Her father is cocoa brown with coarse salt and pepper hair. His nose is wide and his lips full. Very handsome. Tulani has his full lips and a nose of her own. Her hair is cut in a chin length bob. She is beautiful. And damaged.

She sits by herself while her parents talk to Isaac. I am drawn to her. I am officially a stalker.

"I believe you."

"How do I know you're not just saying that to get me to talk so you can run back and tell everyone what I said?"

"You don't." She looks toward her parents.

"I'm a trained dancer. I danced in one video and I got paid. That doesn't mean I deserved what happened to me."

"Tulani. Come here, honey." She hesitates as though she has something to say, but instead, she glides over to her dad with perfect posture. Mr. Bell puts his arm around her shoulder and uses his other hand to brush her hair from her face. She forces a smile for him. That hurts me.

I sit outside the courtroom, vigilantly watching for Terrell to come down the marble hallway. I wouldn't blame him if he blew me off. I'd be sad, but I wouldn't blame him. I dial him about fifty times and text message him. I can't stand not knowing what's going on. I check my bag. My friend is there. I've been doing well mostly because of Angela's meddling, but I'm scared. Aunt Juicie's Bible is also in bag with the note still attached in the inside cover. *For quiet times and times of need.* The bailiff calls my name.

"Can you give me one minute?"

"One minute, Ma'am. And then it's showtime."

The courtroom is cherrywood paneled with brushed silver accents. It reminds me of a wardrobe I'd bought from IKEA. My heart is fluttering. Especially when I see the back of my parents' heads sitting behind Isaac Scholer and Tulani Bell. Rodney and his flock of attorneys sit on the other side facing straight ahead, with Aunt Say, Big Rodney and Kerri in the row directly behind him. I am sworn in and then Isaac asks me about my life with the Barrus's before the rape.

"Pleasant. Good natured and normal."

"Got it. And afterward?"

"Not so much." Aunt Say's eyes are watery and her nose is red and puffy. I feel a mix of contempt and pity.

"Did Rodney harass you afterward? Taunt you, maybe?"

"No, I wouldn't talk to him. So he left me alone for a few months."

"Until?"

"Until he was alone in the house with me."

"You told me Mr. Barrus used a particular phrase with you. Can you recall it at this time?"

"Yes. The second time Rodney raped me, he said you're no different than these other hoes. You want the dick. They all do." Miss Bell nods stiffly.

"Can you tell me why he said that?"

"Because I told him I didn't want it to happen."

"Did you wear revealing clothes in the house?"

"No."

"Not short shorts or mini-skirts?"

"I beg your pardon, Isaac."

"You're a bright woman, Mrs. Lucas," says The Judge. "But answer the question."

"In the summer, sometimes."

"On the day that you say the second rape occurred, where were you when you first came in contact with Mr. Barrus?"

"On the stairs on the way back to my room."

"And he lived where?"

"In the basement."

"So he had no reason to be upstairs."

"None."

"Did you invite Mr. Barrus upstairs?"

"No, he chased me."

"And that's when he made that statement."

"Actually, he forced me to the floor and put his hand under my skirt. When I tried to push him off, that's when he said what he said."

"No further questions."

The Judge waits for Isaac to get back to his seat. Rodney whispers to his attorney.

"Cross examination, Mr. McDougal." Mr. McDougal smoothes the front of his suit and comes out from behind the table.

"Mrs. Lucas. How are you this morning?"

"Fine. Considering." He smiles, giving new meaning to the term pearlie whites.

"Fair enough. You have a history of violence. Don't you Mrs. Lucas?"

"I don't think so."

"You attacked your cousin Kerri at a family function. Is that true?"

"It was self-defense. She attacked my character."

"Yes or no."

"Yes."

"And you attacked my client in the men's locker room at The Garden in New York City after trespassing?"

"No."

"You didn't slap him in the face?"

"Well, yes. But - "

"And did you not say, and I quote, 'I should have killed you', Mrs. Lucas?"

"I said should have."

"Yes or no."

"Yes."

"And did you not scream obscenities at the security guard?"

"So what?"

"Yes or --"

"Yes, yes."

"Well it seems you have animosity toward my client."

"And rightly so."

"Mrs. Lucas. Were you angry with Rodney because he told your parents you were sleeping around?"

"That was news to me until a few months ago."

"Mrs. Lucas, I'm going to have to ask you to please answer yes or no unless asked to elaborate."

"Were you angry with Rodney for telling your parents that you were sleeping around?"

"Yes."

"So now you're getting back at him?"

"No."

"Your cousin, Mrs. Kerri Long, testified that you lied to your parents to go out on clandestine meetings with boys. And Councilwoman Tanisha Banks-Carter confirmed that you would come to her house as a pretense to clandestine meetings."

"Someone has a new vocabulary word, don't they?" A few laughs ripple throughout the courtroom.

"So it's safe to say that you were a liar and a sneak as a teenager."

"No."

"Really? So you didn't go away with Mr. Sherron Banks without letting either your supposed best friend, the esteemed Councilwoman, or your parents know where you were going?"

"I had my reasons."

"And where exactly did you go?"

"To an abortion clinic."

"Interesting. Well, who were you pregnant for?" I steady my voice. Even after all these years, I am embarrassed.

"I don't know."

"You don't know. So you were promiscuous as well. Not exactly a virtuous young lady, huh folks?" He smirks at the jury.

"Opposing counsel has inadvertently brought something to my attention. On the day that the alleged second rape occurred, you claimed my client put his hand under your skirt. What kind of skirt did you have on?" I could have slapped that stupid toupee off Isaac's head.

"A mini skirt."

"Hoping to entice my client?"

"No. It was a hundred degrees outside." Every court show on network television tells you that a question like that should be an objection, but Isaac doesn't make a move.

"Duly noted. Did you go to the hospital after the alleged rape took place?"

"No."

"Not after the first or second so-called instances?"

"Not after any of the repeated occasions, no."

"Why not?"

"Because I thought rape was something that happened with ugly dirty men. Not my cousin. Especially not my favorite cousin. And I didn't think anybody would believe me."

"Isn't it true that you're in the midst of a custody battle?"

"Objection. Irrelevant," I say. The Judge crosses his arms over his chest.

"I'm sorry, Your Honor," I mumble. Isaac scribbles on his yellow legal pad.

"Mr. Scholer, I get the feeling that you're not exactly following the court's proceedings."

"I beg your pardon?"

"Mr. Scholer, you have a job to do! A job that you may lose, if it becomes clear that you do not represent your clients to the best of your ability!"

"Mr. McDougal, please repeat your question." Mr. McDougal smirks.

"Mrs. Lucas, are you going through a custody battle?"

"Objection. Irrelevant," says Isaac.

"Trying to establish behavioral patterns, your Honor."

"Mrs. Lucas, you may answer."

"No."

"Let us admit Exhibit A. A copy of the petition for parental custody, filed in the Supreme Court in Brooklyn, New York."

"Mrs. Lucas, do you care to change your testimony?"

"No."

"So you're sticking with your claims that you are not in the midst of a custody battle?"

"Yes. My ex-husband and I have an understanding."

"Why? Did you threaten him with rape charges as you did my client?"

"Objection!"

"Sustained."

"Mrs. Lucas. Isn't it true you were less than cooperative when Mr. Lucas came to your home to make arrangements?"

"Yes."

"And isn't it true that you and Mr. Lucas had a huge argument at his place of business?"

"Yes."

"So why in the world should we believe anything that comes out of your mouth? You've proven yourself to be uncooperative, confrontational, less than credible, lacking in moral fiber--"

"You want to arrange a clandestine meeting with me later?" The Judge peers over his glasses at me.

"One more snide comment out of you and you will be held in contempt." Terrell peeks into the courtroom and holds up a white envelope.

"You testified earlier that my client had tons of girlfriends, sometimes more than one at a time. So what I want to know is why should we believe my client would want to rape his own cousin?"

"Rape is not about sex, Mr. McDougal. It's about power. Control. But honestly, I don't know why he would want to."

"Me either. But what's more important is: Why would we believe you? I have no further questions."

"But it doesn't matter if you believe me or not."

"I said no further questions."

"You asked me a question, but you didn't let me answer it."

"I did not ask you a question."

"Yes. You asked why would you believe me." The Judge nods emphatically.

"You did ask her a question."

"It was rhetorical."

"You asked."

"Okay, Ms. Lucas. What, pray tell, is your answer to the question?"

"I already said it didn't matter if you believed me." He chuckled and looked at the jury like I had just put all my crazy cards on the table.

"Really? You're a key witness in a trial where my client is being sued for a ridiculous amount of money and may be sent to jail. And since it's obvious you have a vendetta against my client, I find it hard to believe you wouldn't care if the jury accepted your testimony. And that is a statement. In any case, no further questions." He walks back to his seat assured that he has just put me in my place. Me.

"Recross, Mr. Scholer?"

"Uh. Yes, your honor."

"Mrs. Lucas. Why is it that you don't care if the jury does not believe your testimony?" I could kiss him. Or maybe just pat the top of his head.

"Actually, I said I didn't care if Mr. McDougal didn't believe me. I can make the jury believe me because I have evidence that Rodney raped me."

"Objection. This evidence was not produced during discovery."

"She ain't got no proof, man. I didn't do anything to her." Mr. McDougal pats Rodney's forearm. Isaac folds his arms over his chest.

"Mrs. Lucas. Tell me about this proof you have."

I look at my parents sitting in the seat behind Tulani Bell's parents. Angela sits between them pensively watching me. She hasn't said much since learning there's a possibility Terrell is not her father. My father approaches the bailiff. When the bailiff opens the back door, Terrell walks into the courtroom.

"For the Christmas holiday of my senior year, I took my ex-husband, who was my boyfriend at the time, home with me for the holidays. And like most young couples in their early twenties, and very much in love, we couldn't keep our hands off each other. When Rodney came to Christmas that year, he plied my ex-husband with alcohol and forced me to have sex with him again. As a result of one of those two *clandestine* meetings, I did go to the hospital approximately eight and a half months later."

"From time to time, I would wonder about my daughter's paternity, but I would brush it off to have a sense of normalcy and stability in my life, which is what I had with Terrell." The Judge peers over his glasses.

"That doesn't scare me," I say.

"I'm not surprised by that. But can we get to the proof?"

"Oh. Sorry about that. Up until five minutes ago, I wasn't sure, but now I am. My proof has a name. Her name is Angela Monique. And her biological father is Rodney Barrus, Jr." Every mouth in the courtroom drops to the floor.

Then suddenly the chatter is chaotic. Aunt Say cries out, *'Lawd! Oh Lawd!'* And Big Rodney grunts like a boar and Kerri sits there with no expression and Rodney the pig does not squeal, but shifts his eyes back and forth in the Uncle Fred fashion. The Judge slams his gavel down.

"Order!" he shouts. "Order in the court!" He bangs and bangs again.

"Order!" The courtroom noise dwindles to a loud hum.

Rodney trains his eyes on Angela. His face is ashy-looking and he seems to have aged ten years in the last minute or so. The rest of the family is all eyes. The Judge bangs his gavel yet again.

"Order!" The courtroom simmers.

"That's not proof." Terrell hands the envelope to the bailiff. The Judge reads over the documents.

"Mrs. Lucas's proof only states that Mr. Terrell Lucas is not the father. It does not in any way implicate, Mr. Barrus."

"Well then, let's do a test now." Rodney is on his feet.

"You said you forgave me, you bitch!" he shouts. "You're a lying conniving bitch!"

"Forgave you for what, Rodney?" His Uncle Fred's dart back and forth again as he realizes just then that he has exposed his horns.

"Well, Mr. Barrus, in light of this new information, court will be recessed for an hour. The jury will deliberate on the charge of rape and assault in the third degree and come back with a verdict."

Outside the courtroom, Big Rodney snaps his suspenders and hollers for everyone to hear.

"She seduced my boy! She used her womanly ways on him. Everybody know a man can't resist no womanly ways!" I don't know if he's talking about me or Tulani Bell. I don't really care. I step toward him to give him one last taste of MC Lite Brite. But in his face, I see the faded light of a man who is desperately holding on even though it's clear he is at the end of his rope.

ISAAC SCHOLER BUSTS THROUGH the door. "What were you thinking? You could have compromised my client's case!"

"It took over twenty years for him to pay for what he did to me. And I don't think Tulani Bell should have to do the same because you were either too star-struck or dumbstruck to do your job properly."

"I am the District Attorney. Not you."

"She is the victim. Not you." He slams the door. The courthouse lunch sits untouched in the center of the table. The smell of old cole slaw and cold fried chicken permeates the air. Angela stands to the side twirling the ends of her long braids around her finger. Terrell grabs her into a hug.

"Don't be nervous."

I almost expect her to be like me and say she's not nervous. But she is Terrell's girl. Straightforward, no holds barred.

"I can't help it."

"I'm still your Daddy. No matter what that paper says."

"Of course you are," says Angela. He closes his eyes, resting his chin on her forehead. I am sorry for my secrets and lies. I'm not even sure I could ever fix what I'd done to him. My parents quietly hold hands, but they don't dare speak. In fact no one utters another word until the bailiff knocks on the door to tell us it's time to go back.

The courtroom is abuzz with a new chatter. Necks crane and eyes shift back and forth from Angela to Rodney.

"Cheekbones. Definitely the cheekbones..."

"She's tall like him."

"I think she's lying…They should go on Maury."

Rodney stares straight ahead, as though distancing himself from the chaos bubbling around him. Every now and then, he leans in to whisper to his lawyer. His favorite cheerleader sits two rows back, but Aunt Say and Big Rodney remain right behind him.

"Madame Foreman, have you reached a verdict?"

"Yes, your honor. We have."

"Will the defendant please rise?" Rodney stands and brushes his shoulders off. Yes, he does.

"How do you find the defendant?"

"On the charge of rape in the first degree, we the jury find the defendant guilty." Tulani puts her head down. I squeeze the blood out of Terrell's hand.

"Order!" yells The Judge. "Order!"

Aunt Say reaches out to Rodney, who shrugs her off. Kerri stands to the side holding Merri on her hip.

"Kay. I didn't." Kerri switches Merri to the side of her that is furthest away from Rodney. He looks awful right then. Like someone has died. I should be glad but I feel terrible inside.

"Oh, it's like that? You're cut off!" he yells. The bailiff cuffs Rodney.

"Worthless freeloading bitch!" He hollers, true colors shining through.

"You're a dirty fuckin' loser, Rodney! Don't drop the fuckin' soap!" yells Kerri. I don't know where Big Rodney has gone, but Aunt Say sits in the same spot, zoned out to the madness that are her offspring. Terrell zips Angela out of the courtroom before anyone can miss her. He is a special man.

"You did it. You did it!" cries Tanisha. She hugs me so tight I can't speak. Big brother Sha, who I hadn't seen since the melee, stands right behind her. I transfer from Tanisha's arms to his. My mother is coming toward us and although I know she sees Sha and Tanisha, she tries to sneak past, her eyes on the marble floor.

"Ma, you're playin' yourself." She narrows her eyes at me, which I actually find to be quite comical. My father holds his hand out to Sha who takes it in a firm grip.

"My wife and I are sorry for everything that happened."

I can't really hear Sha's response because I'm distracted by Tanisha who has pinched the hell out of my arm.

"Neesh! What the hell?!"

"Girl! Today is your lucky day."

"I know. I can't believe he's been convicted. But damn."

"Yeah. That, too. But that's not what I mean." She points me toward the back of the courtroom.

Corey Robinson walks down the aisle like he is meeting me at the altar. My heart thumps, as does Tootie. Corey Robinson is here. In Houston. For me.

I have just a second to digest it all before Terrell comes back into the courtroom, shoulders squared and deep voiced. More deep than I remember it. He rests his hands on my shoulders.

"Angel and your parents are in the car. Are you ready to go?"

"Why doesn't he just spray the area around you?" whispers Tanisha. I chuckle because she sounds like my other sister, Stacey.

"Miss Sunshine. What kind of thing is that to say?!"

"But it's so obvious," she giggles.

I am still stunned that Corey has come all the way to Houston, Texas. For me! Adrienne Lucas! I get on my tiptoes and kiss his five o'clock shadowed, caramel complected cheek. And then I turn my back on him and sashay out the courtroom doors.

"Ayj. You're not gonna talk to him?"

"I'm over him."

"You're such a liar."

"I know." I stride off with my head held high, across the marble floor, passing the flashing lights and the yelling reporters and the fans and the court staff and the police detail and Kerri, who is giving a live interview, out into the glorious sunshine that I've missed for so long.

And damn, it feels good.

ACKNOWLEDGEMENTS

God, for this gift that I am able to share with my readers; for the past and present support and encouragement especially shared through Cira, Alana, Malaika, Milton, Ernesto, Anthony, Meredith, Sabrina, Donna, Jolene, Kendall, James, Candice, Teresa, Stacey, Patrice, Brianna, Tiffany and Cordenia (every day I'm hustle-in'!); for my boss, Peter and my co-workers at JH; for the knowledge shared through Damion Sincere, Renee Flagler, Moses Miller and Gloria Mallette; and last but not least, for my parents, family and friends who've been hearing about this project for years and still believe in me. I love you.

E-mail questions and comments regarding *Rabbit's Lucky Number* to rabbit@brooklyngirlpublishing.com. We look forward to hearing from you!

www.rainn.org

RAINN | Rape, Abuse & Incest National Network
The Nation's largest anti-sexual assault organization
1.800.656.HOPE

3056298

Made in the USA